AFRICA
A DREAM DEFERRED

BY
JOHN GAY

First Edition 2004

Publisher
The New World African Press
1958 Matador Way #35
Northridge CA 91330

ISBN 0-9717692-8-1

Photographs by Judy and John Gay

Published by the New World African Press
Copyright 2004 by New World African Press
ALL RIGHTS RESERVED

Printed in the United States of America. All rights reserved. No part of this publication may be reproduced or transmitted in any form or by any means, electronic or mechanical, including photocopying, recording, or by an information storage and retrieval system-except by a reviewer.

Although the author and publisher have made every effort to ensure the accuracy and completeness of the materials, the Press assumes no responsibility or errors, inaccuracies, omissions, or any inconsistency herein.

ABOUT THE NEW WORLD AFRICAN PRESS

The New World African Press evolved over a period of fifteen years. Originally, it began as Elsie Mae Enterprises in honor of my own special guiding light, my late mother Elise Mae Holloway. Later Elsie Mae Enterprises was changed to the Boniface I. Obichere Press. This new change was in honor of my mentor, friend, and colleague, who passed from this realm and made his transition to the afterlife in the world of ancestors in 1997.

Finally, the Boniface I. Obichere Press metamorphosed into the New World African Press in 2000. While the name of the Press has gone through several name changes, its mission and purpose have remained the same: to fill the void and neglect left by the major publishing houses; to publish manuscripts that focus on the Diasporic experience in Africa, Europe, and the countries of the New World. While the press is primarily concerned with diasporic issues, it is also committed to publishing non-Diasporic manuscripts and literature such as *Bach: A Fictional Memoir* by Dr. Paul Guggenheim, and *Space: A Journalist Notebook* by DeWayne B. Johnson.

The New World African Press list of books includes the following. Clarence E. Zamba Liberty, *Growth of the Liberian State: An Analysis of Its Historiography* is the first in our Diasporic series. Others include: Herbert H. Booker, *The Noble Drew Ali and the Moorish Science Temple Movement*, and Joseph E. Holloway, *An Introduction to Classical African Civilizations*, *The African American Odyssey: Student's Manual and Study Guide with Text Combined Volume*, and *Neither Black Nor White: The Saga of An American family*. Sakui Malapka's *The Village Boy* is the first in the series of novels about Liberia.

The New World African Press is proud and honored to publish the works of John Gay, *Red Dust on the Green Leaves*, *The Brightening Shadow*, and his latest novel in this series on the Liberian Civil War, *Long Day's Anger*, and now his memoir covering fifty years of experiences in Africa. His latest is *Africa: A Dream Deferred*.

A Dream Deferred
by Langston Hughes

What happens to a dream deferred?
Does it dry up
like a raisin in the sun?
Or fester like a sore--
And then run?
Does it stink like rotten meat?
Or crust and sugar over--
like a syrupy sweet?
Maybe it just sags
like a heavy load.
Or does it explode?

PREFACE

I offer this book to all of you who love Africa, whether you are Africans by birth or not. Please read it, realizing that the story it tells is often painful. You may disagree with some points that I make. If so, please let me know in what ways I have spoken wrongly. I do not mean to denigrate Africa and certainly not the wonderful people I have known and worked with. But I do know that there has been much suffering, and I know also that many, if not most, African societies have failed to realize the potential that I saw when I arrived in 1958, and which most of you also saw when you started your love affair with the continent and its people.

I have drawn from what my family and I learned as we worked and lived in Africa from 1958 until we retired in January 2001. We taught in rural Liberia from 1958 to 1974 as Episcopal missionaries at Cuttington University College, a small but very ambitious American-type liberal arts college. I was head of the social science division and gave courses in European and African history, philosophy, political science, ethics and research methods. I realized very early that I had much more to learn from my African students, who came from at least 10 other countries besides Liberia, than I had to offer them from my very limited and very American education. And so I became deeply involved in research into indigenous knowledge in such areas as mathematics, logic, education, agriculture and health. To a great extent my students not only were my research assistants but did independent research on their own. My wife Judy taught English and theology, and did research in indigenous folklore.

After teaching, studying and writing at Cambridge University in 1974-75, we went to Lesotho, where I took employment with the Food and Agriculture Organization and then the United States Agency for International Development, while Judy completed work for her Cambridge doctorate in social anthropology on women, marriage and migrant labor. After completing my assignments with the development agencies, I taught at the National University of Lesotho for three years in the sociology department, and then spent four years doing research on development issues in Lesotho, Botswana, Ethiopia, Uganda and Tanzania.

Judy and I then once again became missionaries for the Episcopal Church, at the behest of Archbishop Desmond Tutu. We joined a Christian collective in Lesotho, called the Transformation Resource Centre, which was committed to seeking social, political and economic justice in southern Africa. Our fellow workers were a body, ecumenical both theologically and politically, including activists from the African National Congress, the Pan-Africanist Congress and the Black Consciousness Movement. During those exciting six years, I edited the newsletter *Work for Justice* and continued to do what I hoped was socially responsible research on issues related to poverty and development.

When South Africa achieved its independence in 1992, we left the Transformation Resource Centre, while still remaining very close to the community we had helped build. Judy went on to work full-time with the Anglican Church in Lesotho, and was ordained as a priest in 1996. I began full-time research at Sechaba Consultants in Lesotho. Sechaba (the name in the Sesotho language means "people") has been and still is committed to presenting the knowledge, beliefs and socio-economic condition of ordinary people in Lesotho and other southern African countries. Most of our assignments were funded by international agencies, with the support of the Lesotho government. We wrote reports on such issues as poverty, agriculture, education, health, energy, water supply, regional migration, employment and attitudes to democracy.

Judy and I left Africa at the end of January 2001 having reached the age where we must turn over work to others. We left with joy at having spent 42 wonderful years in Africa, but with deep sadness that we, Africans and outsiders alike, had not been able to bring to fruition the dreams and hopes with which we had started our various tasks. This book is the result of my trying to understand just why the Africa we knew and loved has not fulfilled its promise.

Each of the chapters in my book deals with a general theme, a sector of the totality of life and society. These themes are dealt with in sub-sections in a very personal way, drawing on my own experiences in sub-Saharan countries where I have worked. I often come to discouraging and discouraged conclusions, even though I try to point out signs of hope. I want you to feel the pain and the discouragement, but I also want you to help me, and all those others who love Africa, to see how these signs of hope, these sparks of life, can be the basis for a better future in Africa.

What I have said in this book is entirely my responsibility, and I stand for what I have written. Having said that, I wish to thank those who have read sections, or even all, of the book in draft form. They include Al-Hassan Conteh, David Coplan, Martinus Daneel, Elwood Dunn, Judy Gay, Steven Gill, Peter Green, Jean Hay, Joe Holloway, John Humphrey, Paul Jefferson, Gerard Mathot, Jim McCann, Sue Perry, Alan Price, Ted Scudder, Parker Shipton, Herbert Spirer, Gordon Thomasson, Desmond Tutu and Howard Webber. To all of you, many thanks for your patience and your good ideas.

FOREWORD

I have a passing familiarity with much of what John Gay has written about Africa (particularly, Liberia). Before this study, and his well-known books *Red Dust on Green Leaves*, *The Brightening Shadow*, *Long Day's Anger* and *The New Mathematics* and an *Old Culture*, I had the opportunity to read his "A Letter to My Children, With Much Love" (1999), "The 50th Anniversary of the Holy Cross Mission at Bolahun" (1972), and his insights on the requirements for reconstructing Cuttington University College in the aftermath of the civil war in Liberia.

In *Africa: A Dream Deferred*, Gay continues his quest for understanding, and his efforts at interpreting an Africa in which he spent perhaps his entire working life, that is, until now. The thrust is two-fold. On the one hand, there is the appearance of a resurgent Africa following the Second World War, but one that quickly bogs down in value/culture challenges occasioned by encounters with the Western world. On the other hand, there are the glimmers of hope in the midst of "unfulfilled promise" that beckons consolidation from enlightened leadership by Africans and friends of Africa.

Thus, it is that Gay captures the hopes of a decolonizing Africa (modernizing Liberia), the nationalist surge, the development programs, and the transforming intent. Here he articulates the visions of Africa's first generation of leaders—Tubman of Liberia, Nkrumah of Ghana, Kenyatta of Kenya, Nyerere of Tanzania, Toure of Guinea, and numerous others. Yet, once the shroud of the Cold War was removed one discovered what Ali Mazrui has called "a Garden of Eden in decay." As Gay distills his forty-two years of experiences in Africa as missionary in both the religious and secular sense of the words, his work with the Episcopal/Anglican Church and international aid agencies in Liberia, Lesotho, Botswana, Ethiopia, Uganda, Tanzania, and South Africa, he points throughout to "hopeful signs" amid disappointing performances. Thus the old "moral center" goes, ideally to be replaced by a new wholeness; development from below replaces development from above; a personal elitist political system yields to the challenge of internal democratization; and the industrialized world grows more sensitive to the human dimensions of Africa's problems and undertakes to change its partnership relationship accordingly. Might the unanticipated events of 9/11/01 accelerate this latter process? There are mixed signals to date. It remains unclear where one is addressing terrorism's roots or seeking to root out terrorism, unable to distinguish terrorism as symptomatic of malady or terrorism as mindless violence.

John Gay provides in his last chapter a miniature blueprint for the continent, leaving Africans themselves to fill in the details, hopefully more in action than word. Beyond the imperative of international democratization, he sees education and health as "rights not privileges;" and urges African leaders to promote local agriculture, business initiatives, and regional integration; starve wars by addressing small arms proliferation; isolate and indict warlords; repatriate illicit foreign savings; restructure foreign assistance; and effect moral and spiritual renewal with a view to restoring to African lives the intent of our common creator.

In a final "personal postscript" Gay affirms his personal Christian faith, reaffirms and commends to Africa the redemptive power of the Christian Gospel as it faces the momentous challenges of secular and spiritual rebirth and renewal.

Gay's perspectives on Africa are not unlike those of the Englishman, Basil Davidson. He comes to the continent with liberal political credentials, a Christian perspective informed by the social gospel, and insights gleaned from careful study and observation both of indigenous African society, but as well the product of an often uneven power encounter between Africa and the Western world. While his "hopeful signs" are balanced and realistic, for the most part, there may be areas of the text that invite circumspection. As one points out Africa's ills and prescribes remedies, one must do so within clearly understandable parameters—the world as it is, including the challenge of transformational change. One must do this rather than adopt the "kick out the rascals" approach, without a program both "clever" and "sincere" as replacement. Transforming Africa may require nothing less than a marshalling of political will and moral courage on part of political actors both internal and external to the continent.

I feel both humbled and honored by the request of my college professor to write this preface to his reflections on his African odyssey. One hopes that the thinkers and doers of Africa's renaissance will find in the pages that follow perspectives both valid and sincere.

D. Elwood Dunn
University of the South
March 2004

TABLE OF CONTENTS

CHAPTER ONE. A BRAVE START, A ROUGH ROAD	**1**
CHAPTER TWO. A CHANGED MORAL ORDER	**5**
2.1 Reshaping of initiation ceremonies and secret societies	6
2.2 Secularization of traditional art forms	17
2.3 Breakdown of family structures	26
2.4 Emphasis on the individual instead of the community	30
2.5 Loss of local histories	35
2.6 Loss of women's roles	40
2.7 Abuse of tradition to maintain social control	43
2.8 Ethnic and cultural oppression	47
2.9 Hopeful signs	50
CHAPTER THREE. NEGLECT OF INDIGENOUS KNOWLEDGE	**54**
3.1 Destruction of natural forests	54
3.2 Introduction of exotic trees	58
3.3 Loss of environmental diversity	60
3.4 Introduction of cash crops instead of food crops	63
3.5 Creation of single-crop, single-product economies.	67
3.6 Side-lining of indigenous economy	72
3.7 Hopeful signs	74
CHAPTER FOUR. DOMINATION BY ELITES	**77**
4.1 Mis-perception of Africa as a supposed single culture area	77
4.2 Imposition of western democracy	78
4.3 Indirect rule through westernized elite	83
4.4 Split between citizen and subject	86
4.5 Racism and xenophobia	92
4.6 Slave trade	95
4.7 Forced labor	96
4.8 Artificial creation of ethnic groups	96
4.9 Artificial national boundaries	99
4.10 External focus of modern infrastructure	101
4.11 Greed and war	102
4.12 Hopeful signs	105
CHAPTER FIVE. ALIEN EDUCATION SYSTEMS	**108**
5.1 The invention of failure	108
5.2 Emphasis on white-collar employment	111
5.3 Irrelevant curricula	112
5.4 Examinations and paper qualifications	115
5.5 Colonization of the mind.	118
5.6 Consolidation of the elite	120
5.7 Hopeful signs	121

CHAPTER SIX. DEMOGRAPHIC SHIFTS — 123
6.1 Population growth — 123
6.2 Refugees and displaced persons — 125
6.3 Urbanization — 128
6.4 Migrant labor — 132
6.5 Brain drain and labor export — 134
6.6 The effect of convenient transport — 136
6.7 Hopeful signs — 139

CHAPTER SEVEN. RELIGIOUS CONFLICT — 141
7.1 Disparagement of local religious beliefs — 141
7.2 A divided Christianity — 145
7.3 Christian-Muslim conflict — 148
7.4 Multiplication of missionary bodies — 151
7.5 Growth of African-initiated religious groups — 152
7.6 Lavish weddings and funerals — 157
7.7 Hopeful signs — 161

CHAPTER EIGHT. ALIEN MEDICAL SYSTEMS — 163
8.1 Disrespect for traditional healers — 163
8.2 Cure as mechanistic rather than holistic — 165
8.3 Emphasis on cure rather than prevention — 167
8.4 HIV/AIDS — 168
8.5 Introduction of strong alcoholic beverages — 173
8.6 Spread of alien diseases — 175
8.7 Expensive medical care not available to the poor — 178
8.8 Hopeful signs — 180

CHAPTER NINE. WESTERN ECONOMIC CONTROL — 182
9.1 Externally-imposed development schemes — 182
9.2 Loans to create indebtedness — 188
9.3 Export of raw materials — 191
9.4 Displacement of peoples — 196
9.5 Misplaced emphasis on urban development — 200
9.6 Hopeful signs — 202

CHAPTER TEN. IMPOSING WESTERN POLITICAL FORMS — 204
10.1 Disrespect for customary leaders — 204
10.2 Politics without policies — 208
10.3 Political parties as ethnic and social clubs — 210
10.4 Swollen government bureaucracies — 212
10.5 Inconsistent and corrupt borders — 215
10.6 Rulers for life — 216
10.7 Rulers and their yes-men — 218
10.8 Hopeful signs — 219

CHAPTER ELEVEN. CENTRALIZED COMMAND ECONOMIES
11.1 Five-year plans
11.2 Top-down collectivization 2̲
11.3 State control of labor unions 226
11.4 Centralized food distribution 229
11.5 Inappropriate price structures 232
11.6 Expensive prestige projects 233
11.7 Bureaucratic controls on the informal economy 235
11.8 State-controlled media 237
11.9 Hopeful signs 239
CHAPTER TWELVE. INCREASED MILITARIZATION **241**
12.1 Enlarged post-colonial armies and budgets 241
12.2 Alignment with foreign power blocs 245
12.3 Tightened security and suppression of dissent 247
12.4 Military coups 248
12.5 Internal and external conflicts 249
12.6 New/old styles of war 252
12.7 Hopeful signs 255
CHAPTER THIRTEEN. WHERE NEXT, AFRICA? **257**
13.1 Internal democratization 257
13.2 Education and health are rights, not privileges 257
13.3 Serious anti-HIV/AIDS campaign 258
13.4 Promote local agriculture and business initiative 259
13.5 Promote regional integration 259
13.6 Starve wars and isolate warlords 259
13.7 Repatriate illicit foreign savings 260
13.8 Restructure foreign assistance 260
13.9 Moral and spiritual renewal 261
13.10 A personal postscript 261
REFERENCES CITED **263**

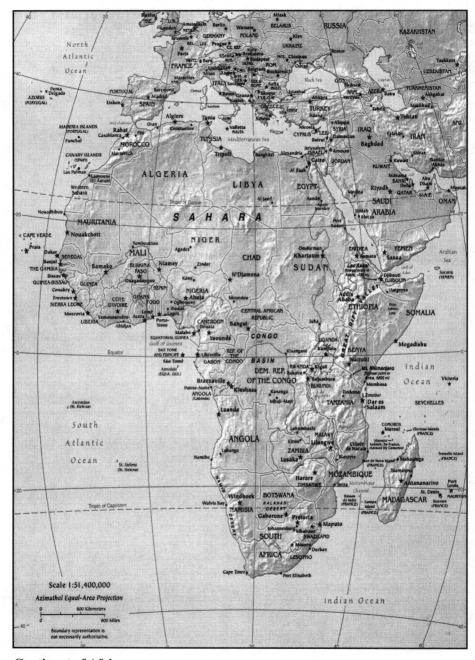

Continent of Africa

CHAPTER ONE. A BRAVE START, A ROUGH ROAD

African Freedom Day 1960

I arrived in Liberia in December 1958. A year earlier, Ghana had joined Liberia and Ethiopia as the only independent, self-governing nations in sub-Saharan Africa. The excitement of a new beginning was heavy in the air as other colonial territories also looked forward to their own independence.

My first serious conversation that same December was with three of the young men who looked forward to creating the future Africa. Kayetan Ngombale, Shabani Kisenge, and Ghisler Mapunda had traveled overland from Tanganyika to start their university education at Cuttington College in rural Liberia. They had attended the Pan-African Congress in Accra in November 1958 and were intoxicated with the promise of a newly free, united, socialist Africa. I was caught up by their excitement and felt that we who were teaching at Cuttington College could help them, and others like them, to build the new society.

What was their dream? Ghana's Kwame Nkrumah, the Osagyefo, the Redeemer, was lighting a fire that would burn across the continent, and these young men were eager to take that fire home to East Africa. They would help their "Teacher," the Mwalimu Julius Nyerere, bring the fire to every homestead in their country. Not only would they bring the reality of freedom to their home, but they would join forces with freedom-loving people across the continent to create a single blazing beacon of hope for the world in the United States of Africa.

I realized what a great privilege I had been given as I joined the vanguard of young people who would build the future. Cuttington College was a small, church-run, American-style liberal arts college established in 1948 in the very heart of Liberia. My wife Judy and I were missionaries for the American Episcopal Church. We had come to Liberia, to Cuttington, at the invitation of the Liberian Church and had committed ourselves to a minimum of six years teaching the new leaders of Africa. We did not know then that we would spend the rest of our active lives in the continent.

At the age of thirty I was little older than our students, some of whom were even my age-mates. Judy, at twenty-five, was certainly younger than many of them. We had more formal education than our students, and so we thought we knew everything worth knowing. All of our education was very American, and we had no qualms about bringing what we knew to people who must certainly need what we believed we were qualified to provide. We had been given a mandate by our own members of a world-wide, educated society. What made this challenge so much more exciting to us than if we were simply providing those tools to American college students was this sense of being "present at the creation," to quote former American Secretary of State Dean Acheson (Acheson 1969). He spoke of the creation of the new post-World War II Western alliance. We believed that we would help create the new Africa.

There was something Wordsworthian in the joy of it all. As he wrote in his *Ode on Intimations of Immortality*, it was

...a time when meadow, grove, and stream,
The earth and every common sight,
To me did seem
Apparelled in celestial light,
The glory and the freshness of a dream.

My wife Judy remembers a line from a sermon she heard as a child: "To be alive in such an age as this is wonderful; to be young—'tis very heaven."

The time certainly seemed right. The vital signs were strong and healthy. The ages of slavery and colonial domination were over; wars seemed no longer necessary. Indeed, the African continent could now fulfill its destiny in the history of the world.

Strong leaders from Senegal (Leopold Senghor) to South Africa (Albert Luthuli), from Kenya (Jomo Kenyatta) to Zambia (Kenneth Kaunda), from Uganda (Milton Obote) to Côte d'Ivoire (Felix Houphuet-Boigny), from Ghana (Kwame Nkrumah) to Tanganyika (Julius Nyerere), from Nigeria (Nnamdi Azikiwe) to Belgian Congo (Patrice Lumumba) could hardly betray the continent that had given them birth. And they would be guided by elder statesmen who knew the problems and pitfalls on the path of national self-government: President William Tubman (Liberia) and Emperor Haile Selassie (Ethiopia).

We might have worried that there were too much leadership and not enough of what I might try to call "followership", but that thought was far from our minds. We admired, even revered these men (not surprisingly, no women among them). A friend told me recently how at the tender eight of eight he had been filled with hope when he first heard Kaunda speaking at a rally.

There was peace almost everywhere in Africa in 1958. The Mau Mau rebellion in Kenya had nearly run its course, and it seemed that the British would soon have to yield power to the local people. There was a sullen peace in South Africa. The Sharpeville massacre was still to come, and young Africans were preparing themselves to play a strong role in changing their country.

And education! Education was the catalyst that would change the face of society. In most countries only a small minority of Africans had been to school, but schools were now being opened at an increasing pace. We at Cuttington College were part of the vanguard providing university education to young people who would then go back to their own countries. They would bring back literacy, insight, and skills to the families who had sent them off with high hopes, first to high school and then to university.

The larger world too was more or less at peace. The Suez Crisis had come and gone, and Nasser was firmly in power. The Korean War had been brought to a stalemate. There was still trouble in Vietnam after the French defeat at Dien Bien Phu, but the big war had not yet started. The Chinese Communists were consolidating their hold on the mainland. The Soviet Union and NATO threatened each other, but the policy of Mutual Assured Destruction by various armories of nuclear weapons appeared to guarantee an uneasy peace. In short, there was space for an African re-birth during which the nations could create their futures without serious outside interference. We could proceed with our task, and we knew that the future lay with us and with those we taught.

Yet it did not work out as we had hoped. I write this in the year 2004 when disaster in almost every African country mocks our great hopes. Sierra Leone is barely recovering from the wreckage left behind by a bloody-handed, almost-leaderless militia. Liberia is almost prostrate in the wake of a ruthless and greedy tyrant who enriched himself from every drop of blood, cut-off hand, and precious diamond. From Senegal to Somalia to South Africa there is hardly a country which has come close to fulfilling the hopes we all shared in those heady days of 1958. Many are far worse off now than they were then, although there are signs of hope, as I will affirm in what follows. Wordsworth continues in his *Ode*:

> *It is not now as it hath been of yore;--*
> *Turn whereso'er I may,*
> *By night or day,*
> *The things which I have seen I now can see no more.*

I will try in what follows to explore some of the reasons for the loss of innocence, for the failure to achieve what seemed so very possible almost half a century earlier in 1958. I have learned much from other scholars and activists and will draw on their writings wherever possible. In particular I commend an excellent summary of informed world-wide opinion put out by the U.N.'s Africa Futures Project in 2002. What I have to say is more personal, but I hope it covers as much ground as the writers of that report.

I will reflect on events and circumstances that I have actually and personally seen and in which I have played an active role. And I will set my experiences in a wider context to the extent that I have kept up with African news. I have been involved in African education and development for more than forty years, and I have worked primarily in eight countries: Botswana, Ethiopia, Lesotho, Liberia, Namibia, South Africa, Tanzania, and Uganda. I have learned much in these and other countries, and I want to share what I have learned with my friends. I still have hope for African nations and peoples, but that hope is much tempered from what it was forty-six years ago.

Historian Edward Tenner calls it "the revenge of unintended consequences" (Tenner 1996). Few of the efforts we and others made in Africa to bring "civilization" were spiteful or selfish. Instead, many of us, including Judy and me, wanted to do the right thing by people whom we came to love.

That the consequences might be harmful to the very people we wanted to help was the farthest thing from our minds. Unfortunately, the thick context of events made it inevitable that our efforts would often produce something very different from, even opposed to, what we had intended. We human beings are nearer to slugs than to God, as someone said. We see only what is immediately in front of us, and even that we do not see clearly. Unintended consequences result because the totality of circumstances—the tightly intertwined network of push and be pushed—suffers a myriad of adjustments in response to any single intervention.

We who came to Africa in 1958 held a very simplistic view of social change. If we did this one good thing then the consequences would be what we intended. If we educated a hundred students from across Africa, we would help build a new world. True—the world we helped build was a new world, but it was very different from what we intended. Chaos theorists, using the work of Lorenz, claim that killing one butterfly in the Amazon can lead to major weather shifts elsewhere in the world (www.zeuscat.com/andrew/chaos/lorenz.html). True or not, our actions at Cuttington, as well as the actions of our fellow missionaries (both sacred and secular), had, and continue to have, serious reverberations that we did not, indeed could not, anticipate.

It was overkill when Dora Taylor, under the pseudonym Nosipho Majeke, pilloried those who took part in the foreign conquest of South Africa as if each and every missionary, politician, soldier, and trader was out to plunder it (Majeke 1952). More balanced is the approach of the Comaroffs, who delicately attempt to understand the motivations and actions of both the missionaries and the astute Tswana as co-creators of a changed world (Comaroff and Comaroff 1991, 1997). They relate the rich context of life in nineteenth-century England to the equally rich setting of the Tswana people and show how the missionary enterprise changed both the missionaries and those being missionized.

I am still a missionary at heart, just as the Christian churches, the World Bank, the United States Agency for International Development, and the United Nations Development Programme continue to be missionaries. Africans who commit their lives to Africa's future have also taken up that mission, and some have been lauded for it. The Zambian Representative to the United Nations praised Nyerere posthumously on his eightieth birthday by saying that Nyerere's generation "had an unshakable belief in their mission and chosen political ideology. They were committed to lead, secure the liberation of Africa and give the new states a new beginning. They did not believe in failure" (www.un.int/zambia/s26.html).

The intention of all of us—Nyerere, Christian churches, United Nations, World Bank, and the thousands who have given their energies and even their lives to Africa—has been and still is to help Africans fulfill their God-given potential as part of a holistic, integrated, global village. The consequences for Africa are often unfortunate, though not universally. Much has gone wrong, yet hope remains. As a Christian, admittedly a very chastened Christian, I have hope. What has happened to weaken my naive hope and replace it with sober but dedicated realism is the story of this book.

CHAPTER TWO. A CHANGED MORAL ORDER

I have been present at, and certainly at times a participant in, a radical change of the moral order that has held African societies together throughout millennia. For some, these changes have been welcome; there are those who say the changes have brought Africans out of a supposed "heart of darkness." Others say that, on the contrary, the changes have broken a moral order that worked well over centuries, first during the eras of relative isolation and then during a five hundred-year hammering by outsiders eager to profit from the opening of a new continent.

I do not claim that the pre-colonial, pre-missionary moral order was perfect, fine-tuned to the specific needs of everyone in the various African societies, but I believe it did maintain a measure of stability in some places. Nor do I claim that there was a common "tradition" that locked people together in a timeless framework over the many centuries prior to the coming of Western and Arab intruders. Furthermore, I do not support the old cliché that we missionaries brought light to the "Dark Continent," though I realize that much of what has made Africa the continent it is now is due to imperialists, Muslim traders, and Christian missionaries.

What I do believe is that in most African societies there was a moral center, and I am concerned about the role we all played in the loss of this moral center in the communities where we worked and lived. I do not deny that there were great benefits to pre-colonial societies derived from contact with other cultures, whether African or otherwise. I also do not deny that moral decay eats at the heart of every society from within. Yet there is always change, sometimes autochthonous, sometimes external. Some change marks real progress in human lives, while other change (or perhaps even the same change) leads to loss and damage.

For an example of pre-colonial disorder, consider the case of the Kpelle-speaking village of Gbansu in rural Liberia where Judy and I spent eight months studying traditional farming in 1974. We know that there was repeated civil war and banditry prior to "pacification" by the Liberian government. An event I am able to document was the end of one of the inter-village wars on 29 May, 1919. How do I know the exact date? That was the very day when Einstein's general theory of relativity was tested by the transit of Mercury across the face of the sun during a total eclipse visible from much of West Africa. In Gbansu, the disappearance of the sun in midday brought the fighting to a halt. The people told us that the eclipse was a great boon, since it stopped bloody slaughter and destruction.

The pre-colonial style of warfare among Kpelle people was straightforward. War chiefs alternated with town elders as rulers of communities. When a war chief ruled, one of his (occasionally *her*) responsibilities was to fight neighboring villages. Gbansu was invaded in May 1919, and the town was burned to the ground by marauding soldiers. It was a harsh and difficult time in Kpelle pre-history. No wonder the population grew slowly. Eclipses could not happen every time there was war.

But I am not talking only about the negative side of traditional Kpelle life. Much of it was sensible and life-affirming. Unfortunately, in many ways we did our best as missionaries and developers to undercut what was good and replace it with a way of life we understood and which benefited us. I do not want to flagellate myself, not only because I do not think I did much damage—after all, I was only a small part of a much larger Euro-American culture of domination—but also because many of those whose culture we undercut were willing victims.

this chapter, I will look at the larger picture of moral change in sub-African societies. I will consider eight features of the history of transplanting ...ing by outsiders of new cultural elements onto old stock. I will also try to why I think each effort, in the end, in some way contributed to the loss of that ...ope we all had in December 1958, despite the very real benefits that also were realized. No one element in the cultural onslaught could have brought about such a collapse by itself, but all were part of the pattern of loss. I will draw on my own experience, but I will refer also to comparable experiences in other areas.

The eight areas are:
    Reshaping of initiation ceremonies and secret societies
    Secularization of art forms
    Breakdown of extended family structure
    Emphasis on the individual instead of the community
    Replacement of local by global histories
    Change in women's roles
    Remaking of "tradition" to maintain social control
    Redefinition of ethnicity and culture.

Each of these eight aspects of cultural change is heavily contested by Africans and outsiders who have lived and worked in Africa. Some speak of these as destructive, leading to moral collapse. Others welcome the fresh wind of change. I tend to see the changes both as inevitable and as leading to Africans being unable to survive in a harsh, competitive world of rapid technological and social change. I claim that these changes have contributed materially to much of the failure of African societies and to their inability to be what they still have it within themselves to be. Yet I also claim there is still hope for new ways of life to grow within the shells of the old.

2.1 Reshaping of initiation ceremonies and secret societies.

Every society in the world has its ceremonies and institutions by which girls become women and boys become men. Too often, foreign presence and intervention have damaged the social fiber by alienating people from their accustomed coming-of-age procedures. New initiation rites and new secret societies have replaced the old; the new is sometimes beneficial, but often destructive to what had been of great value. I was present at such ceremonies in Liberia, Lesotho, and Tanzania and have read about them in many other countries. For as long as anyone knows, Poro and Sande societies have been the glue holding together communities in the Mande-speaking areas of Liberia, Sierra Leone, and Guinea. The village chiefs and elders may be the public face of discipline and law, but when the going gets tough, cases are referred to the less visible leaders deep within the hierarchy of a forest-based society. These leaders, called *zoes*, are usually blacksmiths, hunters, or farmers in everyday life.

The *zoes* manage the schools every boy and girl in Kpelle society must enter at some time before puberty. Traditionally, children on the verge of puberty attended these schools, held deep within the forest behind forbidding woven fences, boys for four years and girls for three. During that time, the children are considered to have been eaten by the "Big Thing." They have been removed from their childhood world,

Liberian initiation school ceremony

and for their time in bush school they are no longer part of their families. Upon graduation they emerge as adults, having incorporated in their lives the heritage of the community. They have been marked as full members of society by scars across their bodies, representing the teeth marks of the "Big Thing." They have been taught how to grow rice, how to climb palm trees, how to raise children, how to speak in proverbs. They are now adults, and they must respect the social order that maintains the village, not perfectly to be sure, but certainly within limits that define effective social control.

What happened to these schools when we outsiders came to disturb their world? The first serious challenge came from Western Euro-American classrooms, which brought a competing vision of what education should provide. Literacy became a requirement, replacing the old ability to speak and sing and declaim in the grand manner of their fathers and mothers. The history of the tight-knit family into which they were first born as children and re-born as initiated adults was replaced by what rural Liberians came contemptuously to call "book." I have tried to tell the story of both the old and the new ways in my three novels *Red Dust on the Green Leaves, The Brightening Shadow* and *Long Day's Anger*(Gay 2002a, 2002b, 2004).

David Diop, the Senegalese poet, speaks in his poem *The Vultures:*

Of foreigners who did not seem human,
who knew all the books but did not know love (Diop 163:145).

The consequence is that now young Africans are initiated into the knowledge of books, but lose their heritage.

One example from the early 1960s happened in Sinyea, the village next to Cuttington College. Sinyea opened a primary school in December 1958, shortly after I arrived. The late President Tubman, who was renowned as an African statesman and considered (often literally) by many Liberians to be their father, opened the school and dedicated it to his Unification Policy, whereby every Liberian would be a full part of the civil society.

In a 1955 speech inaugurating his policy, Tubman said that "representation and other responsibilities of Government cannot be properly and effectively discharged where educational and health facilities are not fully available on a basis of need and equality to fit and prepare men for leadership" (Smith 1964:98). What he meant, and what we wished to implement, was that all children in Liberia, from whatever background, should complete a full primary education within the American educational system that Liberia had inherited as part of its legacy from the nineteenth-century United States.

The meaning of this policy for specific children at a specific time and place was clear and led modernizers to take strong action to ensure that Tubman's vision would be implemented. However, in November 1964, Mrs. Rose Sambolah, the principal of the Sinyea school, was challenged by the chief *zoe* of the initiation school in Balama, the village just beyond Sinyea along a bush path into the interior. He wanted to take prepubescent boys from the Sinyea elementary school and put them instead into the bush so that they could become adults in the customary way. The children were about to write their end-of-year examinations, which were due at the beginning of December. Mrs. Sambolah gave a firm no to his request, saying that the children could only go into the bush in mid-December. Otherwise they would lose the entire year of school, which in practice meant they would most likely drop out permanently.

The *zoe* was equally insistent and had the authority of village tradition on his side. It would be easy for him to organize what Rose Sambolah would have called kidnapping by going to the children's homes at night and taking them forcibly into the bush. The parents would not have dared resist, much less the children. The confrontation quickly became a crisis.

The incident was resolved only when one of our Cuttington students, Arthur Kulah, intervened. He had been helping the children with their studies and their play after school. Also a member of the secret society, he spoke to the *zoe* and managed to persuade him to postpone entrance into the Poro bush. He pointed out that the government also had power and that any *zoe* who denied government authority could get into trouble. The *zoe* backed down and agreed to let the children wait beyond the normal date of entry, which was traditionally timed to coincide with the end of the rice harvest and the arrival of the dry season. In the process, he was forced to agree that these same boys could return to school in March and would not have to remain for the four years he normally would have required. Kulah later became Methodist bishop of Liberia as well as the author of a brave and hopeful look at Liberia's future (Kulah 1999).

So what was wrong? Initiation was maintained; the secret societies continued to function. Children, in theory, could have the best of both worlds. Serious clashes between most of the churches and the traditional secret societies were not the issue. Only a few fringe churches, such as the Swedish Pentecostal church in the far north of the country, excommunicated members who joined the secret societies. The mainline churches welcomed those who had received initiation. My principal research colleague, John Kellemu, who went on to become a Lutheran minister, was also high in the Poro system. He was able to advise us on the depth and accuracy of our research, particularly in order to prevent us from revealing or distorting Poro secrets. We were grateful for his "quality control," and the Poro officials were grateful that we did not stumble into a serious breach of rural etiquette.

Entering initiation school in Liberia

The deep problem was the Poro and the Sande were, in the end, emasculated. Poro initiation school had adjusted its entry date to fit the opinions of a woman from the coast who had herself not attended any initiation school. It had agreed to truncate the time from four years to four months. In this case Poro had bowed to the higher authority of government and the Western, so-called *kwii* way. It was the beginning of the end for all that the chief *zoe* stood for in his task of teaching new generations the Kpelle way.

Why would that be bad? Tubman's vision was of a society of equals, all schooled according to requirements of the new world, all prepared to take their place in the Western community of literate "book" people, the very community which we at Cuttington College were doing our best to promote. We would eventually admit into Cuttington a few of the students who had finished the Sinyea elementary school and had gone on to complete high school. We would give them a first-class Western-type education, and we would have gone one further step along the road toward realizing the dream that had inspired Ngombale, Kisenge, and Mapunda, my students who had been so inspired at the Pan-African Congress in Accra.

The problem was that so many children did nothing of the kind. Some of them dragged themselves to school and back each day for a few months, then missed a few days here and there, and finally dropped out entirely. Others were like the seed that Jesus mentioned which was sown on stony ground. They did well for a year or two, but then failed to pass the exams. They might try again, only to fail a second time. And then they too dropped out. Only a very small minority, some think as small as 10 percent of those who entered first grade, would make it through sixth grade. And of these only a small minority could afford to leave Sinyea or Balama and go to a boarding high school somewhere else in Liberia. Even those who could pay the fees and deny their family the farm labor, so much needed in a subsistence agricultural society, often could not survive the rigorous competition of six years of high school. Finally, of those who by hard work and good luck graduated from high school, Cuttington was in a position to enroll only a tiny minority as candidates for a university degree. There were less than two million people in Liberia in the 1960s, of whom more than half were under eighteen. In those early years, Cuttington could accept annually no more than 100 to150 and the University of Liberia perhaps twice or three times that number.

The rest were caught in a limbo not of their making. They may have had three or four months of initiation school, but they had not been steeped in the full heritage of their own Kpelle or other indigenous people. They were equally only very lightly initiated into the mysteries of the Western *kwii* world. They were not really children of two worlds, but were rather, in a serious way, children of no world at all.

What has happened to these children of no world? Some have become the fighters in Liberia's civil wars, wars that have spilled over first into Sierra Leone, then into Guinea and most recently into Côte d'Ivoire. It has been well documented that the young men who joined Charles Taylor, his unsuccessful rivals in the carnage of the 1990s, and then the more successful rebels of the 2000s, were those who could not make it in the modern world and who were at the same time no longer at home in a functioning rural village.

I met some of the survivors at a training school in Gbarnga in rural Liberia. They were the very sorts of young people described in a CARE report as former child soldiers for whom "programs attempt to identify [those] who have been exposed to extreme violence and provide relevant educational opportunities for them" (Harwood and Anis, 2001). They had nothing to show for their part in the war, nothing to show for the little education they had received before the war, and they were not part of any viable village community. And yet they were much better off than the amputees and beggars I saw in Monrovia in 2001, who were doing nothing, because there was nothing they could do.

Stephen Ellis spoke eloquently in 1995 of the role that Poro could play in the Liberian civil war, a war which shows no sign of stopping even after the departure of

Charles Taylor. He said, "The Poro society is essentially a system of socio-political control based on communication with the invisible world... [M]ediation with the invisible...appears to offer the only realistic solution to Liberia's crisis" (Ellis 1995:196). He added the churches to the mix when he said, "The spirit world is the only domain in which constructive action is still detectable, and in this a leading role may fall to the churches" (Ellis 1995:197). In my view, the constructive collaboration of indigenous and Western spirituality is needed to bring eventual peace.

A similar phenomenon was seen in Sierra Leone as its people worked for peace. The Kamajor are traditional hunters in the Mende ethnic group who have used their commitment to Poro to defend civil society. William Reno (Reno 2003) points out that "youth were recruited with the approval and consent of traditional authorities, and organized into bands of 'traditional hunters'. This practice gave fighters a high level of commitment and a stake in obedience to local social strictures governing the use of violence, thus protecting local communities upon which they relied for support from atrocities." As I see it, the tenuous and still-uncertain return of Sierra Leone to peace and order has depended in part on the collaboration between the indigenous secret societies and the coastal Christian government.

That collaboration unfortunately ran aground on March 2003 with the arrest by the United Nations War Crimes Tribunal of Sam Hinga Norman, Sierra Leone's Minister of Internal Affairs. The Kamajors, led by Mr. Norman, committed their share of atrocities during the civil war. Now they too are being called before the bar, just as are leading members of the Revolutionary United Front, which Norman and the Kamajors opposed. Norman's trial is proceeding by fits and starts, even though he sacked his defense lawyers in June 2004.

The Charles Taylor government, which professed to be Christian, tried to join forces with the powerful secret societies of the interior in the way that Stephen Ellis suggests. But his greed for power and wealth rendered his Christian commitment marginal at best and at worst, pure hypocrisy. He proclaimed himself to be "Dahkpannah," which means the chief *zoe* of all the secret societies in Liberia (Anderson 1998). In his case it was not collaboration, but illegitimate co-opting of the Poro by the *kwii* government, very much in the same way that previous presidents of Liberia declared themselves to be the heads of secret societies in which they had never been properly initiated. The Poro then becomes only a tool of government, not an independent force.

Liberian presidents, including Charles Taylor, have tried to co-opt the churches and reduce them to docile instruments of public policy. Fortunately, some mainline churches have refused to be bought out by the government, although the more evangelical and pentecostal churches have accepted presidential largesse. Paul Gifford documents the surrender of many right-wing church groups to Samuel Doe (Gifford 1993).

The same was true of Charles Taylor; he drew criticism from articulate self-confessed atheists, who often see through religiosity. The website www.atheists.org put the matter very well: "During a [2002] 'Liberia For Jesus' rally, Taylor collapsed onto the ground, and declared 'We shall confess our sins before God, (and) ask him to heal our land.' While Taylor is putting on the masque of public religiosity and trying to turn his nation into a theocracy, however, watch dog groups say that he is looting Liberia's wealth, aiding terrorists and violating human rights on a massive scale."

Under such circumstances, Stephen Ellis's optimism for a peace-promoting collaboration in Liberia between the church and the indigenous secret societies was unlikely to be realized. Now that Charles Gyude Bryant has become interim Head of State, there may be hope, particularly if both institutions—the Poro and the Christian church—can stay alive and independent of government. Bryant is an active Christian, a long-serving lay leader in the Episcopal Church, a person who has all the qualifications needed to bring Liberia back to life. But he must have the support of a way of life that pre-dated Liberia as a nation and that still exists in rural villages. The Christian church and the traditional secret societies need each other; otherwise, the unraveling of Liberian society will continue, the result of civil war fueled by unscrupulous leaders and ignorant militias.

Liberia and Sierra Leone are not the only countries with a rich indigenous heritage of initiation rites. Our Western world is replete with them. I was a Boy Scout, though not very successful, and I bravely, if incompetently, led a Cub Scout troop when my youngest son was in primary school. Admittedly, what I did was tame stuff compared with the four intense years of Poro in rural Liberia. Nonetheless, there are many like me who do their little bit in passing on a heritage to our American children.

Africa is no different; its various cultures have helped children become full members of the community for centuries. Yet most of these initiation rites are under threat. In Liberia, however, the Poro is not dead. Most churches never really turned their backs on the Poro, and it appears that there is a chance for a rapprochement between Christian churches and the indigenous institutions of socialization. The potential still exists, though now rarely practiced, for children to grow up to respect both traditions.

Basotho initiate singing his praises

In Lesotho, the so-called "circumcision schools" are shorter, but they fulfill many of the same purposes as the Kpelle bush schools. They teach discipline, they impart the history of the Basotho people and of the specific sub-clans, they prepare children for marriage, and they demonstrate the hard task of winning a living from the severe mountain landscape. The boys are circumcised in order to make them men and are expected to sing poems at the graduation ceremony in praise of their courage in the face of hardship. However, unlike in Liberia, early missionaries in Lesotho decided that joining the initiation schools was against the Gospel. As a result, families had to choose between loyalty to their Basotho past or to a Christian future. This created a lose-lose situation in Lesotho in contrast to Liberia's solution, which gave a few children the possibility of a win-win way of life. Those Basotho who chose to have their children enter the initiation school forfeited the right to send children to Western school, and vice versa. Thus, an unhealthy split grew between those who had "lost their tails," as new initiates are described, and those who are still called "dogs," because they have gone only to the Western school.

This enmity continues to the present day. Not long ago, a Christian catechist strayed too close to an initiation school and was almost beaten to death by the trainees. Increasingly, because schooling is becoming more expensive and less a guarantee of a good job, poor rural children are once again choosing the traditional way, thereby widening the gap between the two ways of life. Many fall into the trap of belonging to no world at all, mostly because they fail to jump over the hurdles required by the Western school system, a means of initiation I discuss in a later chapter.

On the other hand, there is no reason why the two worlds cannot offer joint allegiance and membership to Basotho youth. Possibly, looking to the old ways is a transient phenomenon, soon to be overcome as government schooling becomes universally available. The unanswered question is whether the initiation school, in its modern resistance to Westernization, grows out of a deep Sesotho malaise or whether it is only a despairing pretense because of failure to succeed in the "modern" money economy. In the meantime, violence and within-culture enmity increase.

I remember vividly an incident when a teenager from Soweto was visiting us in Lesotho. My wife and I took him for a trip to the mountains where he and his friends enjoyed swimming at the foot of a waterfall. Suddenly a group of young initiates and their teacher appeared, marching determinedly toward the children. They were legitimately terrified because of the very real danger of being abducted on the spot for initiation. Trembling, I stood between them and the advancing crowd of young men, who were covered with red ochre, clad in red blankets, and carrying menacing knobkerries. Nothing untoward happened; the initiates changed their course, I quickly got the Soweto boy and his friends out of the water, and all was well. What is sad and disturbing is that all might not have been well.

Stories are told almost monthly about the mismatch between initiation societies and the modern community in southern Africa, both in Lesotho and in the neighboring Eastern Cape province of South Africa, reflecting to the present day the distinction between "Red" and "School." The Red are those who have, often for good reason, rejected the new world, which promises a better life, but fails to deliver it to the great majority. The conflict is described beautifully in the novel The *Heart of Redness* (Mda 2000), contrasting "believers" and "unbelievers." The believers in Mda's book, which is set both in the mid-nineteenth century and at the end of the twentieth century, reject the modern world and all that it purports to bring, while the unbelievers accept British colonial rule and rapid modernization.

Basotho initiates painted with red ochre

The reality for many "red" people is a tragic encounter with circumcision ceremonies. The health department in South Africa's Eastern Cape reported forty-five deaths due to botched circumcisions in 2002, more than at any time since record-keeping started in 1995 (/allafrica.com/stories/200212190002.html). Another sixty-eight were admitted to hospital for problems arising from such circumcisions. Circumcision school "owners" resist being supervised by the public health service, and even more strongly resist having the operation done in public hospitals.

This is in strong contrast to the situation as I remember it in Liberia before the civil war began. In rural Liberia, with church approval, initiated nurses visited the initiation lodges to make sure that circumcisions were performed under sanitary conditions. So far this has proved impossible in southern Africa because churches have denounced the "heathenism" of initiation schools, and traditional believers have resented church interference in their affairs.

In his novel, Mda attempts a rapprochement between Red and School. The character of Camagu, a Western-educated development "expert," marries a woman from the believer group instead of the university-trained school principal who seemed a natural match for him. His intention is to have the best of both worlds—traditional Red belief and environmentally sound Western business practice. His "solution" may be overly simple, and he has also been criticized for neglecting to address the HIV/AIDS pandemic and thus glossing over the most serious problem faced in today's South Africa (Rush 2003).

Whether such a meeting of minds and hearts may one day be possible in southern Africa depends on both sides working together to bring meaning to young people who are not equipped to make it in a highly competitive economic setting. Yet being "Red" is not an inevitable barrier to full participation in the rapidly changing and unfolding new southern Africa. Good will and intelligence on both sides are needed to ensure that any such barrier is torn down.

What I saw in Tanzania, during a two-day visit to Maasai herders at the southern extreme of their nomadic range, was indeed sad. Here was a society trying very hard to maintain traditional ways of life in a hostile world. I spent a day with herders and their animals on the Usangu plain, where evidence suggests the future is bleak. As the populations of both the Maasai and their cattle grew, they were forced to migrate south and west, only to come up against the mountains of Mbeya where no herding is possible. To the west were the Nyamwezi cattle herders, firmly in possession of traditional grazing lands. These Maasai, the front edge of a migratory people, were trapped. Some Maasai settled in villages, though others resisted. At the time of my visit, they were beginning to grow crops and to send their children to school.

Maasai girl inspecting new initiates

As a result, the initiation ceremony I attended was a drunken travesty of what I imagine took place in the past. The same dances were held with the same remarkable leaps into the air by young boys. The young people sized each other up as possible partners. But there was an air of unreality about it. The only sober person at the party was the elder of the community, who confided to me that their way of life was over. The ceremonies—to which I was an unexpected visitor, not simply a tourist, since I was investigating development possibilities in the area—were somehow only a sham, and the drunkenness hid the sham from all except the sober elder.

A Maasai, commenting on his own society through the Internet, says, "We are told to abandon our way of life and seek the external culture of imperialism, because it is 'superior to ours.' On the contrary, many of us see this idea as a crime against our humanity. Our culture is just as important to us as it is to everyone else around the world." He quotes a Maasai saying: "It takes one day to destroy a house but to build a new one will take months, perhaps years. If we destroy our way of life to construct a new one, it will take thousands of years" (maasai-infoline.org/Maasaiceremonies.html).

Can the good life that the Maasai have known over many centuries, a good life that cannot survive the rapid changes taking place in Kenya and Tanzania, be merged smoothly with a new kind of good life? A Maasai, writing for the World Bank, says, "Their knowledge and practices are empirical, based on continuous observation and their close attachment to and utter dependence on natural resources. The knowledge is stored in cultural and religious beliefs, taboos, folklore or myths as much as in the individuals' practical experience. Knowledge is imparted in the youth through a phased childhood and adolescence." He goes on to ask "whether the Maasai's distinct culture will have endowed them with the flexibility and adaptability to cope with the new conditions without losing their identity" (www.worldbank.org/afr/ik/ikpacks/tanzania.htm). Maasai in both Kenya and Tanzania have been the objects of mission work by secular developers and Christian evangelists for more than one hundred years. It is critical that all those who are concerned with Maasai well-being in an uncertain world find these ways to cope.

Another pervasive problem is female genital mutilation, or clitoridectomy, a widespread practice in Africa closely tied to initiation. James Ngugi (now writing as Ngugi wa Thiong'o) in his marvelous novel *The River Between* (Ngugi 1965) depicts the terrible conflict regarding the practice within the hearts of young Gikuyu women. The old people say that a woman must be cut, and the churches speak against the practice. The custom continues across much of tropical Africa, in some places in the name of Islam and in others in the name of tradition.

There are women who defend the practice in the public arena, as in this revealing comment quoted by Amnesty International from Mrs. Njeri, a Kenyan: "Circumcision makes women clean, promotes virginity and chastity and guards young girls from sexual frustration by deadening their sexual appetite" (www.amnesty.org/ailib/intcam/femgen/). Amnesty International explains further why various cultures defend the practice; adherents claim that not only does clitoridectomy protect chastity, it keeps young women away from sex entirely until their arranged marriages. Traditionalists assert that in their cultures a girl cannot be married if she has not been cut.

Nonetheless, there is widespread opposition among African women to the practice. The issue is whether becoming a fully respected adult woman depends on having the clitoris cut at the time of puberty. Genital mutilation has been described by many as a crime against humanity and a gross violation of human rights. In the same Amnesty International report, Sudanese medical doctor Nahid Toubia says that genital mutilation "represents a human tragedy and must not be used to set Africans against non-Africans, one religious group against the other, or even women against men."

Sadly, there appears to be another side to the question of patriarchal control over women. The proportion of people infected with HIV/AIDS in North Africa and the Middle East is far below that reported for most of Africa south of the equator. A recent report from the region reports only 443,000 who are HIV-positive in the region (http://allafrica.com/stories/200302140563.html). Some have challenged this figure, claiming it is too low. It is not impossible that the severe restrictions women in these nations, many of whom practice genital mutilation, restrict the spread of AIDS. It is striking that such a high proportion of southern Africa are HIV-positive. For example, at the end of 2001, 51 percent women in Lesotho ages fifteen to twenty-four were HIV-positive. This figure is for a society where rape, sexual violence and a generally relaxed attitude toward sex prevail. Surely, however, there must be a better way to prevent AIDS than doing horrible things to women.

In all four cases—in Liberia, in Lesotho, in Tanzania, and with widespread female mutilation—the rites of passage and ceremonies of adulthood have fallen into contradiction with the social realities of a continually encroaching modern world. In Liberia, the Western school reduced the Poro and Sande bush schools to a shorter, weaker imitation of the bush schools of the past. In Lesotho and South Africa, the conflict between church and circumcision school weakened each institution, leading to a deep rift in the nation. In Tanzania, the Maasai went through motions which were rooted in a way of life they could no longer sustain. Finally, the new world of female equality and liberation cannot accommodate an ancient practice which was designed to keep women in sexual bondage.

Yet real harm is done when initiation rituals and customs such as these are lost. It is my contention that this loss is at least part of the reason why the dream of the new Africa, which we all held with such fervor in 1960, has not been realized. Archimedes said that with a place to stand and a lever he could move anything. Without a place to stand, however, it is not possible. One such place to stand is provided by an initiation rite which welcomes children into adulthood. These children and, in fact, all people become human beings through the act of induction into the community. The Sesotho proverb *motho ke motho ka batho* can loosely be translated, "A person is a person through other people." That "becoming of a person" takes place in many ways, of course, but a principal way in every society is through rites of passage.

The loss of rites of passage is the loss of the social glue that gives stability and security to life. No longer do old sanctions restrain alienated individuals from doing whatever they wish. In the case of Liberian civil war, a perhaps overly optimistic Stephen Ellis implies that after the terrible breakdown of all values and all inwardly accepted social controls, the old alliance between missionary and Poro/Sande societies might bring back social harmony. The partial success of the Kamajors in Sierra Leone in helping bring peace may grow out of the realization that old and new forces must work together to prevent chaos. It could happen in Liberia.

What are the implications for comparable situations in Lesotho? I think the same alliances could be helpful. The Lesotho Evangelical Church has taken a small step forward by calling its conference center a *mophato*, meaning the hut where initiation takes place. So far, however, the churches have not taken the radical step of making their peace with the old way of life so that the new can build on the old. Unfortunately, the result means social strife, with the unschooled initiation school ignoring and breaking the norms of the schooled world, leading to an increase in class-driven crime.

For example, a profoundly disturbing pattern emerged from a study I carried out in Lesotho in 2000. Groups of up to ten ordinary villagers were asked to sort cards, each naming a strategy to escape from poverty (Gay and Hall 2000: 152ff). The strategies fell into five clusters, of which four made good sense as areas of life within which people might better their lot in socially responsible ways. These four were agriculture, wage employment, family relations, and government structures.

The fifth cluster was a catch-all collection of marginally or patently illegal ways to get ahead. Foremost among these was the brewing and selling of beer; also included were marijuana production, prostitution, theft, street trading, hawking, renting properties, small businesses, pensions, politics—and initiation school. These activities compose the so-called informal sector, which throughout the Two-Thirds World is the survival strategy of those without the resources of land, capital, or skill. That the initiation school is identified with this group shows its marginality in a divided society. Petty crime and livestock theft are the revenge of the underclass against the upper and middle classes who have pushed them out. Young men are trained in the initiation schools to be fighters; they are trained to make their way in a hostile world.

Much the same is true in the Eastern Cape Province of South Africa, where the initiation school provides recruits to the rapidly increasing crime problem. No longer does the circumcision school serve as the base upon which a newly maturing adult can stand. Rather, it tells him that he is marginal and gives him the tools and the ethos with which to fight a system which he will never fully be able to join.

I saw members of the Maasai band with whom I celebrated the initiation drinking themselves into a stupor while the elder who guided me through the ceremonies lamented the future. But what are the alternatives for the young Maasai who has maintained his ties with the old ways, but who sees that such ties are not viable in the long term? I learned that some Maasai had split off from the main group and were planting crops, sending their children to government school, and seeking employment, but they were no longer attending the traditional ceremonies. As these Maasai diverge onto different paths, the followers of the old way seem doomed to enter a world that has no place for them.

As for young women who break loose from the constraints imposed on them by the impossible and demeaning practice of genital mutilation, the worry is that they will be freed from more than merely the practice of clitoridectomy. With both men and women released from the otherwise lamentable restrictions of a strong patriarchy, there is little to restrain their sexuality, whether benign or otherwise. I think of Yeats' wonderful poem, *A Prayer for my Daughter*, in which he asks,

> *And may her bridegroom bring her to a house*
> *Where all's accustomed, ceremonious;*
> *For arrogance and hatred are the wares*
> *Peddled in the thoroughfares.*
> *How but in custom and in ceremony*
> *Are innocence and beauty born?*
> *Ceremony's a name for the rich horn,*
> *And custom for the spreading laurel tree. (Yeats 1953:187)*

Yeats, of course, spoke out of an arrogant and class-bound disrespect for ordinary folk, but his prayer rings true for the many young people in the world who have lost their roots. The challenge for those of us who love Africa is to help her people find ways to marry "custom and ceremony" with the new, modern world, while at the same time rejecting what the early 20th-century British colonial ruler and theoretician Lord Lugard spoke of as ways which are "repugnant to humanity"

(Collins 1970:98). Surely female genital mutilation is repugnant to humanity, but what is needed is a way to retain and enhance humanity without having to agree that Mrs. Njeri spoke out of a different wisdom than the wisdom of individual human rights.

If customary traditional societies no longer provide the foundation stone for children's lives as they enter adulthood, then other forms of association will take their place. Christian churches have tried hard to build such communities. Missiologist Titus Presler shows how the Zimbabwean *pungwe*, or night vigil, provided an anchor and a focus for the liberation struggle during the war of independence and how it now binds Christians together in a community of faith (Presler 1999).

An example from what was then the Belgian Congo was the *Jamaa* movement, in which Catholics and their families were initiated into a tightly-knit body. Women had a "living encounter" with Christ, and men with Mary. A series of initiations led to a final stage of union in which the priest and the families within the chapter lived and worked and prayed together, often to the exclusion of the outside world. Members shared all possessions and all activities in a spirit similar to that of the early church described in the Acts of the Apostles in the Christian Bible. The object of the movement was for its members to find total healing and no longer fear or covet the outside world (de Craemer 1977).

African independent churches continue to flourish across the continent, and most require some form of initiation into membership. I worshiped with a Zionist church in Lesotho in early 2003 and was present when new members were baptized in the river that divides Lesotho from South Africa. It was clear that the initiation was intended to heal, to separate the members from the world, and to bring them into a new fellowship. The initiation into this group was not as severe as that of the *Jamaa* movement, but it clearly gave its members a family to help sustain them in their encounters with a harsh and unforgiving world.

It is, however, not only the church which provides new and modern associations within which young Africans find solace and security. There are recurrent reports of students forming secret societies at African universities. Perhaps the most notorious are found in Nigeria. The BBC reported on 19 June 2002 that at least seventeen people were killed and several injured when members of a secret student society opened fire with guns at a university in southeastern Nigeria. It has been widely reported that these societies have terrorized many campuses in Nigeria and have even forced faculty members to accede to their power.

In summary, the human desire for membership and solidarity in groups that help their members to be human expresses itself in both customary and modern forms. Such societies can both benefit and harm society at large. For Africa to move out of the slough of despond, into which much of the continent seems to have fallen, requires creative rebuilding of the foundations which enable children to become adults in a strong, life-affirming manner. Initiation has always been and remains a cornerstone for that foundation.

2.2 Secularization of traditional art forms.

Visual art. As I write these pages, I look up from my computer and see on my wall a Dan secret society mask from Liberia and Bambara fertility figures from Mali. I enjoy them and find them beautiful. They enrich my house and make me feel that I am part of Africa. On the living room wall is a warm, round, moon-faced Baoule mask from Côte d'Ivoire, a mask that Judy calls our "Mona Lisa" because of the enigmatic half-smile and despite the horns that belie the clearly feminine face.

Because of photographs in scholarly books, I know that these masks have been made in the traditional style, unlike some of the tourist art I have bought elsewhere. Our particular exemplars of these traditional styles may not have been made for ceremonial use, but ceremonial or not, they represent the art of pre-colonial Africa.

Some would call what I have done a rape of traditional African art, not only by collecting and displaying the pieces, but also through books on my shelf which have captured the souls of the art in photographs open to anyone and everyone. I remember one of the first times I tried to photograph some women crossing the Cuttington campus. They hid their faces, claiming that my camera would steal their inner being. Might they have been right? Is it indeed inevitable that we outsiders will steal their souls as further gratuitous damage on top of our theft of their land, their resources, and their children?

Before the devastation of the civil war, Cuttington College had a museum, built to hold the best items from a truckload of masks, statues, and carvings that had been brought to us by an itinerant Muslim trader. He had obviously ransacked villages throughout West Africa, buying anything he could find, ranging from fine, old authentic ceremonial objects to tourist junk. We agreed to buy the truckload for about $10,000, which in the 1960s must have seemed a princely sum to the trader. We set aside items of museum quality and then sold the rest of the pieces to ourselves in order to make up the $10,000 we had spent. Was this also a rape—this time of a higher magnitude?

I remember an illiterate rural Liberian who visited the museum. He was horrified at what we had done. He believed that the museum was full of magic and mystery, and he objected to our displaying these materials. I do not remember that he threatened us, but he went away full of fear and resentment.

Tanzanian woman making a pot

He was defeated, just as traditional people across the world are defeated when their cultures become a show-and-tell museum. In the 1930s, people were killed because they revealed the secrets of their communities. Dr. George Harley, the pioneer medical doctor in the far interior of Liberia, collected the best masks that the Mano and Gio people had to offer and gave them to the permanent collection at Harvard's Peabody Museum. It is generally believed that at least one of his informants was killed for their roles in selling this art and culture to an outsider. I myself bought a few hand masks from the village elder of Gbansu; he got into trouble with the village, but since the hand masks were only talismans for individuals and not for the whole village, the trouble was not so serious.

Tragically for Cuttington and its attempt

to honor the artists of Liberia's rich past, the museum we created was looted during the civil war of the 1990s. Some pieces have found their way into the international art market, but most have been lost, probably forever. Was it perhaps the revenge of the artists? I do not want to speculate. But no longer is Cuttington able to hold up to its visitors a mirror to the past—for good or for ill.

What is happening now? I have regularly attended the Grahamstown Arts Festival, held every July in the South African university town. In addition to the music, dance, drama, lectures, and films that fill every waking hour, there is a large market providing stalls to traders from all over Africa. Many of these traders bring truckloads of commercially-produced African masks and carvings, some of which I bought because I liked their style. The traders purchase these items in bulk in villages across West and Central Africa, where they are carved and painted by skilled craftsmen brought up in a tradition that is almost, but not quite, dead. In Johannesburg in 2003, I found the same traders, now no longer itinerant, selling their wares in a huge crafts market.

The power has inevitably gone out of such objects. They are no longer serious religious and ceremonial art—they are artifacts, curios, trade goods, things to satisfy the curiosity of foreigners like myself. Neither are the forests where the trees grew any longer places of awe and mystery, but are instead desecrated, as the wood which once made masks is cut down to supply furniture to luxury-loving Europeans and Asians. Of course, I am not saying anything new. The same complaint has been made over the years both by foreign collectors and by people who mourn the loss of their traditions.

More important are the consequences for today's Africa. Throughout the world, a holy object is supposed to have power to guide people's lives. When a holy object loses its power, as has happened across Africa, then people are left with one less reference point to guide them. The enthusiasm of iconoclasts notwithstanding, most people need visual symbols. The enacted art of a mask on a raffia-covered dancer in rural Liberia has been potent—but what happens when its potency dies?

The recent civil war in Liberia and the current war in Sierra Leone show how new symbols are created when old symbols die. Rebels dress themselves in powerful, but very new, costumes. The more conventional warriors wear camouflage uniforms, but others go much further. General "Butt Naked" was one of the rebels—his battle dress was captured in his battle name. Others wear women's dresses or wigs. Skulls and other human bones decorate some warriors. Here is power without restraint, when bloodthirsty rebels abandon the old symbols and baptize new ones in the blood of their opponents. Did we prepare the way by secularizing the old art forms? I would not be surprised.

And yet art has proved to be a remarkably powerful tool in the liberation struggle. Whereas the old art, the indigenous art of pre-colonial peoples, has mutated into cross-cultural chic, new art is continually emerging from Africa. The African National Congress recognized the importance of visual art as it carried on the struggle in South Africa. Not only did it promote posters and paintings, and even graffiti, as weapons against apartheid, but it made sure that the outside world would refuse to buy and exhibit mainstream white South African art. In 1989, the National Executive Committee of the ANC issued a public statement saying, "An important and dynamic dimension of this democratic offensive against the structures and institutions of apartheid colonialism is the sphere of culture—embracing the arts, other intellectual pursuits and sports. Cultural activity has won and already occupies an important position as an integral part of our overall strategy for national liberation and democracy" (www.anc.org.za/ancdocs/pr/1989/pr0500.html).

During the apartheid era, photography was one of the few visual arts where black artists were able to make an impact on the larger public. Peter Magubane was one of the first to break with conventional law-abiding photography. He had been sent to photograph the Sharpville massacre in 1960 and was so shaken by the event that he later said, "From that day I made up my mind that I shall think of my pictures first before anything. I no longer get shocked; I am a feeling-less beast while taking photographs. It is only after I complete my assignment that I think of the dangers that surrounded me, the tragedies that befell my people."

Magubane went on to work for that late great newspaper *The Rand Daily Mail*, only to be imprisoned for his work in the late 1960s. He was released after 589 days in jail and then made his international reputation both as a photographer and as a human being for his marvelous shots of the June 1976 Soweto uprising (www.marekinc.com/HumExcellenceRSA090301.html). I saw his pictures in the Hector Petersen museum in Soweto in January 2003 and realized then how important good art had been in the struggle.

William Kentridge and Jane Alexander are representative of post-apartheid white South African art, vibrant in their clean lines, but also compelling in their presentation of the realities of the "bad old days." I was moved and sobered by the black-and-white animation that Kentridge did as a backdrop to a production of the play *Ubu and the Truth Commission* at the Grahamstown Festival. The play filled in the gap of a hundred years since the original Ubu play was written (Shattuck 1965). Ubu was a foul-mouthed, self-centered, avaricious and utterly disgusting person who made himself king in his own fantasy world. Kentridge translates the story into the apartheid era with Ubu enjoying his lusty consumption of all that a down-trodden black society can offer him. In the end he faces the Truth Commission, takes a symbolic shower, accepts his role as an exploiter and sails off into the sunset, free of any obligations to make the new world better than the old.

Jane Alexander has created powerful life-size sculptures to show the reality of white domination and black suffering. One I remember most vividly is entitled *Butcher Boys* and shows three nude men with bulls' heads, seated on a bench and presumably relaxing before their next venture into the butchery of black Africans. Another shows an ill-dressed black man sitting hopefully before a television set, wistfully hoping that the white world might offer him something. Her portrayal of a black nanny and a white baby on a park bench brings to life the drudgery of black domestic servants.

Thus, African art is not only the time-honored heritage of pre-colonial sculpture, remarkable as that may be. It is also part of the ongoing fight for freedom and justice in Africa. I still remember with awe the remarkable art of the Ethiopia that fought for its liberation over many centuries, not just in the relatively short half-century that has given me a home in Africa. In Ethiopia I saw the brave wall paintings in a remarkable monastic church on an island in Lake Tana, paintings which held up high the power of Christianity in a part of the continent where Islam threatened to conquer all opposing religions. I saw also a startling wall mosaic in the headquarters of the Economic Community of Africa in Addis Ababa. There in brilliant colors was St. George, the patron saint of Ethiopia, slaying the dragon, but this time not just the conventional icon. The dragon who was shrinking from St. George's blows was huddled far down in the southern corner of an otherwise free African continent, so that the whole mosaic brought Christian and African liberation into one vivid im

This vision of liberating Christianity is one that has stuck with me ove years. Our faith has almost always expressed itself visually. May it continue to do so, and may it help Africans find images that can sustain them and carry them into a brave new future.

Music. We outsiders have done our best to remove the numinous from traditional African music. Yet the heart of African indigenous music is not dead in the same way that I fear the heart of African indigenous sculpture is dead. Beautiful sounds are coming out of Senegal and Mali and are widely popular elsewhere in the world. In Lesotho there is *famo* music, sung by migrant workers to the accompaniment of drum and accordion. Ghanaian highlife is still alive and well. Fela Kuti's irreverent and caustic protest songs were instrumental in bringing the collapse of the military government in Nigeria. Fortunately, it is hard to kill music even on those sad occasion when it is hijacked and turned into Muzak.

Liberian drummers

Today, what is missing from much African music is the spiritual heart that made its hearers stop and listen. Performance is now a commodity rather than a communal event. The best musicians go on world tours and record for audiences who can buy CDs. What such musicians often fail to do is to speak directly to the hearts of their own people. The commercialization that has killed traditional sculpture is beginning to happen to music, with formula songs being turned out on assembly line for money. People buy it because they like it, but such music is no longer rooted in their inner lives. There is a great difference between passive audiences listening to a performance and active participation by people in a vital and living culture that is their own. When the latter is lost, then society loses a great deal, and the door is opened to hedonism and social disintegration.

Judy and I tape-recorded traditional Kpelle music all through our stay in Liberia. I find the music beautiful and at its best, deep and unforgettable. After making many recordings, only once did the ancestors have their revenge. I caught on tape the sweet but haunting sounds of a flute accompanying the "Big Thing" as he came into the village long after midnight to celebrate the death of a leader in the Poro society. The tape was good, but now it is the only tape I cannot find anywhere in my belongings—I would like to believe that the tape vanished because I overstepped the limits of decency by making the recording.

There is a deep continuity between jazz and the public Kpelle music—but, strikingly, not the secret society music, which we might overhear on moonlit nights in Gbansu. On such nights the whole village would be alive and alert to the drums and horns of the village musicians. Fortunately, African traditional music has remained alive in American, and now world-wide, jazz. Yet the best of American jazz could hardly equal the rhythmic complexity of what we heard. Unfortunately, contemporary American jazz does not by and large speak to most Africans. Rather, they have been caught by music like rap and kwaito, music which speaks to and reinforces the alienation which has been forced upon them by generations of racial and economic exploitation. To be bad is to be good in this new inversion of values. Even more problematic is the music of rebel soldiers, such as the frightening and ominous martial chanting of Jonas Savimbe's now defeated UNITA militia in Angola.

The great alternative in much of Africa is the music of the church. Whereas popular music has become far too fully a performance art, church music is alive across the continent. Every church in Lesotho, no matter how small, has a choir, and some of them sing very well indeed.

Secular choirs are also popular, and one of the leading recreations in much of southern Africa is the choir concert. Zakes Mda memorialized such an event in his novel, *The Heart of Redness*. His description rings very true for those of us who have attended many such concerts. Several choirs will meet for an evening, sometimes even a full night, of singing. They challenge each other to sing songs, both familiar and new, and the audience responds to the occasion by paying ever larger sums first for a given choir to sing a number, and then for that choir to stop if the audience is not satisfied.

Choir music is drawn from any and every source—traditional songs, folk music, hymns, newly composed four-part choruses, selections from the classical repertoire. Choir members are enthusiastic about preparing for both informal concerts, such as I mention above, and for more formal concerts.

In Lesotho, I had the great privilege of conducting the Maseru Singers, a group of Africans and expatriates. An especially moving occasion was *Bach's St. Matthew Passion*, a work demanding two adult choirs, a children's choir, and two orchestras. We found the choirs in Lesotho: the Maseru Singers, a local church choir, and a children's group from a local primary school.

But where were we to find orchestras in the isolated and beleaguered country of Lesotho? I had learned earlier that there existed a Soweto Symphony Orchestra, a group of musicians who were playing wonderful music together in the wasteland of the biggest apartheid black "location." They played on instruments that would be scorned by a junior high school orchestra in the U.S., not because they did not know any better, but because they could not obtain anything better. Not everyone is as fortunate as the great South African jazz trumpeter Hugh Masekela, who was given his first instrument by the legendary Anglican priest Fr. Trevor Huddleston.

The conductor of the Soweto Symphony had learned his art by donning a janitor's uniform and sweeping while the South African Broadcasting Company orchestra rehearsed. We in Lesotho and the Soweto group rejoiced in making each other's acquaintance and in performing together in Lesotho, a country which was an island of non-racial sanity.

But how to find a second orchestra? We contacted players from the orchestra—all white, of course—of the Orange Free State, based in the heartland of white Afrikaner South Africa. They agreed to join us for the concert, and so, black and white, we put together what I remember as an inspiring, even though perhaps not technically very good, performance of the *St. Matthew Passion*. I chose to introduce the occasion, which took place toward the very climax of the anti-apartheid era, by dedicating the concert to the memory of those who had died in the struggle for freedom. I know that at least one of the Afrikaners in the orchestra objected in his heart, but we proceeded nonetheless.

What I rejoice about in the aftermath is that four of the string players went on to form the Soweto String Quartet, which is now one of the leading ensembles in the new South Africa. And a second violinist, Sibongile Mngoma, who doubled as an alto for some of the solo sections of the piece, has blossomed into a formidable musician in both the classical and the popular repertoire. What a joy it was for me to work with such people and to see how music has spoken to and helped to liberate the people, both black and white, of South Africa.

I must conclude by discussing that most evocative of all African songs, Nkosi Sikelele Africa, which has become the national anthem not only of South Africa but also of several other African countries. We first sang it in Liberia in 1960 at the time of the Sharpville Massacre, using the words "God bless our native Africa." It became the rallying cry of the ANC, who sang it in Lesotho when they needed to boost their morale, such as when Oliver Tambo made the very risky flight into Lesotho to celebrate the funeral of forty-two people killed by the South African Defense Force. I heard the song most recently on the BBC in March 2003 sung by a group of teachers in Tanzania who were protesting low wages. Music has been very important in the liberation of Africa, and that great song proves it so.

Dance. Dance too has gone through a great change in recent years. In Ethiopia, I witnessed the slow, solemn dance of elderly men at a feast in honor of the Virgin Mary. I was there as a visiting researcher; the event was not put on for any outside spectator. The men, dressed in long white robes, carried large drums and prayer sticks and moved slowly in a great circle while the replica of the Ark of the Covenant was brought from the church and displayed with great reverence. The movement was slow and beautiful and culminated in an ecstasy of deep singing and deeper drum beats.

I have also shared in a secular, but nonetheless very communal, night of dance in Gbansu. Everyone, young and old, male and female, danced together to the beat of complex drum rhythms, and the community became one thing. I felt very privileged to be part of the occasion.

A sad and wistful imitation occurs when African high school or university students put on a drama and include ritualized traditional dances. The occasions always involve a student dressed in skins and carrying a fly whisk, which he waves in mock ferocity while the rest of the students, clad in what they think is traditional dress, dance around him. The artificiality, indeed phoniness, of the occasion is obvious. I have seen such performances in Liberia and Lesotho, and they were stamped by the same cookie cutter. They look back to the past hopefully and yet without actual hope, since the students are trying to recapture something that is lost. Authenticity is gone, because the students have been thoroughly weaned out of a culture which they can only vaguely remember. What they do is in the end only a parody of what once was real.

Yet new dance emerges out of new contexts. What is unfortunate is that the new dance forms mostly represent protest and anger. The toyi-toyi in South Africa is charged with energy and has become a vehicle for rebels who very much have a cause. The toyi-toyi frightens white conservatives for natural and obvious reasons. I remember a cartoon in a South African newspaper showing a white man entering a dance school and asking shyly, "Can you teach me to toyi-toyi?" The answer is clear—this dance has to come out of deep feelings of oppression and need.

More frightening is the dance of death, inflaming so much of Africa today.

Pictures of rebels training and fighting in the Democratic Republic of Congo, in Sierra Leone, and in Liberia show how the human spirit can be captured by a demonic energy, lived out in dance. I saw the same frightening energy just below my house in Maseru, Lesotho in September 1998 when protesting youth (many of them hired to take part) sang and danced at the gates of the royal palace. They worked themselves up into a frenzy, which erupted into the looting and burning of shops and buildings along the main street of Maseru.

A more positive use of dance is emerging in the new southern Africa. Dance groups have sprung up in every corner of the region, and many have performed at various festivals. Lesotho has now established its own Morija Arts Festival, just as South Africa has Grahamstown. Among the vibrant groups at both festivals have been young dancers from Soweto. Vincent Mantsoe, recipient of the Young Artist Award in the mid-1990s, performed in Grahamstown and has gone on to be a major force in South African dance. His performances have the grace and life of a professional choreographer who combines Western technique and the raw power of life in the black townships.

Poetry and rhetoric. Poetry also became part of the liberation struggle when it was taken away from griots, praise singers, and new initiates. Poetry played a vital role during the liberation struggle, but afterward, as the higher rhetoric was replaced by the hypnotic rantings of demagogues, something very new and dangerous happened. At its best, demagoguery can be impressive; in Liberia, when President Tubman "got carried away," we realized the power of a master orator. But when the substance of what he said was destructive, as happened in his later years, then the oratory became dangerous.

We taught our students at Cuttington the value of high rhetoric. Research that my colleagues and I did in rural Liberia showed the real power of rhetoric in finding solutions to what were called "palavers," cases brought to chiefs and elders for wise mediation. But the student speeches were often parodies, just as their dance-and-drama performances were parodies.

Such empty rhetoric is exemplified by a great line in Wole Soyinka's play *The Lion and the Jewel*. The schoolteacher tries to impress Sidi, the village beauty, with his English vocabulary. After a torrent of multi-syllabic nonsense, Sidi asks, "Is the bag empty? Why did you stop?" to which Lakunle replies, "I own only the Shorter Companion Dictionary, but I have ordered The Longer One—you wait!" (Soyinka 1963:7).

What we heard at Cuttington is echoed in Lesotho. The English language newspapers have regular contributors who have almost nothing to say and say it in a great many words. There are admittedly some writers who make very good sense, but they are in a minority. Such meaningless posturing leads to a degrading of speech and language, and that leads in the end to the destruction of rational argument. Connoisseurs of political discourse, in whatever country, would not be surprised by the existence of such nonsense, but its extent and richness might amaze them.

Demagogues flourish when sense and sensibility die. Pronouncements from Charles Taylor in Liberia and now in exile in Nigeria, the late Foday Sankoh in Sierra Leone, former president Daniel Arap Moi in Kenya, the late Laurent Kabila in the Democratic Republic of Congo (formerly known as Zaire) and Robert Mugabe in Zimbabwe, to name only a few, are depressing in their emotional appeal and intellectual vacuity. Traditional poetry and rhetoric have been swallowed up by the new and meaningless rhetoric, which African leaders have learned from foreign teachers. The hope for rational, policy-oriented discourse inevitably fades in the face of such populism, and the unfortunate result is repression and, eventually, war.

Street poetry, spoken more than written, shows one way forward. Mzwakhe Mbuli, released in November 2003 from prison for alleged bank robbery, made a marvelous beginning with his vigorous and vital oral poetry. He was called on by Nelson Mandela to recite at his 1994 presidential inauguration. His poem was strong and forthright, typical of what he declaimed throughout the struggle for freedom, landing him in jail once before.

Mzwakhe's poem *Our Music* sets forth what I have been saying about hope for the survival and growth of the arts in Africa:

> *Our music is traditional*
> *Our music is inspirational*
> *Our music is spiritual*
> *Our music is therapeutic*
> *Our music is rich and soul uplifting*
>
> *Our music is our culture*
> *Our music is our entertainment*
> *Our music is our heritage*
> *Our music is our identity*
> *Our music is our pride*
> *Our music is rich and soul uplifting*
>
> *We accord solemn tribute to our martyrs through our music*
> *We praise and worship through our music*
> *We celebrate significant historic events through our music*
> *We send our messages through our music*
> *We communicate through our music*
> *Yes, our music is rich, real, sweet and soul uplifting*
>
> *I talk about traditional songs and dance*
> *I talk about wedding songs and love*
> *I talk about freedom songs and Chimurenga*
> *I talk about healing songs and spiritual power*
> *I talk about songs of war and victory*
> *Indeed, our music is rich, real, sweet and soul uplifting*
>
> *Africa is ours*
> *Africa Day is ours*
> *This continent is ours*
> *The only continent in the world*
> *That is shaped like a question mark*
>
> *The only continent in the world*
> *That is shaped like a question mark*
> *Indeed, our music is rich, real, sweet and soul uplifting.*

Mzwahke's poetry and his fight to be released from what many see as an unjust sentence can be found on the website www.mzwakhe.org/. He may or may not have robbed a bank, as the courts claim. What is clear is that he is a creative voice helping Africans to speak out loud and clear. That there are many young, vital voices in Africa breaking through the fog of tired rhetoric is also clear. May we listen to them and find hope.

2.3 Breakdown of family structures.

Basic assumptions about kinship and authority vary greatly across the African continent, with each society organizing family life in its own way. The traditional Kpelle family differs greatly from the traditional Basotho family. The Basotho may find the Kpelle way confusing and vice versa, but for each, accustomed way of life makes sense and contributes to social stability.

Additionally, family structures are changing across Africa, moving from customary polygyny to the missionary-sponsored nuclear family and finally to the present-day international pattern of cohabitation and single-parent families. I call it the "Coca-Cola-ization" of African family life, following a comment I heard in a shop in Palapye in eastern Botswana. I was very thirsty, and not being a fan of fizzy drinks, I asked the shopkeeper if he had any juice. He said he had only Coke, and when I complained about it, he said, "Coca-Cola is our national drink." I was in Botswana, so I should behave like the Batswana.

In fact, Botswana goes much further than the other African countries I know in giving up both polygyny and the nuclear family. I met many women there, including several working on my research project, who said they had no intention of marrying. They did not want to spend their lives with drunken, irresponsible husbands. They wanted children, but did not want to be burdened with the males who impregnated them.

One terrible consequence of this change in family patterns is the march of HIV/AIDS across Botswana. At the end of 2003, adult prevalence there was 37.3 percent, and it may well be higher as I write this in 2004. Much the same is true in Lesotho, though not to the same degree; the rate there in July 2004, according to the *New York Times*, (20 July, 2004, p. 1) is 28% for working age adults. I cannot claim a direct causal relation between family breakdown and AIDS, but it is clear from data collected by Sechaba Consultants that there was a dramatic drop in the percentage of women in the young adult age group who said they were married at the same time that AIDS prevalence went up. In 1994, 60 percent of women ages twenty to twenty-four said they were married; the figure dropped to 48 percent in 1999. In the twenty-five to forty-nine year age bracket, grouped in five-year increments, the percentages dropped from the mid-70s to the mid-60s. The pattern only stabilized with older women, most of whom were grandmothers (Gay et al 1990; Gay and Hall 1994; Gay and Hall 2000).

I do not know the situation in civil war Liberia, although it was clear even when I taught there that marriages were far from stable. Carolyn Bledsoe's research there in the 1970s showed that marriage patterns were changing rapidly; the closer a community was to the money economy, the more women were opting out of the old polygyny. I saw the beginnings of such change in Gbansu, although the change was nowhere near as advanced as Bledsoe reported from the mining community where she did part of her research (Bledsoe 1980).

Today the AIDS prevalence rate in Liberia is high and growing. According to UNAIDS, the rate among women attending ante-natal clinics in 1999 was 12.7 percent; no later data are available. A report issued in Monrovia in 2001 includes what the authors call "family disorganization" as a factor leading to the spread of HIV/AIDS (Otti and Barh 2001:33). A woman is quoted as saying, "Marriage nowadays is ornamental as compared to the days of old when marriage was respected and dowry paid." The high prevalence of HIV/AIDS in Liberia cannot be blamed solely on changing marital patterns, as Otti and Barh also point out. Nonetheless, marital breakdown is surely one important reason.

It is important, however, to see another side of the story. It has been said that the greatest risk a woman runs of HIV/AIDS infection comes from sleeping with her husband. In such cases the marriage has not broken down, but the husband is unfaithful and brings HIV/AIDS home to the family. The *New Internationalist* for June 2002 says, "According to UNAIDS, up to 80 percent of HIV-positive women in long-term relationships acquired the virus from their partners. This in a society where men having multiple sex partners is the accepted norm. Ironically, marriage is one of the greatest risk factors for women today" (www.newint.org/nissue346/state.htm).

I want to look more closely at the patterns of infidelity and the breakdown of marriage as well as at the present and future consequences to Africa of this shift in family life. I cannot survey the entire continent, so I confine myself to those situations and places I know.

Let me begin with a marriage and family pattern that superficially appeared to work. One day I asked Old Man Benjamin, the Gbansu village elder who sold me hand masks, to gather his family together for a group photograph. I had been taking pictures around the village and was giving copies to my friends there, and I knew that Ben liked putting snapshots up on his wall. I assumed he would take some time to assemble his wives and children and perhaps a few other slightly more remote relatives. Not at all! He simply called together anyone he could see and had them pose, with him as the centerpiece.

Who were they? Some were his biological children, others were somehow in his lineage, but still others had no relation at all to him that I could identify. From his point of view, they were all his family, because he was the village elder and was responsible for them all. Moreover, as I looked more closely into the overall genealogy of the village, I found that essentially everyone there, and many in neighboring villages, could be considered part of the elder's extended (indeed, very extended) family through marriage, patron-client relations, and distant, formalized "uncle-nephew" ties.

I looked more closely into the matter so I could understand what he meant by family. Ben had four wives for whom he had paid bridewealth. Each of these wives had children and also had blood relatives in the village. All belonged to his family, because the Kpelle kinship system does not make rigid distinctions between male and female lines. However, since Ben was the elder of the village, all others in the village were part of his larger family. In most of these cases, Ben was able to fashion a linkage of some sort through his ancestry and the ancestry of these other men and women.

But that was not all. Before the war, each rural Kpelle village was surrounded by a network of small hamlets settled by senior village residents, usually to make it easier to keep careful watch over a farm. Ben was no exception. He had

Liberian village elder and family

built himself a house near his cocoa, coffee, and rubber trees and near his rice farm, and he had populated the village with his relatives. In order to find "relatives" willing to work for him at his farm village, he married more women from Gbansu and then farmed them out to newcomers who did not have the money or other resources to marry. These newcomers were then part of Ben's family, because they were beholden to him for their wives, who were somehow also Ben's wives.

The other senior men in the village had similar retinues—several wives and their children as well as clients who attached themselves to their senior "Big Men." At a higher level, even beyond Gbansu, there were other even bigger "Big Men," such as the local clan chief who exercised authority over Ben and his townsmates. Doubtless, this man in turn considered Ben to be part of his family.

The person at the apex of the network of marriage relations, who in the early 1930s, interestingly, was a woman, takes authority over the whole Kpelle region. The case of Madame Suakoko is revealing. She "married" many wives so that her family relationships could be solidified. Even into the late 1990s the rivalry for authority in the area was between her putative descendants. She may have "fathered" them, but she clearly did not "mother" them.

The implication for family relationships when the web begins to unravel and there is no center is a loose collection of isolated strings, some still tied together in sub-webs but others floating loose. The pattern is like that when I have broken real spider webs and seen them lose their shape and coherence, leaving the spider adrift and the filaments of his web just a disconnected nuisance.

How has the Christian church intervened in and affected the complex system of customary marriage under the leadership of a "Big Man"? It started by insisting that marriage is a relation between one man and one woman without dealing with the breakdown of the social order that inevitably comes with isolating families from each other. Mongo Beti's wonderful novel *King Lazarus* makes the point beautifully. The king of the area in Cameroon is deathly ill and is persuaded by missionaries to give up all but one of his wives so that he can be baptized and go to heaven. He does so, but instead of entering heaven monogamous he recovers and does not die. All his relatives then descend on him in what a Catholic missionary in the book calls "a collective nervous breakdown" for having violated the community of whi/ titular and symbolic head. In the end, in the interests of social harmony, h' back his wives (Beti 1960:153).

I was born into a one-man, one-wife culture, and I am very happy with my marriage. I rejoice in the wonderful fifty years Judy and I have spent together. But I am now less certain that I would urge my rural Liberian friends to go the same route. It may well be good for a community to remain united through dominant figures, even if they are usually sexually aggressive men. The early missionaries condemned overt polygyny out of hand, but I am fairly sure that the covert polygyny that resulted from their insistence on formal monogamy is worse than the orderly social structure they undermined. It is true that multiple marriages are more likely to spread AIDS than faithful monogamy, but I have to admit that the AIDS incidence is least in those (admittedly Muslim) areas where polygyny is rigorously enforced, and informal polygyny punished by law. Obviously, I am still confused.

I think of Moorosi, a young Mosotho who grew up in our family. He is a happily married man with a lovely daughter. Recently, his brother was killed in a barroom quarrel, leaving behind his pregnant wife and infant child. Formerly, the custom would have been for Moorosi to have taken his brother's wife as his own second wife and to have raised the two children as his own. However, Moorosi has been well trained in Western ways, is an active church member and has no intention whatever to follow the tradition. In fact, it makes life much easier for him than if he had had to marry his dead brother's wife. Doubtless, she too would not want to have to marry Moorosi. But whether that is a good resolution of the problem is not clear to me. The woman was left to her own resources, pregnant and raising a one-year-old child. Were the old ways to continue, she would be secure and would have the help of Moorosi's wife Mary as she struggled to raise her children. Now she is alone.

One negative consequence of the shift away from customary marriage is that tiny family units have to work their way through their problems alone, which brings to mind another case in Lesotho. The parents of a young friend of ours have long since separated and may even have died; he is not sure where his father is. His wife also has no parents to whom she can turn. They are both second-generation victims of nuclear families gone wrong. They have two children of their own and are raising another child who was brought into the world by his sister, who has no husband. They are in effect children adrift in a world without structure.

I think that a good case can be made that Western Christendom has imposed on African communities a marriage system that is only doubtfully able to provide security and help to the children of a changing world. Faithful, monogamous marriage, in which husband and wife leave their parents to form a new and separate social unit, is great if it works, but much of the time in current Western society it does not work. Perhaps it did in earlier days, but now in Europe and America isolation and loneliness are almost the rule. We have interpreted Genesis 2:24, which says that husband and wife must leave their parents, to mean they must leave their family. The choice to be isolated in a lonely world has not proved a wise choice in many American or European families. Has it been a good idea in Africa? I am not sure, but I think possibly not.

The example given by all too many missionary families leaves much to be desired. Two of the families with whom we lived and worked in Liberia have been broken by divorce. Both men left their wives for pretty, young secretaries. Both were ordained missionaries, both proclaimed the virtues of the new, better way of marriage, and neither was able to carry through in his own marriage.

The extreme disruption caused by migrant labor in southern Africa is another contributor to the breakdown of family life. For more than a hundred years, Basotho men have left their families to work in the South African mines. Nowadays they can return home on a monthly basis, but before South Africa won its struggle for democracy in the early 1990s, annual visits were all that most men were allowed. The result was marital chaos. Men would take girlfriends, or even boyfriends, near the mine while their wives would often succumb to the blandishments of men who stayed home. Apartheid was wicked in very many ways, and its demise has brought many blessings, not the least of which is at least a partial improvement in the lives of married men and women. That the improvement is only partial for Basotho is due to the national boundary, which makes it difficult for Lesotho citizens to make their homes in South Africa, despite the fact that the South African elite have built their homes on the backs of Basotho labor.

What are the implications for the breakdown of the social and political order where these conditions prevail? An important factor that makes a state cohere, that allows development and progress, is the presence of stable families. Men and women who depend on each other and on the larger society around them for a healthy home life and a good start for the next generation are needed to promote a good future for all. Where these conditions are absent and where it is each person for herself or himself, then the web of society is broken.

2.4 Emphasis on the individual instead of the community.

Like Sesotho, most Bantu languages have a concept meaning "a person is a person by people." John Donne put it this way: "No man is an island." In other words, we are what we are because of our relations with others. The term used most commonly in southern Africa for this concept is *ubuntu*, loosely translated "human-ness." Cognates of the same concept exist in almost every southern, central, and eastern African language. Yet the almost inevitable consequence of new family structures has been the shift away from family and community solidarity to the cult of the individual.

The *ubuntu* ideal is being lost to a large extent because of a new individualistic value system that came with the missionaries. One of the first ways it happens is when a person is taken out of his birth community and religion to be baptized. For example, I am sure that the baptism and confirmation accepted by the young Tanganyikan, Shabani Kisenge, did not take root in his life, because it did not involve the rest of his extended community. I have a photograph of his confirmation at Cuttington College. He is standing in front of the chapel with a disparate collection of village people who shared almost no cultural ties with him. The act of committing himself to Christ and the church was more a piece of theater than a piece of community solidarity. It is probably no wonder that he fell away. We failed to integrate him into a living family of Christians.

We humans are herd animals. It is the rare one of us who can take a Nietzschean stand and be a lone hero. I resonate with the Lone Ranger image more than most people do, certainly more than my wife, but I know I need a community to support me in what I am doing. A common 1960s slogan in America was "Do your own thing." Yet in the Western lifestyle we have introduced in Liberia and Lesotho that idealizes the Lone Ranger, the each-person-for-himself model all too often yields to family breakdown and real loneliness.

A young Liberian confessed in a class I taught on Christian ethics that his real worry about graduating and getting a job was that he would have to support a huge extended family. He hoped that he might leave Liberia or at least be posted to a location far from his home where he could be free from the crowd of relatives who would appear at his door on payday. Of course, he had depended on members of the same family to support him when he was at university, but now he hoped to escape and become his own man.

A hustler I met in Tanzania fit the model in a curious and ironic way. He was the village chief, but his main interest was self-aggrandizement, certainly at the expense of the villagers and even at the expense of his own wife. He had arranged for the village to buy grinding mills so that they would not have to beat their rice, maize, and millet in mortars. He was clearly making a substantial profit from these mills. Yet when I visited his house, I met his wife pounding rice in a mortar. I asked him why he did not use the mills at home. His answer was very simple. He pointed to his wife and said, "I have my own mill."

His connivance at exploiting his fellow villagers was so obvious that even he realized we would give a bad report on him to the government. Our task was to assess the level of rural development, particularly within the *ujamaa* system pioneered by President Nyerere. My research assistants and I were visiting seven different villages in southwest Tanzania, two of which in fact adhered quite well to Nyerere's ideal. But this case was clearly different. The chief knew it, we knew it, and he knew that we knew it. Here was a classic case of leadership exploiting people for its own benefit and for the benefit of political party leaders.

What did he do to cover his tracks? In seeming sincerity and politeness he offered us a large bag of rice to take back to Mbeya, the regional headquarters. My research assistants, all Tanzanians, and I looked at each other and realized immediately what was happening. We were being bribed not to report unfavorably on this village. We had been accustomed to receiving the occasional small gift of food in a village—a bowl of porridge, a bunch of bananas, even a chicken—to make us more comfortable while we were doing our three or four days of work in the village. But here was a substantial gift at the end of our time there. There was no hesitation among any of us; we turned him down politely but firmly. In fact, our report on that village was quite harsh.

This village chief was a "modern" man in that he saw his fellow villagers as subjects to be exploited and not as part of his extended humanity. Exploitation of others is as old as the human race, and the traditional Bantu sense of *ubuntu* is often forgotten. But this case seemed different. The man had been appointed chief of the village by a political party that in theory was trying to create "African socialism." And he was supported by his fellow political appointees in the exploitation process.

How had the community fallen into such a trap? I learned that this village was in fact not a "real" village. It was the product of the "villagization" policy introduced by Nyerere and his political party, which had been at first called the Tanganyika African National Union and then Chama cha Mapinduzi. The theory was persuasive. Many households in rural Tanzania were scattered across the countryside where people cultivated their farms and grazed their animals. Such households had very little access to social services, and so their children did not attend school; they had no means to bring their produce to market, they could not receive medical attention, and they could be only marginally part of the larger political, economic, and social reconstruction of the nation.

In the interests of *ubuntu*, people were to be brought together where they could live as a large extended family, with social services being laid on that could not have been provided to the myriad of small isolated homesteads. They would be given political indoctrination and would be organized into what were called "ten-cells," whereby each ten families would be instructed how to make their own decisions on development within the village and even within the larger region.

In this particular village, *ujamaa* was singularly devoid of *ubuntu*, and people's lives were being ruined. We saw abandoned houses outside the village, houses which had once been fine dwellings. Instead, people were living in close proximity in unpleasant, windowless houses. Who was benefiting? Certainly not the people. Rather, the beneficiaries were the political appointees for whom villagers were a cash crop to be exploited.

There was so much of this across Tanzania that it is no wonder Nyerere felt he had failed. Nyerere himself eventually abandoned the system and even had the courage to give up his presidency. He acknowledged that his idealism had failed, and that the system had become a means of exploiting and impoverishing people who previously had at least grown their own food and kept themselves alive on their individual homestead plots. It is immensely to his credit that he resigned. In far too many other African countries he would have bluffed his way through, surrounding himself with sycophants and enforcing his authority through the same crowd of political appointees who were destroying the rural way of life.

The deep irony of the situation I saw in this village is that dehumanization was taking place in the name of a new concept of family. The political leaders of the village were economically rational, modern men—in fact, all were men—who knew how to use the ideology to their own selfish ends. The top-down imposition of a beautiful ideal killed the possibility of achieving that very ideal, which was at least potentially present in the customary system. This situation clearly shows that, when scheming economic rationality implements a theoretical construct without weaving the ideal into the existing fabric of life, the result is alienation.

I saw another example of the isolation of a person from the community in a village near the border of Tanzania with Malawi. One man found a way to get around the enforced collectivization of agriculture in the area. People were supposed to sell their cash crops to the government, which would then bring them their payment several months later. The problem for the people was that inflation would eat up their profits by the time the payments were made.

This man offered to buy crops with immediate cash payment at a rate well below the going market rate. He grew rich in the process and was both hated and needed by his fellow villagers. In fact, my research assistants and I could hardly say he belonged to the community. He lived at one end of the village where he bought and stored his purchases before selling them across the border to Malawi. The Songwe River was not a mighty flood, and even I was able to walk across by jumping from rock to rock. Malawi was a free-market country, at that time under the authoritarian right-wing rule of Hastings Banda, and welcomed the chance to undercut Tanzania's socialism by interfering with the official Tanzanian economy.

Once again, the irony was heavy. Tanzania had introduced a socialist economy in order to benefit the people. Instead, the people were hurt by it due to incompetence and long delays coupled with high inflation. As a result, the pure, naked exploitation by a man, for whom his neighbors were only a source of cash income, provided a service that the socialist *ubuntu* government could not.

Fortunately, the community spirit has never been lost entirely. I have seen the remnants of African *ubuntu* in every country in which I have lived or visited. Certainly in Gbansu, the truly poor and disabled were cared for. The blind old man who lived in a shanty at the edge of the village was given food. In return, he wove chicken baskets, in which people took their chickens to the farm and back when the farming season was in full swing. The musician whose photograph graces our living room wall, being quite mad, never bothered to make his own rice farm. Instead, he played for every cooperative work group, and in return he was provided food.

The only real exception in Gbansu, in many ways not really an exception, was an older man whose children had abandoned him as a nasty and unpleasant father. His wife had either died or moved away; I am not sure which. In any event, he was alone, and the village people had little use for him, because they said he was selfish. At an age when he should have enjoyed some rest, being cared for by his children, he still had to do his full turn as a member of the cooperative work group. He may have been paying for his sins, but he was not allowed to starve.

In Lesotho the spirit of mutual forbearance and sharing has died in many areas of life. Anyone in the village who is too successful and who thus sticks out from the common mass becomes a target. Cattle may be let loose in his field to eat the green maize. His peaches may be picked by village children. In the worst case I have heard, a wealthy man's new borehole was filled with stones to prevent him from drawing water for his new pig farm.

But the truly poor are not allowed to starve. I have calculated the proportion of what I call "aid givers" and "aid receivers." Aid receivers are those who need help in order to survive, defined by me as households with income of less than 50 Maloti (equal to about U.S. $6 in 2000) per person per month (Gay and Hall 2000:151-152). They are almost all helped by their neighbors or relatives along with a minimal supplement from government largesse. Aid givers are families with at least 100 Maloti per month per member. They are often quite poor themselves, but almost every Basotho family helps people who are even poorer. Fortunately in 1999, our research confirmed that there were still more potential aid givers than aid receivers. At that time we found no one who was actually starving, confirming that sharing is still possible. I fear for the future, if income and food production decline, if AIDS becomes worse, and if people have nowhere to turn for support.

The case of a man, his wife, and two small children who were living in a tiny, round hut in a rural village illustrates the still-existing safety net. They had almost nothing to call their own and slept on the bare floor. At least the hut itself was sturdy, as it must be in the bitter winters that come to Lesotho. I tried to find how they survived, since they have no field, only a tiny plot around their house, and no employment. I was told that the man takes care of his neighbor's donkey and in return gets food for the children. The neighbor was not what I would have called a wealthy man, although he had a more substantial house than the poor man and had some cash income, but he realized his responsibility as an aid giver and did not let his neighbor starve.

The one case of true destitution I remember was a family in Maseru living in a broken-down one-room brick house. One wall was entirely open to the air, and the only bed in the two-meter-by-three-meter room was a broken spring on which a mad brother was lying and moaning to himself. The two young children were sent out on the street to beg. In this case, a charitable woman (herself somewhat mad) was trying to rescue the children and take them to her shelter.

True destitution may well come if the number of aid receivers ever exceeds the number of potential aid givers. That prospect is not impossible. Many are deeply concerned that Africans will be unable to feed themselves in the near future. The e-journal *New Agriculturalist on-line* made a grim prediction in their first issue of 2002:

> Deaths from HIV/AIDS has already deprived the 25 most HIV/AIDS-affected countries in Africa of seven million workers and, according to FAO estimates, could kill a further 16 million by 2020. The demographic, social, economic and political consequences will be catastrophic if no mitigating factors lessen the pandemic. The impact of HIV/AIDS goes well beyond health costs and losses of skilled labour; its impact is having a devastating effect on food security, as many hundreds of thousands of people in rural areas have become infected and too ill to work (www.new-agri.co.uk/02-1/develop/dev02.html).

As food production goes down, as employment drops, and as AIDS-related deaths of people in their productive adult years increase, then society may reach the point where the not-so-poor are no longer able to care for the truly poor.

Future Harvest points out, "To make ends meet, many families are simply selling off livestock, including draft animals used to prepare land for planting. The practice, known as 'capital stripping,' is normally seen only in times of famine." (www.futureharvest.org/health/aids_feature.shtml). When the assets are gone, there is no source for mutual support. If this eventuality is combined with attitudes like those of the Liberian student who did not want to help his numerous relatives, then heaven help countries like Lesotho. African society may well fall into the terrible trap of man-eat-man poverty that Colin Turnbull described among the Ik in northern Uganda (Turnbull 1973).

Ubuntu may be dying, but it is not dead yet. Unfortunately, there are voices in Africa proposing the harsh, fierce way of competitive capitalism as the only way forward. A Kenyan, James Shikwati, said in 2000, "Africans tend to think *en masse*; they think and reason as a community, a clan, and/or a tribe. This has held captive the creative potential of individuals. This has bogged down the entrepreneur spirit whereby individuals are forced to follow tribal whims." He goes on to denigrate *ubuntu* and then urge Africans to "Raise the standard of individualism and objectivism in Africa and African talent will emerge" (www.irenkenya.org/articles/shikwati_jul00.htm).

The cult of individual identity, individual conversion, individual competition, and individual success or failure has not fully taken root in the countries I have visited. Rather, some African communities continue to retain at least vestiges of what in pre-colonial times was a genuine stress on communal, not just individual, well-being. Whether African communalism and family-hood can thrive in the future is an open question. Shikwati is not an isolated voice. The elite, who are the "citizens" of whom historian Mahmoud Mamdani speaks (Mamdani 1996), are often hard-bitten capitalists.

The debate rages now in South Africa, where the African National Congress is struggling to keep within its ranks the energetic entrepreneurial black capitalists, the forces of the Congress of South African Trade Unions, and the members of the Communist Party who worked together to achieve the victory over apartheid. Many believe that a split is inevitable, leading to a realignment of politics in the post-apartheid society. The right wing of the ANC objected strongly to the two-day walkout by COSATU in October 2002 in protest of the privatization of state assets, while many on the left wing praised the action. Nelson Mandela intervened in December 2002 to try to heal the rift so that solidarity could be maintained (marxist.com/Africa/cosatu_gs2002_report2.html).

At issue is the long-term question of socialism and African development. Will African customary family unity, indeed, will *ubuntu* survive? In my view, the struggle within the ruling ANC in South Africa is a skirmish in the war for the soul as well as for the body of Africa. Will the terrible threat of AIDS, hunger, and poverty drive Africans to choose the harsh road of survival-of-the-fittest capitalism? Or will they find ways to share what little they have and still keep their essential humanity? I do not know.

2.5 Loss of local histories.

A family gains an identity through its shared history. So does a community, and so also does a nation. When the family breaks down, it loses its rootedness in history. The history may be deep, as in some West African countries, but it may also be shallow, reaching back at most two or three generations.

One example is from Lesotho, whose history is encapsulated in the story of Moshoeshoe I, the wise and farsighted leader who brought the nation into existence at a time of drought, war, and chaos. His was a minor clan in a welter of competing sub-groups, some of them bearers of Sotho-Tswana inheritance and some simply remnants of ethnic and social disorder. He brought them all together, and in so doing created the people who are now called Basotho (Gill 1993). This history is very important to the present-day Basotho, who look back to the early nineteenth century as their founding period. It is true that some myths reach well before the time of Moshoeshoe, but they are neither widely believed nor operative in shaping people's lives.

What is more important to most Basotho is their place in the history of the last 200 years. They know who they are in relation to their South African neighbors, and they cherish their national identity. Basotho on the Lesotho side of the border celebrate never having been incorporated into South Africa, despite the knowledge that there are more Basotho in South Africa than in Lesotho itself. Successive victories over the Afrikaners and then the British also remain important. These victories helped shape the pride and self-consciousness that made Lesotho into a nation. Yet some Basotho are now saying that they should take their rightful place as part of the region, even if it means being incorporated at long last into a non-racial, democratic South Africa. In a 1997 survey, 41 percent of Basotho adults said they would like Lesotho to be part of South Africa (McDonald et al. 1998: 27).

There are many peoples in Africa who are less fortunate than the Basotho, because their local histories have been or are in the process of being lost. A young man I had the privilege of teaching at the Anglican Theological College in Grahamstown, South Africa, had lost his moorings in a shifting world, because he did not truly know who he was. He spoke Afrikaans, the language of those who conquered his presumably Khoisan ancestors not long after the Dutch landed at the

Cape of Good Hope in the mid-seventeenth century. He knows nothing of the language and culture of his ancestors, and it hurts him. I loaned him a book on Khoisan society, detailing its shift from a semi-nomadic pastoral society to slavery and finally to official categorization as a marginal group lying between blacks and whites. Reading the book was painful to him.

In general, those of mixed-race in South Africa want to know who they are. I have been told by mixed-race friends that under apartheid they were not white enough, and now under the new democratic government they are not black enough. A sign on the door of a "Coloured" student at the Theological College showed three placards: "Black", "White," and "Coloured." Under the Black and White signs were doors leading to separate toilets. There was no door under the "Coloured" sign. My young friend knew he must accept himself as a South African or else reconcile himself to being nothing, and the debate was hot in his soul.

Another descendant of the indigenous population of southern Africa was a student of mine at the National University of Lesotho. His face had the typical high cheekbones, slightly slanted eyes, and light skin color of people commonly called Bushmen. Yet he knew nothing of his ancestry, except that the Basotho had overrun the mountains of Lesotho trying to find space for their farms and their cattle after their expulsion from the plains of what became the Orange Free State. In the process, Basotho made the mountain Bushmen into clients or in many cases killed them and married the women, leaving no remnant of Bushmen culture. After hearing me lecture on the disappearance of the hunting and gathering populations of southern Africa, my student stood up in class and told his fellow students that when he looks in the mirror in the morning, he sees a Bushman, but that he knows nothing of what that should mean to him. His history has disappeared. He must now be a Mosotho, or else he too is nothing. He also keenly felt this debate in his soul.

A young man who was my co-worker in Ethiopia faced a comparable anguish. He came from a minority ethnic group and resented the dominant Amhara and Tigre peoples. His history had been swallowed up by the ruling class of an empire that to this day pretends to be a unified nation.

At least Lesotho and Ethiopia have a dominant African ethnic group complete with a full and proud history, a history which unites them as peoples. Tanzania has tried to join this club by making a serious effort to create a common history, uniting hundreds of diverse groups under the banner of Swahili culture. In one village where I worked, adults were proudly completing their Swahili literacy courses and were being given diplomas that marked them as full members of an emerging society. Even there local histories were being lost, and the individualism coming from the top did not yet allow the people I met to achieve full status as part of one country with a common history. The transition period is very difficult in which people abandon one identity without fully accepting a new one.

I met one elderly Tanzanian who resisted the creation of a new society if it meant destruction of the old. He told me that Nyerere should never have left his own community, where he would have been a hereditary chief. If he had stayed where he belonged, he could have made rain through his inherited power, and the country would not now be suffering drought. I read into his remarks something that he did not intend explicitly, but may have underlain his ideas: the real drought in Tanzania was a lack of respect for what went before. Instead of enriching the grand tradition out of which he was born, Nyerere was imposing new ideas on his people and, in so doing, impoverishing it.

Telling stories in rural Liberia

The situation in Liberia is much more problematic. The public history tells of the pioneers who came across the sea in the early nineteenth century to settle what was then the Pepper Coast. Members of the indigenous ethnic groups are being asked to incorporate into their history people who helped defeat their ancestors. One example is a woman named Matilda Newport, who fired a cannon with a burning coal from her pipe in order to ward off an attack from the De people; another is the almost-white first president, Joseph Jenkins Roberts. Not included are stalwarts such as Samoure Touré, who nearly established a state that would have included much of Liberia's northeast interior, or Madame Suakoko, whom I have already mentioned as the leading power among Kpelle-speaking peoples in the 1920s and 1930s. In no way are the heroes and heroines of indigenous life included in the myths that celebrate and unify Liberia.

How have we, as outsiders, contributed to the marginalizing of people's own stories? In one way, we have acquiesced to the hegemony of the West simply through our power, our language, our money, and our offers of escape. We see ethnic groups as remnants, not as mainstream social structures. It is much easier for us to identify with the Western-educated English- or French-speaking elites than with people who seem unable to make it in a competitive, globalized world. And we do our best in schools and the workplace to free them from the supposed shackles of being "bush" or "country."

Additionally, we study their histories as academic curiosities. My student with the Bushman features was taught about his ancestors as if they were creatures from a dim and distant past, which unfortunately in many ways they are. And even where the marginal "bush" culture is still alive, its history is of little importance to the "developed" or even to the "developing" world. Only when the lid blows off are such people taken seriously. The leaders I knew in the Poro secret society in Liberia were good people, but very marginal to the dominant political culture. They were not schooled in the Western tradition and were committed to maintaining what little they could salvage of a dying way of life. It is only when they suddenly become of strategic importance, as in the case of the Kamajors of Sierra Leone, that people take them seriously. It was predictable that the Kamajor leader Sam Hinga Norma was indicted for war crimes; it is easy to predict that his people will once again be pushed to the margins of society and forgotten.

I can see a strong incentive for such people to resist with all their being the blandishments of Western hegemonic cultures in shaping new African nations. It is not surprising that disaffected Africans from Dakar to Mombasa to Cape Town protested against American arrogance in pretending to fight for Iraqi freedom as missiles and bombs rained down on Baghdad. They sensed that the United States is engaged in rewriting world history, whereby American arrogance and hegemony replace local pride and local identity. They may have little knowledge and indeed care very little about Saddam Hussein as a particularly vicious dictator. Why should

I was in remote rural Liberia in late 2001 and saw a poster of Osama bin Laden on a wall and a proudly-worn T-shirt showing a picture of the radical rap singer Tupac Shakur. I am sure he had no knowledge of Tupac Amaru and the struggle of the Incas against the Spanish in the sixteenth century. But I am also sure that he understood the power of the radical anti-establishment rap of Amaru's namesake in the twentieth century, a namesake who also died a disgraceful death.

Tupac in Liberia

Rural people know that few of their number will gain entry to the elite. Most who enter school will drop out as failures without employment, no longer rooted in their indigenous way of life. Why not resist? Even worse, why not strike out wildly and chaotically to take for oneself at least a few of the good things of life? Why not resist the high capitalist world that promises them nothing but failure?

This feeling of hopelessness is especially prevalent among those who have tried but failed to walk the road to elite status. On the other side are those who have kept their history and their way of life somewhat intact; they are less likely to engage in the kind of wild violence that severely damaged the facilities at Cuttington College during the civil war. Once again, in early 2003, Cuttington College was attacked as gangs of thugs, from both the government and the rebel sides, fought for control of the towns and villages along the main road to the interior. It was not the local people who did the major harm, though they did their share of the looting when lawlessness broke out. Rather, those who join the armies and fight the wars are the failures who have lost their history, their rootedness, and who are willing to follow a demagogue who promises them the moon. The militias who fought for Charles Taylor in the 1990s and the militias who fought against Taylor in the 2000s are people without roots.

Similarly, the ordinary Basotho, who continue to farm increasingly unproductive fields or who make a marginal living in urban, whether formal or informal sector, employment, were not the ones who burned and looted Maseru in September 1998. The school drop-outs, the unemployed young men, and the gullible fortune seekers who listened to demagogues, gathered at the royal palace in Maseru in August and then were worked into a frenzy leading to the riots that so badly set back Lesotho's economy.

Was their behavior irrational and counter-productive? From the national perspective, of course it was. From their perspective, they had nothing to lose and may have even gained a little by their actions. They were not part of a rooted culture, had no hope of employment, and had not made it through the stringent requirements of the educational system. Why not riot? Perhaps they could take home a few looted goods. Perhaps the rabble rouser who inflamed them in the first place might win the day and give them jobs as part of his retinue. Even if none of these dreams were realized, at least they could have a rousing good time letting off their frustrations burning a town that gave them no welcome and no comfort. They were attracted by the promises of out-of-power politicians who knew they had not won the recent election and used disaffected people as tools in a direct-action bid for power.

I am speaking of the young people who did the rioting, not of the demagogues who led them, who had a clear vision of where they were going. The demagogues knew their history and wanted to take power to remake Lesotho in their own way. They used young people as a temporary pseudo-extended family to help them achieve goals profoundly unlinked to the nation as a whole. The demagogues had chosen to separate themselves from the main stream of national history in order to create a new history for themselves. Power, not community, was their goal, and the young people fell into their trap.

There have been moments in recent African development when even the leaders lost their sense of history. Côte d'Ivoire has been part of a broad West African culture region for as long as history can give evidence. In pre-colonial days, the forest, the savannah, and the Sahel were integrated at least economically, and often politically. The French colonial empire maintained the unity of the region against local warlords such as Samoure Touré, who wanted to unite the area under his own empire. Under the wise old tyrant Felix Houphouet-Boigny, Côte d'Ivoire kept the unity by becoming the dominant economic and political force of the region while at the same time respecting the historic rights of people to enter freely from neighboring Burkina Faso, Mali, and Guinea. In my view, it was the new government's shortsighted and narrow, ethnic fear of outsiders that led to the 2002 civil war in Côte d'Ivoire. Ivoirité is a new concept without historical roots, and the excluded inevitably rose up against being kept out of their accustomed economic and political role in the country (www.observer.co.uk/Print/0,3858,4601937,00.html).

Had the leaders of Côte d'Ivoire been willing to listen to the bearers of local history, they might have acted differently. In much of West Africa these are the griots, who are trained to bring the past to the attention of the present. Their role "was to preserve the oral traditions and ensure that the community knew well of its ancestors, as well as the function of the mainstream society. The person, whom the griot was tutoring or counseling, would use his knowledge and apply it to everyday situations in hopes of making sense. Griots present a situation from the past by telling stories, something the people can relate to, and teaching them how to apply the moral or lesson in the story to everyday situations" (www.cocc.edu/cagatucci/classes/hum211/students/smith.htm). Had those lessons been heard, Côte d'Ivoire might not be in the mess it finds itself in as I write these words.

South Africa is also trying to recover a history that has meaning for the post-apartheid generation. I visited three powerfully moving museums in January 2003: the Robben Island prison just west of the Cape Town harbor, the District Six Museum in the center of Cape Town, and the Hector Pietersen Museum in Soweto. In no way do they gloss over the atrocities of times now gone. The heroes and the villains are present in vivid photographs; patient and thorough explanations are given both on the walls and by guides who have themselves been through the struggle. Even more striking is that the ANC government has chosen not to tear down old statues or replace old street names. Admittedly, some towns have been given what seem to be new names, but in most cases these are the names by which the original inhabitants would have referred to them.

The Truth and Reconciliation Commission, which submitted its final report on 21 March 2003, was committed to making the truth known about the horrors of apartheid. Very few atrocities have been ignored. Admittedly the ANC tried to have the report toned down so that its own bad behavior in the prison camps of Angola could be forgotten, but history has been preserved intact, and in that way the people have been served.

2.6 Changes in women's roles.

In many cases men have taken the lead in recreating the social order. In the new Africa, women have often been left behind, certainly in relation to the status they had in pre-colonial times. Liberia has been an exception recently, but even there women have lost out in crucial battles for control.

Rural Liberian senior women

One example is found in the rural area near Cuttington College in Liberia, where the successors of the chief and war leader Madame Suakoko have been men. Her influence remains, but as a figure from the past, not as a real guide for the future. What may have been the last exercise of authority by women in that community came during the burial of the powerful chief of Sinyea, the village immediately behind the college. Old man Sebe Dorweh, the chief and the father of Philip Sebe who at one point became acting town chief, was a friend of ours. His aunt, Nepee, was the leader of the women's society in the village and exercised considerable authority behind the scenes.

What happened when Sebe Dorweh died was that the women took control of the funeral. They said, quite correctly, that it was their time to control the secret societies. In theory, women control the forest for the six years when they hold their initiation schools, three years for preparation and three years when the girls are inside the fence. Then men have the forest for eight years, four years of preparation and four years of school. Sebe Dorweh died during the women's period. Village elders debated about who should hold the funeral, but the women prevailed, I think to a large extent because of the influence of women's society leader, Nepee.

The roughly equal status of women's and men's secret societies seems to have faded into the background, at least as I read the news. We hear almost nothing about the Sande society, the women's stronghold. The wars in Sierra Leone and Liberia involve men, and the men's Poro society appears to be dominant. When Charles Taylor announced that he was now the head of Poro nationally, there was no mention of Sande. When I attended a meeting of senior people in Sinyea at the end of 1997 there were no women at the meeting. These situations may be signs of a temporary imbalance due to war, but I tend to think otherwise.

In the meantime, rape and other forms of violence against women have increased sharply. Young girls were captured to provide services, both domestic and sexual, for the militias in the civil wars in Liberia and Sierra Leone. Very recently, Liberians United for Reconciliation and Democracy (LURD) and MODEL (Movement for Democracy in Liberia) rebels in Liberia were said to carry on the same practices that Charles Taylor's ruffians used in the 1990s. For example, on 6 March 2003, Human Rights Watch reported on the atrocities committed in Liberia by both government and rebel soldiers. To a horrifying extent these atrocities are against women who have been captured and then forced to serve as sex slaves.

The situation in Sierra Leone was also horrible during that cou[ntry's] threatening civil war. Physicians for Human Rights report that "internall[y] women and girls in Sierra Leone have suffered an extraordinary level of [?] violence and other gross human rights violations during their country's civil war, with half of those who said they came into contact with RUF (Revolutionary United Front) forces reporting sexual violence" (Physicians for Human Rights 2002).

Elsewhere in West Africa, women are still being sold as prostitutes, some to as far away as Europe. Reportedly, "Togolese citizens are trafficked to Côte d'Ivoire, Gabon, Nigeria, the Middle East (specifically Saudi Arabia and Kuwait), and Europe (primarily France and Germany) for indentured or domestic servitude, farm labour, and sexual exploitation" (U.S. Dept. of State 2001). Such reports are commonplace. Nigerians and Sudanese have been accused of selling women as slaves wherever they could find a market. Slavery for these women normally means both domestic service and sexual exploitation. Most recently, the Janjaweed militia in western Sudan have used rape as a tool of conquest.

At the same time, women are struggling to regain their rightful place, both in politics and in economics. The only serious candidate to oppose Charles Taylor in the 1997 elections was a woman, Ellen Johnson-Sirleaf. She had all the right qualifications for the job, far more than Taylor himself, except that she was not a warlord. I would like to think she might have won the election had it taken place in peacetime. She was a viable candidate for the post of interim Head of State during the negotiations in Accra after the exile of Charles Taylor, but apparently she may have been considered to deeply involved in politics to be a neutral manager of the transition to democracy.

Women are also seeking their rights in other African countries. Under laws promulgated by the British and confirmed by the independent Kenyan government—laws which purportedly reflected traditional customary law—women's property belongs to their families and not to themselves. In March 2003, Human Rights Watch took up cases of women whose husbands die and who are left either without resources or who become unwilling wives of their husbands' close male relatives. In Lesotho, women are demanding the right to enter marriage "out of community of property," which means they have a legal right to their salaries and possessions.

Similarly women are moving into positions of power in South Africa. Not only is the speaker of the South African National Assembly a woman, Frene Ginwala, but also "Of the 490 members who were elected to the National Assembly and the Senate (now the National Council of Provinces) in April 1994, 117 were women: 109 in the National Assembly and eight in the Senate" (www.idea.int/women/parl/studies5a.htm). And, for better or for worse, Winnie Madikezela-Mandela remains a powerful political force in that country. She manages to escape jail regularly, despite being convicted, and comes back seemingly with more popularity after each brush with the law.

The place of women in Lesotho significantly diminished with the coming of the British colonial presence. Customary authority in village life has always given women a place parallel to that of men. The women's initiation ceremonies were important, and women had the right to manage cases that transgressed their rights. Less is heard now about the *khotla ea basali*, the women's court. Instead, women are playing their political and legal roles in the villages as substitutes for the men only when the men (who by heredity should be chiefs) are away or sick or dead. No woman seems to be in authority by her own right, not even the powerful Chief

Mantatisi, who was regent for her teenage son, Sekonyela, during the pre-colonial period. Only in the spiritual world, as with the female prophet Mantsopa during the time of Moshoeshoe, could a woman assume authority without standing in for a male relative.

The underlying reason for this shift, as I see it, is that colonial authorities, as well as missionaries, brought with them assumptions about the role of women that were imposed on local people. They institutionalized a legal system that made women subordinate to men rather than parallel to them in their own "separate but equal" areas of life.

In Lesotho, under the cover of this imposition of male dominance, there still remain many ways in which women have authority. Particularly, as a result of the migrant labor system, women manage households and make agricultural decisions. Additionally, in part because of the migrant labor system, but also because boys are expected to work as shepherds in the mountains, Basotho women have a much higher mean level of education than men. In surveys conducted by Sechaba Consultants (Gay et al. 1991; Gay and Hall 1994; Gay and Hall 2000) women older than eighteen consistently had about one and a half more years of school than their male counterparts.

More recently, women are more likely than men to find employment in factories, particularly textile factories. But these areas of authority and economic power have not yet resulted in redressing the legal balance. Women are not allowed to own bank accounts or take loans without the approval of their husbands. Men can even order their wives' employers to dismiss them, as I saw in one startling case involving a female employee of the Ministry of Agriculture. This is another reason, beyond simply men's drunken violence against women, that educated and sophisticated Basotho women today are increasingly avoiding marriage.

What are the implications for social stability? Where women are denied their full role, power structures depend more on the use of force than on persuasion. A social system where equality between the sexes was present would be less likely to fall into the violence and chaos prevalent in so many African countries, though I must admit that women in high places are often as ruthless as their male counterparts.

A survey was taken in 1999 and 2000, under the auspices of Michigan State University and the Institute for Democracy in South Africa, by a consortium of scholars in twelve African countries regarding attitudes toward democracy (www.afrobarometer.org). Altogether, 21,531 randomly selected adults were interviewed in Botswana, Ghana, Lesotho, Malawi, Mali, Namibia, Nigeria, South Africa, Tanzania, Uganda, Zambia, and Zimbabwe. In general, women were much less politically active and much less well informed about politics than men. The southern African countries were less biased toward men than the other countries, but even there, women—despite their relative equality in education—were less interested in politics and political discussions than men and were less well informed about public affairs.

I have used the Afrobarometer survey to develop a scale which measures well-being in relation to democracy. The survey shows that men are consistently higher on the scale than women in all of the African countries surveyed (Gay 2003). This scale takes into account five factors: political awareness, economic well-being, social linkages, information access, and personal security. In every case the women fall short of the men in achieving the extent of freedom which can lead to real development, an argument made persuasively by the Nobel Prize-winning economist (Sen 1999). The difference between men and women, perhaps not surprisingly due to the strong Muslim presence there, is greatest in Mali and Nigeria, and least in Lesotho, South Africa, and Namibia.

2.7 Abuse of tradition to maintain social control.

Male dominance. An important element in the oppression of women is the device of claiming "tradition" to justify male dominance. "It is our African culture" is the reason I have heard so many times for women to be kept "in their place." Students have told me that men may sleep around, while their wives must remain faithful. Thus, the operative moral standard for men is different from that for women, and the justification is drawn from the past.

Violence against women comes under that same appeal to the past; that a man is free to beat his wife is justified, since the man is the head of the household. A young man whose wife has left him told me it was all right to beat his wife when she failed to do what he wanted. Yet some women fight back. In one extreme case in Lesotho, the wife poured kerosene over her abusive, drunken husband and set him alight. But such cases are rare.

More normal is the case of a man in a village where I had been working. He came home from the mines one night to find his wife sleeping with another man from the same village. He beat the wife and warned her and also warned the chief that if it ever happened again he would kill both of them. He returned to the mines and came back a few weeks later for another unannounced leave. He entered the house and again found the two of them in bed together. Without a word, he grabbed an axe and killed them both. He went immediately to the chief, woke him up, and told what he had done. He was never charged for the double murder. After all, from the male point of view, he had announced what he would do, and he did it. From the chief's point of view, he did what was right and necessary, and his action could not be called murder.

"Tradition" appears to be used by some as a precedent from yesterday to justify today's action, whether yesterday is taken literally or simply as any time in the remembered past. It is thus highly selective and is applied to the needs of the moment. In this sense, tradition is like the appeal to precedent in Western law; the trick is to find the precedent to suit the need of the moment. Common law in the United States and England has systematized precedent in order to obtain a degree of consistency in application of the law. In oral tradition, such a systematization is not possible. I remember reading about a land inheritance case in Nigeria for which colonial documents were found that contradicted what villagers believed to be the "tradition". What the parties who had a strong self-interest in the case "remembered" was exactly the opposite of what members of their family had declared to the court a generation earlier.

Fatou Sow, a Senegalese sociologist, spoke at Rutgers University in 2000 on the changing place of women in African political life. She speaks of today's African nations that "have restructured their hierarchical, social and family systems according to their religious patriarchal ideologies (Islam and Christianity), colonial legislation and their new political order. In this, African women have been deprived of their position, their participation and their autonomy in the management of these spheres. They have been confined to the social sphere that has become private" (www.africansocieties.org /n1/paginaarticolo3.htm). As a result, she claims that many men, whether professors or journalists, still believe that women should take their proper place in the home rather than in public life.

This conventional wisdom, that women's place is in the home, is being rejected widely, at least in public statements. A few groups, however, still publicly proclaim the belief, expressed by a fundamentalist web-site: "As Christians the Bible makes it clear that women are not to be pastors or teach or even speak in the Church, as an authority over the man (1 Tim. 2:11-15; 1Cor. 14:34,35). The feminists cannot change the teachings to fit their beliefs. Christian churches in South Africa will be affected by government regulations that will be increasing over time, to a degree that will eventually outlaw the churches entirely" (hometown.aol.com/mdeubig/newsitem1.htm). It is to be hoped that such voices will eventually disappear, and that Christian churches in South Africa will not only flourish but will welcome the new freedom of women.

To the best of my knowledge, I do not find support for the belief that African traditional culture consigns women to a subordinate role as housekeepers and servants to men. I believe, as Dr. Sow says, that this belief has been foisted on Africans by religious institutions, both Christian and Muslim. Certainly, African development has been hindered by preventing half its population from sharing in the process. I can only hope this reason for Africa's decline will soon be pushed aside. There are too many other serious issues facing Africa to allow gender prejudice to hold her back.

African time. Some people refer to a concept they call "African time" in which being late to a meeting is considered part of "African culture." A flagrant example of this patronizing attitude came from Andrew Natsios, head of the U.S. Agency for International Development. In a June 2001hearing before the U.S. House of Representatives he said African people "do not know what watches and clocks are" as a reason for not giving AIDS medication to Africans (www.house.gov/international_relations/democratic/hearing_060701.pdf).

I remember one occasion when the agricultural development project on which I was working scheduled a meeting in a rural village for 9:00 a.m. I was told by the expatriates working for the project, all of them white Europeans, that there was no point in arriving before 10:00 a.m. because of "African time." I was not happy with the idea, and so I made a point of being at the meeting at 9:00 a.m. sharp. Most of the local people were present, and we all had to wait until the other project staff arrived an hour or so late. In this way, the supposed tradition that meetings always start late was confirmed, through a decision made by the expatriates. The members of the project staff were so insistent on being late, because they wanted to check their mail, make telephone calls, and make sure the office work was going well. Moreover, they wanted to assert their authority. The overt excuse was a patronizing nod to "African culture" and "African time."

A few days later, many of the same Basotho who attended the project meeting were called by their village chief to discuss the reason why there had been such an extensive and damaging hail storm the previous afternoon. The chief invited them to a meeting at 6:00 a.m., and they were there exactly on time. The issue was very important to them, since they were afraid that someone in the village had violated a traditional taboo. There was no appeal to some mythical "African time" in this case. The issue mattered to everyone, and they arrived in time to air all the dirty laundry of the village. In fact, laundry was the issue, since one woman was reported to have hung out her laundry at an inappropriate time, thus calling down the hail.

A friend pointed out what should have been obvious to me after working for more than forty years in Africa; namely, that meetings are often more about showing status and consolidating patron-client structures than they are about conducting business. The chief in the hail-damaged village used the occasion not only to root out the cause of the storm but also to consolidate his power.

I remember another example from the National University of Lesotho. A power-hungry academic (who is now a senior Minister in the Zimbabwe government) waited until the very end of a meeting of a major university committee to point out that the agenda had not been published the requisite number of days in advance, and therefore the proceedings were invalid. He won his point, he forced the other senior academics to wait the required time before the meeting could be reconstituted, and with great personal satisfaction he saw all the same conclusions reached at a time of his own setting. His colleagues were furious, but his power was untouched, and henceforth the university staff, out of fear, showed him more respect than they ever had before.

This use of official meetings for consolidating personal power rather than for achieving needed results is not confined to African countries. We do it in the American Congress, and the British do it in their Parliament. My impression, however, is that such maneuvering is much more common in Africa, and in some cases is the only way the game is played. Moreover, in African countries, short-term expatriates have little need to gain "power points," and thus become impatient with locals playing the meeting game, even though at home they might well choose to do the same thing themselves.

Dr. Bedford Umez, a Nigerian, argues against the idea of "African time," calling it instead "selective punctuality." He says that his own people do it to each other, and he asserts that the reason behind it is a deep inferiority complex. The same Nigerians who would be on time for something that mattered to them will arrive two or three hours late for something organized by other Nigerians. He says that once Africans decolonize their own minds, this will end the demeaning and counter-productive habit that is called "African time" (www.angelfire.com/tx/bumez/culture.html).

I agree in large measure with Dr. Umez and would go even further to point out that the inferiority is enhanced by the response of critics from outside Africa. It takes two parties to achieve effective colonization of the mind: the colonizer and the colonized. Once they work together in a synergistic way, then such stereotypes as "African time" take deep root.

Supporting these ideas is an objective test of time perception in studies I carried out in Liberia in the 1960s. We found that non-literate Kpelle-speaking adults in rural Liberia measured time in ways that made cultural sense. They responded punctually to the natural indicators of time of day and time of year. Moreover, when tested to find the ability to estimate the amount of time it would take to pace a certain distance, they were more accurate than American adults (Gay and Cole 1967:71-75). In short, there is no intrinsic cultural basis for a poor sense of time. Instead, the arrogance of outsiders and the felt inferiority of insiders feed on each other and produce the myth of "African time."

African science. Many people I have met believe in what they call "African science," by which they mean a power over nature. I have seen this supposed power in action on several occasions, some very impressive and some rather pathetic. In all cases, however, I believe this "power," if it really exists, is used as a means of social control.

I am not referring to the real scientific impulse which has been as much a part of life in Africa as anywhere in the world. Certainly, the people with whom I have worked are committed to the rational study of nature. My work in Liberia and Lesotho shows that rural farmers practice their own form of serious science when they need it in order to manage their environment (Gay 1983). I am talking instead about something quite different, something more like the superstitious fear of the "occult," which can be seen in every society.

One sobering example involves trial by ordeal. A Liberian friend of mine owned a chicken farm. She employed a local manager who, in her opinion, had stolen money. He denied it, and in the end both agreed to hire an "ordeal doctor." I was present as a witness. The ordeal man heated a cutlass red hot and announced that if applied to the leg of an innocent person no harm would be done, but that the guilty person would be badly burned. Both parties agreed to the test. He rubbed a liquid on the legs of the two parties and then on his own leg, seemingly the same liquid in all three cases. He applied the fiery red cutlass to his own leg first, and nothing happened. He reheated it and applied it to my friend's leg, and still nothing happened. I watched closely and could see that, in fact, her skin was depressed where the cutlass touched it. In short, he was not faking the physical contact of hot iron with flesh. He then turned to the accused person, applied the reheated iron, and at once the flesh sizzled and smoked. Guilt was established.

Trial by ordeal in Liberia

How do I, with my rationalistic Western mindset, explain what I saw? I do not explain it, but I am convinced that somehow the ordeal doctor had either been paid to find the suspect guilty or had figured out by psychological signs that he was guilty. He must have applied the iron somehow in a different way to obtain different results. His ability to control other people through his ordeal procedures was confirmed.

A more confusing example of the appeal to tradition lies in the broadly conceived area of "medicine." The use of herbs, bones, sand, spittle, blood, and even body parts—to name just a few of the physical objects that may be brought into play—brings power to the "doctors" and allows them to control others. A particularly poignant and powerful case was brought to a friend of mine, a medical doctor. Two powerful "doctors" were competing for status in a rural village in Liberia. One came to my friend in terror. He said the other had defeated him in the struggle, and that he now realized he must die spitting blood in the next thunderstorm. My friend admitted him to the hospital for observation, but could find nothing wrong. A thunderstorm came up in a few days, and, in fact, the man died spitting blood. The Western doctor who treated him could only conclude that he had frightened himself to death. The victor in the struggle used customary beliefs to kill the loser.

While I was studying small-scale informal businesses in Botswana, I worked closely with members of the African-initiated Johane we Masowe Church, because they were among the most effective informal sector business people in the country. Much of the power the elders of the church held over their followers was derived from their control over medicine. Believers were not allowed to seek medical care from

Western doctors or nurses; instead, they had to find it within the community. In this case, the tradition was not very old, going back only to the 1930s, when according to their tradition, Johane had died and gone to heaven. When he came back to life after three days in heaven he told his followers that they must not use Western medicine. Social control was guaranteed through adherence to the culture and beliefs of the movement. When I asked what happened to young people who broke away from the church, I was told about a man who had left the fellowship. He had gone to school, used modern medicines, and was now a hopeless drunkard. He no longer was supported by the group and had to find his own way in a hostile world.

A pathetic case of the use of supposed control over nature is seen in the case of a friend of mine, a spiritual healer in Liberia, who attempted to show me his power. Unfortunately, he was drunk at the time. He sat on his "throne" in his office, the throne being a bucket seat he had rescued from a plane crash, the office a mud-and-thatch hut. He performed for me the magic that he often used to impress local people with his power, but he fumbled it badly. The coin that he had hidden in a folded sheet of Arabic writing slipped and fell on the floor while he was trying to make it disappear. Poor man! He often came to my house for aspirin for his headaches (perhaps caused by too much strong drink).

In the worst case, which fortunately I have never witnessed, young people are persuaded that charms rubbed on their bodies will protect them from bullets so they can go fearlessly into battle. I was told about the 1905 Maji-Maji rebellion in southwest Tanzania by an old man who remembered seeing soldiers use the medicine who were then killed by German gunfire. The same beliefs are held by many fighters today in Africa, including those in the renewed Mai-Mai movement in eastern Democratic Republic of Congo. In more benign cases, soccer players go into games protected by medicines that will help them win. In one case that I did know about, both teams bought medicines from the same doctor!

Social control is the name of the game in all these examples. "African culture," as interpreted by men, leads to control over women; as interpreted by expatriates, it leads to patronizing and demeaning attitudes toward "African time"; and as interpreted by customary healers and religious leaders, it leads to dominance over the lives of people in their charge. The net result is that ideology is used to suppress people and force them to behave in a certain way, thus keeping them from creative thought and action.

2.8 Ethnic and cultural oppression.

The moral order in any society is a complex balance of often very different individuals, families, and communities. A healthy society manages to find places for almost any group, including the most obviously deviant. For some, that place may well be in detention or hospital or in isolation from the rest of the society. In truly sick societies, such as Nazi Germany—or more recently, Rwanda and Burundi—the hatred of the different leads to genocide. Fortunately, in my work I have not experienced these horrors personally.

However, in African countries where I have lived, I have observed the tendency to reject those who are different. This was most obvious in South Africa where the dominant white community oppressed the majority of the nation, which was African, Asian, and mixed-race peoples. Fortunately, the overt racism I saw in South Africa is now discredited and even illegal, although, of course, racism continues under the surface.

More disturbing is the increasing xenophobia in South Africa. I have worked with the Southern African Migration Project for the past few years, and one of our principal findings was that people who move from one country to another are by and large decent and hard-working, seeking mainly to find a better place to live and work. Yet they are castigated by the new racists as drug addicts, thieves, job stealers, rapists, and disturbers of the peace. During the hard-core apartheid days, the big worry of whites was the *swart gevaar*, an Afrikaans term meaning "black menace." Today it seems to me that those most concerned about the black menace are blacks, such as Chief Mangosuthu Buthelezi, the leader of the Zulu political party who was also Minister of Home Affairs in South Africa. Many South African blacks forget the help they were given in the liberation struggle by the very people they are now trying to keep out of their country.

In Liberia, where there are at least sixteen linguistic groups (twenty-eight, counting dialects), cultural differences have always been a serious problem. That number does not include the Americo-Liberians, the so-called "Congo people" (descendants of people taken as slaves who were "freed" by the American navy on the Liberian coast in the process of being shipped to the New World), or the Muslim, mostly Mandingo, traders who moved freely between Liberia and the countries to the north. The long-term discrimination against indigenous African people on the part of Americo-Liberians was only very slowly being eliminated through President Tubman's "unification policy." Had the unification policy continued under Tubman's successor, William R. Tolbert, Liberia might not be in the mess we see today. Yet even this policy means unification on the terms of the coastal immigrant aristocracy rather than a merging of cultures on an equal basis. It is true that indigenous people were being welcomed into the elite, but in so doing they had to take on the traits of the elite.

What made the problem so complex was the intricate hierarchy of ethnic groups within the structure outlined above. The Americo-Liberians were graded according to the purity of their American ancestry. A few, like Harry Morris, who owned a large rubber farm outside Monrovia, may have had no indigenous people in his family tree. Most of the others were of mixed ancestry, but even in these cases lines were drawn. Just below Americo-Liberians of mixed descent were the Congo people, who thought of themselves as superior to any indigenous group.

If the ancestry of Americo-Liberians or Congo families included people from the more prestigious ethnic groups, particularly the Vai and Grebo, then they were higher on the ladder than those whose indigenous ancestors came from what some Liberians considered to be lower class ethnic groups, such as Bassa or Kpelle. The Grebo held their heads high because they dominated ethnic politics in Maryland County and were the proud owners of nineteenth-century Anglican prayer books. The Vai were slave holders in the northwest who had their own script into which documents and prayers had been translated. The Kpelle and Bassa were the laborers for the upper classes. More than one Vai person told me how his people had kept Kpelle as slaves and still saw them as inferior.

Even farther from the establishment were the more remote ethnic groups of the interior, who had less contact with the expanding Liberian nation during the nineteenth and early twentieth century. At the very bottom was the Krahn ethnic group residing along the southwest border with Côte d'Ivoire. That the Krahn were the people who would overthrow Tolbert, leading to the brutal and corrupt dictatorship under Samuel Doe, should not have been a surprise. They greatly resented the hegemony of almost everyone else. The only jobs they could get were in the army, and it was the army that provided them with a power base when they took over. There is still a strong undercurrent of hatred and distrust between the Krahn and other ethnic groups, both Americo-Liberian and indigenous.

Following this line of argument, the Mandingo would also have fallen to the bottom, because many of them were itinerant traders whose homes lay elsewhere, in Guinea or even Mali. Yet some had settled in Liberia to make their fortunes, or even to become simple rice farmers; in some cases, they did very well. In their own eyes, the Mandingo were a vastly superior people to "Liberian savages." I remember one Mandingo chief telling me what it is was like in the interior town of Gbarnga when he arrived in the 1920s. He told me, with a straight face, that the "natives" were all naked and that they only began to wear clothing when the Mandingos sold it to them. They saw themselves as civilized in a way superior even to the Americo-Liberians, who were not even true Africans. It must not be forgotten that the great Afro-Caribbean scholar Edward W. Blyden himself praised the Mandingoes as key to the future of Liberia (Blyden 1967).

Mandingo elders in Liberia

I have gone into what may seem unnecessary detail about Liberian hierarchy for the simple reason that much of what has happened since the overthrow and murder of Tolbert can be understood in terms of ethnic politics. The fury displayed by the Krahn under Doe when they executed leading Americo-Liberian politicians grew out of their long-term resentment at being on the bottom of the pile. Their later very uneasy and very temporary alliance with the Mandingos in the United Liberation Movement for Democracy in Liberia (ULIMO) developed because both they and the Mandingo felt left out after it became clear that the mixed-race Americo-Liberian establishment was once again claiming power under Charles Taylor. The death of the Liberia that Tubman dreamed of came about because of the accumulated strain of hatred and anger that could not be resolved through the slow evolution of a truly Liberian nation.

Instead of working toward the unification that Tubman wanted, each player in this sad game sought to suppress the other players or at least to enroll them as subordinates in the quest for power. The process by which society and government continued to unravel up to early 2004. LURD and MODEL seem no different from the National Patriotic Front in their ability to commit atrocities and wreak havoc. They claim to be adhering to the agreements signed in Accra in September 2003, but their child soldiers continue to loot and rape throughout the interior. The rebel groups, moreover, continue to play the ethnic card, with LURD being supported by Mandingoes from Guinea, and MODEL by Krahn people from southeastern Liberia and southwest Côte d'Ivoire.

Similarly, the destruction of Sierra Leone can be understood as a long-term war between the indigenous rural people and the ethnically mixed Krio in and around Freetown. I cannot speak of it in detail since I have not witnessed it first-hand.

Additionally, I fear that the same game is being played elsewhere in Africa, with only a very few countries, such as Lesotho, saved from it by their ethnic homogeneity.

Unfortunately, ethnic homogeneity is no guarantee against oppression. What has happened in Lesotho is another story. It is true that there has been a minor tendency for members of elite clans (particularly those descended from the great king Moshoeshoe I) to lord it over others, as well as a slight tendency for Basotho of Xhosa ancestry to find it difficult to get ahead. But the major source of oppression is economic, with those at the top seriously exploiting those at the bottom. I will discuss this further later on.

But it must not be forgotten that the very ethnic homogeneity which I have praised in Lesotho came at the expense of the indigenous Bushmen whom I mentioned earlier. Moshoeshoe I brought diverse peoples into one nation, but critical to that unification was their common cattle culture. Cattle were the medium of cultural and political exchange, and the Bushmen were, by their very means of living, outside that network. For them cattle were no different from the elands and other antelope which they killed; they were not a resource to be managed and traded. It was structurally inevitable that the Bushmen must either be integrated or driven out. Since there was nowhere to drive them to, as the Basotho gradually occupied the higher and higher mountains, they were destroyed.

I was aware of, but not personally involved in, the numerous ethnic rivalries in Ethiopia, Uganda, and Namibia. Highland Ethiopians felt superior to lowland peoples, Baganda did not want their children to marry Acholi from the north, and the dominant farming and business people in Namibia looked down on the pastoralists and nomads. And in Botswana, where one ethnic group dominates the nation, the same prejudice prevails against the Bushmen and the Herero.

Where does this leave Africa and its peoples? I fear the resurgence of hatred and enmity in countries now more or less at peace, including South Africa and Namibia. And I fear the increase in small-scale as well as large-scale conflict. Ethnicity and race are partly real and partly the invention of Western society, as I will discuss later. The increase in war and hatred has its roots at least partly in genuine African indigenous differences, but this increase also owes much to the Western desire to classify in order to make colonial administration and post-colonial economic control easier. Furthermore it is always easier, even with the best of intentions, to plan and cooperate with people who speak our language, who have a similar education and who understand our cultures. We thus exacerbate the inherited problems of colonialism by too easily working with people like us and ignoring those on the margins.

Moshoeshoe I of Lesotho, President Tubman of Liberia, and President Mandela of South Africa were all on the right track in trying to unify disparate peoples, even though their motivation may not have always been purely altruistic. In order for politicians to succeed, a large measure of self-seeking patronage is needed, if they are to have a following. I fear that the present leadership in most, if not all, African countries fails to follow the best aspects of the leadership provided by men such as Moshoeshoe, Tubman, and Mandela. Instead, self-centered power politics take over, and vision is lost. We are seeing the consequences all around us in today's Africa.

2.9 Hopeful signs.

As I said in the Preface, at the end of each chapter I will summarize the main points and supplement each with what I consider to be signs of hope for a better future in Africa.

Concerning **initiation ceremonies and secret societies**, I can say, though with trepidation and great uncertainty, that the role of the Poro in Liberia may hold out some promise. At their best they represent the stability of the past and seek to sustain a responsible political structure. More hope, in my view, is to be found with the African-instituted churches, which stress commitment and responsibility. I find the theology of some of these groups a bit strange, and some I would reject as not Christian, but often their lives display a sobriety and mutual concern that conventional "modern" Africans do not show. What seems to be needed is a ritual of commitment to the group in order for solidarity to exist.

Furthermore, neither do we want to lose **traditional art forms**, though they cannot simply be copied and still retain their vitality. On the other hand, motifs from the past can inform current art. I have been moved by some of the art on display at the Grahamstown Arts Festival in South Africa, particularly woodcuts produced by young South African artists. The three-dimensional carving of much of Africa may no longer happen, but the two-dimensional incising of feeling and love into a block of wood brings the richness of the past into the flatness of the present. In addition, much of the music coming out of Africa today bridges the generation gap. I was particularly moved by the music of Samite, a Ugandan musician who played, sang, and spoke in a marvelous video entitled *Song of the Refugee* (Samite 1997). He sang of hope in Liberia, Côte d'Ivoire, Ruanda, and Uganda. I heard him perform at the Grahamstown Festival, where a huge audience roared its appreciation as he shaped a deeply Christian message of love in the idiom of traditional Ugandan music. During another year at the Festival, a Ugandan troupe of musicians backed up a Luganda version of Bertholt Brecht's great play *Mother Courage*. Brecht's poetry was transmuted into African idiom.

Art may be flourishing, but **family structures** have certainly suffered, as the uneven transition from polygyny to monogamy and from there to cohabitation takes place across Africa. A moving exception to the seeming decline in family solidarity is the continent-wide response to the AIDS crisis. There are already millions of AIDS orphans, and more are expected over the coming years. However, it appears that in many cases, particularly through grandparents stepping in to help a whole generation of dying young adults, they are adjusting to the crisis by taking in children only remotely related to them, and in some cases not related at all. The love that is shown in these ad hoc responses to tragedy is indeed impressive and may show that the breakdown of the husband-wife relation is being overcome by a re-establishment of larger ties of concern for bereaved relatives and friends.

What remains of great concern is the fate of children who no longer have any living relatives. There, the hope must lie with voluntary non-government organizations. In early 2003, I was particularly moved by the work of HOKISA, an organization in Cape Town providing a home for children living with AIDS, whether their own cases or those of afflicted and dying family members. Also impressive was the day-care center in the East Rand outside Johannesburg, where I saw up to sixty children being cared for by a concerned traditional healer, or *sangoma*. What was sad about her situation was that the staff could not care for the children on weekends so that when Monday came they would arrive hungry and dirty, because there was no one at home.

In this way, the **community** is responding to crises, not only through absorbing AIDS victims into households, but also by not allowing destitution to harden people's hearts. My experience of poor Basotho reaching out to even poorer Basotho is heartening, and, I hope, a paradigm of what can happen elsewhere in Africa as poverty grows. Unfortunately, some situations are almost too desperate even to allow for a humane response, such as the ongoing genocide in Darfur or eastern Democratic Republic of Congo. But my hope is that if peace can be restored, *ubuntu* will revive and people will once again be able to be people.

In 2004, as Liberia lurches from crisis to crisis, from LURD attacks to the return of refugees from Côte d'Ivoire, people are having to open their hearts and their homes to refugees. Tens of thousands of people moved from Gbarnga in the center of Liberia to camps closer to the capital, Monrovia, and even there the attacks and looting continued. Surely there would be immense suffering, more than is even known now, if Liberians of all walks of life were not willing to give at least some comfort and care to displaced persons.

And yet in the midst of all the turmoil, **local histories** need not be lost. One of the most striking successes of the Truth and Reconciliation Commission in South Africa was its preservation of the stories of the apartheid era. Images of the past are always changed, clarified, and simplified, but in the case of South Africa the reality cannot be hidden. It is to be hoped that similar replayings of the past can flourish throughout Africa as peace is eventually restored to troubled communities. Already, Liberians are talking about the necessity to capture the history of the civil war in order to find the pockets of humanity that remained to protect innocent people during that terrible catastrophe. Sierra Leone has recently instituted its Truth and Reconciliation process, and Ghana also is trying to recover a lost generation of history under the post-Jerry Rawlings government.

At the same time, the **role of women** is coming to the fore everywhere, yet the oppressed can only be liberated by their own efforts. Throughout sub-Saharan Africa, with the possible exception of Muslim areas, women are speaking out and carving out their futures. That Ellen Johnson-Sirleaf was the only viable opposition candidate against Charles Taylor in the 1997 election in Liberia speaks volumes. Strong-willed and creative women have risen up in every endeavor, such as Professor Wangari Maathai, who received the prestigious UNEP Sasakawa Environment Prize for environmental protection for helping people plant trees in her native Kenya (www.unep.org/sasakawa2/committee.asp). In addition, Uganda's Seventh Parliament has 74 women members. There are also women cabinet ministers in most countries, and in South Africa in particular, key ministries, such as foreign affairs and health, are headed by women.

The loss of **tradition** is inevitably more problematic. Every articulate African speaks in the name of tradition in one way or another. I see a convergence between the recovery of history and the allegiance to tradition. The two can go together, as is seen in the example of the renewal of the rich Christian past in Ethiopia. Just as the church is gathering strength in post-communist Eastern Europe, so the Ethiopian church is reaching out to try to bring the country together. Moreover, an important debate is taking place in South Africa as to the role of the chieftaincy. It is certainly true that the chiefs maintain the peace and help resolve local conflicts in rural parts of South Africa. Some (sadly, not all) of the chiefs are working hard to modernize the chieftaincy institution so that it can play a constructive role in national as well as local politics.

Ethnic unity within diversity is not an impossible goal. I am very encouraged by what I have seen in Lesotho, where people of different ethnic groups have formed a unified society without suppressing the Xhosa or Ndebele minorities. There remains much ethnic hatred in Liberia, but there are people who are working to overcome the recently ignited quarrels that had begun to disappear under presidents Tubman and Tolbert. The genocide of the early 1990s in Rwanda and Burundi is the stimulus for a serious attempt to bring ethnic groups together. Much credit can be given to former South African president Nelson Mandela, who did much to reconcile white, mixed-race and black in his own country, and who is now determined to bring Hutu and Tutsi together.

In short, I do not see the **breakdown of the moral order** as a hopeless barrier to coming together to build a better future for Africa. In all eight of the areas I have discussed in this chapter, there are signs of hope. May we all see them, hear them, and work to bring them to fruition.

CHAPTER THREE. NEGLECT OF INDIGENOUS KNOWLEDGE

3.1 Destruction of natural forests.

I grew to love the rain forest in Liberia. Our eight-month stay in the remote village of Gbansu included many forays into the forest. It was cool, clean and dark. Wildlife was not evident, although I am sure it was abundant. It was difficult to see more than a few meters into the forest, because of the dense undergrowth and the thick stand of forest trees. Occasionally I would see a few monkeys in the branches and a brightly colored tropical bird. But always there was the buzz, the murmur, the chattering, and the singing of insects and birds. The rain forest is never quiet.

Hunters knew the forest well. Bomo-sii, my teacher and research associate, went hunting many nights and would often manage to bring down a small antelope with his single-barrel shotgun. We had our share of bush meat and enjoyed it, even though we felt the occasional twinge of conscience at killing things wild and beautiful. The forest seemed in those now far-off mid-1970s almost limitless, and we believed that our visits were only to the fringes of an immense expanse of green.

I flew over the forest several times then and was always awed by the clean, unbroken canopy which extends in some cases to almost a hundred meters above the ground. The occasional river cuts through the forest, often almost totally overgrown by trees. Only the major rivers, like the St. Paul, which passes close by Gbansu, leave a clear opening to the sky. Paths are less visible to the air, since most paths in the high forest differ little from the trails made by the larger mammals and have to be re-opened with every passage.

River in Liberia's rain forest

At that time, human society only nibbled at the edge of the forest, keeping its villages and cultivated fields in a restricted area of low bush and occasional small patches of high forest preserved for the initiation schools. The village of Gbansu and its outlying hamlets used an area of about eighty square kilometers, enough space for roughly a thousand people to live in balance with nature. The bush was allowed to grow back for eight to ten years after it had been cleared for rice farming and then was cut and burned again for a new crop. It was rare for people to cut down the high forest, not only because it was hard work but also because it remained an awesome and holy reserve where spirits lived and where wild animals could be hunted and killed. The people of Gbansu, exemplified by my language teacher and guide, knew their forest intimately, knew what it could do for them, but also knew the dangers of abusing it.

For several reasons, however, the situation I saw in Gbansu became inherently unstable. Had the people been left alone, had medical care not been available so that the population remained constant, had commercial agriculture not been introduced along roads built for the purpose, had land not been grabbed by wealthy outsiders, had war not come to the nation, then very likely what we saw could have continued for hundreds of years to come. That was not to be the case, as we see more clearly now than we imagined then.

Cuttington University College, where we taught, was a mere eight hours walk from Gbansu. But the difference between the two areas was vast, most clearly visible when flying from the field near Cuttington to a small airstrip cut out of the bush at the edge of Gbansu. Over Gbansu, the rice crops were a healthy green in contrast to the sickly yellow-green of rice grown in the villages near Cuttington. The slash-and-burn cycle around Cuttington had been reduced to a mere three or four years, which did not allow fertility to be restored to the soil. The result was poor crops, necessitating an even more rapid return to the same site in a few short years.

The reduction of the farm cycle near Cuttington was the inevitable result of its being on the central road leading from Monrovia to the interior and on into Guinea. Adjacent to Cuttington was Phebe Hospital where high-quality medical care kept people from dying of malaria, dysentery, untreated infections, and all the other tropical nasties so common across Liberia. People who graduated from schools in the interior migrated to the main road to set up businesses and build their homes. The combination of increasing population density and non-agricultural uses of the land meant that the old eight- to ten-year farming cycle could not be sustained. The result was a downward spiral evident a quarter of a century ago to any observer.

An example of what I most fear for Liberia was a 1972 Israeli land-clearing and rice-planting project in a small piece of high forest at the end of a road behind Cuttington. The intention was to clear all the trees and undergrowth, plant rice the first year, and thereafter turn it into a coffee plantation. Rice grew reasonably well the first year, but the rains quickly exhausted the soil, carrying the nutrients off into the nearby rivers, nutrients which would otherwise have been captured by the roots which survived the always incomplete burning of the forest in the normal slash-and-burn process. Moreover, the coffee trees did not have the ability to capture nutrition from the air and return it to the soil in the way the forest trees have always done. The result was a bare and stony patch of land that required continual fertilization in order for the coffee trees to bear fruit.

The situation is even worse now. When I flew from Abidjan to Monrovia in October 1997, I could see Liberia's future before my eyes. Almost no high forest remained in what had once been an unbroken expanse of forest in southwestern Côte d'Ivoire that I had driven through in 1966. Instead, I saw a patchwork quilt of small farms, villages and roads. As soon as the plane crossed the Liberian border, I could see what I had known before in Côte d'Ivoire. In Liberia, we flew over dense greenery, from that height a seemingly endless bed of full-grown broccoli and cauliflower. I realized then that the civil war in Liberia had brought at least one good result. The forest remained uncut, with only one overgrown road threading its way through the lavish, undisturbed wilderness.

However, I knew what would come on the basis of what I saw in Côte d'Ivoire. Sadly, my expectations for Liberia are now being realized. The Taylor government leased out large parcels of land to timber companies, with overall control lying in the hands of the Taylor family. Such unchecked greed will soon destroy what civil war and preceding centuries of relative peace left intact. In November 2001 I flew over the same forest that had seemed so beautiful and unbroken in 1997. I saw visible clearings and roads cutting everywhere. I fear that the end result will be even worse than in Côte d'Ivoire, where at least small farms and commercial villages have sprung up to replace the forest.

The Society for the Conservation of Nature, incorporated in the early 1990s, set up the Sapo National Forest not far from the southeast coast of Liberia. This small band of committed conservationists has carried on a brave fight to protect a small portion of forest, known to be one of the last refuges for many rare plants and animals. They were encouraged by the Liberian government within the framework of the Forest Development Authority. In fact, several grants were made to conservation groups through Conservation International and Fauna and Flora International (www. cepf.net).

Forest giant in Liberia

I fear that these grants and this official support by the Liberian government were just window dressing to cover up the intense exploitation of the forest by the Taylor government. In a time of terrible civil war, the Liberian government had the temerity to promote eco-tourism in the very same southeast portion of the country that was being wasted by clear-cutting (www.FOL.org, News from Monrovia and World Press 2003-03-21).

A major indictment of the Liberian government was issued by the Save My Future Foundation in Monrovia (SAMFU 2002) describing the impact not only on the forest but also on the people living in rural southeast Liberia. The Oriental Timber Company was a serious destroyer of the forest, taking out huge amounts of timber without any attempt at ecological protection or restoration. Ivan Watson reported the devastation to nature and human society in stark terms: "The Oriental Timber Company's roads and timber operations have expanded deeper into the rain forest. What was once a towering, untouched jungle habitat of rare forest elephants and pygmy hippopotamuses is now a honeycomb of quarter-mile wide strips of deforested bush and road" (The Boston Globe, May 20, 2001). He quotes local and international authorities regarding the extent of the damage, including Liberian prize-winning ecologist Alex Peal and Reg Hoyt of the Philadelphia Zoo.

In addition, the damage to his beloved Liberia became an important theme in the sermons and speeches of Archbishop Michael Francis, Catholic archbishop in Monrovia for more than twenty-five years and winner of the 1999 Robert F. Kennedy Human Rights Award. At a meeting of the Save My Future Foundation, he said that "it was about time that the forest industry be preserved and judiciously exploited, otherwise, 'our children will find a deserted land.' The solution depends on the cooperation of the common people who are the custodian of the natural resources" (allafrica.com/stories/200301140656.html).

Even CNN has reported on its website about Taylor's continual and very profitable illicit trade of timber for weapons: "Most of the country's timber exports go to China and to Europe, where protesters have demanded action to stop the shipments, accusing Taylor and his associates of ransacking Liberia's forests. In five years, the country's annual timber exports have risen from $5 million to more than $100 million. Investigators allege that Taylor uses the trade to enrich his own personal fortune and to provide cover for arms trafficking" (www.cnn.com/2002/TECH/science/01/13/liberian.timber/). In April 2003, Taylor's government admitted it was selling timber to buy guns, but said it must do so in order to defeat the insurgent LURD forces.

I hope that the new interim government under Bryant will take seriously the task of preserving the forest as an investment in the future of Liberia. I worry, however, that it will be tempted to continue the indiscriminate cutting of valuable forest trees in order to earn resources to finance reconstruction. One way to resist this temptation will be for international agencies in effect to buy back the forest, as they have begun to do with full government support, in Gabon (http://usinfo.state.gov/regional/af/usafr/a3031305.htm).

Liberia is not the only place where I saw the destruction of forests. I was called to Ethiopia by the Food and Agriculture Organization to help analyze data for a reforestation project. There, I could see everywhere the results of what must have been centuries of cutting down indigenous forests. Other disturbing circumstances included the donkeys and humans loaded with charcoal that came into Addis Ababa every day from the surrounding countryside. Additionally, Ethiopia has been severely overpopulated for generations; sadly it is endemic famine and bloody and senseless war that is slowing its population growth.

The Ethiopian landscape I saw showed the scars of intensive cultivation. I visited the highlands village of Ankober where men were out plowing the stony, exhausted soil, hoping to get a bit of barley at their next harvest. I could not imagine that the harvest would be more than a few handfuls, considering the condition of the soil. There, I witnessed a joyous feast dedicated to the Virgin Mary. The feast was surely one of the few occasions of joy in that desolate land. Boston University Africanist Jim McCann, however, points out that it is unlikely trees had formerly grown on those stony fields that seemed to have lost all their topsoil to the intense seasonal rains and to the scouring wind that blew, cold and cutting, the entire time I was there.

Afforestation would be difficult in that place because of extreme poverty and because of the exhausted soil. The project was serious and certainly more wood was needed, but I fear that in some of the areas I saw, it was too late. McCann points out that in other parts of Ethiopia forests do indeed grow very well, too well from the point of view of some local inhabitants (McCann 1999:102). Even in Ankober I saw micro-forests where some trees could flourish, but certainly not on the barren fields.

Plowing stony soil in Ethiopia

Lesotho also has had its share of uncontrolled cutting of its meager cover of shrubs and small trees, mostly along river banks and on the north-facing slopes of hills. Before the first major influx of people at the beginning of the nineteenth century, Lesotho was largely covered in perennial grasses that supported a substantial population of ungulates and their predators. But indigenous trees were also present, and in sheltered environments could grow up to twenty meters high.

Lesotho is cold, and everyone needs fuel in the winter when snow can stay for up to two months in the high mountains. Houses must also be constructed to withstand the winter, and so poles and beams had to be cut from available trees in the early days before South Africa developed its own forestry industry. As a result, the larger trees were very quickly cut down for timber, and shrubs were cut in increasing numbers to provide fuel. The environment deteriorated quickly, erosion spread, and soon people began to realize just what they had done as yields fell and firewood became more and more difficult to locate. Lesotho too has had its afforestation programs, and these have been reasonably successful, to the point where Lesotho is one of the few countries in the world with more trees every year.

There are many examples of the loss of forests across Africa. Loggers are cutting roads and felling trees throughout the great forests of the Congo basin. It is an irony in this situation that the Pygmies, who have always lived in symbiosis with the forest, are now being hired to cut them down (New York Times, 16 February 2003). In Kenya, which once had enlightened policies of forest management both in pre-colonial and colonial times, greedy entrepreneurs are now recklessly cutting its highland forests for profit and for land development (allafrica.com/stories/200301150637.html).

Serious flooding in Mozambique is due in large measure to the deforestation of its highlands and those of its neighbors, South Africa, Swaziland, and Mozambique. "Tree leaves cushion raindrops, allowing more water to enter the soil. Tree roots both stabilize the soil and dry it out. But when uplands are stripped of trees, rainwater, instead of being absorbed, is immediately released to the streams and rivers. The result, observes Janet Abramovitz of the environmental group Worldwatch, is that rains that might have caused small problems now cause floods" (whyfiles.org/107flood/).

Why should I care about the loss of indigenous forests in Africa when the continent is under attack in so many other ways? Why should the destruction of the Sarpo National Park in Liberia worry me when the whole of Liberia is being destroyed by cruel and heartless soldiers? Liberian Archbishop Francis, at the meeting mentioned above of the Save My Future Foundation, came closest to providing an answer: "Our children will find a deserted land," that is, if Africans do not take proper care of their forest resources.

Without resources, there are no sources for livelihood. Without livelihoods, there are no jobs. Without jobs, there is war. A child soldier is quoted in the New York Times, "You get big in war. If there's another war, you will not go there? You will go there. In a war, what we chasing? Isn't it money?" (Sengupta 2003).

Liberia's rich resources of iron, rubber, diamonds, and timber are currently being put to no good use. Instead, they are fueling the ever-spreading West African civil wars. Who is to blame young men for allying themselves with war when they see nothing in their futures except hopeless poverty? Until there are viable alternatives, they will do that which is easiest for them—they will fight.

3.2 Introduction of exotic trees.

In much of Africa, tree-planting has meant the introduction of fast-growing, commercially profitable trees such as eucalyptus, wattle, and pine in southern Africa, and coffee, tea, rubber, and cocoa in tropical Africa. These trees have indeed proved profitable to those who manage large plantations, but they have been of doubtful value to the small holder, and have often harmed the environment.

Eucalyptus has been both praised and censured throughout Africa. Some people say it is the only hope for fuel and poles once the indigenous trees are gone. Others say it further destroys the environment by not allowing other trees to grow alongside it and by sucking all the water from the ground so that grass cannot grow. I was told by villagers in the Luwero Triangle in Uganda that they did not want eucalyptus seedlings, though they were being provided for next to nothing by the government. They feared the tree because of its negative effects on other trees and crops in the area. This was in one of the most fertile and best watered areas of Africa, an area where almost anything will grow and grow well.

I have seen eucalyptus groves in Lesotho and have been torn between liking and hating what I saw. The seedlings grow quickly into big, beautiful trees. They provide much-needed poles and firewood. They turn to coppice when cut so that more wood is available within a short time. But they are thirsty, and they degrade the adjacent soil. I have seen eucalyptus groves where scarcely any green matter grew within four or five meters of the trees.

Lesotho has its own slow-growing trees which could be cultivated and could provide firewood over a long period of growth. What must be done is to plan ahead, which seems beyond the ability of those who create time-limited development projects. An example of such long-thinking comes out of Queens College in Cambridge University. In the 1970s, the Master of the College noticed that the beautiful, large oak beams in the ceiling were beginning to show signs of decay. He contacted the College forester to ask if there were any large old oak trees on College land that could be cut down to provide new beams. The forester indicated that seedling oak trees had been planted five hundred years earlier when the College was being built in order to have wood available when the first set of beams were no longer useable.

Planning far ahead may make little sense to foreign donors who are constrained by the need to show results within a few short years. However, residents of a country must plan for their children, their grandchildren, and for all future generations. Lesotho's own hardwoods can be grown. The same applies to forestry development projects throughout Africa. Afforestation in Ethiopia can be done in a short-sighted way, planting more of the eucalyptus trees that now ring Addis Ababa, or it can be done with an eye to the long term, using indigenous hardwood trees.

The tropical rain forest has highly valuable trees, including Liberian forest giants, such as mahogany and other slow-growing hardwoods that command high prices on the world market. It may seem like a good idea in the short run to plant rubber, coffee, and cocoa, but surely it is not impossible to plant hardwoods for the future, inter-cropping them with the quick-growing commercial trees. It has been proven in Uganda that replanting mahogany in a forest that has been already severely cut is not only possible but also beneficial to the whole ecosystem (www.budongo.org.html). However, as research in Ghana has shown, replanting can only be done by respecting the indigenous mix of insects and disease pests that grew up with the ancient forests over the course of time. Otherwise, artificial plantations, even of familiar indigenous trees, tend to fail (www.itto.or.jp/newsletter/v7n2/06plantation.html).

Additionally, exotic trees can cause serious environmental damage. South Africa is beginning to root out non-indigenous trees in order to allow the local shrubs and trees to recover their dominant status. I was in Cape Town in early 2000 and took a walk up a hill behind the hotel in Hout Bay, where I was staying. I saw evidence of serious efforts to uproot invasive species so that the local vegetation can be restored; at the same time this work provided jobs to out-of-work South Africans. South Africa is no longer willing to plant massive stands of pine, wattle, and eucalyptus since they crowd out the more ecologically friendly and valuable local species; yet much of the damage has already been done, and few natural forests remain. I also saw impressive indigenous forest giants on the south coast at Tsitsikamma, but surrounding them were huge pine plantations which must have replaced tracts of the adjacent natural growth. Must the desire for immediate profits always win?

However, it is not easy to root out invasive species and replace them quickly with native vegetation. A careful study of sequestration of carbon in plants in order to reduce the greenhouse effect has also looked at restoring native forests in South Africa. "As with forest conservation or plantation forestry, assisted forest regeneration could lead to negative social impacts if communities are prevented from changing to preferred land uses in the future. This negative impact also can be reduced by ensuring that the designation of areas for reforestation is consistent with long-term regional land-use plans and that community development priorities are effectively incorporated during project development and implementation" (www.grida.no/climate/ipcc/land_use/284.htm).

In the case of intrusive species or reforestation, it is important to listen to the accumulated experience and wisdom of indigenous experts and of organizations such as Nuffic. Nuffic is committed to the use and dissemination of local knowledge, has experts who have studied this question. It maintains its International Network of Ethnoforestry, "A peer group of concerned foresters, scientists, international agencies, and NGOs working for the documentation, dissemination and integration of indigenous knowledge on forest management with formal forestry, in various cultures and indigenous peoples in different parts of the globe" (www.nuffic.nl/ik-pages/lists.html).

3.3 Loss of environmental diversity.

Dugout canoe on the Okavango

One of the most special and beautiful areas in the world is the Okavango Delta in northwest Botswana. The Okavango River enters Botswana from the highlands of southeast Angola, where it has collected rainfall from a wide catchment. That part of Angola is still reasonably free from erosion, and so the water arrives in Botswana clean, clear, and cold. The river then spreads out into a wide basin, which is as near to completely flat as is possible on this complex and folded planet. The river runs through the Delta, passes by the town of Maun, flows into the Magadigadi Pan near the Orapa diamond mine, and eventually disappears into the Kalahari Desert.

The diversity of the Okavango Delta is wonderful and strange. Birds, fish, reptiles, mammals, trees, and plants are found in abundance there that are found nowhere else in the region. A small indigenous human population lives within the Delta, dependent mostly on fishing and more recently on tourism. We spent three days in the swamp, traveling by day in a dug-out canoe and sleeping at night in camps on the small islands that barely rise above the water. That brief time was an experience of peace and great beauty we will never forget.

Yet the Delta is under threat from "development." Cattle ranchers want more of the surrounding area fenced away from the wild game that has inhabited the area for millennia. Farmers want to take advantage of the annual flood to plant crops on the renewed fertility of the margins of the river. Even more serious, the governments of Botswana and Namibia want to take water from the river for the growing and thirsty populations of their cities and industries.

In 1997, anthropologist and expert on large dams Thayer Scudder led a thirteen-person team to investigate the situation, and found that it is quite unnecessary to take water out. Eventually, the Okavango was declared the largest protected wetland site in the world under the Ramsur Convention, the intergovernmental treaty providing a framework for the conservation of wetlands and their resources. Nevertheless, temptation for misuse is great, and the great Okavango Delta is still in serious danger. As recently as October 2000, The Namibian wrote about Namibia's proposal to cut off the Okavango River as it crosses the Caprivi Strip before it enters Botswana. And in 2003 once again the Namibian government has proposed a scheme to generate electricity from the water entering the swamp (allafrica.com/stories/200302250730.html). Any such loss of the Okavango Delta would be a serious blow to this fragile world's biological diversity.

Since the Basotho established themselves as a nation in what has been called "a ruined paradise," Lesotho has lost almost all its large mammals (Brown 1965: 220-231). I have seen a very few small and medium-sized antelopes in the mountains, and thus was impressed with one chief who forbade his subjects from killing any of the small herd in his area. But this pitiful remnant is nothing compared with reports of the huge herds and flocks in Lesotho prior to the Basotho retreat from aggressive and predatory Afrikaners.

The Basotho once lived in what is now the Free State of South Africa, in an area with enough pasture to support their herds and flocks. As they were forced across the Mohokare River (Caledon, to the white South Africans), the Basotho searched for pasture, which they found only in the mountains. The mountains were originally populated by hunter-gatherer Bushmen, who saw the Basotho livestock as fair game. As has been the case everywhere, the hunter-gatherers lost the battle to the herders, who in the end killed the men and married the women in one of the earliest examples of human genocide.

Goats grazing in Lesotho's mountains

The migration into the mountains also affected much plant life. Lesotho originally was a high grassland covered with sweet palatable vegetation supporting the herbivores that reportedly covered the mountains. These grasses gave way to invasive species from the west, so much so that there are only a few areas where the original grasses still flourish. The fault lies mostly with the overgrazing of cattle, sheep, and goats, as well as the horses and donkeys used by herdsmen for transport. The mountain pastures could not sustain the rapid increase in animals, which quickly ate up the best grasses, right down to the roots.

Sour grasses and inedible grass species from the Karoo to the west replaced the sweet grasses. The new vegetation at least had the virtue of holding the soil in place, but fire, used by shepherds to bring up tender, young grass in the spring, left more and more areas bare of all vegetation. The inevitable result was that early spring winds and summer rains eroded the soil, leaving bare rock where there had formerly been thin topsoil held together by the sturdy root structures of grasses and shrubs.

Additionally, environmentalists in Lesotho are now fighting to save the Maloti minnow. The tiny fish, which lives only in streams high in the mountains, is threatened by the huge Lesotho Highlands Water Project. The resulting man-made lakes will slow or submerge many free-flowing streams and introduce larger, predatory fish into remaining streams. After more than a hundred years of environmental destruction, it seems too late to worry about a tiny fish, but perhaps some concern is better than none. Unfortunately, it is feared that the fish will not survive such radical changes in the environment.

A further consequence is the loss of sponges that hold and filter water and provide a source for springs and rivers at lower elevations. The World Wildlife Fund warns: "The loss of these natural sponges for floodwaters within the river basin increases the risk of extreme floods. WWF argues that many of these problems could be avoided if the recommendations of the first ever World Commission on Dams (WCD) were applied to future dam projects" (sciencepolicy.colorado.edu/ socasp/floods.html). I saw one severely damaged bog on the road to the Highland Water Project dam at Katse; there, water had clearly once been absorbed by the soil, but was now rushing toward the lowlands, where there is often damage from heavy flooding.

In short, environmental diversity has been lost in Lesotho. An entire culture of hunter-gatherers has been destroyed. Grasslands have been reduced to small patches amid large stretches of inedible shrubs. The natural mechanisms for storing and purifying mountain water have been trampled and destroyed. Topsoil has been washed or blown away. Lesotho polymath David Ambrose and his colleagues have told the full story in a recent account of threats to and efforts toward conservation (Ambrose et al., 2000).

Yet efforts are now being made to save endangered species; not just the Maloti minnow, but also remarkable plants such as the spiral aloe, which grows naturally only in the highlands of Lesotho. By 1996, Lesotho had ratified seventeen international conventions on the environment, although admittedly little has been done to implement these conventions (Chakela 1999:199). Such hard work by environmentalists is valuable and must be encouraged. Even so, most of the damage has already been done, and Africa is the poorer for it.

What is the situation in Liberia? If the far eastern timber companies hired by ex-President Charles Taylor and his thugs have their way, they will destroy the rain forest that is the glory of Liberia. It is one of the last of the largely untouched forests once covering coastal West Africa from southern Senegal to Cameroon, where they joined the great forests of the Congo basin. The Society for the Conservation of Nature in Liberia, a small non-governmental organization, struggled bravely through the civil war to protect the Sapo National Forest, located a short distance inland from the Atlantic coast.

One small remnant of a once-great forest cannot compensate for the loss of an entire eco-system. The rain forest is the lungs of the West African climate; the ability of trees to absorb carbon dioxide and breathe out oxygen is critical not only to West Africa but to the world. As the forest shrinks, the rainfall pattern will change, and the desert will advance into the Sahel and the savanna. Even on a local level, one piece of forest is not enough to sustain the wildlife that depends on a large grazing and hunting area. The deep, thick jungles of Liberia support several pygmy species that are found almost nowhere else, including the forest elephant, the so-called "bush cow" or forest buffalo, and the diminutive pygmy hippopotamus. They and their predators need space in which to thrive, and the Sapo National Forest does not provide that space.

There is one case where the rush to exploit a natural resource has possible beneficial consequences. In the Kalahari Desert of South Africa, the San people have been exploited and abused for generations, but their land in much of the Northern Cape Province has remained relatively intact. This is in contrast to comparable land in Botswana, which has almost entirely been given over the cattle ranching.

In the Kalahari, a desert succulent plant has been found to contain chemicals that suppress appetite. According to a New York Times article by Ginger Thompson, the San have used this plant for as long as they can remember to sustain them as they go on long hunting trips (New York Times, 1 April 2003). An agreement has been signed with San authorities allowing the plant to be used to develop drugs that help overfed Europeans and Americans cut down their consumption of rich foods. It is indeed ironic that obese rich people are turning to lean and hungry Africans in order to stop eating too much.

I conclude this section with an anecdote from Uganda. The village where I stayed in Luwero needed an improved water system. Their shallow well gave clear water, but it was not "modern" and did not yield enough water to provide more than a handful of houses with drinking and washing water. Yet the people who used that well wanted it preserved and maintained.

Why were they so concerned? They showed me a small fish that lives in the well. How it got there and how it survives in isolation from every other body of water, I do not know. But the people felt it was very important, perhaps as a guardian of their water supply. Giving up that well, and the fish that lived in it, meant to them the destruction of something valuable. I believe they were quite right, even though their explanation did not sound to me like "science." May that small fish, and its counterparts throughout Africa and the world, live and flourish. If we forget these guardians in our rush to modernize, we do so at our peril.

3.4 Introduction of cash crops instead of food crops.

One of the enduring myths of modernization is that farmers do better to grow cash crops so they can buy both food and consumer goods. There is some truth to this myth, as there is always some truth underlying every myth. Rubber, sugar, cotton, coffee, tea, cocoa, pyrethrum, cut flowers, peanuts, tobacco—all have made some people rich and have fattened government balance sheets. Moreover, if a country produces enough food, in variety, to feed its people, then the use of surplus land for cash crops makes good sense, provided the benefits get back to the people whose land

Tapping rubber in Liberia

is used. What is not clear is if these ordinary people have benefited.

One illustration is the Firestone Rubber Company, which in effect bought Liberia in a debtor's auction and developed the biggest rubber plantations in the world on what had formerly been small-scale cropland. Both Firestone and Goodrich gained control of large tracts of Liberian land as early as the 1920s, when it became clear that natural rubber from Brazil and the Central African rainforests simply could not meet the demand from the rapidly growing automobile industry.

Small holders were paid to grow one last crop of rice on land that was then taken away from them. Afterward, they were employed as rubber tappers, at incredibly low wages, to work on what should have been their own land. Workers ran away to other parts of Liberia, no longer willing to do what amounted to dreary slave labor. Firestone then commissioned rural chiefs to impress and deliver to the plantations local residents, paying an attractive bounty per head. Eventually the industry stabilized and some, mostly poor and landless, workers left their villages and became regularly paid workers (Clower et al. 1966:42, 164).

The big rubber growers have done very well. To those of us who visited in the 1960s and 1970s, the Firestone plantation gave the impression of a vast tidy orchard. Its trees marched down long orderly rows and supposedly happy workers produced the rubber we needed for our tires. The headquarters at Harbel were immaculately tended, with beautiful staff houses, a commissary, and a hotel to meet everyone's needs. In the early 1960s, we went to Harbel for our regular grocery shopping, because we knew we could get American delicacies at prices cheaper than in the Lebanese shops in Gbarnga or Monrovia.

I suffered my first shock of recognition at the manicured inequity of it all when I attended a party at the home of one of the Firestone senior staff. What most upset me was a scavenger hunt organized to find clues all over the plantation. Here we were, wealthy expatriates, using for a game the very milieu in which workers lived and died. I refused to join in and instead stayed at the house until it was time to go back to Cuttington, feeling at the same time self-righteous and foolish.

 At least the Firestone plantation produced maximum income for the owners, modest income for Liberia, and a minimum income for the workers. Far worse were the small-scale local rubber producers in the interior, people who had planted rubber on what had been viable rice-producing fields, rubber that produced very little reward. Moreover, the soil on which rubber is planted soon becomes useless for any other type of crop, turning stony and hard, since rubber is a hydroponic plant, dependent on abundant rainfall and little else.

Liberia is littered with old rubber farms, some of which have been rehabilitated. Few produce at the same high level as Firestone, Goodrich, or the other large private farms, such as that of Harry Morris, the Americo-Liberian capitalist. The rubber companies bought latex from these small farmers, paid them almost nothing for it, and processed it at great profit. The big companies did not care how the small producers managed to produce their little bit of rubber, but they were willing to accept it as it came.

Labor unrest continues, even during the civil war, because of the harsh and unjust conditions under which workers are hired and fired. In September 2002, workers at the Cavalla Rubber Plantation asked their labor union to assist them after being dismissed without severance pay. Just as in the earliest days of Firestone Rubber, however, they could expect little help from the government, which benefits from and condones the exploitation of workers.

Admittedly, the system in Liberia is not as bad as that under King Leopold in the Congo, though the objective is the same: get rubber however you can get it. I am sure Liberia is the poorer for having been a major rubber producer. The people who might have eaten from the soil had to be satisfied with a pittance from rubber income that could not provide them with a true livelihood. Clower and his colleagues calculated that in 1962 rubber tappers earned a daily wage of 45 U.S. cents, plus another 10 cents in food subsidies. Their approximate annual income was $150 (Clower et al. 1962:164 ff). In that same year, the estimated value product per worker per year in what Clower called "tribal farming" was more than twice that amount, at $339. No wonder rural people had to be coerced into jobs as rubber tappers, and no wonder chiefs were being paid an average of about $350 monthly to recruit laborers.

Cocoa and coffee were not as destructive in Liberia as rubber, though my experience was that small-scale producers had problems similar to those of small-scale rubber producers. They planted cocoa and coffee on their land, but made very little out of it. To the best of my knowledge, the reasonably well-run cocoa and coffee plantations at Cuttington regularly lost money; they were not the cash cows that the college had hoped for. Workers had to be paid and the crops had to be picked and processed. The end result was money spent and money lost and more small rural farmers in trouble. The cocoa and coffee groves in Gbansu were all losers, some to the point that people let the trees go back to bush. Small-scale producers on small plots bear the burden of growing the crop and are at the mercy of the world market for what they receive, and when I was working in Liberia there was no world-wide shortage of either commodity. There was no urgency on the part of the coffee and cocoa purchasers to improve the situation.

How can I explain the apparent contradiction between the poverty of the small producer and the wealth of the industry? One of the main strategies of First-World industries investing in Africa is to get raw materials cheap, process them in skillful ways, and then sell the final product at a substantial profit. It is in their interest to ensure that the local farmer is only marginally competent. He does not give up the business, but he produces goods that he cannot process into a commercially marketable product. To the extent that African countries like Liberia continue to sell raw materials to European, American, or Asian manufacturers without processing them locally into commercial products of increased value, the rural farmer becomes more impoverished. Robin Palmer and Neil Parsons, as well as many other scholars, have given striking examples of the process (Palmer and Parsons 1977).

What are needed are skilled business people at the local level, but they are scarce. The cooperative village of Iwala in Tanzania that I visited in 1991 was organized according to President Nyerere's ujamaa theory. It succeeded at business because of its skilled, energetic, and highly motivated village chairman. Its people were adept at growing coffee and maize and even more so at marketing their crops.

They built a large storage shed for their produce and bought more produce from neighboring villages. During my visit there, I heard of their plan to buy a large truck to transport produce to Dar-es-Salaam. Their own goods would be charged a nominal fee for transport, but other villages would pay dearly for the privilege. Thus, this traditionally ujamaa village became purely capitalist in relation to its neighbors.

Unfortunately, Tanzania was not able to reap the real rewards of either maize or coffee, namely, the rewards of processing them into saleable finished products. The efforts of Iwala to make a profit from their energy and skill were not translated into national profits, because, like so many developing countries, Tanzania could only export its raw materials. And those villages, those farmers, like Iwala's neighbors, in the end got very little from these commercial crops. I visited a total of seven rural Tanzanian villages, and it seemed clear to me that the people would have done better to grow food and thereby feed both themselves and others in the nation.

One village in the highlands of the southwest, Tukuyu, successfully grew and sold food crops. With its excellent soil and temperate climate, the villagers grew a surplus of white potatoes, peas and beans—all difficult to grow in the tropics. They were also self-sufficient in milk production. Unfortunately, due to the doctrinaire socialism of Nyerere and his party, they were not allowed to sell them to other people in the region who needed them. My research assistants and I broke the law ourselves when we transported fresh produce back to the district headquarters of Mbeya. We did not mind doing so, because we knew that people in the city were hungry for such vegetable and dairy products.

The one exception to the rule in the Mbeya area was a well-run tea plantation in the highlands of Tukuyu. Here, a tea factory took freshly picked leaves from local farms and processed them into high-quality export-grade tea. Unfortunately, most of the local tea farms in Tanzania were run by either the state or the village committee, who knew little about agricultural management, and the workers were sporadic in their commitment to regular picking. I saw state-run tea plantations where the trees had been allowed to grow wild, and the leaves were no longer worth picking.

There is a long list of similar examples. In Zimbabwe I saw huge farms planted almost entirely with tobacco, upon which the national economy depends heavily. Vast sugar cane plantations cover much of KwaZulu-Natal and Swaziland; at the same time, landless people remain hungry. In Lesotho, many high-quality soils were planted in asparagus, which the Basotho do not eat; it was intended only for export. The typical rural family in Lesotho has about one hectare of land. To turn over a substantial portion of that to an export crop, which in the end produces only very low monetary returns, is an unfortunate and misguided choice.

Overall, I agree with the World Watch Institute: "Many indebted countries turn to export of coffee, bananas, flowers, and other cash crops, often at the expense of their own domestic food supply, in an effort to earn foreign exchange to pay down debt. The main beneficiaries of this export orientation are typically large corporations, foreign investors, and large land owners, and not the rural poor" (lion.meteo.go.ke/cna/impact/hunger.html). For example, flowers are grown in fertile parts of Kenya and Zimbabwe on land that could easily produce food. The New York Times reported on 4 June 2003 the stark contrast between the laborers who produce flowers for the overseas market and the wealthy Europeans who buy them. Workers on these plantations earn at best about $2 per day for a forty-six-hour week, wages that are not enough to feed them, house them and send their children to school. And yet…they have jobs; many of their neighbors do not.

The paradox is that people desperately seek employment from the same companies that human rights activists decry for using what amounts to slave labor. Joan Robinson, a Cambridge University economist is widely quoted as saying, "The misery of being exploited is nothing compared to the misery of not being exploited." I have found different versions of the quotation, but they all have the same message: workers will do whatever they can under almost any circumstances to avoid destitution. I have seen women lining up to take jobs in textile factories that human rights activists in the United States want to close. There is no easy answer.

3.5 Creation of single-crop, single-product economies.

What makes many of these decisions to farm export crops so damaging to hopes for long-term sustainable agriculture is the concentration on single-crop farming. This problem occurs with the cultivation of a single food crop, as in the case of maize in much of southern and eastern Africa. Maize was introduced around 1800 into what is now South Africa and Lesotho by the Portuguese from Mozambique. It has spread widely and is now the preferred staple crop throughout the region.

Maize is a very demanding crop, however, requiring high levels of moisture and nutrients in the soil, unlike its more tolerant counterpart, sorghum. I have heard maize called a "noxious weed" in the context of the semi-arid parts of southern Africa. Yet it is grown year after year by Basotho farmers, with each year's average yield lower than the year before. Sorghum and wheat contribute a small amount to the total cereal-crop production, but maize is by far the most important. As the population grows and the yield declines, Lesotho must import ever larger amounts of maize.

Poor maize crop in Lesotho

Farmers insist on growing the crop despite its low productivity, because people like to eat it, maize porridge is easy to cook, maize can be stored safely, the stalks are good for fodder as well as fuel, and the crop requires little attention.

Other areas are more suited to maize production. The BBC reported that Zambia had a surplus of maize in the 1999-2000 season, though only 6 percent of the land was actually cultivated. In Zambia, diversification into cash crops, as well as other food crops, would make sense. This conclusion is strengthened by the catastrophic shortage of maize in 2002, forcing Zambia to appeal to the World Food Program and other donors for help. Had they diversified earlier, they might have avoided a difficult situation. Once again in 2004 Zambia has a surplus of maize, but I have heard nothing about diversification into other crops. What next year may bring no one can predict, but having more alternatives would be safer than assuming another bumper crop of maize.

What adds to the unfortunate circumstances in Zambia is its history of moving people off farms and into the mining areas in order to promote the copper-mining industry (Palmer and Parsons 1977: 159-161, and passim). After doing so, white commercial farmers, drawn from the British colonial establishment, replaced the local people and became the principal maize growers. The main reason why there is so little protest against these commercial farmers is that there is so much available land. In Zimbabwe, however, a large proportion of the people is landless, and thus they resent the white landowners.

A consequence of mono-cropping is exhaustion of the soil, as is the case in Lesotho. Government and foreign experts have said that chemical fertilizers are the answer, and they have forced both themselves and small farmers into debt through the use of expensive inputs of fertilizer. Our research shows that the more money is spent on agriculture, the more money is lost. Even as far back as the late 1970s it was proven that chemical fertilizers have a negative rate of return on Lesotho's generally poor and exhausted soil. It simply does not pay the poor Mosotho farmer to spend money on his crops. Zero input of fertilizer produces at least some output, while spending money on trying to enrich depleted soils means, in the majority of cases, losing money (Gay and Hall 2000: 84-86).

A new method, which is at the same time an old method, is now being tried in Lesotho. A shrewd farmer named J. J. Machobane insisted even before Lesotho's independence in 1966 that mono-cropping of maize was a mistake. Instead, he suggested a mixed cropping system based on potatoes, but with regular alternation of crops and systematic planting of several crops simultaneously in individual fields. He advised against chemical fertilizers, recommending instead plowing heavy amounts of organic matter into the soil, including animal dung, wood ash, and compost from household waste, leaves, and weeds.

The British agricultural advisors looked down on Machobane and his ideas as being old-fashioned and unscientific. They were victims of the seeming success of Western commercial agriculture, and they were also anxious to market Western products, such as fertilizer and tractors, wherever they could. Anything "traditional" was messy, unscientific, small-scale and linked to a social system that must one day disappear. They were not aware that challenges to the farming systems they were so proud of in their homes in Europe and America would also arise and show that high-input, mechanized mono-cropping was probably wrong there as well.

Machobane's ideas were buried under a pile of government and donor plans, none of which proved viable in the field. After a generation of failed donor-driven agricultural projects, people looked once again at the common sense, simplicity, and social relevance of the Machobane system. It is to be hoped that fields exhausted by years of mono-cropping, including both the high-tech Western system and the low-tech family-based system of "maize, more maize and yet more maize," can be restored to health in this way. The Machobane Foundation is now being given strong support both by donors and, more important, by local farmers, and shows great promise for a future of more productive agriculture. (www.iirr.org/saem/page171-176.htm).

Related to the British desire for "scientific agriculture" is the powerful drive within large agro-businesses to improve traditional farming through the use of fertilizer, irrigation, new seeds, and mechanization. Norman Borlaug, who won the Nobel Peace Prize in 1970 for his work on the "Green Revolution," wrote an editorial published in the 11 July 2003 issue of the New York Times. It urged African farmers to adopt high-tech approaches to farming. He claims that African farmers could double or triple their yields, so that they could not only feed themselves but export crops to the world market.

He is quite right about the loss of soil fertility, the lack of nutrients, the shortage of water, and the difficulty of transport. All these have kept productivity down. I have documented a steady decline in total cereal crop production in Lesotho over the last century; 1973 was the last year that Basotho farmers produced enough maize, sorghum and wheat to feed themselves (Gay and Hall 2000:25). At present, Lesotho produces only about a quarter of what it needs and imports the rest, mostly from South Africa. The only way Lesotho can do this is by what economist Michael Ward many years ago dubbed "hard labor for life." The Basotho must work in the international capitalist system to earn money that will enable them to buy food.

Where I think Borlaug is wrong is in his recommendation that subsistence farmers adopt high-tech agricultural methods. Surveys I have conducted in Lesotho show that cash inputs in traditional farm settings have a negative payoff. The more money a farmer spends on plowing, fertilizer, seed, pesticides, irrigation and hired labor, the more he or she loses, so that there is a negative rate of return. The optimal solutions for rural subsistence farmers are either to do their best with traditional methods and harvest a small amount, which costs them nothing but labor, or give up farming entirely and work for cash. A third option is to shift to the Machobane method or something similar. We should trust African farmers to make the right decision for themselves. Allan Low shows clearly in his book *Agricultural Development in Southern Africa* that rural southern Africans are smart. They will allocate their time to that which produces the greatest net reward.

Tractor plowing in Lesotho

Yet many Africans are now being lured into the purchase of expensive pesticides, fertilizers, tractors, and genetically modified seeds in order to increase yields. In my view, their growing resistance to these technical fixes is quite correct. Only when farmland is taken away from subsistence farmers and given to commercial agro-business do Borlaug's recommendations make sense. The social consequence of such an alienation of land is more serious than the loss of food production, however. The people whose land is lost will move to urban centers where they will become a greater drag on the national economy than they were as minimally productive, part-time subsistence farmers.

Where farming is healthy, it is to a large extent because of diversity. Rural households in villages like Gbansu have an extremely complex farming system based on a slash-and-burn method that unfortunately cannot survive population growth and alternative land use. For what it was (or still is in remote parts of Liberia not yet subjected to "development"), it was effective and formed the basis of a healthy diet.

Rice remains to the present day the main crop in Liberia, but mono-cropping has never been practiced in rural subsistence farm practice. In Gbansu alone I managed to locate 120 different varieties of rice, which were planted according to the soil, weather, and expected harvest date. Moreover, rice was not the only crop in an individual field. Maize, pumpkins, and small vegetables were planted in and among the rice. After the rice was harvested, the field would be used a second year for cassava and other vegetables. In that second year, the bush would begin to grow back, providing shade cover for the new crops. Farm owners generally build a small thatch shelter on the farm to retreat from the regular downpours of the rainy season. Around the shelter they plant a small garden as well as bananas and plantain, which bore fruit

Rice harvest in Liberia

within the two years that a particular piece of land was cultivated.

At times, the farm shelter became the base for a satellite hamlet, in which case slower-bearing trees such as oranges or coconuts were planted. The hamlet al.so provided room for a small cocoa or coffee plantation, although these crops were generally not successful due to management problems and low market prices. To show that the hamlet was truly a home, a kola nut was often planted along with the umbilical cord of a new baby. The kola tree belonged to the new infant throughout life and that person was afterward identified with that farm site.

The same is true elsewhere. Rubber depletes Liberian soil and leaves little nutrition in it for restarting food production. Peanuts in the West African savanna are also very demanding and require increasing levels of fertilization. This does not have to be the case. I was impressed, for example, with the diversity of crops in Luwero in Uganda. The soil there was so fertile that people said they must jump out of the way once they had planted a seed lest the growing plant push them over. It is only war or donor folly that can allow people to be hungry in such a place.

Single-product economies are not only based on agriculture. My impression of Zambia, based on a short visit, is that it has been destroyed by copper. The mines on the copper belt needed workers, and so the British colonizers between 1930 and independence in 1964 actively discouraged people from remaining in their homes and working the land. Better by far, they thought, for men to dig out the copper ore, refine it into relatively pure copper, and sell it (at low prices, compared to the profit that copper products would bring to the foreign owners) to European and American manufacturers. In the end, copper prices have steadily dropped, because more copper is being mined elsewhere and because the electrical industries are finding substitutes. Zambia mortgaged its future against continuing profits from copper without processing the copper itself or diversifying into other activities. When the government sold the copper industry to Anglo-American corporation in South Africa, the Anglo-Americans pulled out of the business after deciding it could not make a profit. The country is now left with huge foreign debts, an ailing mining industry, and poor land use (/news.bbc.co.uk/2/hi/business/2205509.stm).

South Africa is now emerging from its single-product history. From the late nineteenth century until very recently, gold and diamonds were its main exports. Moreover, these commodities were not beneficiated, as jargon puts it, in South Africa but were sent abroad as raw materials, just as the Zambian copper was sent to be processed abroad. Employment in the gold mines was absolutely essential for the Basotho from the very beginning, but now mining employment has seriously declined, from a maximum of about 130,000 workers in the early 1990s to less than 70,000 in 2000 (www.fao.org) and nearer 60,000, according to the Central Bank of Lesotho. I have not been able to find more current statistics, but I anticipate that the number might have fallen to roughly 50,000 by mid-2004.

Diamond mining has only marginally involved the Basotho, but it has been very important to the South African economy through the De Beers Group.

Lesotho has a few diamond-bearing areas, but production has been limited. Botswana is far more fortunate, with two major diamond mines that contribute greatly to the economy. None of these countries, however, has seriously entered the processing industry. South Africa developed a small diamond-cutting industry in the 1980s, but it went broke, as the *Sunday Times* reported in late 2002 (www.suntimes.co.za/2002/04/21/business/news/news16.asp). A few small companies in southern Africa are making gold jewelry, but in most cases African countries are still selling their raw materials to others, notably Italy, Israel, and Belgium. These countries prepare gold and diamonds for the jewelry market and thus make the real profits.

Oil, timber, iron, bauxite, coal, platinum, and uranium are other commercial raw materials that have proved a mixed blessing to African nations. I have already mentioned the destruction of forests, and the resulting permanent loss of environmental richness. Yet instead of exporting furniture or dressed wood, African countries continue to sell raw logs. Their forests are rapidly disappearing, and little profit is being brought to the people whose lands are despoiled.

The papers and radio reports are full of the disasters that oil brings in its train. Nigeria is a special case. In Nigeria, the oil industry is corrupt, explosions have killed many people along the Nigerian oil pipelines, and there has been extreme damage to the fragile wetlands of the Niger Delta. In mid-2004, the Ijaw are still fighting the Itsekeri in the river area and have forced three oil companies to cease their operations.

Additionally, Angola can only maintain its oil industry by in effect ceding Cabinda to the oil companies. What historically has been the most corrupt and vicious of all African nations, Equatorial Guinea, will soon support its corruption and tyranny at a vastly higher level due to discoveries of oil. It may well be better not to have oil than to have it, since the oil-consuming countries have not suffered from the excesses associated with drilling for and exporting oil.

Having marketable raw materials is only a blessing if they can be put to work within the society that owns the materials. In Africa since the time when slaves were the first major export, raw materials have benefited people other than Africans themselves. Economies that depend on the export of an unprocessed raw material, whether it is a food crop, a mineral, or even human beings, are weak, unstable, and always at the mercy of the purchaser. Such economic instability breeds political instability. A continent always at the mercy of foreign nations will never be a continent that enjoys peace and internal development. Where crops, minerals, and people are sent in raw form abroad and re-imported as manufactured foodstuffs, assembly-line machinery, and foreign experts, local economies suffer.

Human beings continue to be exported. A case can be made that Africa's single most important export commodity is people. Certainly, the South African gold industry grew and continues to exist to a large extent because of workers recruited from Lesotho and Mozambique. But at a deeper level, Africans are leaving their home countries, and even their home continent, in ever larger numbers, both to escape ongoing civil turmoil and to find economic improvement abroad. The Southern African Migration Project (SAMP), which I have worked with over the years, continues to provide full documentation regarding migration within and beyond the region (www.queensu.ca/samp/).

Africa's economy continues to be weakened and the continent's health diminished by the exploitation of crops, minerals, and people. The crops fight back by dying and the minerals fight back by being exhausted. People fight back—by fighting.

3.6 Sidelining the indigenous economy.

Every African society has had its own indigenous economic system. Some flourished, allowing the creation of cities and empires. Others were more modest, devoted instead to the well-being of a small, sometimes isolated, community. These economic systems were effective to the extent that they allowed the interchange of goods and services within the community as well as between other communities and societies. Indigenous systems have been marginalized, in fact almost destroyed, by the dominant global economic structures.

Indigenous economies in Africa have historically tied together all the aspects of technology and society into an integrated, organic whole. Enough remained of the old economy in Gbansu, for example, for us to see how it worked. The community was never entirely self-sufficient, even before becoming part of a larger Liberian nation, because certain things could not be found in the eighty square kilometers that made up the village land. For instance, there was no natural salt. In desperation, people boiled and dried banana leaves to get a soda-like residue that gave a bit of flavor. But people preferred to get their salt either from the coast or from the Sahara Desert in exchange for forest goods. What could they sell? Kola nuts were a principal trade item, always welcome, even in the desert. Iron ore was plentiful, and Gbansu's people were noted for smelting iron to make high-quality tools that could be traded for other goods.

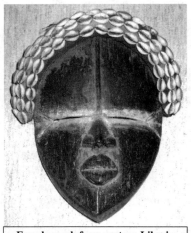

Female mask from eastern Liberia

The Gbansu system was thus largely self-contained, except for salt and a few other minor trade goods. I met a man in Gbansu who was sold in the late 1920s as a laborer, ultimately for shipment to Fernando Po, an island off the coast of Equatorial Guinea, in order to provide salt for the village. Additionally, despite the assertion by a Mandingo elder that before the arrival of Muslim traders in the forest the local people went naked, we know that cotton was locally grown, spun, and woven into durable cloth. There was also a plentiful supply of food of all types needed for good health. Sturdy houses were built from local wood, thatch, and mud. Men hunted with knives and arrows; both men and women fished with nets and with local plants that stunned fish in the water. Palm trees provided material for weaving, palm nuts for cooking, and palm wine for a pleasant, mildly alcoholic drink.

Nor was artistic and spiritual life lacking. Wood carvings from the Liberian interior are among the great art objects of the world. Folk tales and riddles make up an intricate corpus for instruction, entertainment, and reflection. The music of the forest is rich and complex and has been the source of Western jazz. The education of children was the point where the cultural heritage came together, so that the next generation could carry on and improve on what had been given to them in the three or four years of seclusion in bush school.

Much of this interlocking economy was still in place while we lived in Gbansu. The only clear break with the past was that people no longer smelted iron in order to make tools in the blacksmith shop that was still the focus of masculine life. However, we could find slag heaps around the village that had not yet been overgrown with forest vines and shrubs, indicating that iron had been smelted within living memory. In a nearby village I was given a detailed description of the process that enabled blacksmiths to produce iron and steel of various qualities, depending on what it was needed for (see Thomasson 1987).

The hammering of knives, axes, and cutlasses from scrap iron was beginning to die out while I was there. Ready-made tools could be bought at any shop. Despite not being of the same high quality as the locally made tools, they were cheap and required no labor except to keep them sharp. A few people still grew cotton to spin and weave into what we called "country cloth," but the imported cheap cottons cost little and were easy to sew into garments. This resulting clothing wore out much sooner than the indigenous cloth, but it was easily replaced. The walls of houses were still made in the old way, but thatch roofs were falling into disuse, being replaced by inexpensive corrugated iron sheets. Tinned meats made an occasional appearance in the village, particularly as game was harder to find, due largely to over hunting with guns rather than with knives and arrows. Packaged salt was easily available. Palm wine was no longer the drink of choice since the Firestone Rubber Company started selling inexpensive stills that produced raw (to me, undrinkable) rum from sugar cane.

How did people buy all these consumer goods? There was some trade in local goods, such as cloth, bush meat, rice, cocoa, coffee, and kola nuts. But most of the income came from village men who worked as rubber tappers, supplemented by income from a few successful, better-paid migrants. The total annual cash income of the village was just enough to buy the few things people needed. However, the opening wedge of the monetized world had been inserted, and it was clearly only a matter of time until villages such as Gbansu became part of the global rural proletariat.

The Basotho entered the world economy much earlier than the Kpelle-speaking people of Gbansu. Lesotho's very existence was predicated on a complex settlement negotiated by the Afrikaners and the British. Consumer goods were sold in the new country almost as soon as the treaties were signed, and the Basotho very soon found ways to earn money. At first they sold grain to the newly-arrived, unsettled Afrikaner farmers and then to the miners at the newly discovered diamond and gold mines.

Because of Lesotho's initial, indeed foundational, link with the international money economy, its technology has always been part of the Western world. Much that we consider today to be "true Basotho culture" was a product of the mid-nineteenth century. Even so, when the technology brought by the outside world changes, the Basotho must react or lose out. Technological innovation has not been as strong in Lesotho as in Liberia, to a large extent because the Basotho inherited a technological culture from outsiders.

Internal exchange between the Basotho has never been as important as in other parts of Africa. Part of the reason is that theirs was never a market economy. West Africa, where weekly markets are an ancient practice, is a very different society. The larger reason for the lack of a market economy in Lesotho is that most of the exchange has been with traders, employers, and tax officials outside the core of Basotho society. Whereas money to some extent circulates within Kpelle culture, when South African rands arrive in Lesotho, they go out almost immediately with very little internal circulation.

In the case of rural Liberia, indigenous rural technology has yielded slowly, grudgingly, and inevitably to outside forces. By contrast, in Lesotho indigenous technology was largely a product of outside forces. My experience in Ethiopia, Uganda, Tanzania, and Botswana leads me to see their situations as intermediate— somewhere between the situations in Lesotho and rural Liberia. In every case, however, the global economy is slowly and inexorably dominating and replacing the indigenous system.

I am not saying that local is always best and foreign is always worst. Human societies continually learn from each other, often to the benefit of all. I am convinced that for a time in the nineteenth century the Basotho had the best of all worlds, sparked by a strong leader who guided them into selective acceptance of new ideas. Even Kpelle culture was not created from the beginning as an isolated, independent world. It is now understood that iron technology originally came from Egypt. West African rice grew first in the Senegal basin. Bananas came from the Far East by way of Madagascar, and cassava and maize are New World crops. Of importance in these cultural exchanges is the extent to which the recipient culture can use new ideas and new skills without being destroyed in the process.

What are the consequences for Africa of the loss of the best features of indigenous technologies and economies? Surely the answer has to do with the ability of African people to make their mark on the global system, rather than just to submit to it. Selling cash crops and other raw materials in exchange for money and goods without adding value to local resources and materials is to give up the game and guarantee perpetual economic stagnation and defeat. No one can free the oppressed except the oppressed. Clearly, the oppression which Africans now experience is founded in and exacerbated by the loss of their own economies and technologies. They have been unable to seize the occasion and enter the global economic struggle on equal terms with the rest of the world.

In the process, forests are destroyed, and no one gains except big companies and exploitive African rulers. Exotic species are introduced, and the environment suffers, while business people make short-term gains from fast-growing trees and shrubs. Indigenous insights into what can really work within the local environment are lost, as donors and nationals who have been schooled abroad bring pre-packaged technological solutions. Cash crops benefit agri-business, but leave people hungry. Mono-cropping brings short-term profits to companies that do not care about maintenance of the land base and crop diversity. Economic servitude to outside global structures guarantees permanent debt and dependence. The picture has been bleak in recent years, and African economies have declined. But it is important to see the problem as a whole before answers can be found. I have tried here to show what the problems are. I hope and pray that the next generation will find answers.

3.7 Hopeful signs.

At the same time, all is not hopeless. People across Africa are learning once again to use their own knowledge and technology, rather than depending solely on outside assistance. Inventive use of intelligence is not confined to outsiders who think they alone can bring useful new technologies. My African friends and colleagues are working hard and thoughtfully to ameliorate the situation in which they find themselves.

Protection and expansion of **forests** is a major concern in several African countries. I am pleased to know that Lesotho is one of the few countries in the world with a negative rate of deforestation, meaning that more trees are being planted than are being cut down. The project I worked on in Tanzania was committed to afforestation. In addition, South Africa has halted planting of exotic trees in large plantations on the Natal north coast. The Society for Conservation of Nature in Liberia has been granted a substantial award for the work of Alex Peal in maintaining the Sapo National Forest. On a very small scale, I was impressed with the commitment of the Namibian government to protect the stands of indigenous welwitschia in the coastal desert. And the United Nations Environment Programme (UNEP) has a substantial list of success stories across the continent, including even the extremely dry country of Burkina Faso (www.unep.org/unep/envpolimp/techcoop/3.htm).

Exotic trees, despite the bad effects of the ones I have named, can be beneficial. In Lesotho, peach trees are everywhere and are a major source of food and income for many families. A fruit farmer in Mochudi in eastern Botswana grew his fruit trees along the bank, and indeed almost in the bed, of a dry river, in that way tapping the underground moisture and also stabilizing the soil. Bad as some eucalpyts may be, others have been bred which are more friendly to African environments.

Across Africa people are once again husbanding its **environmental diversity**. The Lesotho Highlands Water Project is still trying to hold the line against species extinction, particularly the Maloti minnow. An environmental "hot spot," to use the current jargon, is the escarpment separating Lesotho and South Africa's KwaZulu-Natal Province, which has been the focus for extensive meetings and action programs designed to protect the fragile and often unique vegetation of the high mountains. Declaring the Okavango wetlands as a Ramsaur site in 1997 means that governments will have a much harder time diverting the water to either industry or urban consumption. Environmental protection legislation is gaining ground, even though implementation of the legislation tends to lag behind rhetoric. At the end of 2002 there were ninety-one World Heritage sites in Africa (whc.unesco.org/nwhc/pages/sites/main.htm).

Cash crops can be helpful, provided they do not interfere with growing needed food. Mixed farming, which was looked down upon only ten to fifteen years ago, is gaining favor again. Diversification that includes mixing cash and subsistence crops, can be more profitable than either alone. In Zimbabwe I was impressed by a large farm in the eastern highlands where cut flowers were grown along side vegetables for home consumption. In January 2003 in South Africa, I saw black farmers starting once again to produce successful and profitable garden crops.

On a larger scale, Africans are moving away from **single-product economies**. For far too long, South Africa built its national economy around gold. Now it is producing various manufactured goods and in so doing is becoming a world player. Little Lesotho is doing the same and is host to several textile manufacturers. My wife noticed with pleasure that the trousers she recently bought in Cambridge, Massachusetts carried a "Made in Lesotho" label. In January 2003 the American students I was traveling with visited the factory in Lesotho that produces garments for

Gap. Although the working conditions leave much to be desired, the factory represents an important step toward self-reliance. In agriculture, the Machobane method is being widely adopted in Lesotho.

The **indigenous economy** has never fully died, although in many parts of Africa it has not realized its full potential. Local crafts are a significant business in Namibia, where visitors are able to purchase many different products made from wood or grass. In Lesotho, locally grown mohair is woven into tapestries that command a high price in Europe and America. Better marketing and production standards targeted to outside demand are still in short supply, but realization of the necessity for them is growing. Crafts markets are growing in number and quality in South Africa, as I saw recently in both Cape Town and Johannesburg. I saw sophisticated traditional irrigation systems in Tanzania, which reflect the ability of Africans to develop a technology that uses their own natural resources in their own way. In short, Africans can take over the management of their resources, and in so doing take their future, into their own hands.

Bamboo irrigation pipes in Tanzania

CHAPTER FOUR. DOMINATION BY ELITES

Foreign domination, neo-colonialism, economic imperialism, cultural aggression—all have been blamed for Africa's present sorry state. I fear to venture into such territory, lest I fall into the trap set by those who forget what Africans have done to themselves and consider only what outsiders have done to Africans. Yet there is the opposite temptation: to think only of the folly, the narrow ethnic loyalties, and the corruption of far too many Africans. I am resisting both temptations by choosing to refer as broadly as possible to domination by foreign as well as local elites. Moreover, it should be noted that the foreigners who have sought hegemony over the victims of oppression are often as likely to be African as they are to be European.

It is an escape from the complexities of reality to look at African nations as collections of poor, downtrodden peasants and proletarians ruled by arbitrary, greedy rulers. This may happen, but it is not the only story. There are elites of all sorts—researchers (like me), donors, missionaries (also like me), World Bank and International Monetary Fund (IMF) experts, traditional chiefs, entrepreneurs, creditors, warlords, diplomats, cabinet ministers, been-to's (the Bintu tribe consists of those who have "been to" Europe or America for study), business managers, heads of state, Mafia bosses, bureaucrats, and power brokers, in addition to the usual national and international villains.

In this chapter, I explore how elites have exercised control, often to the detriment of those who must suffer under them. I am not advocating anarchy, tempting as that might be, but rather I am simply pointing out where and in what ways powerful structures and individuals have had serious negative consequences on ordinary people. The big picture is that power brokers in Africa both control and are controlled by their clients; the symbiotic relation between patron and client explains the success of the former and the survival of the latter.

4.1 Misperception of Africa as a single culture area.

What is Africa? The question is often asked whether there really is any unity within the continent. This is an important question for understanding the role of elite forces, since some of the most powerful international elite deal with the continent as a whole. This book does assume an underlying unity for sub-Saharan Africa, but the concept is problematic. Where the concept goes wrong is in assuming there is a unified African reality that can be partitioned and manipulated according to a set of general rules. There may be some overall patterns, but they can only be sifted from extensive study of the forty-three countries and many more culture areas that make up the sub-continent.

I make the common, but admittedly still problematic, assumption that the Africa of the Sahara and the Maghreb are so different from the rest of the continent that northern Africa is more similar to the rest of the Mediterranean world than it is to sub-Saharan Africa. Even in ancient times the Mediterranean was literally "the middle of the earth," with all parties—Greeks, Romans, Egyptians, Phoenicians, and their numerous trading partners both north and south of the sea—viewing North Africa as part of their world. What little was known of sub-Saharan Africa was elaborated into images of wild beasts, some of whom were vaguely, but not very, human.

Even today, the regions below the Sahara are amazingly diverse. But it is also true that the imposition of false unity—for instance, the creation of entities such as Liberia or Nigeria—has had long term negative effects on people whose natural unity was only in the process of emerging. Yet the imposition of a spurious unity is only harmful when those who do the imposing have power. If the elite work their will on those who are unified only because power brokers enforce unification, then damage can be done. For example, the "divide and conquer" strategy has been useful to many, from the conveners of the 1885 Berlin Conference to white South Africans who sowed seeds of dissent by pitting Xhosa against Xhosa. A more immediate danger comes from the ambitious Colonel Ghadafi of Libya, who is the driving force behind a future United States of Africa. His present effort is confined to the new African Union, which replaces the Organization of African Unity.

At the other end of the spectrum, the elite of the movie industry have tried to create an artificial Africa for profit, to the detriment of the wonderful diversity of African peoples. In what was otherwise a good film, *The Color Purple* portrayed a tourist agent's dream that was essentially a pastiche of Africa, composed of thorn bushes, giraffes, and romantic natives. I fear the result of such portrayals is that in the minds of many Americans the picture of Africa is a cookie dough cut-out packaged in sloppy sentimentality. Certainly, there is a business motivation for conjuring up portrayals of a unified Africa, since it would then represent a unified market for products.

4.2 Imposition of Western democracy.

Where has the cookie cutter carved Africa into replicas of a foreign original? Democracy and the nation-state are a good starting point. My own American government, with a measure of good will and several measures of hegemony, has tried to shape African governments according to the American model. The excuse for domination by a foreign power in that case is that democracy must be created in order for Africans to govern themselves.

Americo-Liberian home in Liberia

The classic case of imposition of Western forms occurred in the 1840s when Harvard University legal scholars wrote a constitution for Liberia (Dunn et al. 2001:84-86). Not surprisingly, the constitution was remarkably American. Yet rather than being an instrument for liberty and equality as the Americans had hoped, it was used throughout its life from 1847 to 1986 as an instrument of oppression. The constitution empowered the settlers, who had either been slaves in the United States or had been rescued from slave ships by the American navy, to rule over the indigenous people of the interior. They were able to do so within a seemingly just and impartial framework of law. That framework, however, was derived from the same structures that allowed Americans to destroy Native American culture, enslave Africans, and disenfranchise women.

It was not until 1960 that the structures for self-government were brought to the rural provinces, which were from that date divided into counties, supposedly parallel to the already-existing coastal counties. According to President Tubman's rhetoric, it was designed to emancipate the hinterland, but even in the original coastal counties, constitutional rights belonged only to an educated oligarchy, which had total power over its "native" clients. Administrators were appointed for the new counties, and only in elections for traditional chiefs were any concessions made to democracy. I remember seeing President Tubman In 1971 administer an executive council in Gbarnga, where he made decisions after listening to people's complaints. In his absence, the county superintendent had limited authority but was always subject to central control.

In 1999, I was part of a vigorous debate as scholars from the United States and Africa planned a survey on democracy as understood and practiced in Malawi, Zambia, Zimbabwe, Botswana, Namibia, South Africa, and Lesotho. The debate concerned whether, in constructing the survey questionnaire, the answers would be influenced by using an American model of democracy. Several of us who had lived in Africa for many years said that many American assumptions just did not apply, including fixed borders and a hierarchy of officials with a head-of-state apex. Our point was that governance in Africa is multi-centered, with many different authorities to which people owe allegiance, particularly political allegiance. We eventually managed to modify the survey in the direction of a less well-ordered but more realistic set of questions. An additional five countries—Ghana, Mali, Nigeria, Uganda, and Tanzania—were added to the survey, so that now a twelve-country data base has been constructed and can be consulted (www.afrobarometer.org/results.html). A second round of the Afrobarometer study was completed in 2003, including now 15 countries.

The first survey shows that there is a real desire for democracy in Africa. But it also shows that democracy is conceived very differently in the twelve countries. Most respondents felt that liberty and freedom are most important, but this was stressed most heavily in Malawi, Namibia, South Africa, and Zambia. These countries have recently moved from repressive governments to multi-party democracies.

A populist concept of democracy as government "by the people, of the people, for the people" was second overall in importance but was stressed most heavily by people in Botswana, Lesotho, and Nigeria. These countries have strong local traditions of participatory democracy in pre-colonial times.

Majority rule was the third most important feature listed. This was emphasized most by people in Tanzania and South Africa, reflecting the importance of politics at the local level. Both countries have a history of strong party organization at the grassroots, where majority rule determines the exercise of power. Mali is an interesting case. In that country peace, unity, equality before the law, and economic development were considered most important. Mali has moved from military rule to multi-party democracy in a peaceful way.

Finally, Zimbabwe and Lesotho are countries with the most negative views of democracy. In both cases, governments elected through free parliamentary means have proved unpopular in their exercise of power. I helped conduct and analyze the Lesotho portion of a further survey of democracy in 15 African countries in late 2002 and early 2003. Analysis of the results in Lesotho shows a considerable increase in support for democracy, mostly as a result of the successful elections of May 2002 (Gay and Mattes 2003).

In short, it seems clear that people in the various countries are creating meanings for democracy out of their experiences, whether unfortunate as in Lesotho in 2000 or more optimistic as in Lesotho in 2003, rather than taking Western notions of democracy as a model. One of the latest buzzwords in Western development jargon is "good governance." I have no quarrel with the notion, but I think it is vital to make sure that governance be defined from within the community rather than imposed by the international elite of the developed world and its agents.

The question of democracy—what is it, and how it works—becomes complex in a case like that of Lesotho, where there have been roughly twelve different forms of government since the country came into existence in the early nineteenth century. Starting from the anarchy of a period of drought, warfare, invasion, and clan conflict, Lesotho came into existence as a paramount chieftaincy under the inspired leader Moshoeshoe I. He created a nation out of refugees from the regional wars occurring from 1800 to 1820. Under Moshoeshoe I, the country was a participatory democracy in the sense that all men (but very few women) freely expressed their views and had their voices heard. Shortly before Moshoeshoe's death, the country became a British protectorate, then for a short time a colony, then again a protectorate. Within the framework of indirect rule, the Basotho polity shifted from a paramount chieftaincy to a feudal monarchy under Moshoeshoe's sons and their families. Later, the external system stagnated under the benign neglect of the British.

Colonial officer in Lesotho

Independence came in 1966 with a British-type parliamentary democracy that survived until 1970 when the Prime Minister lost an election, suspended the constitution, and ruled by decree for sixteen years. Then in 1986 the military, supported overtly by South Africa and covertly by America, took over and ruled until 1993, when there was once again a democratic election. At that time Lesotho became in effect a one-party state, since the party that had supported the Prime Minister in 1970 had lost most of its support. The opposition that had gone into exile in 1970 took every seat in parliament because of the first-past-the-post system, and the losers (who might have received about 30 percent of the vote) complained they had been cheated. In one sense, they were right, since they should have had representation. In the other sense, they were wrong, since the election had been free and fair.

A second election in 1998 produced a similar result; the opposition gained one seat. The election may have been technically free and fair, but once again it was a democratic failure, since more than 30 percent of the electorate had no representation. The losing party then mounted protests that led to riots, looting, and burning in three major towns. The country was rescued from a resulting military coup by the intervention of South Africa. The South Africans set up an Interim Political Authority (IPA), which proposed alternatives to the electoral system in order to allow the opposition a voice in parliament. The party that had won the 1998 election was allowed to continue governing, but it was ultimately restricted by obligations to the IPA.

New elections, as mentioned above, took place in 2002 under a modified proportional representation system. Few people initially wanted the elections, for several reasons. The government was satisfied to govern. The opposition stood to gain more political points by asking for elections than they could get from actually holding the elections, which they were certain to lose. The IPA did not want elections, since the members (chosen from all fourteen political parties, including some with essentially no following) could lose their fat salaries.

In the end, the elections did produce useful results, and as I said above, the result has been a boost to the perception of democracy in Lesotho. Altogether, eleven of the political parties contesting the election won seats. Six were left out in the cold, because they did not get enough popular votes to qualify (Transformation Resource Center 2002:6). Subsequently, leaders of the opposition parties have reported their satisfaction at having a forum for expressing their views, even though they did not win the election.

It is no wonder that the Basotho did not give Western answers to questions in the Southern Africa Democracy Barometer. The only times they have lived under a true democracy was when Moshoeshoe I ruled as a paramount chief, and during the brief interlude between independence in 1966 and the coup of 1970. Otherwise, the system has wavered between various non-democratic alternatives, most introduced from abroad. I am encouraged to think that the new system of proportional representation is working better, but in any event it will be because Basotho have worked out a solution that makes sense to them, not a solution imposed by a foreign super-power.

Of the countries where I have worked, only Botswana comes close to a Western model of democracy. Its history is different; it has not suffered the dislocations and false starts of African countries like Lesotho. In nineteenth century Botswana, Khama I and then in the twentieth century his descendent Seretse Khama were low-key monarchs with strong Christian and democratic leanings. Seretse Khama abdicated his hereditary position as chief of the Ngwato people, one of Botswana's leading clans, so he could run for the presidency of the newly declared republic, a post he won by a comfortable margin in the elections of 1966.

Since its founding as an independent nation, Botswana has had a lively multi-party system, although the ruling party has never been seriously challenged for the presidency. As is common in most African countries, the opposition has shown greater strength in urban areas, in part due to education. The Afrobarometer survey shows that in the capital, Gaborone, the higher an individual's level of education, the greater his preference for democracy over authoritarian rule. In other parts of the country there is no clear education-related preference.

Botswana's success as a democracy has been due largely to its economic strength. Cattle have been money-earners for many years, and the low population density means pasture is readily available. The number of cattle is growing, however, and cattle owners may eventually find themselves in trouble as they look for pasture farther into the Kalahari Desert. The government has expelled the indigenous San from the central Kalahari to make room for more cattle grazing, but in mid-2004 the San are suing to regain their land. The other major source of income is diamonds. Fortunately these have been located in concentrated, well-guarded desert locations where wildcat prospecting is not possible.

Confirming the findings of the Afrobarometer Survey, comparisons of Liberia, Lesotho and Botswana point to a highly diverse political environment within which democracy might take root. Additionally, the *ujamaa* experiment in Tanzania shows how a top-down, rigidly controlled participatory democracy proved unable to cope with the economic realities of the country. In Uganda, its no-party system (founded on decentralized village-based decision-making) operates under the clear direction of Yoweri Museveni, the widely popular military ruler who became a civilian after conquering a series of misguided governments. In Ethiopia, two successive coups overthrew a feudal emperor and a ruthless Stalinist in favor of Tigreian highlands hegemony. Yet Ethiopia's new government does not satisfy the southern and eastern ethnic groups absorbed into the empire in the late nineteenth century. In Namibia, one ethnic group—those who idolize the leader, Sam Nujoma— makes up about 70 percent of the country. At the same time, the other ethnic groups in Namibia are broadly dissatisfied with a democracy seemingly destined to elect Nujoma president forever. Finally, in Zambia, Kenneth Kaunda tried to regain power after having resigned the presidency but was hounded by those who defeated him; his opponents even declared him not to be a Zambian.

It is simply not possible, therefore, to provide a model for democracy or any other form of government that is able fit all countries in Africa. The British and French thought they could bring the benefits of London and Paris to Africa when they first administered and then freed their colonies. The Belgians, Portuguese, and Spanish did not care what happened when they left as long as they could get out physically and at the same time maintain their investments. The Russians and Americans did their best to export home-grown political systems and failed roundly. I admit that in many ways I like our American system, and I wish that the best parts of it could be translated to Africa. I also agree with Winston Churchill: whereas democracy is a bad form of government, the others are all worse. But neither it nor any other foreign-made system can be fully imposed upon Africans. The local cultures and histories are far too diverse; ignoring the differences damages the countries that are the targets of misguided good will.

Moreover, there is no single form of democracy appropriate to all countries. The Pan-Africanism proposed repeatedly from Blyden in the nineteenth century to Kwame Nkrumah at the dawn of independence to Colonel Ghadafi today, has never worked. If there is any pattern that is pervasive in Africa, it is that of vertical patron-client linkage, a view shared with many scholars, such as Bratton and van de Walle (1997) and Chabal and Daloz (1999).

A rather sad consequence of the "one continent, one Africa" assumption is the disillusionment that African-Americans feel when they "return home" to Africa. I have known Garveyites and black Jews who came to Liberia thinking that they would find their true home. Their experiences were by and large painful, except for a few who were able to find a niche in the Americo-Liberian elite. I have known black Peace Corps volunteers who were victims of culture shock in both directions. Not only was it hard for them to accept the radical difference between themselves and the Liberians, Basotho, or Ethiopians they met, but it was equally hard for their hosts to understand just how American were their black visitors. The problem is encapsulated in language. Basotho know that white Americans have difficulty learning Sesotho, but at a sub-rational level they expect black Americans to catch on easily. It does not happen.

The overall thesis of this section, that Africa is not a single entity but a complex network with very general "family" relationships, applies to many other issues as well as to democracy, including education, religion, medicine, and economics. In a later chapter I will trace in detail some of the specific consequences of trying to impose democracy. For now, I will point out that when Western elites talk about "African democracy," they make assumptions that simply do not fit reality. Far more to the point is to talk about government as it exists in countries such as Angola and Zimbabwe along with all the other countries in the alphabet soup that is Africa.

4.3 Indirect rule through Westernized elite.

Americo-Liberians have been the hands and voices through which the United States has ruled Liberia. America may have created a political framework for Liberia through its 1847 constitution, but the real power was economic and military and was exercised in Washington. The United States kept the Liberian establishment well outfitted in top hats and protocol, but the profits went overseas and were much higher than the nominal amounts of money given to Liberia as foreign aid.

I shocked a group of wives of USAID experts in the late 1960s by telling them that the bread that America casts on Liberian waters comes back to the U.S. well buttered. They felt that their charitable presence in Liberia was a sacrifice, despite being able (just like the missionaries) to buy anything American they wanted at the Firestone supermarket and through duty-free orders at the main port in Monrovia. Even their husbands at the junior level must have felt strangely warmed by their work in Liberia. Those at the senior level knew better, or would have if they had listened to President Nixon when he said that foreign aid is simply an exercise in American self-interest.

The United States profited from Liberia through its surrogates in Monrovia due to cheap rubber and iron ore. Firestone Tire and Rubber Company struck a hard bargain with Liberia, in order to rescue Liberia from bankruptcy and make immense profits from rubber. "After several years of negotiations, an agreement was finally signed in 1926 granting Firestone a 99-year lease on 1 million acres of land at an annual rent of $.06 per acre. In addition, the company agreed to pay a 1-percent tax on gross income from its Liberian operation." (www.globalsecurity.org/military/library/report/1985/liberia_1_firestone.htm). The details of the Liberian Mining Company, which had exclusive use of 25,000 acres in Bomi Hills in northern Liberia, are troubling indeed. In the course of 27 years of operations from 1951-77, it made huge profits, and paid very low wages to its workers. A balance sheet shows that total sales amounted to about $530 million, at a cost of about $275 million. When the company finally closed its operations in 1977, "it left nothing for the Liberian people except a land destroyed by mining" (pages.prodigy.net/jkess3/Mining.html). as well as the economic choices made abroad how to exploit Liberia's coffee, cocoa, and timber. Political choices were made in Washington so that the United States would have a listening post in Africa through the Voice of America, a relay station for its worldwide spy system, and an airfield from which they could supply "friends" such as UNITA in Angola.

Americo-Liberian dignitary

The U.S. was content for Liberia to do whatever it wished within its own borders, provided foreign economic and political relations were maintained to U.S. specifications and provided nothing was done that appeared to the outside world as "repugnant to humanity," as British imperial officer Lord Lugard put it in the early twentieth century. This American policy fulfilled precisely what lay behind Lugard's indirect rule, including the willingness to take many well-hidden actions that were highly repugnant to humanity.

In the 1930s, the Kru people of Liberia staged a rebellion because of taxation and outside control over local rulers. Historian Ibrahim Sundiata (1980) shows how during that rebellion the American government was initially concerned by atrocities committed by American Colonel Elwood Davis, an immigrant who was responsible for ruthless and callous slaughter of Kru and Bassa people in the center of the country in the 1930s. But by 1934, the U.S. had washed its hands of the whole affair, preferring to listen to the comforting voices of the Liberian government, needed to support Firestone's rubber operations, rather than to the sufferings of ordinary people.

In 1930, when the Liberian government sent workers to Fernando Po in the Gulf of Guinea to grow cocoa, the U.S. collaborated with the League of Nations to condemn forced labor, but only after it became a public scandal. What the Americans government preferred was to maintain a public stance of righteousness but not to worry unduly about what happened behind the scenes. With such a history, it is no wonder that just about the only thing for which Charles Taylor received credit in Liberia was his strongly anti-American stance.

Another example of indirect rule through the local elite is found in Lesotho. As an independent country, Lesotho was intended by South Africa to be a model for the "homelands" they intended to create, but it did not quite work to South Africa's satisfaction. First, foreign donors gave large amounts of foreign aid to Lesotho, and second, the Leabua Jonathan government enjoyed playing South Africa against the rest of the world. Other examples of indirect rule were found in artificial countries such as Transkei, Ciskei, Bophuthatswana, and Venda. I wish I had kept a copy of a cartoon depicting Kaizer Matanzima, nominal president of Transkei, as a megaphone through which South African president P. W. Botha was speaking. In these cases, indirect rule went a step further than imperial theorist Lord Lugard would have liked, because South Africa made no effort to keep its puppet rulers from doing things "repugnant to humanity" in the full glare of international publicity.

Subtle versions of indirect rule are numerous in today's Africa, and none of them benefit the local people. The new elite in South Africa includes wealthy black civil servants and business people. One cynical comment I heard was that today's South Africa is a new example of the Oreo cookie, with black on top, white in the middle and black at the bottom.

The great powers, through the IMF and World Bank, still control the economies of African countries that want inexpensive loans or reduction of foreign debt. Some African countries are in the good books of the big financial institutions, because they are willing to play the game of structural adjustment, under which African governments would privatize state enterprises, seek to recover costs for medical care and education from the consumers, adjust exchange rates to realistic values, and establish firm dates for repayment of long-standing foreign debts. The managing director of the IMF, Horst Köhler, said in September 2002: "There are clear success stories in Africa now, for instance, Tanzania, Mozambique, Uganda, Cameroon, Benin, Ghana, good progress."

(www.imf.org/external/np/tr/2002/tr020919.htm).

I am honestly confused, because I can see merit in both the arguments for and against structural adjustment policies, coming from the right and the left. But one thing is clear; in order to get the kind of economic help they need, African countries must play the international global economic game.

African countries can be hurt by the demands of structural adjustment, at least as it was practiced in the 1990s when "cost recovery" was demanded in education and health. The result was to put education and medicine out of the reach of the poor. Many children drop out of school in Lesotho, because their parents cannot afford school or exam fees. Similarly, the Anglican hospital in Lesotho's remote mountains, which provides the only medical care in a large, sparsely populated area, turns people away who cannot pay the fees the hospital is compelled to charge. Damage has also been done to small businesses. They cannot compete with large international corporations that can inevitably produce goods more cheaply than local entrepreneurs. Global economic growth, on the other hand, is enhanced by structural adjustment and such policies provide jobs for people who might otherwise remain permanently outside the job market. Clearly, structural adjustment policies have had mixed results.

Water is an area of particular concern, even after the IMF supposedly relaxed its most stringent rules for cost recovery. Rainer Hennig, writing in 2001 for the Africa Policy Information Center, reports: "A review of IMF loan policies in forty random countries reveals that, during 2000, IMF loan agreements in 12 countries included conditions imposing water privatization or full cost recovery. In general, it is African countries, and the smallest, poorest and most debt-ridden countries that are being subjected to IMF conditions on water privatization and full cost recovery" (www.africaaction.org/docs01/wat0103.htm). Patrick Bond wrote an angry book just before the August 2002 Johannesburg Conference on Sustainable Development, in which he points out the damage done to ordinary people in South Africa through privatization of water supplies (Bond 2002).

I argue that the many cases of cost recovery and privatization found throughout the continent are classic examples of indirect rule. The major world powers, including the Bretton Woods institutions, the United States, the European Union, and the large transnational corporations, provide rewards to the African leaders who administer their countries in the accepted way. The calls for good governance, fiscal probity, and financial discipline in some ways make sense even to me, but the freedom of African countries to dissent is very limited. The New Economic Program for African Development (NEPAD), supported and partly created by the presidents of South Africa, Nigeria, Senegal, and Algeria, has been criticized as "top-down, non-consultative and so prone to neoliberal economic mistakes that it must be tossed out and a new programme started from scratch," by the generally conservative South African newspaper *Business Day* after the summit meeting of the leaders of the G-8 countries in Canada in June 2002 (news.bbc.co.uk/1/hi/world/africa/2072099.stm).

Many writers, including Patrick Bond, have called NEPAD a new version of neo-colonialism (www.worldsummit2002.org/texts/bondnepadcritique.pdf). I must agree, even though it is clear that African economies are in a mess. The question remains whether outside countries are trying to help Africans clean up or whether the outsiders, themselves largely responsible for the mess, are making it worse with their top-down proposals. These proposals seem more likely to continue the resource flow away from Africa to the developed world than they are to enrich Africa. That, after all, was what indirect rule was designed to do in the first place.

Indirect rule is not only applied from outside the continent, it exists within Africa. At the turn of the twenty-first century, Nigeria and Liberia were engaged in a battle for control of Sierra Leone. The elected government in Freetown was guided by Nigeria, and the rural Revolutionary United Front was guided by Charles Taylor from Liberia. Neither of the parties in Sierra Leone was able to make decisions independently of its backer, and neither backer was strong enough at that point to conquer the other's surrogate government. The result, as in all cases of indirect rule, was that ordinary citizens, and the country as a whole, suffered. The profits to Charles Taylor were blood diamonds and the profit to Nigeria, regional hegemony. Britain had to step in and enforce a peace settlement. At the same time, Nigeria and Liberia failed in their quest for hegemony to a large extent because of internal conflicts in their own countries, conflicts which led to Charles Taylor's removal from power and serious challenges to President Obasanjo's rule in Nigeria.

Indirect rule has become a pattern in the Democratic Republic of Congo (Zaire). The revolutionary armies in the east of the Democratic Republic of Congo still receive their orders and their military supplies from Uganda and Rwanda, despite the continuing denials by both governments. The Kinshasa government became Zimbabwe's client in the year 2000 so that Robert Mugabe could give the orders and reap the profits. A peace settlement has been negotiated in South Africa, which wants to be the power broker, but the settlement seems very shaky as Rwanda and Uganda spar over who is to manage the eastern areas of the country. Even if these countries in fact do withdraw, they will still attempt to manage affairs at a distance. Once again, it is the people of the Congo who suffer. All they can do is to hope they, by good luck, have become clients of the winners, who will then be their patrons and give them a small share of the loot.

The patrimonial system, which remains an underlying theme of this book, operates therefore not only within nations but also between nations. The poor person's patron may be the village big man, but ultimately the patron may also be the foreign power that dictates what the village big man can do for his people. Remember that in Liberia the American government pulled the strings, the village chiefs obeyed, and the poor villager was sent to tap rubber. How different is it now when the big world powers, along with the big powers in Africa, call the tune and the little people dance?

4.4 The split between citizen and subject.

Ugandan scholar Mahmoud Mamdani, in his great book *Citizen and Subject*, has articulated very clearly what I and other Africa-watchers have observed for a long time (Mamdani 1996). He speaks of citizens, who are mostly educated, urban, and politically active, and subjects, who are mostly unschooled, rural, and politically passive. His claim that the subjects are mainly rural is overstated, as I pointed out in a paper based on the Afrobarometer study showing how Amartya Sen's theories are borne out by behavior on the ground. There I say, "Mamdani is correct only to the extent that rural people tend to score significantly, albeit slightly, lower on [a scale measuring political participation, economic wealth, social linkages, information access and personal security] than urban people. In my view the underlying issue is not the geographic location but the level of well-being" (Gay 2003).

Mamdani makes the disturbing claim that apartheid in South Africa resembled the rule of urban elites in other African countries. Citizens are individual actors who play their role in public affairs, while subjects are members of groups, are guided by their leaders, and are not assumed to have individual and distinct voices. Mamdani says the subjects are those who are the victims of this generalized form of apartheid, but this distinction between groups is a reality that exists in many parts of the world, not just in Africa. In my view, where subjects are ruled by citizens, the result is apathy and a low level of development, just as Sen affirms.

I have been in Ethiopia twice. On my first visit emperor in 1963 Haile Selassie was still firmly in charge. He was surrounded by his clique of imperial officials, who were the only "citizens" in Ethiopia. All others were subjects. When I next visited Ethiopia in 1982, the country was rigidly controlled by a small but very different class of "citizens," namely those who were part of Mengistu Haile Mariam's dictatorial Stalinist system. Other people were expected to take orders and were moved about as passive blocks.

The "Lion of Judah" in Ethiopia

When some attempted to assert their independence they were imprisoned and even killed.

The difference between citizen and subject was brought home to me most clearly by observing two resettlement farming areas south of Addis Ababa. The first had been resettled forcibly, mostly by ex-soldiers or urban unemployed. They were certainly subjects in that they had no say about what would be done with them; they were picked up and transported to their new home. The second resettlement area was composed of people who had voluntarily left their crowded home area to find new land. Admittedly, they had little real freedom to participate in the national economy, but they were living their own lives as if they were free people, citizens in their own domain.

The difference between the two areas was striking. The forced resettlement camp was unproductive; the resettled people passively took orders and worked as little as possible. The families that had moved into new land of their own volition were taking charge of their lives in a creative way, administering their own domain, and engaging in productive agriculture.

It is interesting and perhaps even depressing that the same story is being played out again in Ethiopia. It was reported recently on the BBC that people are being moved from areas of high population density in the south to less dense areas in the north. I only hope that the lessons of the Mengistu regime have been learned and that people are not just being moved like so many pawns on a chessboard in order to strengthen the frontier against Eritrea. An uneasy peace prevails on the contested border between Ethiopia and Eritrea, even though the United Nations and the World Court have attempted to resolve the territorial conflict by giving the town of Badame to Eritrea, a decision which Ethiopia is trying to resist.

Rural homesteads in Transkei and Lesotho gave evidence of a similar contrast during the apartheid era. The Transkei homesteads were sullen and sterile. No trees, no grass, and no crops were planted around them, and the houses were painted the same uniform blue and white. As my family and I drove past them we saw hardly any signs of life; there were no children playing or mothers hanging out diapers on clothes lines. The life of a subject ruled by a puppet carrying out the orders of his apartheid masters is indeed sad. Only now, as I saw in my most recent visit to the former Transkei in 2003, are households beginning to show signs of life. The difficulty in creating a vital sense of community development in such areas is evident in Zakes Mda's novel *The Heart of Redness*, which shows how the conflicts of past colonial oppression must be worked out in present community life (Mda 2000).

The plots around rural and peri-urban Lesotho households were, and still are, very different from what I saw in Transkei. Almost all of the Lesotho homes have fruit trees around them, and some have windbreak and shade trees. Most houses have active gardens, growing a wide range of vegetables, including spinach, onions, tomatoes, maize, and pumpkins. When I enter a village, I find activity and vitality. These people are citizens within their own domain and have the right to speak out, to try to influence their government. The task of speaking out has not been easy over recent years, so that democracy has a slightly sour taste to many, but village life remains a domain that government has not destroyed as it did in dislocated South Africa.

The poor in Liberia have suffered greatly since we left the country in 1975. Before that time, the citizen-subject split manifested itself at two different levels: the national and the local. Nationally, the unschooled, poor, mostly rural, mostly indigenous people were subject to the whims and authority of the educated, English-speaking elite. Life was not much better for the poor packed into Monrovia's slums, as I portray in my second of a trilogy of novels, *The Brightening Shadow*, that tell the story of social and cultural change in Liberia in the 1960s and 1970s (Gay: 2002b: 39-40). The on escape route for the poor was for their children to attend school, receive good grades, be admitted to an elite high school, again receive good grades, and then attend university. Those who came from the rural areas and succeeded in completing university became part of an expanded elite, but it must not be forgotten that very few of the rural poor were so lucky. For most people, being poor meant remaining poor, and there was little they could do to better themselves, since the system was stacked against them.

The situation was different at the local level. In remote rural areas, poor farmers could be citizens within their own domain, as I describe in *Red Dust on the Green Leaves*, the first novel of the trilogy (Gay 2002a: 20). In Gbansu, the village where I worked and lived, people exercised political, economic, and social power as players in a complex network, but only within the village or at most within a group of villages. The blacksmith, the herbalist, the farmer, the hunter, the secret society leader, the musician, the weaver, the family elder all shared responsibility for the well-being of the organism that was the village, and none were looked down upon. There, everyone was a citizen, and only the very few who were rejected for serious violation of accepted norms were without power. I fear that this multi-stranded texture may well be dying as the country falls into decay, but in 1974 in Gbansu it was alive and well. Later, I was sad to learn that Gbansu was burned down in the civil war. In 2001, however, I was encouraged by a visit to several other off-the-road villages where the old political structures were then still struggling to survive. I am sure that they too are once again suffering greatly from the renewed civil war. I can only hope that they also are not about to be destroyed , for as the common African proverb puts it, "When elephants fight, it is the grass that suffers."

Unfortunately, poor people in towns along the main motor roads, and even more so in Monrovia, have not been so lucky. They can no longer influence community affairs to the extent that they did in their rural villages, because the real power brokers have now become members of the educated elite. Liberians have a term for them; they call them kwii, a complex concept combining differences of dress, speech, money, employment, status, possessions, and manners. The kwii are the real citizens in these urban areas, and the poor country person is a misfit, without power and opportunity. The slums of Monrovia before the civil war were crowded with people who had left rural areas in hope of bettering themselves, who then failed to achieve even the status they had formerly known in their villages.

Since the civil war, Monrovia's slums have grown so that most of the million or more people who now live in the city and its suburbs are living in misery. Internally displaced people are still fleeing the fighting. A hundred thousand have recently fled to refugee camps in the capital's outlying districts, from which a thousand were kidnaped at the end of March 2003 (allafrica.com/stories/200303310732.html). Moreover, those rural villages that still survive are more dependent on outside assistance than they were before the war, despite the inability of NGOs, foreign donors, and government to provide enough of the necessary aid. When I visited villages in 2001, which I believe may still be threatened by LURD occupation, they were reduced to dependence on aid in most areas of life. Today in 2004 UNMIL troops control most roads and main towns, but ex-combatants still lurk in the bush.

The degree of misery has been increased step by step, first by the shift under Samuel Doe away from political control by the old Americo-Liberian elite and then back to an expanded elite. The new elite in power under Charles Taylor were drawn not only from the old families but also from descendants of the so-called Congo resettlers and from the few rural people who moved up through the system. Each shift in power in Liberia meant a reworking of the elite, so that first one vertical alliance took control and then another. Whoever was in charge, however, concentrated on Monrovia and continued to neglect the rural communities.

Political upheavals have turned matters upside down and inside out, not only in Liberia but elsewhere in Africa. Decentralization remains a dream in most African states, because power can most effectively be exercised at the center, ensuring that most people remain subjects. Liberian academics are urging a change toward decentralization in the political system (Tarr et al. 2002). Even in 1860, prophetic voices, such as American missionary and priest Alexander Crummell, were arguing against an overly centralized Liberian government (Crummell 1969: 39). Unfortunately, power in Liberia still lies with the gun, so that the hopes held by Liberian political scholars and political activists Byron Tarr, Elwood Dunn, and William Allen can only be realized if there is peace. Change for the better will only come when competing patron-client networks agree to become part of a multi-centered system. Until that time, politics will be a zero-sum game, so that if I win, you lose and vice versa.

Botswana is more nearly democratic than the other countries where I worked, and the citizen class is larger and more active. Botswana has two ethnic groups dominating politics, namely the Batswana, who are divided among several major clans, and the Kalanga, who are related to the Shona in Zimbabwe. Both play an active role in politics and compete with each other for power.

There are groups that do not participate in the political debate, notably people I met in the northwest. Left out of the system are the Hurutshe, the Yei, the San, and the Herero. I had no contact with Hurutshe or San, but in my study of small, informal businesses, I met Herero and Yei people. It was clear to me that they were at best second-class citizens, if they could be called citizens at all. The Herero were not poor; they had large herds of cattle that ranged widely across the western Kalahari. They largely ignored the border between Botswana and Namibia, and even when living in their own section of Maun they remained outside the mainstream of society.

Yei household in Botswana

They were the one group I met in Botswana that did not want to cooperate with a survey; they saw it as just another exploitation imposed by the Botswana and Namibian governments. They preferred the anarchy of being desert herders to the oppression they felt as subjects of both and citizens of neither.

The Yei were losers on almost all counts. Some still scratched a doubtful living from barren, dry soil. Others either moved to Maun from the Okavango where they were fishermen or remained in the Okavango living a bare, hand-to-mouth life as tourism and development ate their territory and livelihood. I pitied the Yei people on the northern fringe of Maun where they lived on patches of sand without even the shade that people in the central and southern parts of Maun enjoyed. They begged me to buy their baskets, which are beautiful works of art that sell at high prices in New York City. They are neglected by the Botswana government, which gives the impression of wishing that all hunter and gathering peoples would just disappear.

In a recent study on civil society funded by the British Commonwealth, many Basotho made it clear they are not happy with their status (www.common wealthfoundation.com/information/infosheet49.html). They have not given up, but they want to be acknowledged as citizens. Their status is not as bad as that of South Africans under apartheid and is not as bad as non-kwii Liberians, but they know they are losers.

Our 1999 political opinion survey of seven southern African countries clearly shows Lesotho's disillusionment with democracy. The Basotho score lowest of all the countries in their faith in, understanding of, and hope for democracy (Gay and Green 2001:8). A disturbingly large number of interviewees said they have no access to government and are powerless to change things. They could well be on the way to pure "subject" status. The 2003 democracy survey, however, show an improvement in the situation in Lesotho (Gay and Mattes 2003).

The elite in Lesotho send their children to private schools and seek medical treatment from private doctors, frequently finding both in South Africa. These elite often carry two passports and change identities when they cross the porous border between Lesotho and South Africa. The result is that the elite, who make up the "citizens" class, make decisions and establish policies that favor themselves and bypass the concerns of the poor.

Lesotho's government, its mission schools, and its hospitals are generally neglected, since the elite do not use them. Money counts, and the poor are unable to escape the perpetual trap set for them by the country's inequalities. Lesotho's Gini coefficient, a measure of inequality, is, at .60, one of the highest in the world, higher even than that of South Africa (Gay and Hall 2000:74). The only African country with a higher reported Gini coefficient is Sierra Leone at .63 (www.metafilter.com/mefi/22844), due to the civil war and the resulting destruction of its society. In 2003, South Africa's Gini coefficient is also .60; Uganda's is .38 (www.aegis.com/news/nv/2002/NV020707.html).

Where there is a sharp divide between those with a voice and those without, the voiceless are suffering. They are Mamdani's "subjects," whether rural or urban, and they are indeed oppressed and neglected. People who have no hope of escaping their poverty eventually do not care what happens, and they seek to make their society "ungovernable," to use the phrase so common during the apartheid era. The truly poor have no incentive to work within a system that does nothing for them; when a demagogue incites them to rise up, they do so willingly. When the demagogue provides them with guns to earn their living and drugs to keep them happy, the result is chaos. We saw the beginnings of this chaos in September 1998 in Lesotho, and it required the intervention of the South African and Botswana armies. The intended result was to quell the unrest by turning people's anger against South Africa instead of the Lesotho government. Finally, it is surprising that there are not more Sierra Leones in today's Africa. Where there is a high Gini coefficient, "citizens" flourish and "subjects" languish—until the poor take matters into their own hands.

The recent looting and virtual destruction of the only functioning referral hospital in Liberia illustrates the point. In October and November 2003 soldiers from the various militias, as well as local villagers, took everything from Phebe Hospital, located across the road from Cuttington University College, the very hospital where our youngest son was born. I quote a report written 10 November 2003 by William E. Martin, Administrator, Phebe Hospital & School of Nursing: "[The Out-Patient Department] along the north side of the compound, which had treated hundreds of patients every day, has been completely looted and vandalized. There is no useful equipment left anywhere, and supplies are thrown all over the floor and outside the building. Even the ten exam tables have been destroyed." As of mid-2004, Phebe Hospital is being rehabilitated, and is already serving patients. I indeed hope and pray that this time it will remain intact.

I ask why such vandalism can take place. How can people who would depend on this hospital for precious medical care do such things? The closest I can come to one answer is an incident in 2001 when I visited a village just thirty minutes walk from Phebe Hospital. An old woman was brought to me suffering with what appeared to me to be terminal cancer. She had been to Phebe for treatment, but when her family was told the cost of the surgery required to remove the tumor, they took her home. The family earnestly asked for some money to take her back there. I gave what they asked, but I was also certain they could not afford the follow-up treatment. Perhaps some of her family shared in the looting of the hospital – I have no way to know, of course. Hospitals cannot be blamed for trying to support themselves in the face of never-ending demand by people without resources. Even the IMF insistence on cost-recovery makes rational economic sense. What is not sensible is for health to be a privilege, rather than a right. The World Health Organization spoke at the 1978 Alma-Ata International Conference on Primary Health Care about Health for All by 2000. It has never happened, certainly not in rural Africa and not even in rich America.

Poverty and inability to seek medical care were, of course, not the only reasons for the looting. The looters included drunken and drugged boy soldiers.

Even more, they included commanders who expected to share in the profits from selling the beds, roofing sheets, window glass, copper wires, plumbing fixtures, generator parts, lab equipment, medicines, tools, needles, gas tanks, wooden planks, insulation, water bottles, chairs, computers, books, light fixtures, transformers, spare tires, batteries and whatever else an abandoned hospital might offer. The Administrator reported that trucks from the LURD rebel group were parked at the hospital waiting to take away whatever loot might require heavy transport. At the root, despite human greed, I really do believe is the poverty and desperation, and ultimately the inability to change the situation by rational means, which have fueled so many wars in Africa.

4.5 Racism and xenophobia.

In late 2001, South Africa hosted an international conference on racism and xenophobia. What makes the issue complex in the post-apartheid era is the existence of residual racism on the part of whites and those of mixed race, and the rejection by South African blacks of blacks from elsewhere in Africa. I know people from Central, East and West Africa who have found South Africa a most unpleasant and hostile place. They are rejected because they are too black, because they speak strange languages, because they are seen as thieves and drug dealers, because they are reputed to take jobs from South Africans, but mostly because they are not "us."

Lesotho citizens are not really welcome in South Africa either, though all my Basotho friends have relatives there. There are more Basotho in South Africa than there are in Lesotho, due largely to the theft in the nineteenth century of much of what is now the Free State. The result was that many Sesotho-speaking people remained on their ancestral land as farm workers and servants of the Afrikaners, but not as their own masters. Yet when the Basotho want to cross the border for work, for shopping, to visit relatives, or to seek social services, they meet difficulties. They must wait in long queues for passports to be stamped, they are sent back to Lesotho if they overstay the fourteen-day limit, or they are charged high fees for work and school permits.

The Basotho resent this exclusion, because they remember the long years of apartheid when South African exiles were welcome in Lesotho. They were taken into people's homes, allowed to go to school, given good medical care, and encouraged to find work. Lesotho has always been a haven for refugees, beginning with Moshoeshoe I's open invitation to hungry and homeless people from all ethnic groups to join him. And during the fight to free South Africa from racial injustice, the Basotho played their part, even allowing freedom fighters to operate from their territory.

The struggle has been partially won in South Africa, although there are many who continue to practice racism. The central parts of Ladybrand, just across the border from Lesotho, are still almost all white; blacks live in the "location" north of the central business district, across a mostly unpopulated gully. In butcher shops, blacks are usually served by blacks, and whites by whites. Change is slow, though it is beginning to happen. An important factor leading to change is the increasing dependence of businesses in the border towns of South Africa on Basotho customers. Careful research has shown that "virtually every business and professional leader in [border towns] has important interests, enterprises and associations across the border in Lesotho" (Sechaba 2002:52). These business people are among the strongest advocates of making it easy for Basotho to enter South Africa.

Apartheid in South Africa

What was it like in the bad old days? My first introduction to the region was in Johannesburg in November 1975 while I was waiting for the twice-weekly flight to Maseru. I decided to wander the city just to catch its flavor. I fell in behind a well-dressed white man carrying an attache case. He was walking with a black man, who carried the white man's suitcase at a respectful one pace behind. The comment I heard was, "I don't know why it is, but God just made us more intelligent than you."

I went from that encounter to visit Desmond Tutu at the Anglican cathedral where he was serving as dean. On the notice board was a sign: "All persons welcome at all times." I wonder what the well-dressed white man would have made of Desmond, who has the quickest wit of anyone I have ever known. Desmond once gave a quick riposte when he was blocked by a white man in a covered walkway next to a building under construction. When the white man said "I don't give way to gorillas," Desmond's instant response was to bow and say, "But I do."

I went from Johannesburg directly to the town of Mohale's Hoek in Lesotho to work with the Food and Agriculture Organization and was invited to join the local club. I went to one event only and walked out when I heard members talking about Africans "who had just lost their tails." Not long after, I was driving to Durban and stopped in the South African town of Ladysmith for petrol. The owner saw our Lesotho license plate, asked in a friendly way where we lived, and then said "Oh, when we lived in Mohale's Hoek, there were only five families." He meant white families, of course. On another trip, we traveled with a Mosotho woman who was Judy's research assistant and stopped at St. Lucia Park on the Natal Coast. We were told we could not take servants into the park; when we told the black man at the gate that she was our friend, he was so baffled that he let us in.

To assert that the continuing racism I encountered in South Africa and Lesotho, and even more recently in Namibia, has contributed to decline in Africa is obvious and hardly worth saying. I hope that the World Conference on Racism that took place in Durban South Africa in September 2001 will lead to a better society in that transitional nation. But I see the xenophobia against other Africans as a far worse threat to the future of the continent. The Southern African Migration Project has shown that in most cases the current migration is beneficial to everyone involved. There are always migrants who will take advantage of a new country in order to do damage, but they are a minority among the large numbers who merely wish to use their skills in a new setting.

There is a vast brain drain chain that covers the world. In Africa, the chain starts when people migrate from truly destitute countries such as Liberia, Chad, Democratic Republic of Congo, Sudan, and Somalia to their slightly better-off neighbors, including Côte d'Ivoire, Ghana, Nigeria, and Uganda. From there the next ports of call are often in southern Africa: Zimbabwe, Botswana, Swaziland, and Lesotho. The chain leads next to South Africa, the wealthiest of the African states, after which are Australia, New Zealand, Europe, and North America. Where there is a niche to fill, qualified (or even unqualified) people will fill it.

Escape from Africa is unfortunately biased in favor of white professionals with good connections. A recent report by the Health Systems Trust in South Africa reports that "43% of doctors plan to work overseas after completing their community service. This number has increased from 34% in 1999. More than half of the young, white doctors interviewed intended to work overseas, compared with 10% of African doctors and 40% of coloured and Indian doctors" (news.hst.org.za/view.pjhp3?id'20020402).

Often the brain drain chain becomes a brain gain for the recipient country, whether or not racism is involved. In Lesotho, key posts are filled by Africans from other countries. In Lesotho in mid-2000, the Governor of the Central Bank was a Ghanaian, the head of the Faculty of Agriculture at the university was a Nigerian, and the only orthopedic surgeon was a Sudanese. Headmasters and teachers at high schools are Africans from north of the Limpopo, as are many medical practitioners throughout Lesotho. Lesotho, in turn, has sent some of its best people to South Africa and beyond. In mid-2000 the chief agriculturalist in the Free State was a Mosotho, as was the deputy head of the Development Bank of South Africa. People go where they can improve themselves and where they can provide a service that others need. Breaking the chain by xenophobic restrictions on migration only helps those who cannot withstand competition. It is true that uncontrolled competition can cause harm, particularly to the poorly trained, but tightening borders is not the answer. The answer is competition tempered with job training and job security in recipient countries.

Estimates of the number of Liberians who fled the war range from a few hundred thousand to almost a million. Abroad, they have been victims of anti-foreign feeling, particularly during and after the recent civil war. Many have returned home, but others are still attempting to survive in West African refugee camps. Partly as a result of the influx of Liberians, Côte d'Ivoire became more and more xenophobic during the 1990s. Historically, the border between Liberia and Côte d'Ivoire has been porous, mainly because so much of it is unbroken forest. Moreover, Côte d'Ivoire has always had large numbers of migrants from Ghana and Burkina Faso who came to work on the cocoa, coffee, and palm oil plantations.

When I was in Abidjan in 1997, the taxi driver who took me around the city was a Guinean who had lived in Côte d'Ivoire for many years, because the opportunities there were so much greater than at home. He sent money home regularly and paid an annual visit to his family, but he found his livelihood in Abidjan. The xenophobia, and now the civil war, that has arisen in Côte d'Ivoire (at first in relation to Alassane Ouattara's bid for the presidency and then generally in relation to the definition of "Ivoirité") means that people such as my taxi driver will no longer find good jobs away from home. Dividing Africa into the rich and the poor, due in part to xenophobia, cannot in the end benefit either group.

As a result of the civil war in their own country, many Liberian refugees are still stuck in Côte d'Ivoire, and in Guinea, Sierra Leone, Ghana, and other West African countries. They cannot find work and must sit and rot in boredom, doing nothing. Sometimes their frustration erupts into violence, as happened in April 2003 in the Buduburam camp in Ghana, where several thousand Liberians have been trapped—some for more than ten years.

The Economic Community of West African States is in no real sense a community, since the borders become more rigid every year. Quarrels continue between Guinea and Liberia, Nigeria and Niger, Burkina Faso and Côte d'Ivoire, Senegal and Guinea Bissau, and Mauritania and Senegal, to name only a few. Each xenophobic country thinks it benefits from closed borders, but in the end everyone loses. As of mid-2004, relations between the countries in West Africa have dropped to the lowest levels ever seen.

4.6 Slave trade.

I have not personally seen the slave trade in action, though it apparently still exists in at least four forms. The first occurs in the Sahara and Sahel south of the Sahara, where rural black people are bought by the lighter-skinned Muslim overlords.

Bela slave household in Timbuktu

The other three examples are very close to being slavery. In its second form, women are sent to Europe on false pretenses and then forced into prostitution; in the third, parentless children are bundled aboard ships destined for hard labor in West African nations; in the fourth, children are abducted by militias and either forced to fight or are used for sex.

The only ex-slave I have known personally was the man I mentioned earlier who had been traded in the late 1920s from Gbansu to the coast in return for salt. He was one of many unfortunate people who were shipped from Liberia to Fernando Po, now called Bioko as part of Equatorial Guinea, a country that seems to be just as nasty now as it was in Spanish colonial days. He managed to escape back to Liberia under mysterious circumstances.

My only exposure to the remnants of slavery in Africa came when I visited Timbuktu, once in 1959 and once in 1971. There, the Bela people have customarily been slaves to the Tuareg and lived in small grass and thatch huts outside the main city; they were looked down upon by others. In early 2003, anthropologist Martin Klein explained in a seminar talk at Boston University how everyone in the communities where he lived and worked in Senegal, Guinea, and Mali knew who still had to respect their position as slave families, even though they were technically free.

It is generally known from history how damaging the transatlantic slave trade was in its active period from 1500 to 1850. There is no need to document it here, except to remember that the Africa we see today is only a shadow of what it might have been had slavery not existed. It is important to remember, however, that slavery was not only European in origin. Arabs were great slave traders, and Africans themselves enslaved each other whenever they had the chance. Moreover, free people are people who can fulfill their full potential, and an enslaved society goes nowhere. Countries such as Mauritania, Sudan, and even Nigeria—where women and children are sold abroad—damage themselves by continuing the institution of slavery.

It is important to remember that slavery still exists around the world in one form or another. *Scientific American* published a significant article on slavery in its April 2002 issue showing that every country is still involved, including even the United States (Bales 2002). Bales defines slavery quite legitimately as involuntary servitude from which one cannot escape.

4.7 Forced labor.

When I lived in Gbansu in 1974, forced labor was still alive in the memories of the residents. One man remembered having been forced by soldiers to carry rice from Gbansu to the coast. He and his companions were given two bags of rice each, a load so heavy that they could not put them on their heads by themselves; they needed help to get started. They were not allowed to stop on the way, since it would then be difficult to pick up the bags by themselves. They were beaten if they lagged behind, and at least one of the men died under the strain. They were not paid for their efforts and were expected to make their own way back home.

In the 1920s and 1930s, work on the rubber plantations was another form of forced labor. Chiefs were given a bounty for each laborer they impressed and sent to the rubber farms. In this case, the men got paid for their work, but in the beginning they were not there voluntarily. The result was that they were not able to do the farming they should have done for their families in their villages. This and other forms of forced labor contributed to resentment against the coastal establishment, which eventually fed into the overthrow of the Tolbert government and the civil war of the 1990s.

Slavery and forced labor practices were ended in South Africa in the nineteenth century, but the legacy lives on in the form of farm workers who work for very low wages in return for a place to live and a measure of food and liquor. Many of these farm workers are now elderly and are being forced off the land they have helped cultivate for most of their lives. A comparable situation exists in areas near the Mozambique border, in that illegal immigrants find jobs at very low wages in return for not being forcibly repatriated to their home countries (Mather and Mathebula 2000: 31). Basotho workers find employment in farms just across the border in the Free State or the Eastern Cape, also in return for not being betrayed to immigration authorities. The line between this practice and forced labor is very thin. The absolute necessity of finding work makes it possible for employers, who are members of the elite and thus can bend labor laws, to unmercifully exploit workers.

4.8 Artificial creation of ethnic groups.

"Divide and conquer" is a fundamental rule of top-down politics. People can be managed once they are located in clearly defined groups; such classification was practiced in all the African countries where I worked. The theory of ethnicity is complex. I understand too little of it to enter into the debate, but I have observed what others have theorized about. It is clear to me that decisions have been made by scholars and administrators, who were not part of the group in question, to give that group a separate identity. When an identity is established, by fiat as it were, then the outsiders have power over the group.

Classification has never been a merely abstract, theoretical exercise, and every scientist who wishes to understand and use the things that are part of his discipline must first organize and name them. One of the first tasks given to Adam at the time of creation was to name the animals (Genesis 2:19-20), leading presumably to his having dominion over them (Genesis 1:28). And so it is with human groups. The case so familiar throughout the apartheid era was the governmental classification of South Africans. There were four basic groups—white, Indian, mixed-race and black—as well as subgroups within each main group. Whites were mainly either Afrikaners or English, though the Portuguese had an important place. More remarkable was the status of "honorary white" given to the Japanese but not to the Chinese. Those officially called "Coloured" were of several varieties, including those of mixed race, Cape Malays, Namas and others I do not even know.

Blacks were divided according to their "national" origin. All had their "homelands," where they were supposed to reside when they were not performing a service to whites in the white areas. The basic black language groups were Zulu, Swazi, Xhosa, Sotho, Tswana, Pedi, Venda, Shangaans, and Ndebele, all who were supposed to have an area that belonged to them. Afrikaans and English were not divided into homelands, though some Afrikaners wished it were so. So-called "Coloureds" were everywhere, but Indians were supposed to be confined to certain provinces, and in particular they were not allowed to remain overnight in the Orange Free State.

The system suffered serious strains at the edges. People were classified and reclassified as need and social pressure arose, despite the obvious folly of the entire system. Every year, "Coloureds" became white, blacks became "Coloureds," whites became "Coloureds," and "Coloureds" became black. There were even reclassifications in the mixed-race group, so that Cape Malays became mixed race, and so forth through all the possible permutations and combinations. One example, as late as 1986, was that 506 "Coloureds," fourteen Malayans, nine Indians, seven Chinese and one Griqua were reclassified as whites, and 666 blacks became "Coloured" (www.dadalos.org/int/Menschenrechte.htm).

Additionally, under circumstances of extreme diplomatic necessity, blacks could become honorary whites. I remember the case of the United Nations Development Programme Resident Representative in Lesotho, an African-American, who required emergency medical care in 1978 in Bloemfontein. For diplomatic reasons he was given temporary honorary status as a white. I do not think that they bleached him in the process.

People were required to live in certain areas, take certain jobs, get certain government benefits, and be educated in certain ways. The prospects for blacks were seriously constrained, so that they could rise only so high in society and no higher. Overall development in South Africa was set back greatly by not allowing the majority of the population to share in the benefits of development. The agonies of the anti-apartheid struggle, which kept South Africa from fulfilling its immensely rich potential, hurt everyone: black, white, "Coloured" and Indian.

Only now is South Africa beginning to be what it could have been all along—the engine of economic and social development for the whole continent. But it will not succeed until all ethnic and linguistic groups begin seriously to work together. In some places the effort to cooperate is succeeding. During our January 2003 trip through much of South Africa, we saw one example of progress when we had lunch with the black mayor of Kroonstad and met with his council. It was positive to see what was formerly an entirely Afrikaner town in the Free State now include blacks, whites, and "Coloureds" in its city government. The meeting was chaired by the black mayor, and the other members were clearly eager to work with him to succeed

The racism that so damaged South Africa also spilled over into southwestern Africa (now Namibia) and southern Rhodesia (now Zimbabwe). Both countries had small white populations that tried to create their own social systems with indigenous blacks serving white masters. I am convinced that had the white populations been able to work with the indigenous people as equal partners in integrated nations, these countries would have been better off than they are today. Some have argued that a period of elite domination was necessary in order to build modern infrastructure. Even if that is true, the elite could have been created in a non-racial way. One result, of course, is the terrible backlash that white farmers are now experiencing as Zimbabwe's Robert Mugabe abuses them in order to guarantee his own political survival. Had there not been racism in the first place, then Mugabe's seizure of white-owned farms likely would not have happened.

It is not just in southern Africa that ethnic groups were created in order to make control by elites possible. I read Professor Tarsis Kabwegyere's doctoral dissertation. Tarsis was man with whom I worked in Uganda and who wrote about his own community in southwest Uganda. I was impressed with his clear proof that his "tribe" had not been marked off as having a fixed and separate identity until the British came and decided one was needed. Previously, they had been part of a continuum of peoples with similar dialects and customs within a larger language group.

In Liberia, anthropologists, missionaries, and government officials defined the sixteen (some say, twenty-eight) "tribes" that make up the nation. In this way, the Liberian government created a top-down system of governing that put people in their places under town chiefs, clan chiefs, paramount chiefs, and district administrators. People were identified by dialect as "Kpelle" or "Loma" or "Grebo" or "Krahn," even when the lines dividing them were not clear. There are varieties of Kpelle and Loma that are similar to each other, more so than Kpelle resembles other varieties of Kpelle or Loma other varieties of Loma. But lines were drawn, and these lines have continued to determine social relations. The much more fundamental linguistic lines that existed between Mande, Kwa, and West Atlantic languages were not named and used as means of differentiation, because they did not allow easy demarcation and control.

In southern Africa today, the larger linguistic relations still have great importance. Those South Africans who speak one of the basic nine African languages, as well as citizens of Lesotho, Botswana, and Swaziland, are on one side of a great divide, while blacks from outside these language groups are on the other. These blacks are called by the derogatory term "makwerekwere," perhaps meaning people whose language is unintelligible and full of strange sounds like "kwere-kwere-kwere." Speakers of South African languages are often lighter in skin color than those outside the language group, leading to this linguistic xenophobia. In some instances, South African citizens have been abused or even arrested by other South African blacks who identified them as foreigners, because they were supposedly too dark to be truly South African.

Using an insulting and demeaning identification such as "makwerekwere" is a way to diminish people, to make them into something less than fully human. The term "bushman" also serves that purpose, since it implies a rustic origin. When the Dutch first landed at Cape Town and met the Khoisan, the Dutch called them "Hottentots," an unfriendly and disparaging name. Afrikaners are subjected to the same treatment when they are called "Boers," which means "farmers" and suggests a degree of rural ignorance. In southern Ethiopia, the Oromo people were for a long time called "Galla" by the highlands aristocrats as a way of putting them down. Some of these terms are comparable to more widely known slurs such as Kaffir, Nigger, Wop, Kike, and Coolie.

At the same time, lack of clear identification is problematic for some. My student at the Anglican College of the Transfiguration was clearly of mixed race and also clearly confused. He told me that he has no identity, since he has no link to what he thinks may be his ancestry. He believes he is descended from the Khoisan people, who had originally inhabited what is now the Western Cape. He has hunted for books on their early history, trying to find out who he really is. Cases like his or that of the previously mentioned student at the National University of Lesotho are sad; the pressure to find a group identity is strong. Many are victims of a system that says you are really you only if you can state to what group you belong. The implication is that belonging to a mixed group is not satisfactory.

Surely, the future of the world is that these distinctions will be blurred, if not forgotten. My three sons have chosen the way of diversity, each marrying outside the Anglo-Saxon Protestant community. Our nephew married a woman whose ancestry has most of the colors of the rainbow; she is proud of her black, Amerindian, and Canadian ancestry. This is surely a matter for rejoicing, since it blurs the lines that hard-core racists want to keep to divide us.

We have good friends across Africa who also break down the barriers. Former students of ours at Cuttington University College, Moulai and Ruth Reeves, represent in their family four of the distinct linguistic groups that the Liberian government and the anthropologists were so careful to distinguish. The more these lines are blurred, the more we are one world and the better we will be.

4.9 Artificial national boundaries.

In Africa, families are large and include a wide range of people who might or might not be considered relatives, if looked at according to the narrower Western mindset. When I started my work in a village in the Lesotho foothills, one of my first acts was to interview the matriarch of the village. She demonstrated to me through a series of complex, interlocking genealogies, all of which she had memorized, how everyone in the village was related to everyone else. What her example shows is that whether or not ethnic groups make sense, families certainly are real and of great importance to everyone.

What do family ties have to do with artificial national boundaries? When the British, French, Portuguese, Spanish, German, Americo-Liberian, Arabic, and Ethiopian overlords carved up the African land mass into pieces they could mark on an international map, in every case they cut family ties. The household that became French was divided from the relatives in the household that became Liberian and so forth ad infinitum. The newly proclaimed French subjects in Guinea—even more so the small minority who became citizens—learned in primary school about their ancestors, the Gauls. Just across the border, their brothers and sisters in Liberia learned how in 1822 they had found freedom when former slaves settled in Monrovia. My friends in Gbansu assured me that their home was in Guinea, where their distant relatives still lived, but they were cut off from family by the national border.

The borders in southern Africa are no different. All of my Basotho friends have family members on both sides of the border created to keep the truncated kingdom of Moshoeshoe I safe from the advancing Afrikaners. "Lesotho" is not so much the present nation of Lesotho, but rather is the home of the *bana ba Moshoeshoe*, the children of Moshoeshoe, wherever they may be. This theoretical "Lesotho" may overlap with the home and nation of other people. That is not the issue, however. What is important is that "Lesotho" is where Basotho families live, whether in Lesotho or in their South African towns and villages from the Eastern Cape to the Free State to Johannesburg. Sechaba Consultants concluded that the simplest and least expensive solution to the problem is to allow free passage while retaining some degree of control over import and export of goods (Sechaba 2002).

The Basotho are usually given trouble crossing the border due to tedious bureaucratic rules, but they are much better off than people I know in other African countries. Theological students of mine from Namibia told me of the great difficulties they had communicating with their relatives across the Angolan border, mostly due to the endemic Angolan civil war. A theological educator in northern Uganda told me how the rebellion of the Lord's Resistance Army made life terribly hard for the people of Gulu, many whose children or close relatives had been kidnaped and taken into southern Sudan for military training. Another friend explained how the vast Kariba reservoir has separated members of the Gwembe Tonga ethnic group, who now live on opposite sides of the Zambia-Zimbabwe border.

Other borders are much less problematic and practically non-existent. A Malawian, with whom I have done collaborative research on matters including the question of borders, comes from the southeast of his country. There, the border with Mozambique is simply a highway without checkpoints. The Malawian has family on both sides; he and many other people cross freely for weddings, for school, for shopping, for farming, and for any of the basic matters of life. One brother is Malawian and the other brother is Mozambican, but they are brothers. This situation is fortunate compared to problems experienced elsewhere, because the natural flow of life can continue, uninterrupted by the arbitrary and artificial nation-states created by colonialism.

It is hard for me to find any real advantages accruing to Africans from the creation of these nation-states. The dean of African historians Basil Davidson speaks eloquently of the problem (Davidson 1992). I have learned from him that perhaps the only real beneficiaries are the politicians, who grow fat from the power and privileges they receive, and the foreign powers that milk the economy dry through cheap exports and ruinous debts. The xenophobia mentioned above is exacerbated by these boundaries; it is kept alive and burning by the political rhetoric of leaders who want to retain their ability to exploit their subjects without interference from neighboring leaders.

The painful war between Eritrea and Ethiopia over the impoverished village of Badame shows the folly of these boundaries. Similarly, Nigeria and Cameroon came close to war over the Bakassi peninsula, and even now Nigeria balks at the ruling of the World Court, just as Ethiopia refuses to accept the boundary mediation over Badame. Somalia continues to be plagued by borders that are made and re-made by the various clans who continue ancient warfare into the twenty-first century. Chad and Libya intermittently wage war over the Tibesti area, a war that formally ended in 2002 but still inspires insurgents to try their luck at destabilizing the region. It is indeed a blessing that Botswana and Namibia settled their dispute over an uninhabited island in the Chobi area.

Differences in spoken languages remain one of the principal barriers to communication between groups. In Gbansu, why children of their relatives across the border grow up speaking French in school while their own children grow up speaking English in school is a mystery to both communities. The division of Africa into English, French, Portuguese, Spanish, and Arabic zones has contributed to its failure to develop, though it is true that the current linguistic confusion is in some ways an improvement over the Babel of thousands of different languages prior to colonialism. Perhaps we should be grateful that at least there are fewer language problems than before. We should also be grateful that the indigenous languages still exist to allow family to be family.

4.10 The external focus of modern infrastructure.

Another consequence of foreign intervention is that many African ports, railways, airlines, telephone lines, and even postal systems have been routed through Europe and America rather than through neighboring countries. When I was living in Liberia in the 1960s, I once had to place a call to Sierra Leone. One would think I could have dialed directly. Not at all. The system required that the call go through London and then back to Sierra Leone. On another occasion in 1989 I needed to fly from Liberia to Lesotho. The only convenient route was by way of Europe. From Lesotho, I have always had to first send mail to friends in the United States if I wanted it eventually to reach friends in Liberia.

The reasons for this convoluted, mixed-up infrastructure are economic. African countries are sources of cheap, unrefined raw materials that are sent to developed countries to be refined, manufactured, and then sold, often in the very countries from which the raw materials came. It is thus economically rational for those who build and maintain the infrastructure to minimize the expense of getting coffee, cocoa, rubber, iron, palm oil, or tea to the manufacturer that processes them.

Politics also play their part in this irrational system. Many African countries have stronger links to the parent colonial power than to each other, which means colonial communication links are sturdier than the roads, airlines, telephone systems, and Internet connections between African neighbors.

When I was in Mbeya in southwest Tanzania, I once thought of going to Lesotho by rail. I learned, however, that such a trip was impossible. The Tazara railway stopped in Lusaka. It could not link directly with the former Rhodesian railway, because the two systems had different gauge tracks. Apparently, the original builders saw no reason to make them compatible. They were not designed to serve internal traffic within Africa as much as to facilitate the export of raw materials. The railway built to move iron ore out of Liberia cannot link to the rail system in Guinea, because they are also different gauge tracks.

Highways within and between countries are less developed than major trunk roads to the coast on which goods can be transported in and out of the continent. Cecil Rhodes' vision of a Cape-to-Cairo road and railroad is still waiting to be realized. Paradoxically, it was easier in colonial days to travel between African countries than it is today, not only because of post-colonial wars, but also because there is little incentive and, unfortunately, little money for road maintainance. By 1999, the road I once used to travel from Nairobi to the coast had become impassable due to long-term wear.

Inter-African commerce largely consists of consumer goods being brought back from outside countries rather than effective trade between suppliers and customers within the continent. South Africa is an exception to this pattern, since it has developed an active manufacturing industry. I hope that one day South Africa will be the engine of real inter-African economic growth. The protocol signed by the nations of the Southern African Development Community points in that direction. The basic problem with the protocol is that South Africa is the only powerful economic player in the game. The other countries fear having their infant industries swamped by South African competition.

The most recent effort to link South Africa with Mozambique through the Maputo corridor led to further domination of the Mozambican economy by South Africa. An agreement signed at the end of 2002 allows the South African railway corporation, Spoornet, a fifteen-year concession for transport between South Africa and the port of Maputo. Mozambique will be paid more than $67 million during the contractual period. Once again the big powers are the winners and the small countries are compelled to cooperate in order to make trade possible.

4.11 Greed and war.

Simply, boldly, and basically, the ultimate burden that the elites have imposed on Africa is war. From the elite point of view, war is the ultimate release from all their African burdens. Ordinary people are dragged into wars raging in all parts of the continent. They do not see much benefit in war, but they participate because demagogic leaders, desperate for power, have persuaded or forced them to fight. European war theorist Carl von Clausewitz said, "…war is nothing but a continuation of political intercourse with the admixture of different means" (reference.allrefer.com/encyclopedia/W/war-ent.html).

It is more apt to say that war in Africa is a furtherance of greed by military means. The primary goal of political power in all but a handful of African states has been the enrichment of leaders. A secondary goal is the enrichment of their clients. The general pattern is for the ruler to identify with a particular elite and to make sure that together they benefit from the struggle.

Corruption is often the consequence of success. To the victor belong the spoils, and the spoils are distributed according to who must be paid off, because they would cause more trouble if they were not paid. Political scientists Chabal and Daloz (1999) show how the prize goes to the strongest, while the losers regroup to fight again another day. The leaders of all sides in the struggle benefit, because they have followers who will keep them alive in the hope of profiting from an eventual victory. The patrimonial system only succeeds if clients are paid off. Otherwise, the system breaks down and a new patron takes over. To the victors and, in the case of Africa, to all their clients belong the spoils proportionate to their power in the system.

How have I seen this process at work? When it became apparent that the Americo-Liberian establishment was not invincible, simply by the act of Samuel Doe disemboweling then-President Tolbert, the game was started. There were several abortive attempts to oust Doe during the 1980s, but none succeeded until Charles Taylor mounted a much stronger and better-coordinated attack on the Doe regime. It took almost seven years for the fighting to resolve itself in Taylor's favor, and in the interim there were at least four other warlords struggling for the same prize. Each warlord had his following, and each managed for a time to control a piece of the country. Taylor won because he was able to capture the major population centers and because he was able to deliver the spoils to his followers. He secured control of the timber, gold, and diamond businesses and used the profits to build his power base. In 1997, Taylor won an election, primarily because the people were afraid of the alternatives.

Charles Taylor could have consolidated his gains had he not been so greedy. What made Tubman so successful for so long (from 1944 to 1971) was that he was content to share wealth with a large portion of the population. I flew into Monrovia in 1980 for a conference and sat next to a Lebanese businessman also going to Liberia. I asked him to evaluate the situation now that Samuel Doe had assumed power. In particular, I wanted to know why Tolbert had not been able to retain control. The businessman opened his two hands, palms down, fingers spread wide. He then raked in an imaginary pile of money, allowing much of it to slip between his fingers. "That," he said, "was Tubman's method to ensure that other people got a good share of the revenue." He explained that Tolbert's error was being tight-fisted; money did not slip between his fingers for others to enjoy. In the end, the businessman said, it was greed that killed Tolbert.

I knew that to be true from my experience in Gbansu. Tolbert had expropriated farmland at the village where the trail leading to Gbansu branched from the main road, and he was busily grabbing land from people all along the trail in order to expand his holdings. He was bitterly resented for his greed by the people I spoke with in the Gbansu area.

Admittedly, Tolbert had a sensible vision for solving Liberia's economic and social problems. Sadly, he could not separate personal greed from his plans for development. He was unable to rein in members of his inner circle, and he did not have full control over the remnant members of Tubman's administration. An articulate opposition gained strength, and Tolbert was ineffectual and insensitive in dealing with it.

Grebo warriors at Tubman's funeral

Tubman had enjoyed the good life and had stolen his share of goodies from ordinary people, but he did not alienate people or lose their respect in the process. When he died I was in a remote village in northeast Liberia. A man came running to the house from an even more remote village, crying and shouting, "Our father has died!" He meant it. At the funeral a week or so later, the city of Monrovia was out in force with hardly a voice denouncing Tubman for his misdeeds.

By contrast, few people except for his family and inner circle cried when Tolbert died. Perhaps only the Krahn people from Samuel Doe's home cried when he died. Charles Taylor made his exit in a similar way to that of General Abacha in Nigeria. Before Abacha's death, people proclaimed him their true and perpetual leader. After his sudden death, the streets rang out with rejoicing that the villain was gone. Similarly, there was national relief and joy when Mobutu Sese Seko—the former president of Zaire, now called the Democratic Republic of Congo—was overthrown and then died in exile.

For Charles Taylor, as was true for Jonas Savimbi in Angola, Alfonso Dhlakama in Mozambique, Idi Amin in Uganda, and Foday Sankoh in Sierra Leone, war has been an instrument of achieving greedy ends. Taylor succeeded for his few years in power in Liberia where Alhaji Kromah, Prince Johnson, Roosevelt Johnson, George Boley, and others failed. Taylor was smooth and articulate and tried to appear the statesman, but under the surface he exemplified, as Chabal and Daloz put it, "...disorder as political instrument." He was elected president, as I was told when I visited Liberia shortly after the election, because the people were afraid not to elect him. The choice was peace with Taylor as president—otherwise, war.

Of course, the war continues, despite Taylor's unlamented departure. The rebels in LURD and MODEL understand that many Liberians are fed up with the ongoing tyranny Taylor has imposed on them. Yet it appears that neither rebel group is any better. I have consulted many Liberian friends, and none of them can name a responsible statesman belonging to LURD or MODEL. Both have accepted the peace accords signed in Accra in August 2003, but both also have soldiers actively fighting on the ground in Liberia to gain loot and territory. The big question is whether interim head of State Gyude Bryant will have the strength and the charisma to achieve disarmament, peace and eventual unity.

Yet some warriors do seek peace after victory. I was in Uganda in 1987 shortly after Yoweri Museveni's soldiers finally won victory over the militias of former president Milton Obote and other warlords. He could easily have gone the same route as Taylor, seeking to expand his gains outside Uganda. But at that time he did nothing of the kind. He put his efforts, and the efforts of his soldiers, to work to rebuild the country. I was impressed with what I saw.

Unfortunately, it seems that Museveni has also succumbed to the lure of war as an instrument of greed. His soldiers have invaded the Democratic Republic of Congo in nominal support of the group of rebels fighting against the man who overthrew Mobutu, Laurent Kabila. The prizes are substantial, including diamonds, minerals, and regional power. The chaos of Congo is the chaos of greed, and it seems unlikely that there will be peace in that potentially wealthy country for many years to come. It is a good sign that Kabila's son, Joseph, is trying to repair the damage done by his father. Another good sign is that invading forces are regrouping in their homes. It seems unlikely, however, that the country can ever truly become united, given its sad history. Evidence of this inability was that Joseph Kabila refused to attend the signing of a peace agreement in South Africa in April 2003. More evidence was that eastern Congolese rebel leader Jean-Pierre Bemba refused to attend Kabila's swearing in as president.

It is indeed a blessing that serious war never came to South Africa. Though there were skirmishes and further threats of guerrilla action, apartheid was ended through negotiation. In retrospect, it seems that the leadership avoided war to a large extent because of the good sense of the men who eventually won the Nobel Peace Prize for their efforts—De Klerk, Tutu, and Mandela. Lesotho also narrowly escaped civil war in late 1998 when efforts were made to overthrow the legitimately elected government by force.

Where war has prevailed, Africa has suffered. But where war has been avoided, Africa has prospered. Even without cultural domination, indirect rule, control of subjects by citizens, racism, xenophobia, slavery, forced labor, ethnic classification, arbitrary boundaries, and European control of economic infrastructure, the greed that leads to war would still destroy Africa's chances to become what it has the potential to be.

4.12 Hopeful signs.

The immense diversity that marks today's writings about the continent helps correct the **misperception of Africa as a single culture area**. Some of the writing is good; Basil Davidson is one of my heroes and role models. Some is facile, simplistic, and entertaining but also highly misleading. Journalist Ryszard Kapuscinski should have known better than to make the exaggerated claims about Liberia that it has no public transportation (there are taxis everywhere) and that "the trek from the jungle to Monrovia requires many days of difficult marching across roadless tropical expanses" (Kapuscinski 2000: 244). He does, in his own inaccurate way, make clear the difference between the various parts of Africa where he has worked and traveled.

What is essential is that business people, academics, diplomats, aid workers, missionaries, and the whole array of ordinary people who know and love the continent, make clear the wonder, the beauty, and the variety that is Africa. While this book points out patterns true of many of its various parts, I hope it also reveals the diversity I experienced in the many different countries where I worked.

Western democratic forms are now being modified to take into account African ways of thought and governance. This may not always be good, as in cases where leaders wish to become president-for-life. But there are hopeful signs, such as increased modernization and the adaptation of traditional rule to meet the need for decentralized leadership among local people. The creation of administrative districts in South Africa that include both rural and urban areas is beginning to lead to a more cooperative relation between secular rulers and traditional authorities.

Protests against **indirect rule through elites** are beginning, not only in Seattle and Montreal, but fortunately also in Africa. Ordinary people have voted in democratic elections to remove entrenched oligarchies from power in Senegal, Côte d'Ivoire, Ghana, Malawi, Zambia, and South Africa. What is not yet clear is whether these new governing parties have the courage or the ability to speak for and respect the people who voted for them. Some, notably President Laurent Gbagbo's government in Côte d'Ivoire, have fallen prey to ethnic selfishness. The result has been many months of ongoing civil war in Côte d'Ivoire, leading finally to an ethnically broad-based government, unfortunately not yet stable or secure. It is sad to see the African National Congress falling into line with the big financial powers, particularly in the ongoing procurement of weapons. But it is encouraging that the press has joined opposition parties in speaking out against the power of international financial institutions.

Fewer people must classify themselves as **subjects** now, as more and more ordinary people assume their rightful role as **citizens**. People, even the very poorest, are demanding to be heard rather than just being told what to do. That opposition parties have won victories in so many countries is critical. Even the seemingly anarchic militias that have sprung up where democracy does not exist are signs that the voiceless are tired of always being oppressed. I have personally been encouraged in my survey work by the willingness of ordinary people to answer what must have appeared to them as endless sets of questions, because they hoped that in that way their voices would finally be heard. We researchers who have spent so much time asking ordinary people about their resources, their ideas, their hopes, and their futures have a responsibility to act on what they have told us.

Voices are being raised against **racism**, not only by its victims but also by those who have most benefited from it. Former bastions of white privilege such as the annual Grahamstown Arts Festival are featuring more and more artists from other communities. The audiences are still largely white, but each year we have seen more black audience members. Another unfortunate consequence of inattention to racial discrimination is that blacks were excluded from "high culture" during the apartheid era, and as a result they are not interested in attending today's concerts and plays, even if they can afford them. Symphony orchestras in South Africa are dying at about the same rate that black musicians are being trained to join them.

Elsewhere, xenophobia is growing. It is difficult to find countries that are opening their borders to citizens of other nations. Only Colonel Gadhefi speaks in favor of African unity and openness, and this may be to suit his own ambitions rather than to unify the continent.

Voices, and not only voices but vigorous movements, are being raised against **slavery**, especially as it is practiced in Sudan. I have doubts about the practice of paying to redeem slaves, as some right-wing Christian groups have done, but I praise them for raising the level of awareness. Furthermore, slave trading by the Arab north has increased support for the liberation armies in the south. In West Africa, the trade in women and children has been made more difficult because of adverse publicity. The governments involved, notably Nigeria and Benin, have been forced to speak out, even though it seems clear that senior people in both countries profit from the business of trading slaves.

Forced labor still takes place as a consequence of xenophobic border controls. I have worked in recent years with the Southern African Migration Project; the publicity they have garnered has brought the issue to public attention. Mozambican farm workers in South Africa are now being heard, at least in part because of the research we carried out. Yet hungry, desperate, poor people, many of them refugees, will continue to take demeaning and ill-paid jobs and continue to accept harsh labor conditions if covert permission to cross borders continues to be combined with overt restrictions. As in the American southwest, those migrants which succeed in gaining entry are given the lowest paid jobs, but are not hunted down. They are useful in an economy which needs poor people to do the dirty jobs that citizens and legal residents refuse to do.

There is little hope that the multiplication of **ethnic groups** can be reversed, with the possible exception of South Africa, where there is no longer bureaucratic classification by race. What must be the goal is to reduce the still-continuing use of these labels, not to mention the racism that underlies the divisions between rich and poor. Lesotho is a model, since over its 170-year history, Xhosas, Ndebeles, "Coloureds", and Basotho have lived and worked together without problems. May it happen elsewhere.

It is difficult to find defensible rationalizations for **artificial national boundaries** or ways to adjust borders to satisfy more rational criteria than those used by colonial powers when the borders were first established. But politicians are rarely willing to give up control over even the most unimportant bit of land—witness the bloody dispute between Ethiopia and Eritrea. A good sign, however, came with the resolution by the World Court of the conflicting claims of Botswana and Namibia over an uninhabited island in the Zambezi flood plain. Also holding out promise are the decision to change the Organization of African Unity into a more tightly knit African Union and the creation of regional groups of nations, such as the Southern African Development Community. The nation-states are likely destined to remain forever, but the borders between them can be softened to allow freedom of movement and trade. The East African Federation has revived, albeit to a very limited extent, and the Economic Community of West African States continues to make noises about integration of trade and currencies, despite the civil conflicts plaguing the region. These are moves in the right direction.

Infrastructure construction is beginning to take seriously the links among African nations and not just between Africa and the rest of the world. The Southern African Development Community is encouraging links, such as the Lesotho Highlands Water Project and the rail and road network uniting South Africa and Mozambique. As this infrastructure is built, care must be taken to prevent exploitation of the weak by the strong. If new infrastructure construction is handled wisely, African nations can begin to manage their relations with each other, and foreign powers (the elite that have always ruled Africa) will have less control. Careful management may not completely devolve power from the African elites to ordinary people, but it is a step in the right direction.

I wish I could report progress toward the elimination of **war** as an instrument of oppression and domination. Perhaps the warring parties are serious in saying that they will withdraw from the Democratic Republic of Congo, but I am not convinced. The peace settlement between Ethiopia and Eritrea is more of a truce than true peace, because Ethiopia refuses to accept the Badame decision. Charles Taylor talked peace but made war, just as his militant successors in LURD and MODEL. The ANC in South Africa spends an ever-increasing amount of money on armaments it does not need. At the same time, peacemaking and conflict-resolution groups have sprung up in many countries, particularly through the churches. These groups need all the support they can get so that they can begin to influence public policy. Peace is the only way for Africa to begin to realize the promise we all envisioned when Ghana won its independence in 1957. Since that great event there have been forty-six years of ongoing wars, coups, and mutinies. The genocide in Darfur in western Sudan is the latest horror, but the revulsion of the rest of the world may lead to action to protect the farming communities that are being destroyed by Janjaweed pastoralists. I am hopeful, but I know that history stands against my hope.

CHAPTER FIVE. ALIEN EDUCATION SYSTEMS

Education in preparation for adulthood has always and everywhere been a cornerstone of society. I was most acutely aware of this in Gbansu in Liberia, where in pre-civil war days there was an almost automatic sequence of events leading from birth to adulthood. Education prepared every child to be a full participant in the complex living organism that was the village.

Education began at home with the infant learning language and social behavior. From an early age the child was given tasks to do, leading quickly to sharing the work of farming and house keeping. At about puberty, boys would go to initiation school for four years and girls for three years, during which time they would learn the duties, skills, and arts of adulthood.

Learning never stopped, even after completion of initiation school. For the ordinary person, learning meant becoming a better farmer and a better homemaker, and everyone was expected to work on improving these skills. A few went on to become specialists in hunting, weaving, metal-working, medicine, or government.

5.1 The invention of failure.

A Mosotho child

Schooling is different from education in that education is a lifelong process that is part of every society. Schooling takes place under specific circumstances with defined goals. In the case of the initiation school in Gbansu, the goal was preparation for adult life. Every initiate reached that goal, and there was no such thing as failure short of death, a death communicated to the parents by a broken clay pot at their doorstep.

However, the school system that missionaries and colonialists brought to Africa was different in that it was designed to identify and train people for subaltern roles in the administration of the church, the state, and society. From the very beginning, schools sorted people according to their ability to do the tasks that Europeans and Americans set for them. These tasks were of an entirely different order from the tasks set, for example, by the Gbansu initiation schools. Western-initiated schools required mastery of a European language and simultaneously of reading, writing and arithmetic. These were specialist tasks, which in the earliest literate societies were not done by ordinary people.

In the colonial enterprise, the rules were changed, and the small minority of children who actually entered school were expected to read, write, and do arithmetic. Success came in stages, so that people who did well at one stage were encouraged to learn still more, while people who found a given level too difficult did not go on to the next level. The unfortunate problem has always been that people who did not make it to the next level were branded as failures.

Failure, as I see it, is a necessary part of a system that sets successively higher and yet higher standards for its students. Thus, I speak of the invention of failure, not previously present, since the person in the indigenous system who did not master herbs, hunting, seed selection, or legal rhetoric was nonetheless a full member of society, sharing all its activities and rewards. Such people were by no means failures; they were just not specialists. By contrast, people who "fail" in the Western-created school system are cut off from the rewards that accrue to people who "succeed."

In the African countries where I have lived and worked, failure to succeed in the school system leads to a harsh life. Such people must do the dirty work of society and be content with low recompense. Furthermore, the standard a person must reach in order to enjoy comfort and security has varied over the years. When I first went to Liberia in 1958, a scholar who had finished six years of school was considered a member of the intelligentsia and could command a good job. I remember a government official I met on the Côte d'Ivoire border in 1959. He had finished primary school and was posted to that remote village as the senior Liberian in charge of the area. He had his books with him and begged my friend and me for still more books so that he could continue to live the life of an educated gentleman. We did send him books when we returned from our trip, and I am sure he tried to read them in dim candle-light during the tropical nights.

The situation had changed by the time I left Liberia in 1974. By that time, having a high school diploma was not enough to guarantee a person a good job. College graduates had to hunt for employment, and when I returned to Liberia in 1997, I met Cuttington University College graduates who were running small grocery stores in order to survive.

The civil war has severely damaged the Liberian educational system. Many of the schools I knew about and visited in 2001 closed when people ran for cover. The unemployment rate is staggering; those who manage to finish school cannot find jobs. The CIA World Handbook estimates unemployment at 70 percent (www.cia.gov/cia/publications/factbook). How they arrived at a figure I do not know, and I would guess that it is much too low, particularly as looting and rape continue in the rural areas.

Failure is relative to the market, which sets standards on the basis of supply and demand. However high or low the standard for education is set by the job market, the option of failure is still very real. Those who do not achieve the required results are pushed aside and must find an alternate way to survive. In Lesotho, the job market is different from that in Liberia, because Lesotho has a healthier economy. There, university graduates can generally count on getting a good job; yet even in Lesotho, failure is the kiss of death. As a result, those who fail the Cambridge Overseas School Certificate examination in Lesotho will try again and again to get the needed scores so that they can go on to some form of tertiary education.

I have spoken of the "invention" of failure. The missionaries and colonial officers who brought schooling to Africa wanted to promote at least some people from the customary way of life into the elite to be preachers, teachers, and government officials. Such persons were expected to jump out of their skins and into the ruling class. To use Mamdani's term, they were intended to be the "citizens" in a society organized according to the theory of indirect rule. These early educators gave little thought to the people who would not succeed other than to hope they might learn to read the Bible and write letters. They assumed that such persons would be faithful Christians who would witness to their relatives and neighbors as they melted back into accustomed ways of life.

The trouble was and still is that people who fail in the Western school system cannot always simply go back to the "bush." For the very young who drop out of school in the early years of primary education, this avenue is possible. But for those who have failed to complete primary school or leave after not passing secondary school exams, going home to cut bush, herd animals, and grow subsistence crops is difficult. Not only are they ashamed to return after family, friends, and fellow villagers have supported and encouraged them to find something better than the country way of life, but they have also lost the rhythm and momentum of the village. They become rootless people, no longer the kind of people their parents were and certainly not the kind of people they would like to be in order to enter fully into the (to use the Liberian term) *kwii* life.

A production system that has defective output is an inefficient system. I read about an experiment at an agricultural college that produced larger, meatier, and more productive chickens. The trouble was that despite the high quality of the surviving birds, a very large proportion of the chicks died. The new method for raising chickens was rejected because of its excessive waste.

What I have seen in Liberia and Lesotho is not greatly different from the experiment in chicken-rearing. Our 1999 survey of poverty in Lesotho showed that only 4 percent of those aged nineteen had completed twelve years of high school, and only 12 percent of those aged fourteen had completed seven years of primary school. Of those who attended school, 58 percent had been held back at least one year. Of young people between the ages of eleven and nineteen, about 9 percent had never attended school at all.

Schooling is clearly not an option for all people, and for those who can attend, few finish. In 1996, just over half of the children who entered primary school in Lesotho actually passed their Primary School Leaving Examination, and only about 5 percent of those who enter primary school passed the high school examination (Mathot 2000: 31-32). The 5 percent who complete high school may be well educated, but the 95 percent who drop by the wayside (like the chickens that did not survive the experiment) are defined by society and the economy as failures.

The system is not as wasteful or cruel in the developed world, but even there a dangerously large proportion drop out. I have read shocking statistics about illiteracy and ignorance in the United States. According to the CIA World Handbook, as many as three percent of American adults are in fact illiterate (www.mrdowling.com/800literacy.html), and functional illiteracy is much higher. "The United States Department of Education (1995) released a report that stated that there are 25 million Americans who can not read or write at all. More than 10 million workers lack basic skills in reading, writing, and math and experience difficulty doing their jobs. Approximately 45 million Americans are functional illiterates" (http://www.sarasota.k12.fl.us/sarasota/ whatisprobl.htm).

Failure is still failure, and the experiment is still producing chickens that do not survive. Furthermore, those that fail at education do not die but remain limping and maimed for the rest of their lives, psychologically damaged and unable to get well-paying jobs.

The waste is truly horrifying in countries such as Liberia and Lesotho. From a Western perspective, the great majority of ordinary people in these two countries are failures—and they know it. These people, limping and maimed, form an unemployed and unemployable mass and contribute little to national development. The missionaries and colonial experts who devised the school system inadvertently invented failure and thus must bear much responsibility for the decline and decay seen in Africa. Instead, most of us who have been teachers in Africa, myself included, turn our backs on those we are not able to bring through school to a successful conclusion. Neither do we have any idea how to repair the damage we have done.

5.2 Emphasis on white-collar employment.

The missionaries and colonial officers who first developed the education system in most African countries hoped to train teachers, pastors, and administrators so that the indirect rule system would function efficiently. Elites were necessary if the "natives" were to be ruled efficiently and at minimum cost, thus ensuring that the colonial venture could turn a profit. Similarly, missionaries could not multiply themselves indefinitely, but needed local catechists to maintain their work among converts, and evangelists to carry the message to the heathen. The overt syllabus was to produce trained subordinates, but the hidden syllabus was to guarantee obedience to those in power. In particular, women were expected to submit to male authority, and in some cases mission education for women consisted of training only in basic cooking and housekeeping. I have heard it said that the colonial powers sent "soldiers to conquer their bodies and missionaries to conquer their minds."

It made sense for the first schools to be extremely academic. Good administrators and church leaders had to be fluent in the colonial languages and had to be able to keep good records. The first schools in Liberia even went so far as to train students in classical languages. The leading academic in nineteenth-century Liberia, W. E. Blyden, was a gifted scholar competent in Greek, Hebrew, and Arabic. The situation in Lesotho was less extreme, since the first missionaries were not from the academic elite. But the schools there very quickly became training grounds for those who were intended to be the "citizens."

In order to train mechanics, carpenters, masons, and plumbers for the states created by the colonial venture, some trade schools and training programs were started such as Lovedale in South Africa and Leloaleng in Lesotho. Unfortunately, they were looked down upon in both pre-colonial and post-colonial Africa, including by prospective students, and very few skilled artisans came out of them. In fact, the situation in the home countries was not much different; people in the lower orders there become tradesmen and technicians, while the aristocracy went to university.

The Booker Washington Institute in Liberia was established to train a body of carpenters, bricklayers, mechanics, electricians, and plumbers, but BWI (as it is still called) became more and more academic. Students at Cuttington College who had been to BWI were more interested in their academic knowledge than in their practical and vocational skills. Those who could do so took as many college-preparatory courses as they could, and thus neglected the "mechanical arts." Their reasoning was simple—there was neither money nor prestige in being a carpenter.

Lesotho has done somewhat better than Liberia. The Lesotho Evangelical Church established a vocational training center in southern Lesotho, and the government set up a training institute in Maseru. Both have produced some skilled technicians, but increasingly the leaning of the government training institute is toward becoming a polytechnic, preferring to train engineers rather than craftsmen.

The result is that it is difficult to find skilled workmen to do routine tasks of construction and maintenance. In the most extreme case I remember, I was on a research trip in a mountain village and was staying in a house that had been loaned for several days to my research team. I sat on a rather crude bench, and it broke beneath me. Perhaps I had made a wrong move; perhaps it was poorly made, but I felt responsible, and so I tried to find a carpenter in the village to repair it. In the end, in that village of a hundred households I could find no one with the appropriate tools and skills.

Housing construction is another area of neglect. Many people build their own houses out of available local materials. In traditional rural areas, thatch-roofed rondavels are common and are generally well made. Yet when people attempt to construct a more modern rectangular house with a corrugated iron roof, the job is often badly done. Roofs are nailed on the rafters with inadequate nails, and stones are piled on top to ensure they do not blow off. This works only part of the time; the resulting regular disaster is that strong winds carry roofs away. Furthermore, these houses generally do not have ceilings under the roofs, making them extremely hot in the summer and cold in the winter. The alternative is the traditional thatch-roofed rondavel, which moderates temperature, but it is not fashionable in today's rectangular world.

House construction in Lesotho

An organization that sets an example for others in Africa is Opportunities Industrialization Center International (OICI), founded by the Rev. Leon Sullivan, who also pioneered the famous Sullivan principles used to evaluate companies doing business with South Africa. I encountered OICI people in both Liberia and Lesotho and was impressed with what they were doing. Their primary aim is to train poorly educated and unemployed youth in skills that will give them jobs. In Liberia, despite hindrances to the program due to the civil war, OICI provided training "in various vocational skills training areas (carpentry, electricity, plumbing, masonry, shoemaking and tailoring/fashion design), and in various agro-based vocational trade areas (building trade, animal science, metal works)" (www.oicinternational.org/pro_librea.htm). OICI renovated four centers for training that had been ruined. I hope the renewed fighting will not discourage OICI from continuing when fighting stops, because theirs is the kind of help Liberia needs to get going again.

In Lesotho, with World Bank help, OICI runs two activities: a "building trades center that trains young men and women in carpentry, masonry, plumbing and sheet-metal work. The second is an entrepreneurship and small business development component that provides training and assistance, at various locations, in business and financial management, marketing, bookkeeping, middle management upgrading, and self-employment instruction for Lesotho OIC's building trades trainees" (www.oicinternational.org/pro_lesotho.htm).

5.3 Irrelevant curricula.

What OICI is doing is what governments often fail to do. Official Ministry of Education curricula can promote or hinder development, depending on their relevance to the needs of the nation. There are many different points of view on this question, of course. Some still say that the classical education that nurtured the British Empire (and also nurtured W. E. Blyden in Liberia) is the key to full realization of potential.

I must admit I have leanings in that direction. I wish that more of our leaders understood the history of human efforts to build a good society. Some knowledge of Plato, Aristotle, St. Augustine, Hobbes, Locke, Adam Smith, John Stuart Mill, Marx, and Reinhold Niebuhr would go a long way toward educating those who would pretend to rule us. Great African thinkers, including Blyden, Fanon, Nkrumah, Nyerere, and Mandela, should be prescribed reading for the next generation of politically ambitious Africans. When I was teaching at Cuttington and then at the National University of Lesotho, I required my students to read the words of these thinkers rather than watered-down summaries about them.

But wait. I give myself away in the last paragraph. I am talking about the Europeanized leaders, the "citizens," the white-collar managerial class. The curriculum I describe is what the elite use and benefit from. But ordinary people, those who fail the examinations intended to weed out non-leaders, do not benefit from such a curriculum. Most of what they study in the lower grades is designed to prepare them for the final stages of education when they are supposedly ready to read the words of the great thinkers, but they never reach those final stages.

Kwame Nkrumah fell into that trap when he wrote his last book, *Consciencism* (Nkrumah 1970). It is a tightly-argued, complex piece of philosophical reasoning suitable only for well-trained intellectuals. I myself did not get much out of it when I tried to read it, but perhaps it is just not my style. The point is that those whose minds and hearts he wanted to awaken, to conscientise, are not just the tiny elite who can read his book (or the books of Plato and his followers), but rather the ordinary folk who become failures because they cannot fight their way through the book-oriented, European-language-written, abstracted-out-of-local-context school syllabus.

Some have argued that the bookish curriculum of the lower grades at least prepares people to think for themselves and to have some comprehension of democracy. Unfortunately, this is by and large not the case. In our political opinion survey in Lesotho, the results belie the hope that schools are providing education for democracy. Respondents with less than a high school education had a much weaker concept of democracy than those with at least a high school education and were bitter about the possibility of Lesotho ever achieving anything of the sort (Gay and Green 2001).

School in Luwero Tanzania

Teaching students to think for themselves is difficult when teachers are over-worked, under-trained, harassed, and dealing with large classes of bored pupils. Teachers in those situations resort to methods such as rote learning, beating students who do not obey orders, and requiring regurgitation at exam time. Helping students think for themselves is a luxury that can only be realized when class size is small, when there is enough time to prepare for exams, when students are pre-selected (as they are in elite schools), and when teachers understand what they are teaching. Unfortunately, that long list of conditions is rarely met, and usually only for the wealthy.

I am not saying that there is an easy answer, an easy alternative curriculum.

I was impressed during my brief three months in Tanzania that the government was seriously trying to find an alternative. Tanzania's 1967 Arusha Declaration, whose main goal was to achieve Julius Nyerere's vision of an egalitarian socialist society, had been issued some years earlier. One of the ways to achieve that goal was to implement universal free education as well as literacy in Swahili for those beyond school age, and officials in the Ministry of Education genuinely were trying to bring a new curriculum into being.

The problem lies in the inbuilt inertia of the system. I have been told that it takes up to thirty minutes to turn a supertanker around when it is under full steam. I know that when I used to sail along the Maine coast, turning or stopping even the lightest of boats required planning at least a minute ahead. Similarly, turning around an educational system is an almost impossible task with classes full of teachers trained in the old way, with college tutors who train teachers to do what they were taught, and with civil servants who follow the infamous rule that all initiative is dangerous.

As part of the African Mathematics Curriculum team in 1963 and 1964, I helped write new teacher-training books for Liberia. I then helped introduce the new materials at the teacher-training level and in primary schools in Liberia. The primary-school phase of the exercise was an almost complete failure. Very few teachers, except a few Peace Corps volunteers and a Liberian teacher I had trained, understood what was going on. The idea that mathematics was something to be discovered, not just learned by heart, did not penetrate the minds of either teachers or students. Clearly, we did not approach the matter correctly. I know from my research that rural Liberians, though unschooled, can do mathematical operations in their own setting, but the transfer to an academic mode did not take place (Gay and Cole 1967). I really don't know why we failed, why an exercise that started with such good will and high skill left students and teachers cold.

I can think of no easy answer to the problem. But one possible answer may lie in the fact that the Western-oriented school system has been in place for two hundred years in most African countries. Those for whom it has provided entry into the elite see no reason to replace it with broad-based popular education, built on new and modern theories of education. They send their children to special elite schools where success is almost guaranteed. The result is class formation, whereby those who are "citizens" reproduce themselves in their children. It is true that some children from remote villages are fortunate to pass exams, enabling them to enter the elite. One of my former students at the National University of Lesotho grew up in the distant mountains and proved so competent in school that he finally took his M.Phil. at Cambridge University. He served as the Principal Secretary in the Ministry of Education before going on to become Government Secretary.

Sadly, such examples are rare, since the majority of poor children stop far short of completing secondary school. The schools they attend are of poor quality, and the pass rate is very low. A few high schools in Lesotho have mastered the art of preparing children to pass the Cambridge Overseas School Certificate and have corresponding high pass rates. Schools that do not know the art produce failures and, in some cases, nothing but failures.

Some other form of schooling must be found so that the system is not committed to the formation of two classes: the elite and the failures. Perhaps the example of the initiation school could be applied, in which children would learn basic survival skills, and only a few specialists would go on to study academic subjects.

My quite impractical and impossible dream of such a school system would require practical technical skills, including carpentry, masonry, mechanics, electricity, plumbing, farming, cooking, and sewing, to name only a few, for both boys and girls. Basic literacy, computer skills, health, human biology, and numeracy would be required as necessary adjuncts to the technical skills. Optional electives could be offered after school or in the evenings for those who want to learn literature, history, advanced mathematics, art, music, science, or economics. No special privileges would accrue to those who opted for such subjects, nor would people who excelled in them be given special honors and high salaries.

Sawyers in Tanzania

I realize that such a scheme is madness, given the way the world works today. As it is, those with academic qualifications can find their niche in the world-wide bureaucracy, do only what the job description requires, receive a regular salary, and then retire on a comfortable pension. Artisans, on the other hand, have little security and must be energetic, focused, and driven in order not to fail. As a friend of mine pointed out, it is obvious which alternative most young African students will choose.

A system where technicians flourish and white-collar workers struggle clearly can never be adopted in Western nations. It would be class suicide. All the more, such a system cannot be introduced in African countries as long as the Western world promotes the standard academic curriculum. Even the suggestion of such a system would be decried as prejudice against Africans and a new version of Bantu education.

Despite the impossibility of such a suggestion, which is not far from what Nyerere wanted when he authorized the Arusha Declaration, something must be done to stop the terrible waste that takes place in African schools. We have created a monster in the present system that casts out most school children, so that only a lucky few can get jobs and become citizens. This monster has done more than most of the other structures I have pointed to in this book to diminish and destroy the potential for Africa's advancement. I am grateful to such groups as OICI for believing that other approaches are possible.

5.4 Examinations and paper qualifications.

Closely related to irrelevant curricula are examinations and the paper qualifications that prove that one is not a "failure." It is perhaps inevitable that a structured curriculum requires criteria by which one is accepted and then pushed on to the next level. It is also important that these be as objective as possible, not subject to the personal whims of the examiner, and that they be documented in a public manner.

So why am I complaining about the exam and certificate system, when I have just complained about the system that makes them necessary? We must not forget that the ultimate aim of schools today is to use the curriculum as a means to pass standardized examinations, which are mainly written exams, rather than to demonstrate practical skills. I object to the over use, wrong use, and abuse of the classes-lectures-books-examinations system, which I claim has hindered African development. I have witnessed examples of all three misuses of the system in my time in Africa.

What do I mean by the over use of exams and certificates? Many people assume that passing an exam and holding a paper qualification demonstrates knowledge and wisdom. The agricultural extension service in Lesotho is an excellent case in point. Young Basotho who have completed three years in agricultural college often know very little about real farming. The majority of these students do not have fields of their own and have had little real experience in carrying out the tasks about which they so glibly advise mature farmers. They have passed exams based on a bookish curriculum, but are not required to prove that they are able to make a living on the land.

I remember attending a meeting where a young man was lecturing farmers about when to plant their crops. The farmers were present because they hoped that by attending they might get government-subsidized plowing on their fields. They dutifully listened to what the extension agent told them, but it was clear to me that he had not said anything they did not already know. His was book knowledge; theirs was experience.

It is not only the young products of the agricultural college who are useless in giving advice. Foreign farm advisors in Lesotho fall into the trap of thinking they know everything about farming, when in fact they do not comprehend local conditions. This type of arrogance is a misuse of degrees and qualifications.

An American agricultural engineer came to Lesotho to give advice about plowing fields. Unfortunately, just as he was about to start his demonstrations, his tractor broke down—not an uncommon event in Lesotho, where the terrain is rough and uneven. I advised him that he should go ahead with his demonstration using oxen rather than the tractor, since the great majority of the local Basotho farmers use oxen. He was grossly insulted, acting as if I had told him that all his degrees and experience were useless. He was not willing to adapt to the experience of local farmers and use the equipment they use; doubtless he went to the correct universities and was taught by scientists who had done the practical field research.

My point is that such research is likely to be irrelevant to the conditions on the ground in Africa. I once asked a wise old hand in the development business what would be the best approach to helping Basotho improve their farming. He thought about the question deeply and said, "Rent a piece of land, buy two oxen and a plough, grow maize for a couple of years, and then start giving advice."

A postscript to the story about the American agricultural engineer is the finding, confirmed repeatedly by other farm management economists in Lesotho, that the more a farmer spends on high-tech tractor plowing the more negative the economic return (Gay and Hall 2000:84-86). The same thing is true with mono-cropping and the use of fertilizer and pesticides. I cannot go into the details of agronomy, because I am not a professional, but I can say that our surveys have shown that spending money on these high-tech approaches is a sure way to guarantee financial loss. Basotho farmers, as I pointed out in the chapter on indigenous technologies, know better—at least until they are brainwashed by foreign experts with degrees or by government agents with subsidies.

I have already mentioned the case of J. J. Machobane, whose indigenous system of mixed cropping and organic farming was rejected by the British during the colonial era. The foreign experts had all the degrees, but Machobane had the vision and the experience to develop a system that is correct for Lesotho.

I encountered a similar problem in Botswana. Patrick van Rensburg, a long term resident there, developed a system of Brigades for training young people in many of the practical skills needed for balanced national growth. He won the Stockholm-based Right Livelihood Award in 1981 for his efforts (www.rightlivelihood.se/recip/van-rensburg.htm). He insisted that these skills could be learned on the job by young people who did not need to follow the tedious and often unrewarding route of academic schooling.

The Brigades were achieving some real successes, but then the government stepped in to regularize and institutionalize the underlying teaching program. They wanted the young people to have certificates that would qualify them in the eyes of contractors and employers, and so they looked abroad for an organization to give a stamp of approval. They found the London City and Guilds, which has for many years certified the level of training of British mechanics, carpenters, electricians, plumbers, and bricklayers.

What happened? The system that van Rensburg developed was taken out of his hands and made part of the government bureaucracy. Immediately the students began to want formal qualifications, and those who failed to get official certificates could no longer find work. The Brigades died, and with them died a way to give the "failures" a viable way to make a living. Clearly this is the wrong way to use the system of examinations and certificates.

Further abuses of the system arise in many other ways. Bribes may be passed, politics may determine who will receive certificates, fly-by-night "colleges" may promise instant results, and family ties may serve as substitute certificates. Such cases are all too common in every country in the world, not just in Africa, and everywhere it occurs development is hindered and efficiency compromised.

More to the point is the abuse of the system found in the idea of cost recovery in social services. The International Monetary Fund has urged poor countries to make their educational and medical systems as nearly self-supporting as possible. This means that the family must have the cash to send the child to school. In some cases, free primary education has been introduced, as happened in Lesotho in 2000 and Kenya in 2003. The next step is free compulsory schooling, but that most likely is far in the future.

The most serious problem introduced by cost recovery is the requirement that students pay fees in order to take their examinations. In Lesotho it now costs more than the equivalent of U.S. $100 to take the final examinations at the end of high school. In a country where more than half the households live on less than U.S. $100 per person per year, there is simply no means for poor children to take these exams. Many find the money from friends or relatives or donors, but there is no guarantee that such money can be found. In short, successful completion of high school is a privilege reserved for those with enough money, not a right given to every child. There are also examinations given before the final high school exam, and these too require money. The requisite certificate can only be obtained if the student's family can afford it.

These exams, moreover, are biased toward the academically proficient. Only a few high schools in Lesotho produce consistent success, and there are some that rarely produce even one graduate able to pass the examination. Entry into high-quality schools is restricted to those who have done well in primary school. More often that not, they are children who have attended English-medium schools rather than Sesotho-medium schools. As might be expected, the English-medium schools are more expensive than their Sesotho-medium counterparts. Once again, it is the wealthy who get ahead, and the poor are left behind. This leads to deep structural abuse of the exam system as a way to get the certificates needed for success.

The same problems exist in Liberia. Only the truly wealthy can pass the West African Exam Council tests, which qualify a student for university. Only the wealthy are able to attend the few good high schools that have survived the civil war. The remainder must resort to other means of getting ahead. One way out of the trap is fraud, which led the Exam Council to issue a stern warning before the 2001 exams took place (allafrica.com/stories/200105070332.html).

Another artificial way to get ahead is by attending "universities" offering degrees of doubtful value. Within the last few years, several new "universities" have been opened in Liberia by various churches. I saw one of these institutions when I visited the country in 1997. It was a ramshackle old building in the center of Monrovia without library or permanent faculty members. Even the recently revived Cuttington University College, where I taught for so many years, reopened with the barest minimum of facilities. Most of its lecturers are part-time civil servants who come up-country from Monrovia to help out and in the process supplement their meager salaries. The University of Liberia is in worse condition. Its 2002 academic year was postponed several times due to lack of money for faculty salaries.

These institutions, both the established and the new church "universities," offer degrees that are inevitably of doubtful value, even if their students have legitimately finished high school. Yet degrees are a necessity if students do not want to automatically enter the ranks of the unemployed. The result is that it matters little, within the desperation of post-civil-war Liberia, that the degrees may represent little or no learning. I should not be so judgmental, since the country must make a new beginning. What is disturbing is the tremendous pressure on educators to grant degrees to their students and in so doing violate what they know are proper academic standards. Far more appropriate to the situation in that war-torn country would be the bottom-up reconstruction of a good primary and later a secondary school system, with qualified students being trained at the tertiary level elsewhere in West Africa.

What are the deep disadvantages of an exam-based school system? It is focused on written, literate knowledge rather than on knowledge that enables people to do something with their hands, as OICI is trying to teach. Without proper support from the rest of the educational system, exam-based schooling promotes the idea that students can only learn by being taught rather than by doing. The system is self-perpetuating and leads to the formation of a class structure in which those who do well in the school system are able to send their children to elite schools where they can reap the benefits of their parents' privileges. The system is designed to allow some to succeed at the expense of others. At best it stresses competition and at worst, hatred and war. It rewards conformity and downplays critical self-awareness. In the end, it teaches people not so much to know as to pass.

5.5 Colonization of the mind.

The era when African societies were explicitly the colonies of European powers has ended. Yet the colonial era is by no means over. Economic colonization is one thing, and I will discuss it in detail later. At this point, the colonization I wish to discuss is a colonization of the mind, encompassing the far-reaching Western values and technology have upon the nations of Africa.

Let me summarize what I have said so far in this chapter. First, the possibility and, indeed, the pervasive actuality of failure have been the first and main legacy of the Western, colonial educational system in Africa. Societies have been torn asunder to the extent that participation in public affairs and civil society depends on success in foreign-based schooling. Children who do not make it in the system know they are forever cut off from the rewards accruing to children who pass their exams. These children are branded as failures, and the only alternatives for them are acceptance of a low status in society, flight from the centers of power into the remote rural areas, or crime. In fact, as a friend of mine noted, crime is a very rational response by those whose failure in the main-line schools means they are forced to find alternatives. Crime satisfies needs, brings status, and allows entry into a new and different patron-client network, in which one may eventually become the leader one could never be in normative society.

Second, those who succeed in the school system are trained primarily for white-collar employment, which in most cases means entry into the bureaucracy. The schools understands what is needed in order to fill jobs first created by colonial powers and later left to local people to carry out the normal tasks of government, church, school, hospital, and business. Such people have become full, but nonetheless subaltern, members of the establishment. Yet the real economic and political power remains elsewhere, often in the colonial nation itself but equally as often in a global interlocking directorate of power brokers. Therefore, the minds of white collar workers are set to perform the tasks for which their education has trained them. They maintain the worldwide bureaucratic network at the local post-colonial level, which the colonial powers left as their primary heritage, and find their niche in the global patron-client network.

Third, the curriculum that created the subaltern bureaucracy, which is perpetuated by teachers who belong to that bureaucracy, is irrelevant to the needs of the "failures." Students are not trained to be useful adults, but rather become part of the large pool of willing bodies from which successful leaders are selected. The "failures" are cast out of the system, having achieved only minimal literacy and numeracy and, at the same time, few fundamental life skills. They have been in effect brain-washed into believing that the only education worth having is the same Western education that discards them. They fall into the trap of self-rejection, and consequently they drift into the world of subsistence agriculture, informal sector enterprise, and crime.

Fourth, the vital necessity of making it in the formal, Western-oriented neo-colonial world means that there is a high premium placed on certificates and qualifications. What these products of the school system can do is less important than what credentials they carry and the clothes they wear. This reliance on paper certificates and exam results is the final capitulation to the colonial powers.

The huge number of Africans who have been forced to settle outside their home countries suffers peculiarly from the domination of foreign ways. There are more refugees in Africa than anywhere in the world, and many of them are suffering displacement in refugee camps where they lose their identity and become aliens without a real home to call their own. They start out keeping the vision of home alive, but as the years go on—whether they are Liberians in the camps of Côte d'Ivoire,

Rwandans in the camps of Tanzania, or Sudanese in the camps of Ethiopia—they gradually lose hope.

Different are the members of the diaspora who have taken up permanent residence or have taken citizenship abroad. In some cases they have reached the end of the brain drain chain and are well integrated into European or American society. There are thousands of Liberians who have settled in the United States and have no intention of returning home. Similarly, South Africans of all races have emigrated to the United States, the United Kingdom, Australia, or New Zealand. These people are all consciously, and in many cases enthusiastically, becoming Yanks, Brits or Aussies. They see no hope for their own countries, and they have turned their backs on them. Much of their contact with home happens when sending desperately needed money back to relatives who have not yet found the way to leave. Dr. Marcus Dahn, a candidate for president in the forthcoming Liberian election, claims there are 250,000 Liberians residing in the United States, an estimate which I find plausible, though it cannot be proved (www.newdemocrat.org/ Stories/DahnBallots.htm).

5.6 Consolidation of the elite.

The end product of the alien educational system is the preservation and consolidation of the elite discussed in the previous chapter. Failure is a way of ensuring that the ranks of the elite are kept small. White-collar employment, as the ideal reward for success in school, ensures that those skilled in other trades receive only a small share of the rewards accruing to success. The result is a huge salary disparity between white collar workers and artisans. Irrelevant curricula mean that students who could acquire useful mechanical skills are pushed out of the schools before they can fulfill their potential. Exams and certificates further entrench and consolidate the power of those who have mastered the irrelevancies of the standard school system and have become white-collar workers. The final blow is to break the spirit of those who fail by pointing out to them, subtly or not, that their minds are irrevocably unsuited to the global world.

Liberian official

Those who are excluded become the 70 percent of all Basotho identified in our recent survey as poor. They become the unemployed crowding the slums and squatter settlements of Johannesburg, Cape Town, and Durban. They become the unsuccessful rural peasants moved from resettlement camp to resettlement camp in Ethiopia who eventually become cannon fodder in the war with Eritrea. They become the rural farmers of Tanzania forced into villages in order to produce agricultural commodities for export. They become the rejected minority ethnic groups of Botswana who do not share in the wealth of diamonds and cattle. And, most ominously, they become the recruits for ruthless demagogues and warlords such as Charles Taylor in Liberia and Foday Sankoh in Sierra Leone. These people are the rejects from an alien school system, and when worse finally reaches worst, they are prepared to bring down the whole structure. After all, they have nothing to lose, since everything they might have had has been taken away from them.

5.7 Hopeful signs.

Nyerere's Arusha Declaration was a sign that **failure** in the conventional academic system need not be the end of the line. His vision is still alive, although I must admit that there are few trying to implement his ideas. In South Africa, the ideology of the Pan-African Congress promotes the well-being of the poor and disadvantaged. I do not like the racism inherent in their traditional Africa-for-the-Africans approach, but I appreciate their concern for those who do not make it in the conventional system. We can learn from them.

White-collar employment need not be the only source of rewards in society. Toward the end of our stay in Lesotho in 2001, dependence on skilled artisans for plumbing, electricity, auto mechanics, and construction was growing. And, as the infrastructure in urban areas becomes more complex, there will be more need—and thus greater reward—for people who know how to fix things. I must admit, however, that currently the only technical, hands-on people well compensated for their skills are medical doctors. Other skilled artisans could create guilds and unions in order to promote their image and increase their fees. Opportunities Industrial Center International would likely support that goal. The problem is that skilled workers have little political or economic power.

Many educators have tried to move away from **irrelevant curricula**. Though we failed in the 1960s with the African Mathematics Curriculum, our vision made sense. Lesotho's Curriculum Development Centre keeps working to improve what is taught in classrooms. I am particularly impressed with the efforts they are making in the area of development studies, following the lead of Janet Stuart of Sussex University. Science educators in Lesotho and other African countries are exploring hands-on approaches through action research. Tsepo Mokuku pioneered the way toward environmental education in Lesotho in his doctoral dissertation (Mokuku 1999). The South African Technikons, which are practical university-level institutions designed to train skilled engineers and technicians, are also indications of a welcome change in educational philosophy.

Examinations and paper qualifications are still highly praised and desired, but there are growing exceptions to the insistence on rigid requirements. I mentioned the Machobane system, which has the wonderful advantage that it works. South Africa has introduced what they call "Outcomes Based Education" in which certificates and degrees will represent real achievement, not just paper qualifications. Medical doctors are increasingly listening to traditional healers, who have in the past been ignored because of their lack of "scientific" training. This could lead to recognized certificates for the healers. I cannot always support the remedies of the herbalist or spiritual healer, but I am learning to be more respectful of the ability of non-professionals to meet people's spiritual as well as physical needs. Another striking example of these non-professionals is found in the rapid growth of African-initiated churches led by charismatic individuals without theological degrees.

The African Renascence that has been promoted by and is so important to leaders like Thabo Mbeki in South Africa contributes to the **decolonization of the mind**. Steve Biko gave his life in order to persuade his fellow blacks in South Africa that they have as much dignity and inherent worth as the whites who had so long oppressed them. Recent African literature is full of examples of authors wishing to break the domination of Western forms. Some, like Ngugi wa Thiongo, for a time gave up writing only in English. I was often frustrated in Lesotho in meetings where the Basotho refused to speak English, leaving me to swim or, as most often happened, sink. It was good for them and doubtlessly good for me. President Chissano of Mozambique set an example for his fellow leaders by giving his address at the July 2004 meeting of the African Union in Swahili rather than a European language.

Ultimately, the real challenge is to break the power of the elite, an **elite** that has perpetuated itself through an educational system that kept its supporters in power and prevented outsiders from gaining access to the rewards of an open society. I have said before and now say again that the political and military ferment across Africa is due largely to the desire of the marginal to break the power of those in charge. Much of the warfare in Africa today is, sadly, very destructive. Yet the impulse behind both war and crime is the desire to correct the imbalance of an elite that took quick advantage of independence, created its patron-client networks, and in so doing ensured the survival not only of itself but of its progeny in perpetuity. It has often been said that only the disadvantaged can break their chains of oppression. They are doing it all across Africa, and it is up to all of us who care for the long-term future of Africa to help them do it in constructive ways so that when they win—and win they will—they do not become the next generation of oppressors.

CHAPTER SIX. DEMOGRAPHIC SHIFTS

The size and distribution of populations in the countries where I worked have changed dramatically in the course of my forty-two years in Africa. Currently, there are countries where population growth is a problem, while in others declining population may become a problem in the near future. Population changes also come when people tend to go where they think they can find a good living, which creates a serious problem when no good living is to be had. The current demographic change that bodes most ill for Africa's future is the loss of its most actively productive people to HIV/AIDS.

Yet the problem is not so much demographic shifts as it is population changes that undercut efforts at improving life at the local, regional, or national level. Not only does AIDS reduce the supply of able-bodied productive adults, but urbanization and migration often move such adults from the places where they are needed for economic survival, particularly in productive sectors such as subsistence farming. Forced movements of peoples due to war further diminish a society's ability to support itself and make it more dependent on external assistance.

1960s aerial view of Liberian village

In this chapter I draw for the most part from personal experience over several years of work in Liberia, Lesotho, South Africa, and Botswana. I refer to other countries only when describing how their struggle with problems of population growth and decline continues to block development.

6.1 Population growth.

In Lesotho, South Africa, and Botswana, population growth in the last century continued at a steady rate of between 2 percent and 3 percent per year, but the rate is likely to slow down and even turn negative due to deaths from HIV/AIDS. Rough estimates of the drop in life expectancy indicate that, whereas people born in 1990 could look forward to more than sixty years of life, now the figure is nearer forty. Most southern African countries have escaped the horrors of war, which is an everyday worry across much of the rest of the continent, but they have their own war to fight against an enemy far more insidious. Every day almost 2,000 people in the three most southern countries in Africa become infected with the virus, and about 800 people die daily, according to calculations based on UNAIDS estimates. Life expectancy in Lesotho in 2004, according to the World Health Organization, is now only thirtsix years, whereas in the late 1990s life expectancy was a more encouraging fifty-one years (UNAIDS, July 2004).

The pandemic is not so great—yet—that the population has actually begun decreasing, but it could happen in the future. According to sociologists Barnett and Whiteside, sometime in 2003, Botswana, South Africa, and Zimbabwe should have negative growth rates of 0.1 percent to 0.3 percent (Barnett and Whiteside 2002:

177). In 2001, 2.2 million people died in Africa from AIDS; of these AIDS deaths, 360,000 occurred in South Africa (www.avert.org/subadeaths.htm). AIDS was the cause of 8.7 percent of all deaths in South Africa in 2001 (www.unaidstts.org/news/news_details.cfm?newsId'100).

What is of more significance than absolute numbers is the selective mortality of people in their economically productive years. There are already many families in Lesotho consisting of elderly grandmothers and orphaned children, a phenomenon widely reported in the southern African region. In early 2003, the representative of the United Nations Development Programme in Lesotho Scholastica Kimarya estimated that as many as one out of every five children in Lesotho has already become an orphan, largely due to AIDS (allafrica.com/stories/200301190087.html). Orphans are considered to be children under fifteen who have lost either both parents or a mother to AIDS. Estimates in July 2004 are 100,000 orphans in Lesotho (New York Times, 20 July 2004).

Lesotho has a long tradition, built around the cultural homogeneity of this single-language nation, of helping those who need help. In particular, the Basotho are accustomed to grandparents raising their grandchildren. Until 2000, enough people had incomes that allowed them to support destitute relatives and friends, but when the there are more orphans than there are grandparents or other relatives to care for them, trouble is inevitable.

What is most worrisome is that the ratio of potential aid-givers to those who are in need of help may slip below unity, implying that there would be more people who cannot feed themselves than those who can help out. We know that each migrant worker, who for more than a century helped make South Africa's gold industry possible, helps roughly ten other people. Between 1995 and 2000, the number of miners (out of a national population of roughly two million) has dropped from about 120,000 to just 60,000, implying that more than half a million Basotho have potentially lost their source of support. Of course, some have found other jobs, but in most cases the jobs are poorly rewarded and often temporary. The number of miners continues to decline, with an annual loss of mining jobs of about 5 percent (Central Bank of Lesotho 2001:27).

South Africa and Botswana face different problems. Both countries have self-generating economies, unlike Lesotho whose economy is almost totally dependent on South Africa. The question for South Africa and Botswana is whether they can continue to create employment for the roughly half million people who enter the job market each year. Subsistence farming has reached its limit in both countries, just as it has in Lesotho, which means finding more work for those who must enter the job market. The Congress of South African Trade Unions (COSATU) and the South African Communist Party continue to battle with their partner, the African National Congress, to find the best way to make the economy expand and thus create more jobs.

The situation in Liberia is quite different. According to Northwestern University economist Clower's estimate, it once had steady population growth, starting at a population of 1.0 million in 1960 and growing to 2.1 million by 1984, using Liberian census figures. Had the 1989-1996 civil war not taken place and the growth rate remained steady at about 3.1 percent per annum, the population in 1998 would have approached 3.2 million. United Nations surveys, according to Liberian demographer Al-Hassan Conteh, suggest a much smaller than expected population in existence in 1998 of about 2.7 million. The World Gazetteer estimates the population in Liberia at about 2.8 million in 2003. Estimates are that 200,000 died during the war, accounting for about 40 percent of the deficit. The remaining shortfall is likely due to disease and a declining birth rate.

United Nations surveys suggest that 700,000 Liberians were still displaced as refugees outside the country in 1998. The U.N. High Commission on Refugees estimates that at the end of the year 2000 the numbers were reduced. There were approximately 124,000 Liberian refugees in Guinea; 118,000 in Côte d'Ivoire; 9,000 in Ghana; 7,000 in Sierra Leone; and, remarkably, almost 11,000 in the United States. According to Amnesty International's 2003 Annual Report, "By the end of 2002, there were an estimated 130,000 internally displaced people in established camps, while another 200,000 remained in conflict areas where humanitarian access was severely restricted."

6.2 Refugees and displaced persons.

After the elections of 1997, people in Liberia's rural areas tried to return to some degree of self-sufficiency, but both the damaged infrastructure left by the war and the ongoing threat of more fighting made such efforts difficult. The U.N. High Commission for Refugees said that in 1999, of the 110,000 internally displaced Liberians 13,000 had returned to rural areas, which at least was a step toward righting the imbalance. Unfortunately by late 2003 many of those returnees have surely fled their villages once again to seek refuge from the militias which continue to devastate the country.

Displaced persons camp in Liberia

Some people from the interior attempted to sell foodstuffs at various markets around the country, including in Monrovia, but the amount was insignificant in comparison with the need.

When I visited it in 2001 the country was desperately in need of food assistance. In 2004, the food shortage is even more dire. The number of markets I saw on the periphery of Monrovia has reduced as less food comes from the interior. Moreover, humanitarian organizations may refuse to distribute food to Liberia due to political instability and danger to aid workers. By 2002, the number of people needing food had quadrupled to about 250,000. World Food Program Country Representative, Justin Bagirishya, said in late April 2003, "If there is no security guarantee minimizing the risks of further attacks, it will be impossible for further assistance" (UN Integrated Regional Information Networks/All Africa Global Media via COMTEX). November 2003 BBC reports indicate that the food shortage has become even worse.

To make the situation worse, Liberian exiles in Guinea and Côte d'Ivoire are not allowed to work. Few of them have been allowed to make farms, so that they too are dependent on food aid. In addition, there are tens of thousands of refugees from Sierra Leone in various camps in northern Liberia. Moreover, the border trade with neighboring countries has all but stopped because of the ongoing fighting in Liberia and within its three immediate neighbors. In short, the humanitarian situation is disastrous. Most displaced people are located where they cannot really help themselves or the national economy, and the population movements have left almost everyone involved in a worse condition than they were before the war.

Humanitarian assistance has played a vital role in disaster areas such as Liberia. I have seen it also help in Ethiopia and Uganda. Yet I have serious questions concerning the effectiveness and benefits brought by such aid, even though it keeps people alive. Humanitarian aid can in some cases prolong a disaster, though it may ameliorate the problem in the short run. Aid can also be used wrongly, either by the donor or by the recipient.

During the Liberian civil war, generous donors contributed food, clothing, and money for internal refugees. Evidence soon emerged that warlords had looted the food supplies and had used them for their soldiers. The soldiers did not receive a salary; rather, they stole in order to survive. In 1997, some donors decided it was better not to give aid than to have it misused, a decision supported by refugees in Tubmanburg in northern Liberia. Tubmanburg residents decided they would be safer and better able to support themselves if they were not the recipients of tempting, easily stolen aid. In 2003, LURD rebels attacked refugee camps just outside Monrovia in order to steal food aid, furthering the unwillingness of donor agencies to distribute food to those in need.

Additionally, refugee camps scattered across much of West Africa are engines for underdevelopment. Thousands of Liberians now living in places such as Danane in Côte d'Ivoire, a village I visited in 1959 under better circumstances, could be given land and tools so they can feed themselves. Instead, the xenophobia that has twisted the minds and hearts of many in Côte d'Ivoire has made if difficult for refugees to do anything for themselves, causing them to become permanent charity cases.

It is not just in Liberia where Africans continue to be displaced from their homes. The United Nations High Commission for Refugees (UNHCR) estimated in June 2003 that it was serving the needs of 4.6 million people in Africa alone. They come from the West African forest zone, the great lakes region of East Africa, the Democratic Republic of Congo, Sudan, and the horn of Africa. There are refugees in other areas as well. The numbers fleeing Zimbabwe are increasing rapidly, for example. In some places the situation is improving, such as in Angola, which is now at peace after decades of fighting.

The UNHCR is committed only to helping people who have crossed international boundaries in order to escape hunger, disease, war, persecution, and disaster. Yet many displaced people never leave their own countries. Monrovia is crowded with Liberians who fled fighting near their homes for the relative security of the capital. Before the death of Savimbi, Luanda hosted many who had escaped the horrors of war in the Angolan interior.

The Red Cross and Red Crescent, the World Food Programme, and many NGOs have responded to the needs of displaced persons. People who must flee their homes simply cannot grow anything of their own, and thus they must be fed. Yet these agencies do not always merely provide food to those suffering famine, as so often has happened in rural Ethiopia. Efforts have been made in some refugee camps for self-reliant development. This is especially necessary in cases where the second generation of refugees finds no hope of ever returning home. There is a huge refugee camp at Kakuma in northern Kenya where tens of thousands of southern Sudanese make their homes and wait for eventual peace. Many have been resettled in the

United States, particularly the famous "Lost Boys," but most wait...and wait.

The displaced do not just seek safety and survival in refugee camps or in cities. Some take the more drastic step of fleeing their countries, even fleeing Africa, to find better economic and social conditions. In my research with the Southern African Migration Project, I studied the situation of cross-border economic migrants in South Africa. These migrants come from Mozambique and Zimbabwe out of desperation. They cross the border illegally, often risking the dangers of wild animals in South Africa's Kruger Park or the crocodiles invisible in the muddy waters of the Limpopo River. Many make it across the border safely only to be found and sent back home, where they often turn around and cross again the next day. Many find homes with friends or relatives in South Africa and disappear from sight; their success encourages comrades sent back home to try yet again.

Economic migrants enter South Africa from much more distant corners of Africa. I spent an evening in Johannesburg in 1999 with a group of West Africans. They were concentrated in the Hillbrow section of the city, and I was told that some run-down hotels were almost exclusively occupied by Nigerians. Many were legitimately qualified immigrants, examples of South Africa's "brain gain," but others had come in illegally. I remember listening to one such Nigerian at the airport in Johannesburg arguing his right to enter the country. I fear he was sent back, because it sounded as if he did not have a case that could convince a tough-minded immigration officer.

The ultimate goal for many Africans is Europe or America. In our 1997 survey we asked Basotho where they would like to live if they could leave their home and where they realistically expected they would be able to live. Realistic expectations concentrated on South Africa and Botswana. But the dream for many was to escape Africa entirely. Forty percent of respondents in a survey of educated Basotho hoped to move to South Africa and another 32 percent to Botswana, but a solid 23 percent said they look forward to getting out of Africa entirely. This was not a typical population, but it does show a strong desire for a better life found away from the struggles in Lesotho.

Continuing to reach the headlines are stories about economic migrants who try to find their way to Europe across the Mediterranean. In June 2003, at least three thousand African refugees reached the shores of Lampedusa, an Italian island not far from the Libyan shore. One ship sank with about two hundred people on board. Packed onto overcrowded, unseaworthy ships were people from North, West and Central Africa as well as from the Middle East. The Italians have been divided in their response. Some open their hearts and share their resources, while the xenophobic Minister for Reforms, Umberto Bossi, tried to stop migrants from making the dangerous journey in the first place.

Many also attempt the dangerous crossing from the Spanish enclaves of Melilla and Ceuta on the Moroccan coast. Spain does its best to stop these migrants and has camps where refugees are detained until they can be sent back to Africa. The migrants often pay high prices—in 2001 as high as $1,500—for a boat journey that ultimately may or may not get them to their cherished destination.

6.3 Urbanization.

Urbanization is another form of migration. Even during our time in Liberia in the 1960s and 1970s, there was a steady drift toward the city; Monrovia was much larger when we left than when we arrived. This drift to Monrovia turned into a flood in the course of the civil war, so that Monrovia's population rose from about 100,000 in 1975 to roughly a million by 1997. An estimated additional half million people fled into exile during the war, mostly into neighboring West African countries, so that overall the rural population of Liberia dropped from a million in 1962 to just 700,000 in 1997.

Monrovia in the 1960s

The population of Liberia in 2003 is about 2.8 million, of whom 1.3 million live in greater Monrovia (www.world-gazetteer.com/c/c_lr.htm). In 2003, tens of thousands of refugees crowded into camps in and around Monrovia, so that the city I saw in late 2001 has become even more crowded than what I remember.

The massive over-population of Monrovia is due in part to foreign assistance. If there were no food aid for the city, it is quite likely that some, perhaps many, would die, but it is also likely that many would return to depopulated rural villages where there is at least the possibility of growing something to feed their families. There is no municipal electricity, not enough water, and an increasing rubbish and waste problem in the city. Certainly the incidence of disease in Monrovia is growing, and the medical system is not able to cope. One of the goals of the new interim government is to persuade as many people as possible to return to their rural homes, where they may find survival more possible.

And yet I certainly would not want to go home to a rural village where civil war and starvation are ever-present threats. Forcing people to return to their rural villages is often inhuman, and except in desperate circumstances I cannot support it. I have seen the results of forced resettlement in Ethiopia, and not all were good. Yet voluntary resettlement can work, provided people make their own decision to move and are given the means to do it. Much of rural Liberia is now empty of people, leaving the still-surviving logging companies to destroy the forest cover as fast as they can. If the war was to end and people were settled in these areas, with schools and medical facilities available, they could do something for themselves. As it is, they are becoming perpetual victims of international charity.

Monrovia has always been a singularly unproductive city, if productivity is measured in hard economic terms. Even before the civil war there were very few viable enterprises: a fish processing company, a cement factory, a paint factory, a brewery, and a bottling plant, and they had declined during the regime of Samuel Doe. The owner of the paint factory was one of the first people shot by Doe once he finished disemboweling President Tolbert. Some of Monrovia's other commercial ventures at the time were import-export businesses, managing the shipment of iron ore, rubber, timber, and bringing in consumer goods, including rice, which was not grown in sufficient quantities in the interior. There is far less business activity in Monrovia today. The only significant enterprise to continue unscathed during and after the war was the brewery, which all sides in the conflict relied on to give them a bit of comfort during the dark days of fighting.

A friend who read this paragraph asked me the obvious question: why does Monrovia exist at all? The answer is that it exists mainly for political reasons. Not only is it the final refuge for the displaced who flee the war, but it is the center for important patron-client networks. It is in Monrovia that the negotiations for power take place, and any politician who in better times was "exiled" to other areas in the country is now out of the loop. Additionally, in a normal free market economy, one would expect the economic nodes of power to co-exist with the political nodes. That has not been the case in Liberia, because economic clout has always been exercised from outside the country, working through politicians as their clients—the very clients who then become the patrons for the rest of the country.

Yet this disconnect between foreign economic clout and on-the-ground economic reality was part of what made Monrovia a vital city. It was a main port of entry for dollars and dollar-based products into West Africa. Even during the civil war the Free Port of Monrovia was a locus of economic activities, which were often connected with support of the forces of the Economic Community of West Africa as it tried to keep the peace. The port and foreign soldiers helped create a parallel economy for many of the people who crowded into the city without visible means of support. It is still the only port of entry into Liberia for food and humanitarian supplies. Gyude Bryant, chairman of the interim government, can draw on his extensive experience importing and exporting through the port, and for that reason alone may be the right person for the job.

There is no way Monrovia can produce enough food for even a small proportion of its citizens, and it is clear that a service, economy as opposed to a productive economy had to dominate if people were to survive. Even when its population was a tenth of what it is now, the city relied on imported rice and some fruits and vegetables from the interior. The surrounding countryside is sandy and infertile; the richer forest soils begin about twenty kilometers into the interior. Not only can Monrovia residents not grow food for themselves, but they cannot find employment that allows them to buy food.

Food market in peri-urban Monrovia

Urban growth in southern Africa is a quite different phenomenon. Gaborone, the capital of Botswana, is one example. In 1971 it had only about 60,000 residents. It had grown greatly by the time I lived there in 1982-84, and in 2003, according to the World Gazetteer its population had grown to 195,000. The total population of Botswana is 1.76 million. Maseru in Lesotho is another example, having grown from 37,000 at independence in 1966 to 174,000 in 2003. The greater Maseru area is estimated to have more than 250,000 residents.

While apartheid was still the rule in South Africa, blacks were not allowed to live in the cities unless they could demonstrate they were making useful contributions to the lives of whites. Otherwise, they were required to live in the so-called "homelands." Once apartheid ended, the floodgates were opened. Blacks began to move in large numbers to urban areas if they had work and to squatter

Apartheid relocation in South Africa

settlements if they were without employment or other resources. For many who had been previously forced into rural homelands, the city was the only way ahead, since they had no land and no work where they lived. Many had once had fields, but they had been taken away during the period of land grabbing by whites, who had been granted control over 83 percent of South African land despite being just 17 percent of the population.

As a result, in a situation quite different from that in Lesotho and Botswana, the 1990s was a time of rapid, yet marginally supportable, urban growth in South Africa. Those who moved into Gaborone and Maseru were able to find land and build modest houses, whereas South African squatter settlements are inhumane and shocking. And in Maseru there are jobs to be found for those fortunate enough to work in the textile factories. There are almost no "slums" in either Gaborone or Maseru, while they are ever-present in the areas surrounding Johannesburg, Pretoria, Cape Town, and Durban. On this basis, I was able to say in the Sechaba Consultants report on poverty in 2000 that Lesotho's poverty was in no way comparable to that in the worst of South Africa's shanty towns. Factories are being built in South Africa that can hire some who crowd the cities. Yet, in general, the numbers of urban migrants in the region greatly exceed the available work.

The question then remains: what is the developmental impact of urban growth in Botswana, Lesotho, and South Africa? Urban growth is inevitable, is necessary and, in the end, is probably useful. There may be negative effects in the short run, since people who cannot find work in the cities might have done better to stay in their rural homes. This is probably true for some families, but overall the families that have moved to towns are doing better for themselves and are also doing something useful for the country. It must not be forgotten that the situation in southern Africa is totally different from the situation in Liberia, where urbanization is an almost total disaster.

Why is this so? The main reason is that rural subsistence agriculture is unproductive in all three southern African countries. In Lesotho I saw small-scale, rural dry-land farming become less productive each year. I saw the same situation in Botswana during parts of three farming seasons in the early 1980s. In addition to what I've seen with my own eyes, there are reports confirming that the only really productive rural agriculture in South Africa is done by large-scale commercial farmers. Farming increasingly has become a science and is no longer an art practiced by rural people such as those I knew in Gbansu in Liberia.

Not only are there few prospects for making a living on small rural holdings southern Africa, but job prospects and good social services are only likely to be found in the towns and cities. People know this and move in large numbers to where they can find schools for their children, clinics for their sick, and jobs for the adults. Obviously many fail to find these services, but enough succeed that the prospect is attractive.

Yet I do not want to be misunderstood. Some people like farming and are good at it. I remember two farmers in the village of Qalaheng in Lesotho. They had identical fields next to each other of the same size and soil quality. One man produced more than a hundred bags of maize on his field, while the other got only about two bags. Why? The second man explained. He said that the first man, Mooqo Moqomisa, worked hard, very hard, but he himself, however, was simply not prepared to put in that effort. In my experience not more than about 5 percent of rural farmers have any interest in the hard year-round effort required to get anything out of the exhausted rural soil in Lesotho. Let the 5 percent remain if they want to; they can be productive, even on the worst and most depleted soils. As for the 95 percent, they do not want to farm, they do not do it well, and there are no jobs for them in the rural areas. The towns are saturated, and job opportunities are scarce. One alternative is for them to rent their land to good farmers and then work as day laborers on what is really their own land. This is already happening, but is clearly not ideal.

Oxen plowing in Lesotho

There is another sense in which I do not want to be misunderstood. Certainly subsistence agriculture, under the right conditions, is essential to national survival. Those conditions, however, simply do not exist in rural Lesotho, rural South Africa or rural Botswana. They may, however, exist in peri-urban areas, provided households can acquire land holdings of about 800 to 1000 square meters. For example, greater Maseru has become a large agricultural village. Even though there may be 250,000 inhabitants, I would guess that the majority live on sites where urban farming can be practiced. All that urban farmers need is fencing, water, and weekend time available for cultivation. Lesotho, similar to certain parts of South Africa, receives reasonably good rainfall. Water can be stored in inexpensive ferro-cement tanks, big plastic water tanks, and small backyard dams. Not everyone does so, but they can. Water is also available through the municipal system, though some complain that purified water should not be used for crops.

Lesotho's urban residents and land owners have by and large responded positively to rural people's choice to move to the towns and to their demands for large house sites. Some in the officialdom of Lesotho complain that good agricultural land is being taken out of production by the progressive cutting of fields into house sites. I claim this is not true, and in fact most of these same officials agree with me in practice by acquiring sites from the very fields that they claim should be allowed to remain intact. I do not know the situation in Botswana in recent years, although I know that rural dry-land farming is very unproductive. As for South Africa, allowing people to settle on tiny plots without any potential for urban agriculture seems to be a serious mistake. And yet even these tiny plots are now showing signs of very intensive urban gardening, as people begin to realize that even with only a few square meters something can grow.

Urban growth can be a good and useful thing. In countries torn by war like Liberia, however, it leads to disaster. In South Africa, not enough thought is being given to large-scale urban planning, whereby families can have plots large enough to allow them to grow at least part of what they need to survive. One missing factor is a water policy that uses run-off or recycled water for urban economic activity, including farming and small business. One resource that Lesotho has in abundance is gravity, and that resource can be used to collect and store water for the irrigation of urban plots.

6.4 Migrant labor.

By horse to the mines

Migrant labor has been a dominant feature of the economy of many African countries. Lesotho has built a national way of life out of migrant labor, beginning in the last quarter of the nineteenth century. Men went to the newly-opened gold mines in South Africa, first to trade their grain and animals and then to work. The Basotho have been part of the money economy since that time, and their "peasant" status has declined year by year. The underlying reasons for the shift "from granary to labor reserve," as British anthropologist Colin Murray put it, are that South Africa needed cheap black labor, while at the same time fields in Lesotho were exhausted from over cropping (Lye and Murray:136ff).

Migration in Lesotho skipped the internal stage, namely a migration from rural to urban areas within national borders, that some experts claim must always precede international migration. There were no urban areas to migrate to in Lesotho until after independence in 1966. Instead, people in all parts of Lesotho were recruited for South Africa's gold mines, and to a lesser extent for farms and the railway; the only significant correlation with the type of person being chosen for recruitment was his distance to the nearest South African railway station. And once airplane travel to the mountains became common, recruitment from remote airstrips was as common as recruitment from lowland centers adjacent to the border.

The effect of migrant labor from Lesotho to South Africa has been mixed. Without the gold mines, it is clear that Lesotho would not have received the massive injections of cash that have made it a lower middle-income African country. Yet migration has caused great harm to domestic life. Marriages were unstable, because husbands could only come home at rare intervals (Gay 1980). The 1990s were better, because men could make monthly visits home, but before that time men stayed away for up to a year at a time. The trip home was often difficult and costly, and men often waited until they had accumulated enough money to buy cattle to bring back to the village.

Furthermore, life in the single-sex mine hostels was grim and even inhuman. Dozens were crammed into the same large dormitory room, often sleeping in three layer cubicles built against the wall. Men found prostitutes or even second wives in the vicinity of the mine for sexual relief and often sought male partners within the mine compound.

Conditions in the mines were marked not only by the grim hostel life, but also by the dangerous and difficult work underground. Even today, mine accidents are frequent, and men are often killed on duty. Before the National Union of Mineworkers was able to exercise some control over mine conditions, those who were seriously injured in the apartheid era were sent back to Lesotho with minimal compensation. In 1976, I rode into the remote mountains in a mine-management Land Rover that was bringing a disabled miner back to his family. The compensation given to the man was minimal, and the white men driving the car felt very pleased with themselves for giving him a free ride home. That he was permanently disabled did not seem to bother them.

Botswana had less migrant labor than Lesotho, although men did leave that country for the mines. One reason why there was less migration was that the Batswana were more involved with their cattle, cattle which even today remain far more profitable there than in Lesotho. Yet those men who did migrate, mainly to the mines, suffered in all the same ways as the Basotho.

Migrant labor was also a pattern among South Africans, particularly before the end of apartheid. Both men and women were allowed to work in the white areas, provided they could get the proper certificates. They were not allowed to bring their "superfluous appendages," as South African law described their families, and so could rarely have a decent family life. Women who worked as domestic servants were separated from the rest of their families, and some could not even go home on weekends, since the "madams" wanted them to be on duty seven days a week. They lived in tiny servants' quarters at the back of the houses. When their men visited them at night it was strictly illegal, and often both men and women were arrested for contravening the Group Areas Act.

The ultimate symbol of apartheid was the pass people had to carry to show their right to be where they were found. We were still in Liberia at the time of the Sharpeville massacre in 1960 in which sixty-nine people were killed when South African police opened fire on demonstrators in a protest instigated by the decision of women to burn their passes. I remember the unfeeling conservatism of one of our young priests at Cuttington who saw no reason for us to protest something as far away as in South Africa. He felt we should attend to our own business. At the time we did not know that we would one day play a role in fighting apartheid from inside Lesotho.

The devastation that apartheid imposed on South African society is obvious and widely known. What must not be forgotten in the present context is that migrant labor was one of the principal supports of the white economy, and that the blacks who were at the heart of the migrant system got almost nothing out of it but misery.

Migrant labor in Liberia was a very different experience, occurring mostly in the rubber plantations. At first this onerous task was imposed on rural village men through the iniquitous forced labor system, which ensured that some men were also taken out of Liberia and forced onto the cocoa plantations of Fernando Po. Later, migration to the rubber plantations became voluntary and migration to Fernando Po was stopped (Sundiata: 58ff). Tapping rubber became a way for men to earn something toward the provision of their households and the education of their children. It remained throughout its history, however, an exploitative and demeaning system.

Migration to the towns and cities was not common in the early history of Liberia. As people became more educated and wanted opportunities for their families that rural villages could not provide, rural to urban movement became more common. Our research in Gbansu in 1974 revealed that a surprising number of Gbansu citizens were living in Monrovia. The pattern was the same in Lesotho and Botswana, where the cities have grown rapidly. South Africa, however, did not allow such movement until apartheid had died.

Movement to Monrovia, and to a lesser extent other towns, was a home-grown and probably inevitable phenomenon up to the time of the civil war. Villages in the bush lost their skilled and educated people, so that rural subsistence life grew more and more dependent on the less skilled, the women, and the old folks. It was the rare person who succeeded in school or at a job who was also willing to go back to the village and assist in development.

The civil war changed all that. People fled from the attacking militias, knowing full well that if they stayed to meet them they could be killed or severely injured. Their possessions were stolen, including even the rice that remained to be harvested on their farms. All the animals were killed and eaten, and houses were torched. The civil war created a forced march out of the firing line and into safe havens. There was internal displacement for those who remained in Liberia and external flight for those who left the country. The result was the de-population of the hinterland and the creation of swollen cities and refugee camps. It could not be called migrant labor, since there was no work to be found.

6.5 Brain drain and labor export.

During the period from 1980 to 2003 in Liberia, the great majority of people with marketable skills left the country; most left Africa entirely. I fear that in the end what we accomplished at Cuttington University College was the preparation of graduates sufficiently well qualified to escape the dreary and life-destroying consequences of remaining in Liberia. We inadvertently supplied skilled workers to the job markets of Europe and America.

That was not our original intention, though in retrospect we might have realized what we were doing. I was Dean of Instruction for my first two years at Cuttington, and I remember being determined that the education we provided would be on a par with that of any good small American liberal arts college. In particular, I pressed for the maintenance of standards, so that our graduates could enter graduate school in the United States without fear of failure.

I like to think that we achieved our goal, though in the end the goal may have been counter-productive for Liberia, since our graduates are in senior positions in the United States. One is a dean at Rutgers University. Another is a senior member of the political science department at the University of the South. A third is an award-winning journalist in the Washington area. A fourth has built a distinguished ecumenical career in the church, first in Africa and then internationally, and is now rector of a church in the United States. A fifth is a senior administrator of the music department of the University of Arizona. There are many other examples. Unfortunately, those few Liberians able to afford escape from West Africa are the very ones whose abilities were most needed. They are the elite who had good jobs and enough money in the bank or under their mattresses to leave. There are tens of thousands of Liberians in the United States; the majority are either citizens or have long-term residence permits.

Between 15,000 and 20,000 Liberian expatriates are eligible for what the U.S. government calls Temporary Protected Status (U.S. Department of Justice, September 2002). They are desperately trying to have this status changed to a permanent one. They were allowed to remain while the civil war continued, but once the election of 1997 confirmed that the war was over, they were expected to return home. Few want to, for obvious reasons. In addition to the continuing threat of war, there are almost no social services in Liberia. Many lost their homes and investments and would find it difficult, however qualified they may be, to get permanent jobs and to settle into stable communities. Only in late 2003 are a few skilled Liberians beginning to return home, with the hope that the Bryant government will make life bearable again.

They and people like them must return if the country is ever to make a fresh start, and yet they believe, no doubt correctly, that if they do return they will be shunted aside or perhaps harmed or even killed. On the other hand, the United States benefits greatly from their presence, because most of them are well-educated, able-bodied, and able to fit into the American economy in the same way as those with green cards and citizenship papers.

I find it difficult to give examples of those trained at Cuttington who stayed in Liberia. They are there, and some are performing important services to the country, but there are not enough of them. Unfortunately, they also include the former director of Liberia's police and a financial advisor to Charles Taylor who was thrown out of South Africa for corrupt dealings in oil (www.chico.mweb.co.za/mg/news/98sep2/15sep-liberia_shaw.html).

Another example of the civil war brain drain from Liberia is two Basotho friends who have returned to Lesotho. They moved to Liberia in 1970 to attend Cuttington University College; one became a medical doctor and the other a school principal, and both planned to remain indefinitely, thinking that their prospects in Liberia were better than in the beleaguered Lesotho. Both fled from Liberia on the last available plane before the airport at Robertsfield was overrun by Charles Taylor's army in June 1990. They are now contributing to Lesotho's national growth.

I do not blame those who remain outside Liberia. If I were in their shoes, I would not return until I was sure that some degree of economic normality had been restored. I most admire the good people who remained in Liberia; what is sobering is the difficulty I have had in locating such people—people who could help rebuild Liberian society. At Cuttington we made it easy for our graduates to find good jobs abroad, because we taught them well. We assisted in colonizing their minds, and we gave them the skills to be more than just subaltern representatives of foreign powers.

Liberian graduates

Fixed permanently in my mind is an image from December 1959, at the dance the night before graduation. Except for the smell of the tropical night and the presence of ragged children from the nearby village hoping that some chicken bones might be thrown their way, we could have been at any graduation ball in the United States. The students were dressed impeccably in suits and ball gowns; some were even in evening clothes. This was a time when President Tubman only received daytime guests in striped trousers and morning coat and evening guests in full formal attire. Our students knew how to fit into that society, including those who had grown up in the village that had sent its barefoot children to beg for scraps. The graduates dancing that night (and giving bones to the children) were the leaders we had hoped would bring Liberia into full democracy, economic growth, and rural development.

I am very happy that at least some have remained at home. I rejoice at the commitment of Dr. Walter

Gwenigale to Phebe Hospital, at the willingness of Abioseh Flemister to leave her family in the United States in order to serve as a priest in Côte d'Ivoire and then in Liberia, at the devotion of Dr. Melvin Mason, and then Dr. Henrique Tokpa, who undertook the heart-breaking task of rebuilding Cuttington, at the dedication of Edward Yarkpazua in bringing Lutheran World Relief food and tools to rural people in his native Lofa County, and at the honesty of Varni Sherman in maintaining the integrity of the legal system. Nonetheless, I realize that only a few broke the easy mold they could have fallen into by remaining in the United States.

I have described the Liberian situation at some length because I know the details. What has happened in Lesotho is not greatly different. We have traced graduates of local tertiary institutions and found that many have gone to South Africa to work. A 1998 survey found that two-thirds of the professionals interviewed by us at Sechaba Consultants have given at least some thought to moving to another country to work, indicating South Africa and Botswana as their most likely destinations (Gay 1999: Tables 6, 7). More than half feel it likely they will move within two years (Gay 1999: Table 9).

The Lesotho government has given generous bursaries for study outside the country. It is no surprise that many of them have remained out of the country and have even refused to repay the loans they were given to supplement the bursaries. There are very few Basotho medical doctors within the official government system. Those remaining in the country work for a time for the Ministry of Health and then tend to drift into private practice. Estimates are that half of those fully qualified as doctors are working outside the country. The same is true of nurses. In 1989, the National Health Training Centre reported that its graduates were going to South Africa to work rather than remain in frustrating circumstances in Lesotho (*Work for Justice* 22:10).

The brain drain is not necessarily a bad thing if professionals remain within the region. I see Lesotho in effect as part of South Africa, and I expect that relation to be formalized within the next ten years or so. Thus, I am not too upset when Basotho doctors, teachers, lawyers, or accountants find better-paying jobs next door. I am actually more upset that qualified Basotho are not willing to work in remote rural areas, whether in Lesotho or in South Africa. They want the bright lights and prospect of promotion afforded by living in the cities. As a result, doctors from tropical African countries take the jobs in the Lesotho interior. The brain drain from Nigeria, Ghana, Sudan, Kenya, Uganda, and Tanzania leads to Lesotho, where conditions are distinctly better than at home. They are in turn replaced by skilled people from still poorer countries. Overall, Africa loses its best and brightest, just as Liberia has lost the graduates from Cuttington who made us so proud. The negative impact is lessened somewhat by the willingness of Africans from other countries to fill posts left vacant through the brain drain to South Africa and abroad. But the balance remains negative, and the decline in Africa that is the theme of this book continues unabated.

6.6 The effect of convenient transport.

Even in the distant past, getting from here to there in Africa was possible, including to and from the remote corners of the continent. According to my friends in Gbansu, the bush trails that still exist in Liberia allow people to walk long distances; they were never totally isolated. Whether people were forced to march

Bush trail in Liberia

with rice to the coast, or they walked voluntarily to take jobs at the Firestone Rubber Plantation, the trails were there. Graham Greene's wonderful book *Journey without Maps* (Greene 1936), which is still perhaps the best single introduction to the totality of Liberia, tells of his trip from the Sierra Leone border to the Liberian coast circa 1933. He and his cousin found it possible in the course of several weeks to cover a large portion of the interior without benefit of motor roads.

Lesotho also had routes accessible on foot or on horseback leading into the remotest parts of the mountains. And even before the Basotho entered the country, the Bushmen knew the mountains well and had established settlements throughout them.

Yet the most remarkable story of pre-modern migration, which I encountered in southwestern Tanzania, is the one often told about the Ngoni trek in the early nineteenth century. The villagers along the Songwe River, which forms the border with Malawi and Zambia, still know by fearsome repute the story of the fierce Ngoni warriors. They know the story of how the Ngoni burned their villages and raped their women, and how some remained behind to marry the women they had raped, while others moved on. That the Ngoni covered in a few years a distance on foot equal to half the length of the continent, from the coast of Natal as far as Lake Victoria, shows that migration does not have to occur at a glacial pace.

My point is not that modern transport has utterly changed the African landscape, with its tarred roads and overcrowded mini-buses; instead, it is that modern transport has greatly speeded up the process of migration. There were movements of peoples all the way back to the first proto-humans who spread out of Africa to cover the entire globe. Moshoeshoe I took several weeks on horseback with a missionary friend to make his first extended tour of the country (Arbousset 1991). Now, nowhere in Lesotho is more than a day's trip by car (in some places followed by a trip by horse) from the capital, Maseru. Now, a one-hour Mission Aviation mercy flight or Lesotho government helicopter ride will bring a visitor to any village in the country.

Lesotho Airways in mountains

The same is true of every part of the continent. David Livingstone wandered Botswana for several months before he finally discovered Lake Ngami in western Botswana, where the waters that drain much of southeastern Angola finally sink into the sands of the Kalahari. I was able to take a two-hour side trip by Land Rover from Maun, where I was doing research on small businesses, just to see the place and find out whether people were still able to catch fish and sell them to neighboring villages. Unfortunately, the lake was completely dry when I went there, but signs advertising fresh fish were still visible.

The obvious question for African development concerns the impact of vastly improved transport systems. The naive assumption is that the availability of roads and vehicles, not to mention planes and ships, has been of great benefit to Africa. This is clearly true if one accepts that commerce, education, health, Christian missions, and good government have benefited people who would otherwise not have shared in these improvements in their lives. I do not deny it.

But I must also point out the negative side of the transport systems. They have been instrumental in allowing all the changes I have discussed in this chapter. Historian Tenner, who has explained so clearly the idea of unexpected consequences which follow upon innovations, provides the key to understanding the very mixed blessing of good roads in Africa. He shows in many different contexts how good ideas do not always lead to good results (Tenner 1996).

Population growth has been accelerated by the provision of good medical care, education, and economic development, all of which have needed good roads and fast vehicles. Equally, the epidemics that have so hurt Africa are spread by available transport. The cholera epidemic that covered the continent apparently started when Guinean students flew home from the U.S.S.R. in 1970 and brought the disease with them (Stock 1976:36ff). The dependence of the current HIV/AIDS epidemic on transport systems has been well documented. In our research in 1996 in the mountains of Lesotho, we found an incidence of roughly 10 percent of HIV infection along the main mountain road. There were no cases in mountain villages far from the road.

Yet humanitarian responses to disaster are only possible through the new modes of transport. Before such transportation was available, victims of famine, flood, and war died more or less unnoticed. Most of the time, victims can move rapidly to centers where they can conveniently get food aid, but where they are unable to rebuild their lives. They remain as permanent refugees and must be fed forever. The worst-case scenario, however, is when roads are unsafe due to ongoing fighting, as is the case in Liberia, eastern Congo, and northern Uganda.

Urbanization would never have happened without a convenient way to link rural and urban areas. Even in pre-colonial days the rise of cities such as Timbuktu depended on convenient camel and boat travel in the Sahel. Today, the uncontrolled growth of slum areas around South Africa's major cities is an inevitable consequence of cheap mini-bus transport from the rural homes people have abandoned.

Clearly, migrant labor is only possible when good roads allow movement back and forth between the rural home and the urban workplace. Yet there is the negative consequence of families being divided between work and home. Another is the mounting rate of accidents, many of them fatal, on roads across Africa. Over and over, people are killed by speeding and overcrowded vehicles. We have lost friends on what are seemingly the best roads in South Africa and Lesotho. The same story is told everywhere where there is dependence on fast public transportation. Sub-Saharan Africa has more than ten times as many fatalities per vehicle as the developed

Bus near-accident in Lesotho

world (safety.fhwa.dot.gov/fourthlevel/chap2.htm). The annual fatality rate in the U.S., according to various websites, is between 1.8 and 3.0 fatalities per 10,000 vehicles, and many other nations have been accidental records than the US. There are frightening statistics from sub-Saharan Africa, however. Malawi and Togo head the list at 245. Relatively well-developed South Africa is still high at 16 fatalities per 10,000 vehicles. Furthermore, the brain drain moves mostly by road, but the brains are at great risk. The risk is exacerbated when people enter a new society and culture not familiar to them (www.roads.dft.gov.uk/roadsafety/research19/05.htm).

Demographic shifts are greatly magnified by the availability of road and vehicle networks. For good or for ill, today's Africa is what it is to a large extent because of convenient transport. But clearly the impact is not entirely beneficial, even though on balance the gains may outweigh the losses.

6.7 Hopeful signs.

There is strong evidence that higher education leads to smaller families. In this way **population growth** will tend to slow down as schooling becomes more widespread. There are still many poorly educated people across Africa, but where there is no war, more children are attending school than in earlier generations. One source of slowed population growth cannot be a source of joy, namely, the HIV/AIDS epidemic. But a hopeful side-effect of the anti-AIDS campaign will likely be a dramatic increase in the number of people using condoms, thus not only preventing HIV infection, but also limiting births.

Disaster assistance continues throughout the continent, and I cannot regret that. What I hope for, however, is more careful and selective use of food aid. Already the World Food Program has restricted its food donations in war areas. That may be a disaster for people caught in the middle, but it will also limit the ability of warlords to finance their armies with stolen food.

South Africa is one country where serious efforts are being made to coordinate and ameliorate **urban growth**. It is sad to hear of shacks being torn down, when they are built in the wrong places such as next to rivers that flood regularly. I have seen them, and I can support the seemingly Draconian policy of tearing them down. I have also been impressed with the quality of peri-urban housing projects in many parts of South Africa.

Lesotho is an even better model, because in that country urban growth does not mean the growth of slums. Individual home owners have plots sufficiently large to allow small vegetable gardens. In most cases, they can get full title to their land, though admittedly through quasi-legal means.

The end of apartheid in South Africa brought great improvement to the families of **migrant workers**. No longer are they prevented from bringing their families to visit or live with them, and no longer are they restricted to one visit home annually. Additionally, the research done through the Southern African Migration Project opened the way to more humane border controls.

Against common consensus regarding the **brain drain**, I think movement of skilled workers across borders to places where they can make a better living is a good thing. I do not think people should be restricted to working only where they grew up. Yet it is also a good thing that countries such as South Africa are improving the working conditions of professionals in order to respect their skills, experience, and training.

Transport systems are a mixed blessing in Africa. We are all pleased when we hear, for instance, that the Congo River is once again open to traffic, or that Mozambique and South Africa are linked by rail and high-speed toll road. But our pleasure must be supplemented by serious traffic control. I praise South Africa for being one of the first countries in the world to forbid the use of hand-held cell phones while driving, a restriction the United States is just getting around to implementing. I also praise South Africa for stringent laws against drunk driving. Finally, South Africa has instituted strict guidelines on the type, use, and maintenance of taxis, combis, and mini-buses. We all hope that such laws will spread across the continent to help curb the carnage taking place on Africa's roads.

CHAPTER SEVEN. RELIGIOUS CONFLICT

It has been said that Africans are incurably religious. That is probably true of all humanity, but since the Enlightenment, Europeans and Americans have tried to put the idea in doubt. Africa may not yet have reached a similar state of "enlightenment." Personally, I hope not. One Mosotho once told me that he had heard there were Americans who did not believe in God and wanted to know if such a thing could be true. I had to tell him the truth about the growing agnosticism and atheism in my home country.

But religion all too frequently has had a negative influence in sub-Saharan African societies. Too few people think that "what I believe" and "what you believe" can co-exist in peace or that people might even agree at levels too deep to comprehend In this chapter I consider local opposed to regional belief systems, divisions within the Christian community, the multiplication of missionary bodies, the African-initiated churches, relations with Islam, and finally, as a case study, the ubiquity of feasts and expensive celebrations among all religious groups.

7.1 Disparagement of local religious beliefs.

Religious beliefs everywhere are a curious mixture of the very private, the local, and the universal. The experience of God does not follow the rule books of any form of organized religion. I am a Christian, and I believe that God has spoken to me and guided me, and my family, over the years. I believe that God led us to Liberia and that God has continued to direct our ways. But that does not mean that God speaks to everyone in the same way. God makes the rules, and people learn the rules after the fact. We neither learn all the rules nor do we learn the exceptions, and so we try to impose our interpretations of the rules on God to make sure God does not surprise us by seeming to break them.

In what ways did Judy and I try to put God into a straitjacket? Early in our Liberian life, we went on Sundays after church to the tiny village of Plato-ta to teach Sunday school. We told Bible stories in a classic missionary fashion to a captive audience of children and a few adults who joined us in the thatch-roofed and open-sided "palaver house" to escape the hot sun and the boredom of a Sunday afternoon. Whose stories were we telling? Surely not our personal stories or the stories of the people to whom we were preaching. We were telling the great old stories—Moses and the Ten Commandments, David and the Ark of the Covenant, Jesus and the feeding of the five thousand, Paul and his missionary journeys—which we hoped would resonate with our audience's own experiences.

Unfortunately, we did not bother to ask about the experiences of the people who sat in the palaver house on those hot Sunday afternoons. We did not seek the intensely personal stories of their own encounters with God. We did not explore what the community knew of God prior to the coming of other missionaries who, like us, had told stories of Moses, David, Jesus and Paul.

It was not until much later that we began to realize that Kpelle people had met God through their ancestors, through the spirits of the forest, through the drums and flutes that spoke so eloquently of a powerful but hidden spirit world, through the hand masks that encapsulated a person's reality in a carved piece of wood, through the scars on a man's back that continually reminded him of the terrible teeth of the "Big Thing" that had eaten him, and through the medicines that continually crossed the boundaries between spirit and flesh, boundaries that are so important to all who insist on being descendants of Descartes.

It was not only in Plato-ta on Sunday afternoons that we ignored the presence of God in the lives of the people we met in rural Liberia. We did the same in the classroom and chapel at Cuttington College. There, the stories we told were more complex, but still they were stories from an alien culture.

I taught the history of philosophy during those early years at Cuttington. But whose philosophy? It was the philosophy reified and made into the foundation of our Western Euro-American life, the philosophy of Socrates, Augustine, Descartes, and Bertrand Russell. The students ate up what I taught and what they read, and came back for more (unlike the children of Plato-ta, who were bored with our re-telling of the stories of Moses, David, Jesus and Paul). They rightly or wrongly saw these as foundational narratives of what it means to be part of Euro-American culture. In one lecture in 1959, I outlined the ideas of Plotinus; the students were so fascinated that they insisted I meet them at night to continue the discussion. Their interest showed the level of intellectual discourse at Cuttington in those heady days—but not that I had tapped into the deep groundwater of the life and experience of these students.

The chapel was no different, just less entertaining. We required students to attend Sunday church as well as a regular morning assembly with prayers and announcements. I had the good sense at the time to object. I felt we could not impose belief on anyone. I was overruled by the rest of the faculty, and certainly also by the administration and the remote ecclesiastical hierarchy that composed the Board of Trustees. So we continued to make the students go through the motions of Christian commitment.

Chapel service at Cuttington College

Had I wished to do so, I would have had freedom in the classroom, even in those early days, to explore the students' beliefs, despite chapel services being firmly tied to imported Western religion. As I look back, what really redeemed those years was not so much the teaching I was doing but rather my commitment to research, whereby my students and I looked closely outside the classroom into African ways of thinking and doing. In that shared research, I certainly learned that the intellectual and spiritual baggage I had brought to Africa was very different from the reality we met in rural Liberian villages.

It was, however, only much later during my time at Cuttington that I finally began to ask what the students themselves, their families, their societies, and their nations believed. Unfortunately, that only happened after I had been teaching for almost ten years, despite having done research on secular aspects of local culture. I may have been a good social scientist, but even then my research was still from the outside in, with students as my partners in what was an alien exercise. God most certainly carried an American passport during my teaching and early research years.

What were the effects on students of living on an island of Western Christianity in the midst of rural African villages? Some came from Christian families with a longer history of serious Christian faith than that of most American families. Some became enthusiastic, committed Christians, albeit with a deeply

Western flavor. Some had the integrity to speak their own mind, whether to accept or to reject what we said. The great majority were simply caught in the middle, having lost their ties to tradition, whether that tradition was indigenous religion or Western Christianity. They had become children of no world, not children of two worlds.

I remember a sermon I gave in the U.S. on our first trip back, referring to Jesus' story of the house inhabited by a demon. After the demon was expelled, it was not replaced by something better, and it returned with seven of its friends, so that the house was worse off than before. My sermon was misguided in many ways, but underneath the nonsense that the indigenous society was somehow demon-led and the nonsense that we outsiders could sweep the place clean was a truth: that spirit (and not just nature) hates a vacuum.

Who were these people caught in the middle between traditional belief and enthusiastic acceptance of Western Christianity? One was Lakidzani, whom I met in Botswana in 1982. He was one of my research assistants in a study of small-scale informal sector business people. He had completed high school, but had not done sufficiently well to go on to university. He spoke good English and was willing to interview entrepreneurs, who ranged from tough-minded watch salesmen to women who brewed traditional beer to shaven-headed, full-bearded patriarchs of the Johane Masowe Apostles church.

Lakidzani had no roots, no beliefs, and no ties to anything. He drank heavily and slept around with any willing young woman. I once talked to him about Christianity, and it turned out he had never heard of Easter. He was a product of empty alienation. In stark contrast, the patriarchs of the Johane Masowe church he and I interviewed in our research project led far more personally integrated and whole lives. Poor Lakidzani never had a chance, and I guess that by this time he has likely died of AIDS.

But even at the university level, the loss of a meaningful, powerful faith destroyed people. I remember Shabani Kisenge, the young man from Tanganyika who was one of the trio that had first put the flame of African freedom in my heart and mind in December 1958. Kisenge grew up a Muslim, but at Cuttington he was baptized and became a Christian. Disillusionment set in after a year or so, not only because of the insincerity and hypocrisy of so many Christians he met, but also because it was clear to him that Cuttington College, situated in the heart of conservative, Western-oriented Liberia, was not going to lead the way to a socialist United States of Africa. Before he graduated, Kisenge helped organize an overland escape party from Liberia through Guinea and eventually to Eastern Europe, where a number of our students completed their education, having lost faith in what we stood for in our complacent capitalist Christian college.

I met Kisenge again in Dakar in January 1965, where he was continuing his degree program at the University of Dakar. He was almost ashamed at having been baptized in 1960, and when we parted ways, both of us were sad and rather wistful. I heard that eventually he became a minor bureaucrat in Tanzania. I heard that another of the trio, Ghisler Mapunda, enrolled at the Patrice Lumumba Freedom University in Moscow where he did brilliantly, but where he became a hopeless alcoholic. He made his way back to Tanzania, where drink and obscurity awaited him. I met the third of the trio, Kayetan Ngombale, in 1981 in Mbeya in southwest Tanzania, where he was District Commissioner. I heard whispered comments suggesting that he had grown corrupt during his time in office while at the same time administering a policy of socialist austerity for the people under him.

None of the three was able to find a life-giving faith at Cuttington. All three lost the religious foundations with which they began their lives. As I look back at the wasted opportunity to make a real difference in their lives and in the lives they in turn would touch, I can see that I never found a way to help them link their starting point in life with where they were at Cuttington or with where I hoped they would go in life. They, of course, may have seen things quite differently. They may have thought they took what was useful to them from Cuttington while rejecting the excess baggage—baggage I personally consider vital to a good life.

It was only ten years later that I first taught a course at Cuttington on African traditional religion and philosophy. I was joined in that course by a remarkable group of African students from many different countries, and together we tried to work out just what were their origins and how they could put them to work for the future. It was too late for my three pioneers, but the course may have made a difference to some other students. One thing I do know—teaching the course made a difference in my life. I began to see how African and Christian culture had the potential one day to be part of a new synthesis. I sincerely and deeply hope for that new synthesis to become a reality.

Spirit healers in Lesotho

One result of the disparagement of local religious beliefs is that the number of adherents of African traditional religions has declined over the past century. According to Barrett's World Christian Encyclopedia, the percentage of believers in the indigenous faiths has dropped from near 90 percent in 1900 to an estimate of less than 10 percent in many sub-Saharan countries (www.afrikaworld.net/afrel/Statistics.htm). Benin has the largest percentage of traditional believers, mostly due to the presence of Vodun, which forms the framework of daily life for more than half the population. The religion and its offshoots have spread to the New World, particularly Brazil, Haiti, and Cuba, where there are many practitioners of Vodun and Orisha.

I have begun to learn something about inculturation as a way for Christianity and African traditional societies to create something new together. For example, the Communion of the Saints in European Christianity is strikingly similar to the extended family of the ancestors, the living dead, in Africa. Only recently have I seen that the Spirit blows where she wishes and how she wishes. Only recently have I understood that God does not abandon any human being, but is present wherever and whenever people lift up their eyes and hearts.

What happens to people like Lakidzani is that they either drift aimlessly, drinking and going from woman to woman, and eventually die, or they find themselves drawn to the evils seen all too widely in today's Africa. They find another spirit, an alien and evil spirit. Being caught in the middle, if they are caught up by the power of a demagogue, they turn to horrors such as the RUF in Sierra Leone or the Interahamwe in Rwanda. They see no reason not to do so.

Indeed, we may have swept the house clean, not of devils but of honest God-given spirits, and in so doing we have left it open to real devils. My question is, can a young African caught in this process really be the child of two worlds, or must he become a child of no world? Some people claim that a real synthesis of cultures is impossible. I do not agree. The history of the world has been a panorama of cultures that have merged and grown into something new. Just as monoculture leads to serious problems in farming, the same happens in human society. I hope and pray that African Christians can enrich their worship and their communal life by seeking what is permanently vital and rich from African heritage. I am encouraged by the work of Archbishop Fidele Dirokpa in developing an indigenous service of Holy Communion for Anglican churches in the Democratic Republic of Congo (www.congochurchassn.org.uk/nletters/n47provn.htm).

Yet there are also problems with what I call "both-and" Christians. Difficulties arise when indigenous spirituality and Christian faith are practiced in a

Zionist healing service in Lesotho

divided mind and heart. Many of the people I have worshiped with in Lesotho and Liberia live and pray on both sides of an unnecessarily divided consciousness. The Christian church, which nominally claims more than 90 percent of the population of Lesotho, has turned its back on the deep Christian spirituality that informed missionary work in the 1830s, which remains alive in the hearts and minds of many church-goers. This has led to a deep split in the consciousness of the Basotho, who constitute a majority of the nation. They go to church regularly and expect to be baptized, married, and buried in a Christian church. They also believe strongly in the presence of their ancestors. They know that when they dream of a deceased relative they must slaughter an animal in order to provide that person comfort and security. Ideally, they sacrifice an ox, whose skin is made into a blanket to keep the ancestor warm. The mainline Christian churches have officially rejected this practice, but it continues to the present day, often in disguised form.

The mainline churches also forget the healing power of the spirits and the ancestors. Too many main-stream church services are proper, insipid and boring. If people want to experience the reality of spirit-led intervention in their lives they go to the traditional healers or to the independent Zionist or charismatic churches, where they can find comfort and release. What is needed is for the church to integrate both the past and the present into one way of worship.

7.2 A divided Christianity.

The deepest manifestation that I know of the failure of the mainline churches to reach the hearts and minds of people is the unresolved bitterness resulting from the 1970 coup in Lesotho, when the Roman Catholic-oriented Basotho National Party (BNP) took the government by force from the Protestant-oriented Basutoland Congress Party (BCP). By the time of independence in 1966, the mainline churches, rather than being instruments of God's love, had become in effect clans identified with specific political parties. As a result, the churches were not able to help their members reach out to one another to heal their broken society.

How did the churches become clans? Beginning in the 1820s, the nation of

Lesotho was an amalgam of various patrilineal and patriarchal Sotho-speaking clans to which were added refugees from other southern African ethnic groups. The great leader Moshoeshoe I united these clans and refugee bodies into a nation and did his best to create a united society that minimized differences. He wanted all of his people—all those who had clung to his leadership during a period of drought, during inter-tribal war, during threats from Zulus in the east and Afrikaners in the west, and during the resulting famines—to come together as one people.

He did remarkably well at uniting people and at creating a nation where there had been none before. In secular life, he governed through the use of a national meeting called a pitso where everyone's voice could be heard regardless of origin. In the religious sphere, he was open to Christianity but resisted the divisive influence of the early missionaries who were at times more concerned about fighting each other than in bringing people to God. Shortly before his death, the missionaries wanted to baptize him. He was willing, but he insisted that they all baptize him together. The missionaries refused, preferring to bicker among themselves, and Moshoeshoe died unbaptised. In Ntsu Mokhehle's account of his life, Moshoeshoe is reported to have said of the missionaries: "It is wise that we take a good care of these men. They come from their own homes bitterly divided. And if we should not be watchful over their acts, they shall divide this nation to its utter ruin." (Mokhehle 1976: 92-93)

I like to think that Moshoeshoe went to heaven, baptised "by intention," as liberal theologians might say. What might have happened when the missionaries who had refused to baptize him arrived to seek entrance into heaven? If St. Peter turned to Moshoeshoe to see if they should be forgiven and thus admitted to the holy company, Moshoeshoe might have said something like this: "They were good people. They tried to help us the best way they could, but they just did not understand what they were doing. Let them in." The more extreme critics of these early missionaries would have called them manipulative and exploitative instruments of colonialism. That may well be objectively true, but I would strongly challenge those who impute such subjective motives to the early missionaries who brought Christianity to Lesotho. Rather, the blame should fall on the Western governments and financial institutions that encouraged the separate missionary groups to compete for power.

Regardless of motivation, the divisiveness has done its damage in Lesotho. Families, often by accident of who went where first, quickly chose which missionary to follow. This was contrary to the ecumenical spirit of Moshoeshoe I. Since then, children of one church have tended to remain in that church with one very important exception—a woman who marries outside her family's church joins her husband's church. Church membership thus is an exact parallel to patrilineal clan membership, which is passed on by the father, with women who marry outside of their birth clan changing their clan membership. According to a survey I helped conduct in 1999, Roman Catholics comprise about 44 percent of the population of Lesotho, members of the Lesotho Evangelical Church about 25 percent, and Anglicans about 13 percent.

Many Catholics have identified themselves with the traditional chiefs and the BNP. Members of the Lesotho Evangelical Church, on the other hand, have tended to be loyal to the commoner movement and to the BCP. The BNP won by a slim majority the election held in 1965 on the eve of independence. The second election in 1970 was won by the BCP, but their victory was taken from them by a BNP coup. Parties lined up and churches lined up, and the family and clan system was the only winner. The ideas that political loyalty would be dictated by policies for social betterment and that church loyalty would be dictated by theological conviction were forgotten.

What happened in Lesotho is not just an aberration due to peculiar Basotho behavior. Family-hood, as expressed in clan membership, is the deepest form of religious observance among traditional Basotho, as it is among many African ethnic groups. A family is linked together by its ancestors, who continue to watch over the children and their children's children. Christian missionaries came preaching a new way of life, whereby in theory a person left mother and father, brother and sister, to follow Christ. From the very beginning, the missionaries insisted that Christians reject what they called "ancestor worship." The paradox, the unintended consequence that took revenge on missionaries who rejected the forms of overt traditional belief, was that family-hood quickly took precedence over conscious decision and faith.

What then happens when people need to express their deepest convictions? An event I recently heard about illustrates the point. A young Mosotho woman was caring for the child of Christian friends, but five times in the same night—or so she said—she dreamed of her dead mother calling for her. The young woman left her employment the next morning to return to her ancestral home. The power of the ancestor transcended the power of commitment to a job and of commitment to the overt Christian community that had recommended her for this job. People respond to the atavistic call of the ancestors rather than to the immediate demands of their public life.

The mainline churches are unable to deal with such deep questions, since they have rejected from the start the basis of Basotho (I would even dare to say African) religion. Most people remain in the mainline churches, because they are the clans into which they are born and married. But some leave when the tension becomes too great and turn instead to the independent Zionist or spiritual churches where respect to the ancestors can be spoken out loud. Others live and pray and worship with the mainline churches in the day, but at night they go to churches that can satisfy their deep needs. Still others are attracted by the brash Casio organ music of the American-financed "born-again" churches.

What is the implication for reconciliation in a divided society? The churches in Lesotho are part of the problem, rather than part of the solution, to use Eldredge Cleaver's now overused phrase. They are supposed to contribute to national rebuilding, but instead continue to fight each other over wrongs done as long ago as 1970. The failure of missionaries to realize that family is the basis of Basotho religious belief and practice has led directly to the impasse that threatens to continue dividing Lesotho into warring factions.

It was sad to see Catholic nuns in September 1998 preparing food for BNP youth who had barricaded themselves at the royal palace in order to bring down the government that had won the May 1998 parliamentary election by a margin of 79 seats for the ruling party to one for the BNP. It is still sad to listen to senior BCP politicians berating the opposition in the name of religion.

Thus, in Lesotho the unintended consequences of religious intolerance exist to this very day and can be traced to mistaken missionary attitudes. Indeed, the unintended consequences of failing to listen to African spirituality are present everywhere on the continent. The poet Birago Diop spoke directly to the point, and we would do well to listen:

> *Listen more to things*
> *Than to words that are said.*
> *The water's voice sings*

*And the flame cries
And the wind that brings
The woods to sighs
Is the breathing of the dead...
Those who are dead have never gone away.
They are in the shadows darkening around,
They are in the shadows fading into day,
The dead are not under the ground.
They are in the trees that quiver,
They are in the woods that weep,
They are in the waters of the rivers,
They are in the waters that sleep.
They are in the crowds, they are in the homestead.
The dead are never dead.*

It is we, rather, who are dead if we fail to hear these voices and if we stop the ears of African students and church members so that they can no longer hear their ancestors speak. The revenge of the ancestors is clearly known by those who have ears to hear and eyes to see. There is a way forward, if we only listen to African Christians. In a wonderful new book, *Jesus of Africa: Voices of Contemporary African Christology*, Diane Stinton quotes believers in Ghana and Kenya who see Jesus as indeed an ancestor.

7.3 Christian-Muslim conflict.

In Gbansu we saw the Christian-Muslim conflict on a very small scale, but there was conflict nonetheless. Seku Dorleh was the natural candidate for the post of village chief there. He was bright, thoughtful, well-liked, and from a good family, but he was a Muslim. The Christians and the traditional believers in the village said he could not be chief because he was not allowed by his religion to participate in the customary ceremonies.

Muslims at prayer

Muslims had moved into the village over the past several generations and were well-established. There was a Mandingo "quarter" where the predominantly Muslim members of the Mandingo ethnic group built their houses. Mandingoes were the last of the Mande-speaking ethnic groups to enter Liberia over the course of the pre-colonial period and had been the last to establish a kingdom that included part of what eventually became Liberia. In the late nineteenth century, the Muslim leader Samore Touré conquered much of what is now Guinea, Côte d'Ivoire, eastern Sierra Leone, and northeastern Liberia. He was defeated by the French in 1898 and exiled to Gabon. His legacy remains in much of the forest region, and Mandingoes continue their movement into areas that were colonized by Christian Europe and America.

I mentioned earlier the elderly Muslim trader in central Liberia who believed the Mandingoes had brought civilization to a backward and primitive tribe. I was told similar stories in southwestern Tanzania about Somali immigrants who had brought the arts of civilization to the indigenous people of the area. In this case, they said that the "savages" did not even have fire, but ate their food raw.

In Liberia the relation between Muslim and Christian was made more complex by the hegemony of the Vai people in the northwest, a large proportion of whom are Muslim. They still see themselves as the natural aristocrats among the various ethnic and linguistic groups. They developed their own script in the 1820s and to this day have used it for letters and record-keeping. The script is a source of great pride. According to linguist Saki Mafundikwa, "The Vai syllabary was devised by Momolu Duwalu Bukele in 1830 near Cape Mount in Liberia. It was actually adapted from ancient ideographs that had been in use two centuries before and is still prevalent today where Vais use it for informal correspondence" (www.ziva.org.zw/afrikan.htm). Moreover, in pre-colonial days the Vai kept slaves, many of whom were captured from Kpelle villages in times of war.

Liberia is at the boundary between the largely Christian and traditional-believing people of the forest and the largely Muslim people of the savanna and the Sahel. Enmity between the two groups continues, as I saw when I was in Liberia in 1997. Muslims fought on the losing side during the civil war of the early 1990s and in 1997 were just beginning to re-establish their long dominance of small-scale Liberian trade. They were looked upon with deep suspicion by the Taylor government, which was nominally Christian, and they were not welcomed with much enthusiasm by members of the more settled ethnic groups.

The northeast corner of Liberia, where it meets Sierra Leone and Guinea, remains an area of great turmoil, much of it stemming from Christian-Muslim antagonism. During the civil war, Muslims burned and ransacked Christian churches in major towns. Muslim Mandingoes are the majority of the warriors in the LURD rebel group who invaded Liberia, apparently from Guinea, in order to overthrow Taylor's government and who would like to think of themselves as a government-in-waiting. In mid-2004 this area is still not under NUMIL control.

Three vignettes set the Christian-Muslim struggle in Liberia in context. In the first, a group of Mandingoes came back to Gbarnga at the end of the civil war in April 1997 and slaughtered a cow in order to celebrate the reopening of the mosque. The Christians in Gbarnga were very suspicious that the Muslims were using the occasion to make medicine against them, and so they forced the Muslims to stop their celebration.

In the second, a young man from Bolahun, where we had spent much time visiting the Order of the Holy Cross, had joined the Order despite growing up a Muslim. He went to be with the Order in South Africa and in mid-2000 came back to visit his family in northeastern Liberia. As an ex-Muslim, now a Christian aspirant to monastic vows, he told me that he was in serious danger from the Mandingoes who were creating havoc in the area.

Finally, and most extraordinarily, President Tubman once made a public statement condemning fundamentalist Muslim (and I think also Christian) efforts to stop traditional secret society ceremonies. "After all," he said, "Liberia is a Christian country." Tubman wanted Liberians to work and live together to create a unified society, and identifying Christianity with traditional culture was, from his perspective as a Methodist lay preacher, one way to do so.

The religious conflict continues to plague other parts of Africa, as is evident from the news. It spills over into ethnic quarrels, as I learned when a friend from southern Uganda told me that it would be fine if his daughter wanted to marry an American or a South African, but as for northern Ugandans, absolutely not. He saw the northern Ugandans as savages, as people who would support Idi Amin and doubtlessly do worse than Amin had done. His bias was palpable and his prejudice against northern "tribes" was severe.

In Nigeria, Islam is particularly radical. The outrage at the Miss World beauty contest that was to be held there during Ramadan in late 2002 would likely not have happened in other West African countries where Islam is more relaxed. But in northern Nigeria, Sharia law is now becoming the norm for many states, and Christians are suffering under it. Riots have broken out in many cities, and the Christian-Muslim divide becomes more rigid. Certainly in the violence that took place in the 2003 election in Nigeria, the conflict between faiths was a major factor.

Mosque in Djenne, Mali

Yet in Liberia, when Christians and Muslims cooperated, development moved ahead. The Muslim trader in Gbarnga who thought he was bringing civilization to naked savages was correct in the sense that he was expanding the horizons and opportunities of rural Liberians who had previously known little about the larger world. Samore Touré was not far wrong when he tried to create a West African forest kingdom in order to resist foreign colonial conquest. Nations that are predominantly or complete Muslim have much lower infection rates of HIV/AIDS, which may be one positive consequence of their rigid restrictions on women. Senegal in particular has a very low prevalence of HIV, which President Abdulaye Wade said was due in part to the influence of Muslim clerics: "In the struggle against AIDS, Senegal engaged religious leaders in a cooperative process. Islam in our country is tolerant and liberal, so we were able to organize public conferences where the Imams took the floor and asked the people to do everything they could to fight HIV/AIDS" (www.undp.org/dpa/choices/2000/December/senegal.htm).

But where the conflict between Christianity and Islam has issued in open warfare, the chances of ordinary people to live better were dashed. The conflicts in Liberia since 1990 are not solely the fruits of Muslim-Christian rivalry, but that rivalry has made the situation much worse than it would otherwise have been, particularly during the fighting in Lofa County. Similarly, the rivalry between Muslims and Christians in Sudan plays a major role in the continuing civil war in the south. What makes the situation worse is that each religion creates its own patron-client network, whereby poor people are recruited through the promise of support and a better livelihood.

The Western Cape in South Africa is entering at this point in history a difficult time of religious struggle. Over the past few years there have been regular reports of the activities of PAGAD (People Against Gangsterism and Drugs).

PAGAD is fighting what might have in the past been gang turf wars, but which recently have become inter-faith struggles. Lesotho has been spared this sort of perversion of religion, but Islam is on the move in the region. So far there have been a small number of converts, but Muslims could use them to enter a more militant phase. At present, Muslims are offering scholarships to Basotho not only for foreign study but also for school in Lesotho. If the offer is sweet enough, the temptation to leave a dispirited Christian church might be overwhelming.

I have not seen many Muslim fundamentalists where I worked. The older tradition in Liberia, as in most of the other countries where I have worked, has been for the religions to live and let live, to learn from each other, and to contribute what they can to national development. Unfortunately, fundamentalism is growing in the world, and the chances are high for Christian and Muslim conflict, which has worsened in response to the Reinhard Bonnke Christian crusades in northern Nigeria. In Senegal, President Abdoulaye Wade, a Muslim, is married to a Christian and practices policies of harmony. Senegal's liberal and humanitarian policies could be drowned and lost if Christians and Muslims follow the pattern expressed in the mutually reinforcing hatred of people like Pat Robertson and some Muslims who respond in kind. Robertson's anti-Islamic phobia has even led him to defend Charles Taylor of Liberia as a warrior for Christianity. According to Sonja Barisic of the Associated Press, on his 700 Club broadcast, Robertson said President Bush was "undermining a Christian, Baptist president to bring in Muslim rebels" by rejecting Taylor (www.kansascity.com/mld/kansascity/news/breaking_news/6273906.htm).

7.4 Multiplication of missionary bodies

The record of the mainline Christian denominations in Africa has not been so bad in recent years. They share, they cooperate, and they respect each other. In Lesotho the long-standing tensions between Catholic, Anglican and Protestant have lessened, and cooperation is growing. The King has been a Catholic, but has worked closely with the other churches.

King Moshoeshoe, Desmond Tutu, Protestant doctor at ecumenical meeting

Perhaps we have grown somewhat wiser in the years since those early divisive missionary forays, such as when French Catholics and Anglicans competed for the allegiance of the Kabaka, the hereditary rulers of the Baganda people of Uganda.

Today the troublesome groups are the fringe churches and sects, fundamentalist, often charismatic, often (but not always, to be sure) very right-wing in their politics. Of particular concern in Lesotho, for example, is the Universal Church of Christ, pandering to greed and fear among members of other churches and those who are not church members. This "church" operates in storefronts on the main road just south of the city center and in the bus stop. It attracts members by its promise of "health and wealth," if they contribute generously to the leaders of the church.

Another cluster of fundamentalist bodies has grown up in Lesotho, partly in relation to Reinhard Bonnke's evangelistic campaigns. Many are linked to American or South African Pentecostal groups. They are well-funded, and they appeal to those who like loud Casio organ music and fiery preaching. They are not as crass as the Universal Church of Christ, but they certainly do not promote social concern. They cooperate neither with the mainline churches nor with the African-initiated churches. Their members believe they have been saved by acceptance of a narrow creed, normally focused on a literal interpretation of the Bible, and they tend to be little interested in social and political questions.

In addition to Christians who preach a truncated gospel of happiness, wealth, and emotional excitement, there are other missionary groups who have invaded Africa with alien, non-Christian gospels. The Jehovah's Witnesses are active in Maseru, preaching on street corners and knocking on people's doors to indoctrinate them into what seems to me to be a heretical and divisive distortion of Christianity. At the very minimum, I think believers in God should be willing to pray together for the peace and salvation of the world. I remember asking one Witness who had entered my house to pray with me that we might share a few moments in the presence of God. His response was, "I am not allowed to pray with unbelievers." My response was, "If you cannot pray with me, then there is no point in your talking with me."

Mormons are another blight on the Christian landscape. Young, well-scrubbed "elders" walk the streets of Maseru in their white shirts, dark ties, and prominent name tags, hoping to convert people away from the Christianity which is the faith of almost all Basotho. Fortunately, in a recent survey I found no one who admitted to being a Mormon, just as no one admitted to being a Jehovah's Witness.

I object to groups such as the Mormons, the Jehovah's Witnesses, and the Universal Church of Christ because they deny the fundamentals of historic Christian faith and break the unity of Christian brothers and sisters. They choose a piece of God's reality, and make it into the whole. Having done so, they then deny the rest of us who are struggling to live a Christian life entrance into the kingdom of God. If Christianity is to be a vital force in the midst of daily life, then it should not be broken into competing and mutually contradictory pieces, and much less into heretical backwaters of the main stream of faith.

There are, of course, exceptions. The missionaries I have met from the Mennonite church in the United States and Canada are doing important work. They come to Lesotho and other African countries prepared to help existing churches do their work better and thus be more faithful witnesses to their Lord. Workers from the Mennonite Central Committee helped us in the ecumenical quest for social and economic justice at the Transformation Resource Centre. We were Catholics, Anglicans, Methodists, and members of the Lesotho Evangelical Church working together to proclaim God's love and justice, and the Mennonites came out to share our task, not to start yet another church or denomination.

Mennonites also helped train pastors in the African-initiated churches, men and women of little formal education but great faith. These Christians welcomed outside support, because the outsider was not trying to wean them away from their own, often not well-educated, but very real faith. Rather, the outsider, the self-giving missionary, was helping them to be more fully what they had within them to become.

7.5 Growth of African-initiated religious groups.

Europe and America set an example that has been followed all too enthusiastically by African Christians. In Europe and America, to a large extent as a consequence of the Reformation, the Body of Christ has been broken into many fragments. To be sure, there were splits within the Christian family much earlier, even during the time of the New Testament, when the Apostle Paul bemoaned the fact that there were groups loyal to him and others loyal to Apollos or Cephas or even simply to Christ. The Church in Rome took leadership very early, but even the fact of leadership implied the possibility of fission, and fissions came aplenty, in the form of heretical sects and eventually in the form of the Eastern Orthodox Church.

Certain of these offshoots of the main Christian body were in Africa even from a very early date. Nestorian Christians flourished in Egypt and later in Ethiopia. Carthage saw the rise of other sects, including the Montanists and the Donatists. These divisions in the Christian body contributed to the decline of Christianity, the overthrow of Roman hegemony, and the rise of Islam in North Africa.

Where the Christian faith was most vital, it supported the renewal of society in Europe, leading eventually to the rebirth of culture and society and knowledge in the Western world. Where Christianity was weak and divided, the consequences were decay and decline. I know that I am going directly against the theories of Edward Gibbon in his History of the Decline and Fall of the Roman Empire (Gibbon 1995), and also against the denigration of Christianity in Gore Vidal's novel Julian (Vidal 1981). My view is quite different, namely, that when the Christian church has been true to itself and its founder, it has made life richer and better for the people it serves, both at home and in new places where it sent missionaries.

Many missionaries did not embody the Christian faith in the way I wish they had. I include myself in that camp. The inability of Christianity to serve Africa has been partly due to its failure to recognize and build upon the best that African tradition has offered. It has also partly been due to the proliferation of Christian sects, many of whom sent missionaries to confound and confuse the work of other missionaries, whom they considered at best to be misguided and at worst to be agents of the devil. No one has benefited from these in-group quarrels, certainly not the churches themselves, and even more importantly not the societies to which the churches were sent. Some might say that African traditions have benefited from Christian divisiveness, which gave these belief systems space in which to strengthen and develop.

The example set by European and American churches, as Moshoeshoe I predicted, has led to serious divisions within the African churches. The African churches responded by saying to the foreign churches (perhaps quite justifiably), "a plague on all your houses"; they then set about creating their own Christian bodies. There are now thousands of African-initiated churches (the acronym AIC formerly meant "African independent churches," which is not as accurate as the new version).

Basotho Zionists praying at the river

Assessing, evaluating, and judging these churches is difficult and even arrogant. They must be seen in the context of the rise of churches of the same type in the United States, of which there are as many, if not more, as those in Africa. It is my sense that in both cases the end result has been on balance negative, though there have been AICs that have brought benefit to church and society. On the other hand, it is possible to believe that the full richness of the Christian faith is best served by the kaleidoscopic interplay of all the versions of the faith that jostle each other in today's African world. There is evidence that the AICs have provided much-needed social protection and cohesion to Africans against the corrosive influence of a rapidly changing world, particularly to those who are poorly educated and who are making at best a marginal living.

Many of the African-initiated churches, including the church of Johane Masowe that Lakidzani helped me understand, turned their back on the allurements of mainstream Western society. Masowe, according to what his church members told me, which was confirmed by the research of Clive Dillon-Malone, died in the 1930s in a village near Salisbury (now Harare) in what was then Southern Rhodesia (Dillon-Malone 2000). He told his followers that he had gone to heaven and been given a charge by God to return to earth to save his people. He came back to life after three days and gave his followers strict rules that they were not to attend school, were not to use medicines, were not to drink, and were to engage in only a limited range of occupations: basket-making, tin-smithing, carpentry, market selling, and car repair. The men were to be absolute heads of their households, were to marry many wives (who were required to wear white dresses and take orders from their husbands), and were to protect their children from the corrosive Westernization that was destroying their society.

The MaZezuru (as they were called in Botswana) spread out until they were established from Port Elizabeth in South Africa to Nairobi in Kenya. They were the most successful, hard-working, and serious business people we met on that research study, and when I compared Lakidzani with them, I realized just what Johane was trying to save his people from.

I am of two minds about the church of Johane Masowe, the group which preaches isolation from main-stream urban society. They are the most productive small informal business people I have encountered in my research, but their contribution to the larger community consists only of the metal boxes and woven baskets they sell. They live clean lives. They do not drink, they do not smoke (and to continue the cliché, they probably do not dance and do not joke). On the other hand, they keep their children from going to school and their members from seeking medical care.

The unwillingness to use medicine is a very interesting aspect of many AICs. There is a common tendency to require their members to rely solely on prayer rather than to allow them to seek scientific healing. One man I spoke with in Botswana implied that going to the doctor shows lack of faith in God, who alone can heal.

My experience in Lesotho is that ordinary Christians who are members of mainstream Christian denominations seem to visit doctors for any and every small medical problem. Perhaps the AIC members are at least partly correct in thinking that healing can come through inner spiritual resources rather than only through the scientific magic of external healers. The healers of choice need not be scientifically Western-trained doctors and nurses, but may also include herbalists and diviners.

I think the difference between the African-initiated churches and the mainline churches is that AIC members locate their faith inside the community to which they have given their lives. These churches supply meaning to the lives of their members. Not only do these members not need to look outside, but they are specifically required not to do so. A member of the Masowe church in Botswana described the son of a church member. He had left the church, gone to school, built a business, made money, started drinking, and had eventually lost everything. For my informant, the lesson was clear. This man had fallen away from the faith community and in the end deserved what he got.

When I was in Maun in northwestern Botswana, I stayed with a family that belonged to the Zion Christian Church, which is perhaps the biggest African-initiated church in southern Africa. They were more part of the ordinary world than were the Masowe members, but still their allegiance was to the church, not to the world. Healing in this case also was found in the church. I worshiped with them one evening, and was moved by their vital togetherness. They prayed for each other, shared a common sacrament of tea and coffee, and were an island of general sanity and sobriety in a troubled and confused city.

Despite my being impressed with these groups and the lives they lived, I have to admit to a conventional view of medicine. I was brought up in the United States, and my parents did all the conventional things, training me well so that I would be able to do the same for my children. Christian Science (a classic American-initiated church) was very strange to us, clearly nonsensical and wrong. Thus, I believe that Western medicine is essential to development and modernization, which includes health, in Africa. My instinct is to say that the AICs (both American and African) are blocking progress, promoting disease, and undercutting the initiatives of missions, donor agencies, and governments.

My view was supported by a sad event I witnessed in Maseru in January 2003. I was worshiping with a typical AIC in a full-day service, complete with several bishops and archbishops. The high point of the day was a baptism and healing service in the Caledon River. The entire worshiping body walked to the river and several people were baptized, after which members of the congregation were brought to the river to be healed. A disabled man, full of faith, was dipped seven times in the water, was brought out coughing and gasping...and was not healed. We drove him home, and it was clear he was emotionally broken by having entered the water in faith and then emerging with his disabilities unchanged.

Zionists praying over children

I may be correct in my skepticism, but I may also very well be wrong. It would be worth studying the health of members of the Masowe church, of the Zion Christian Church (ZCC), of the Church of the Lord Aladura in Nigeria, indeed of AICs all over Africa that deny Western medicine. Is it possible that their health is as good as or better than in the rest of African society? It is likely that they are less often victims of HIV/AIDS, because they live in self-contained communities. But until it is proven that their alternative to scientific medicine is at least as good as what they reject, my conviction remains that these fragments of the Body of Christ have been part of Africa's decline.

Not only do these churches resist Western medicine, but some are also opposed to Western schooling. My Masowe friends did not allow their children to attend Botswana government schools. Their argument is that the children would be lost to the faith, since they would pick up habits and beliefs that lead to sin. They provided enough schooling within the community for people to be able to read the Bible, but in their view more is unnecessary and harmful.

I do not know enough about other AICs to say whether Western schooling is discouraged, but my intuition is that they sympathize with the Masowe stance. In a recent survey we at Sechaba Consultants carried out in Lesotho, members of the African-initiated churches had significantly lower levels of schooling than members of the mainstream mission-initiated churches. This may relate to poverty, since the mean income per member of the mission-initiated churches is significantly higher than the mean income per member of the AIC churches. It is quite likely that these facts go together, but it is not clear whether membership in an AIC leads to poverty and low levels of schooling or whether the poor and poorly educated tend to join AICs rather than mainline churches.

There is thus at least a possibility that AIC membership may lead to a lower level of development, although the connection is not firm. The negative attitude toward education of at least some of the churches, combined with the wide-spread negative attitude toward health care, supports this conclusion.

In most cases, AICs have cut themselves off from the main currents of society. This is strongly the case for the members of the Masowe church, but it is also true among the members of the Zion Christian Church. My hosts in Maun made it clear that national politics were not of interest. They were not concerned with political parties, national development, social justice, or governance. As members of the lower middle class, they were interested in the immediate issues of their lives in community. The great national events were replaced in their minds by the great annual meeting of all members of the ZCC at Moria in South Africa's Northern Cape Province.

Surveys I helped administer in Lesotho in 2000 and 2003 regarding political opinions showed that people who identify themselves first and foremost as Christians (rather than as farmers, poor persons, or members of a clan) are less likely to discuss politics with friends. It is commonly said in Lesotho that national politics are dirty and corrupt, and many church people, especially those in the AICs, avoid them.

This phenomenon was particularly apparent during the apartheid years. When my wife and I were working with the Transformation Resource Centre, we tried hard to arouse interest among Christians about the struggle against racial injustice, both in Lesotho and in South Africa. Unfortunately, church people were often indifferent to the big picture. Those who were willing to join the struggle were almost always from the mainline mission-founded churches. It was a great disappointment to many of us involved in the struggle that the ZCC refused to get involved. I remember the sadness we felt when we read that the ZCC's annual meeting at Moria had been addressed by then-president of South Africa, P. W. Botha. He was received as the legitimate and respected head of the country, despite that essentially all members of the ZCC were black and were suffering under the system that Botha so efficiently administered.

During apartheid, two fundamental statements of Christian resistance were issued: the *Kairos Document* of 1985 (Institute for Contextual Theology 1986) and *The Road to Damascus* of 1989 (Institute for Contextual Theology 1989). Both pamphlets urged Christians to struggle against political and economic injustice and oppression. Both statements were critical in the task of seeking a better world. Both documents were signed by Christians willing to stand up and be counted. Yet few from the AICs signed either document. Of the original list of 153 signatories to the

Social justice workshop in rural Lesotho

Kairos Document, I am confident that almost all those who signed were from the mission-initiated churches. The five hundred who signed *The Road to Damascus* included only seventeen whose church affiliation was even remotely related to the AICs, and of those seventeen, eight were from the Order of Ethiopia, at that time a constituent part of the Anglican Church of the Province of Southern Africa.

Obviously, further study of this question is needed. Membership in the African-initiated churches seems to mean dropping out of the mainstream of national development. To the extent that a united Christian voice on fundamental questions such as health, education, and democracy is vital to bringing Africa back from the abyss, then the AICs are not helping and may in fact be hindering that process.

Yet it can be argued that by remaining outside national political activity, these churches are retaining their integrity as well as their African sense of community. By relying on and respecting their own intra-church patron-client networks, they escape entanglements in ethnic, religious, and political inter-group fights. A more wholesome African political milieu may emerge as such groups work through issues of leadership, consensus, and democracy on their own without having to adopt political structures imported from abroad. Such groups often are vital to overcoming the social disorganization and anomie that characterize much of Africa today.

I am persuaded by the assertion, independently presented by two friends who read the first draft of this chapter, that Christianity during the early years of the Roman Empire resisted Roman colonialism by discovering new ways to organize their life together. My friends' idea is that the AICs may well be doing the same thing in Africa that early Christians did in Rome, in this case resisting the imperial ethos brought by British, French, Belgian, Portuguese, and American overlords.

7.6 Lavish weddings and funerals.

Every family in the world uses weddings and funerals to mark the stages of life. Families are created by marriages and are reorganized by funerals. Everywhere, people marry, children are born, and people die. The cycle of birth and death is a universal and integral part of life. Children practice getting married, with great hopes for their future lives.

Why then would I say that weddings and funerals contribute to the African decline? My explanation is two-fold. First, Lavish weddings (called "white weddings") and funerals further accentuate the growing divide between rich and poor across Africa. Second, the not-quite-poor feel compelled to spend their small savings on a display of false affluence that leaves them almost permanently in debt. Only occasionally do families have the good sense to back off from the financial burdens that feasts impose on them.

Moorosi, the young Mosotho who grew up with our family ever since his mother worked for us both in our garden and then inside our house, suffered the loss

Mock wedding in Lesotho

of an older brother in mid-2000. The brother, who had dropped out of university due to heavy drinking, had tried to reform, but this time his luck ran out. He was drinking in a local beer hall, when an old acquaintance, also drinking, decided to take revenge for a long-remembered insult. The friend pulled out a knife, as unfortunately often happens in Lesotho, and stabbed Moorosi's brother three times. The brother died within a short time, and the killer turned himself in at the local police station to face an uncertain future.

Moorosi is now a secondary school teacher, and his wife is supporting the family as a primary school teacher. At the time of the murder they had a three-year-old daughter, and they were trying hard to establish themselves in a small three-room house they built on the edge of Maseru. They could ill afford the expense, yet they were culturally obliged to give Moorosi's brother an elaborate funeral. Not only did the costs eat away at their meager savings, but they also had to assume partial financial responsibility for the brother's pregnant wife and year-old child.

The rest of the family shared the expenses, but Moorosi's mother is a poorly-paid domestic worker in South Africa and his father is an even more-poorly-paid pastor of a tiny African-initiated church. The older sister has a small income as a teacher, but is a single mother who must care for her children. The younger brother was preparing for his own wedding and had no surplus. The youngest sister had just finished teacher training and was looking for a job as a primary school teacher. The obligation of an elaborate funeral exhausted the few resources they all hoped to use to build their lives.

The younger brother's wedding was scheduled for the next month. The family made the wise decision to scale down the wedding expenses. When Moorosi married, the event had been lavish, though their money was limited. His wife Mary rented a beautiful dress, they borrowed sleek cars from friends and employers, and they laid on a full feast for several hundred guests. Moorosi and Mary cherish the memory, but it set back their finances to the point that they had to borrow money to build their house.

We urged Moorosi and Molapo, the younger brother, to be sensible and spend a minimum on the wedding, and they finally agreed. We were unable to persuade them to reduce the expense of the funeral because of severe cultural pressures from friends and relatives. Had they gone ahead with a full "white wedding" for Molapo, the family would have been unable to continue to pay for Moorosi's schooling, not to mention other expenses that come up on a daily basis.

I told this story in detail, because it illustrates the pressures African families feel

White wedding in Lesotho

everywhere. Capital accumulation, to use the jargon, is essential if families are to better themselves, but capital is often dissipated through cultural requirements society places on them.

These events, the brother's funeral and the weddings of Moorosi and Molapo, were in fact small-scale in comparison with many other feasts. When MaSongoa, who had at one point also worked in our garden, died in a rural village, her husband slaughtered two big cattle and several sheep in order to feed several hundred guests from his and neighboring villages.

The husband, Ntate Tobe, a partly disabled ex-miner, was largely supported by his wife, who sold fruit at the gate of the National University of Lesotho after she left our employ. Their family scratched a living from three unproductive fields and regularly came to us for money to buy seeds and fertilizer. How he could afford to slaughter these animals is not clear to me, even with the funds he had invested over the years in a local burial society. The burial society paid for one of the animals, but the other was taken directly out of his small herd, an animal that should have been there to help plough his fields when the next season came. He was left with neither a wife to support him nor enough animals to plough. He was also left with the heavy burden of finding school fees for his children and for the orphaned children of his brother.

MaSongoa's funeral was the very opposite of capital accumulation; it was capital dissipation. Just as it also was for Moorosi's family, so is capital dissipation at the heart of the problem of elaborate weddings and funerals. It is no wonder that an Anglican bishop in Kenya pleaded with his congregation to simplify these rites, no wonder also that an Anglican bishop in Nigeria required funerals be held no later than a few days after the death. Furthermore, as AIDS deaths become more and more frequent, capital dissipation because of funerals is increasing out of proportion to funds available.

A Kenyan Christian said it very well in a letter to the Kenyan Daily Nation in January 2001:

> Through funerals, we Kenyans have hijacked the gospel. The richer and more popular the deceased was, the greater the crowd that attends funerals. They often offer the best platform for pot-bellied Kenyans to be in the limelight. The Anglican Church should be congratulated for articulating a stand against ostentatious funerals for their members. This is because when the poor Lazaruses of this country die, we pay very little attention. Church weddings have become the devil's industry. Most church weddings portray filthy waste, and yet the pastors do not care about this un-Godly behavior simply because funerals and weddings offer them the best opportunity to be at the centre of everything.

Yet it is important to see who benefits from such ostentatious displays. The first group is the poor in the community. Anyone within walking distance is welcome to share in the feast. At many of the urban funerals I have attended in Lesotho there were three tables of food. The head table, often in the house, was restricted to family, clergy, and senior guests. The second table, usually outside but still within range of the elite guests, provided more or less the same food, but it was served on plastic plates with plastic forks and eaten in tents erected in the yard. The third table was in the back of the house, and there the neighborhood poor were served. They had to take their plates and stand outside to eat the food. There may well have been a difference in the menu for the third group, with more traditional food and less elegance, but always there was plenty of meat for everyone. I calculated in one study that a principal source of protein for the truly poor is the meat served at feasts, meat they would otherwise never get. Even at rural funerals, senior family members and important guests are given preferential treatment, but nonetheless, ordinary folk get a good meal.

Another group benefiting from feasts is the extended family, which lives with the household for several days before and after the event. They help prepare the food, and in the process eat more than they might get at home. If the family is wealthy, the extended family is joined by those who hire out their services as cooks and caterers.

In short, weddings and funerals are opportunities for the redistribution of wealth that might otherwise be used for building up family capital. One of the great virtues of life in Lesotho is that the poor are not allowed to starve, but are always provided with something to help them survive from those with slightly more than themselves.

My experience of feasts in other African countries confirms what I found in Lesotho. The feasts in Liberia, which often took place at the end of initiation school or at funerals, were similar to those in Lesotho. Perhaps the main difference was that the redistribution of resources was from adults to young children, who were often fed only after adults had eaten. My Zion Christian Church hosts in Maun, Botswana held a funeral feast that mirrored almost exactly my Lesotho experiences. The feast for the Virgin Mary I attended in Ankober in the Ethiopian highlands was another occasion where the merely poor shared with the very poor. I was informed that those who attended may never see meat except when they attend a Coptic Church festival.

There is another benefit of the African wedding and funeral feasts. The extended family is not only fed at the occasion, but is strengthened and nourished as a living organism. Those who attend the wedding help to cement the new family firmly into the existing body of parents, grandparents, cousins, brothers, sisters, nephews, and nieces, not to mention even more distant relatives who are loosely called parents, brothers, or sisters. The extended family is a mutual support society whose members can call on each other whenever help is needed. Anything owned by one member must be, at least in theory, shared with the other members. This is the ultimate patron-client network, the patrimony that is literally a patrimony.

Obviously, this emphasis on extended family ties brings both benefit and harm, and I can argue for both sides. It is certainly good for a family to care about all its members. It is certainly good when a destitute relative is given a good meal at a lavish feast. It is good that a family member can invite himself or herself to a family home or business to prevent starvation. So many in American society lose their connections with their larger family when key members die. After my mother and her sisters died, I no longer kept in touch with my cousins on that side of the family, though I know that there are many of them living somewhere in the United States. Not so in African societies, where ties are kept, rehearsed for the edification of the children, and renewed when a wedding or a funeral takes place. This is clearly a benefit.

The harm arises from the inability to accumulate capital. Continually sharing wealth with extended family makes it difficult to build a resource base for business. Even if a family starts a business, often the shelves or the cash boxes are fair game for less wealthy relatives. No one starves, but the engine for economic growth never gets put into high gear. The net effect is that the economy is never kick-started. Moorosi, for example, has been trying to build a second small house on his site outside Maseru. He wants to rent it to people newly arriving in Maseru. He keeps postponing the construction, even though he has already laid the foundation, because his money keeps getting used for family matters. If he were harsh and stingy, he would be earning extra money now from a rental property. He is not.

Given the larger economic framework in which Africa must work, the fact that Moorosi and his millions of loyal counterparts across the continent are not building a solid economic base means that African nations (which are made up out of millions of people like Moorosi) will never be able to compete on equal terms with more aggressively capitalist nations. They will always be the poor relations of the world, always selling their labor and their raw materials, but never building the base so necessary for a strong, productive economy.

The decline of Africa can therefore be traced at least in part to Africa's virtues. Eat, drink, marry, and be buried, secure in the knowledge that your family will never let you down, but certain also that you cannot win in the harsh world of global capitalism.

7.7 Hopeful signs.

It is encouraging that Christians in Africa are bringing **local religious beliefs** to light and are incorporating them into worship and doctrine. When Desmond Tutu's successor as head of the Anglican Church in southern Africa, Archbishop Njongonkulu Ndungane, was still bishop of Kimberley and Kuruman, he proposed that the Anglican service of Holy Communion include specific reference to the ancestors. The Catholic Bishops' Conference in South Africa has also made a conscious effort to accept officially many of the beliefs that ordinary Catholics have brought with them to church. Inculturation is alive and well in Africa and is the medium by which still-alien versions of Christianity learn from indigenous spirituality.

Archbishop Ndungane

The deep **divisions within Christendom** persist across Africa. But I remain hopeful that we can work through our differences and find ways to live together as Christians, even though we may not actually form institutional unions among churches. Church unions might not be a desirable goal, however, if there is value in different Christian bodies emphasizing different aspects of the complex reality of a God who is present in the world in so many different ways. Christian councils, as well as interfaith bodies, are present in most countries. In South Africa the major denominations are present in the Christian Council, including, at the extremes, Catholics and Dutch Reformed. And the African-initiated churches are themselves coming together to form interchurch bodies.

It is very hard for **Christians and Muslims** to live and work together, given the enmity and open warfare in so much of Africa. Yet I find hope in the prevailing harmony in much of West Africa, excluding Nigeria. When I was living in Liberia, Muslims and Christians may have disagreed, but they were willing to live in harmony with each other. And wisdom was prevalent in exchanges between Christians and Muslims in an interfaith coalition that worked to put in place conditions for a lasting peace in post-Taylor Liberia. In South Africa also, with the exception of the more violent Muslims in Cape Town, Christians and Muslims have agreed to cooperate in social and economic matters.

There are too many **missionary bodies** working and competing in Africa. The old tradition of comity, whereby only one church body would work in a given area, has broken down. I point to the Mennonites and the Quakers as counter-examples. Believers from both groups in Lesotho have worked closely with all other Christian groups, but without attempting to form their own churches. They meet privately in homes with fellow believers, but they do not advertise themselves as churches attempting to win converts. Since according to our surveys the Basotho are already nominally more than 95 percent Christian, Quakers and Mennonites have taken the better road. Would that the rest of us could follow. We did try at the Transformation Resource Centre, but we need to do more.

I have already indicated my ambivalence about **African-initiated churches**. They are divisive, but they maintain African culture and tradition. They do not care about big issues of politics and economics, but they bring people together in harmonious ways within the confines of their fellowships. They often oppose Western medicine and education, but they are exploring alternatives to the Western systems that are both too expensive for most people and cause those who drop out to see themselves as failures. They are thus both signs of hope and occasions for concern.

Finally, voices are now attacking the waste of resources on **lavish weddings and funerals**. Admittedly, some benefit comes from these events, particularly for the very poor who may depend on weddings and funerals for much needed protein. But more and more leaders have urged their followers, both from the pulpit and in the press, to cut back on unnecessary expenses. Burial societies, which traditionally have provided funds for funerals, now have to be more cautious in what they will support in this time of numerous AIDS-related deaths. The HIV/AIDS epidemic may have one small benefit in that people simply cannot afford to bury the rapidly increasing number of corpses in ways that respect tradition.

CHAPTER EIGHT. ALIEN MEDICAL SYSTEMS

I cannot speak as a medical professional, and so I approach this chapter with some trepidation. I hope I am not one of the fools who rush in where competent people would stay outside. I have, however, seen enough of the medical establishment in the countries where I have worked to say a few things.

Circumstances and organizations that have been a great blessing to Africa were first the missionary-inspired drive and more recently the concern for better medical practice of government, the World Health Organization, and such private bodies as Doctors without Borders. Until recently, people have tended to live longer and healthier lives. In the pre-HIV/AIDS years, people could expect most of their children to survive to adulthood. I cannot but be grateful for the increase in longevity resulting from Western medicine, nor do I think that the Africans I know would think otherwise.

Serious problems remain, however, that are perhaps the unintended consequences of the very excellence of the systems that were introduced. Such problems are also the consequences that inevitably come with the complex Euro-American medical foundation on which Third-World medicine has been built. The knowledge of herbs and other traditional remedies that has accumulated over the centuries is neglected, medical personnel attend to the specific physical problem and not to the whole person, preventive medicine is neglected, new diseases including HIV/AIDS enter unprepared communities, alcoholism spreads, and costs spiral out of control.

Colonial powers depended primarily on medical missionaries to bring new practices and belief systems that were more than merely technical. In Liberia the archetypal missionary doctor was George W. Harley, who brought Western medicine to the far interior, but who was also a pioneer anthropologist, art historian, and Christian evangelist. It is not right to think of medicine as only the cool, technically sophisticated enterprise so commonly thought of as the ideal in Europe and America. Ideally what the Christian mission should have brought, and sometimes in fact did bring, was a combination of healing, prevention, evangelism, service, research, and exploration.

There were problems derived from this complex combination of motivations. I recognize the fundamental importance of Western medicine in bringing health, as well as science, to Africa, but I must also show how the problems accompanying Western medicine may have slowed Africa's development or even exacerbated its decline as it is examined in this book.

8.1 Disrespect for traditional healers.

I have known a few traditional healers and have come to respect some of them, although not in all ways, and certainly not all of them. Dr. Harley certainly respected his counterpart doctors among the Mano ethnic group in Liberia, as discussed in his pioneering book Native African Medicine (Harley 1941). I have already mentioned Kutukpu, who lived in the village of Balama, about an hour's walk from Cuttington. He was a delightful fraud, but I am sure that he helped people in that village, mostly psychologically and spiritually. It seems, according to my friends in the village, that his main role was giving psychological encouragement to families who want to get pregnant.

Kutukpu the healer in his office

Another healer I knew was Maletsoai in the mountains of Lesotho. She lived on a hill opposite the village of Mphaki, sufficiently far from the other households to give her a certain mystique. People had to cross the river from the main village and then climb the hill to find her. She used salt as her main remedy, hence her name, which literally means "mother of salt." She believed strong enemas have great curative power. In some cases her cure may have caused more problems than it solved, but it helped in enough cases that people continued to use her services. She doubtlessly mixed the spiritual with the physical, something not enough Western doctors are willing to do. Today, medicine is often mechanistic and reductionist, a stance the early missionary doctors never took.

Fr. Buasono was another spiritual healer who ran an immensely popular clinic in a Lesotho village where I lived and worked. He was a French Canadian Roman Catholic priest whose French name was transformed into a meaningful Sesotho equivalent. Patients came to him from distant parts of South Africa, and he relieved them of their physical as well as spiritual burdens. There was clearly a good deal of fraudulence in his practice. He had an assistant who sat in the queue with other patients and innocently asked them what their trouble was. He would then excuse himself and quietly slip inside to inform the priest why such-and-such a person, wearing such-and-such clothing, had come. Fr. Buasono would then astound the patient by giving a diagnosis even before the person spoke. He also had sleight-of-hand tricks by which he was able to pull small snakes or other witchcraft paraphernalia from the patient's body. The important thing is that he healed people, not everyone, or even a majority of his patients, but certainly some. Those he did heal went away rejoicing and told their friends.

Healer's house in Tanzania

In a Tanzanian village I met a mature, gracious traditional healer. The government nurse in the same village was an unimpressive young woman who sat dispiritedly in a drab and dirty clinic. The healer had a beautiful house; in it were a variety of herbs and other traditional remedies. I know that I would have preferred him to treat my ailments than trust them to whatever the young nurse was providing.

It is sad that there is a serious lack of understanding and trust between the traditional herbalists and spiritual healers and the Western-trained medical professionals. Only rarely have I seen the gap bridged, and in those cases both sides benefited.

An area in which the traditional healer functions well is that of spiritual and emotional counsel and comfort. If infertility is in part the result of anxiety, which I understand is sometimes the case, then Kutupku was of real help to distraught couples. If bowel dysfunction can be helped by enemas administered by someone with care and experience, then Maletsoai was helpful. Fr. Buasono was a master at spiritual and psychological counsel, as I realized from the one time I spoke with him. If he needed to pull a few fast tricks to accomplish some good, then maybe I should not criticize. An herbalist who has a clean house and knows the whole pharmacopeia of traditional plants is better than a poorly trained nurse.

I remember one case where the two traditions met. A friend of mine who ran the clinic at Cuttington, Dr. John Stewart, attested to the skill of a traditional healer with whom he was unwittingly in competition. A man with a broken leg was brought in a hammock to Dr. Stewart, who said that he must be put into a cast and traction for six weeks before he could move. The family of the man refused and said they would take him to the village bonesetter instead. In six weeks the man walked back to Dr. Stewart's clinic under his own power, perfectly healed. John told me that he could never have produced such quick and perfect results using the methods he was taught in medical school.

The bonesetter could not fully reveal his secrets, because they were said to be part of the lore of a secret society of healers. It is quite possible that part of what helped him to heal people was the power of secrecy. Beryl Bellman discusses the importance of secrecy in rural Liberia in his book *Village of Curers and Assassins*. According to Bellman, not speaking about important matters is key to ensuring their power (Bellman 1975).

Dr. Stewart learned that the broken leg was wrapped in leaves of various types and then strapped tight with vines. The man was allowed to move about cautiously. At the same time, the leg of a chicken was broken. The man was then told that when the chicken could walk he could take off the leaves and vines. The prescription was followed and the man was cured. Dr. Stewart said that in the future he would send people with simple fractures to the traditional healer. Compound fractures (fractures where the skin is broken) were a different problem and could not be healed in the traditional way.

8.2 Cure as mechanistic rather than holistic.

I remember seeking help from two medical doctors in Liberia, both trained in the United States and both missionaries for the Lutheran church. One doctor in effect asked me, "What is wrong with you?" while the other doctor asked me, "What is wrong with your back?" The first treated me as a person, questioning me and involving me in the process of diagnosis. The second treated me as a mechanical system, did his thing, and let me go. I have to admit that both doctors cured me of an ailment, but I left the first secure in the knowledge that I had been more than an animal with symptoms. Yet I must also confess that the second doctor was a very good technician, and his skill with back ailments was impressive. Doubtless, we need both.

The evident popularity of spiritual healers, indeed of spiritual churches, in many African countries derives in my view from their involvement with the whole person as well as the family and community. It is not at all surprising that the church of Johane Masowe in Botswana forbids its members from seeking medical care outside the church. For this church, healing means becoming once again a healthy part of a well-knit, sharing community and not just an organism whose cuts, tears, and malfunctions are patched up by outsiders.

The believers in that church gave me the strong sense that it would be a betrayal of community solidarity to seek medical care from a non-believer. The implication to the community would be that the resources of the church were insufficient and that the teachings of Johane Masowe were not enough to keep the family of his followers together.

In times of desperation, members of such a church, or indeed followers of any spiritual believer, may seek outside assistance, often too late to benefit from the technical expertise of Western doctors. Many medical professionals have told me of their frustration in being unable to save sick people who could have been healed had they come in time. Their reluctance to seek Western treatment stems from the patients' confidence in the community to which they belong and in their realization that a new form of treatment may breach that trust. The outsider may treat the disease but not the people, who thus move one step further away from the community that made them into persons in the first place. I have already quoted the Sesotho belief that *motho ke motho ka batho*, "a person is a person by people". In Sesotho, the foreigner is named in a different noun class than the Mosotho, and is thus not a person in the full sense. The foreign doctor has never become an insider, and treatment by the foreign doctor removes some of the humanity of the person treated.

It is difficult for an outsider to enter fully into the life of a new community. The medical doctor, as does any foreigner, must seek slowly and carefully to understand what it is to be a Mosotho or a Muganda. The understandable fallback position, before this has been achieved, is to treat the symptoms rather than the person. The tragedy is that treating symptoms all too often remains the only approach. Thus, medicine does not move beyond mechanism to the holistic way of seeing the disease as a cultural phenomenon and not just a physical malfunction. For example, the Zionists I met in Botswana who drink tea or coffee at their evening service were seeking not only healing, but affirmation of their membership in the church. In the same way, the Cherubim and Seraphim church members in a village near Phebe Hospital in Liberia relied on prayers to heal them.

Western medicine surely has been a great boon and blessing in Africa. But those who brought Western medicine have in effect insisted that its adoption means acceptance of a new worldview and entrance into a new society. Not enough effort has been made, though efforts still can be made, to reshape Western medicine so that it can be part of the new hybrid Western-cum-African culture. Theologians have spoken of inculturation as a necessity if the church is ever to be rooted in local African culture. The same is true of medicine.

The example of the Poro and Sande societies in Liberia shows how the new medical culture can reach across the barriers to enter the deep aspects of an old culture. These societies are still central to boys and girls becoming adult members of their community. Children are taken deep into the forest to be initiated into what it means to be a Kpelle or Loma or Mende person. They are isolated for up to three years for girls and four years for boys (although much less in recent years). During the initiation time, some children fall prey to disease and accident.

The Lutheran Church in Liberia had the good sense to realize the importance of the Poro and Sande. Some of their Liberian nurses were members of the society and arrangements were made for these nurses to go behind the fence to treat children who needed medical help. They did not enter the Poro or Sande bush as outsiders, as foreign professionals wearing white uniforms. They went as members who had some additional skills to offer in the process of helping children become adults.

Sadly, the case is just the opposite with initiation schools for boys among the Xhosa people of South Africa's Eastern Cape and on the southern fringes of Lesotho. As I pointed out earlier, every year boys die from badly botched circumcisions carried out by semiliterate men without benefit of antiseptic practices and clean razor blades. Recently, the terrible scourge of HIV/AIDS has added to the danger of careless circumcision, because of the possibility for the virus to be spread by cutting boy after boy with the same unsterilized instruments. Yet the initiation school leaders and the Western medical people are unable to work together, to a large extent because the churches have refused to accept the validity of initiation in the customs and traditions of the peoples to whom they were sent.

I think that my point is clear. Whether foreigners by birth or indigenous people who have effectively made themselves into foreigners by adopting the lifestyle of the new medical tradition, outsiders who insist on seeing disease as a set of physical symptoms to be treated by mechanistic interventions will be resisted by people who care deeply about the wholeness of their culture. They will only use outside help as a last resort. It is simply not right to ask people to give up being who they consider themselves to be in order to cure them. At the same time, health practitioners cannot be expected to adopt wholly the lifestyles of the people with whom they work.

8.3 Emphasis on cure rather than prevention.

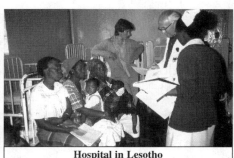
Hospital in Lesotho

A medical doctor in Liberia once told me that he was tired of trying to catch bodies falling off a cliff above him. Instead, he wanted to climb the cliff and build a fence so that people would not fall. The metaphor was quite clear. He wanted to do preventive rather than curative medicine. Day after day people came to his clinic with malaria, dysentery, syphilis, infections, and a whole host of tropical diseases and other afflictions. He gave them medicine, bound up their wounds, and sent them home to get sick again with the same ailments.

This pattern shows further the external, unassimilated character of Western medicine in Africa. The most recent occurrence of the disease is relieved, but the disease resurfaces as soon as the person is back home. The mosquitoes that carry the malaria parasite still bite, the water people drink is still full of bacteria and amoeba, the sexual behavior of people leads them back to the same infected partners, cuts and wounds continue to be treated in an unsanitary way. The lifestyles of the people have not changed, and they return again and again to the doctor until finally they give up trying. The public health approach, which fortunately is taking hold, is to provide anti-malarials, kill mosquitoes, demonstrate convenient and inexpensive ways to purify water, teach people about safe sex, and promote antiseptic care of cuts and sores.

But public health, if it is to be effective, must break through the wall of cultural difference. How people sleep at night, what regular medicines they are willing to take, how they manage their drinking water, how they engage in sex and mating rituals, and how they keep their bodies clean, are all deeply rooted in culture. Public health programs can only succeed if they become enculturated. The need for inculturation imposes a double burden on the medical profession, not only to break away from purely curative medicine, but to integrate the preventive practices into the lives of ordinary people. If doing the latter requires asking people to "jump out of their skins" and become someone else, it will not work.

The simple case of cleanliness is a good example. The rural Liberians with whom we lived for eight months in 1974 were among the cleanest people I have ever encountered. Two baths a day were the norm for people in Gbansu, a habit which we very quickly adopted. The hot, sticky, humid weather made baths a great pleasure, particularly after a day of hard work in the forest. The houses were swept daily, and the yards immediately around the houses were kept free from grass and refuse. Beds were regularly taken out of the house in order to rid them of the omnipresent insects. But this habit of cleanliness did not extend to the utensils they used or the water they drank. People could have boiled water for drinking and washing, because there was plenty of firewood in the ever-encroaching forest, but they did not.

The standards of personal hygiene were very different in Ethiopia. I was quite willing to live and sleep in a Liberian rural thatch house and often did, although I would not drink the water. Yet I would have found it difficult to live and sleep in the rural houses I visited in Ethiopia where people shared their living accommodations with their livestock. Yet there, to the best of my knowledge, the water supply, at least in the high mountains where I did field work, was clean.

To persuade rural Liberians to boil drinking water or to persuade rural Ethiopians to keep their animals outside and to clean their houses is difficult. Certainly, for well-fed and well-housed expatriates to give public health lectures would be useless. The change—for in my opinion change is indeed necessary in both these cases—has to be rooted within the culture. Such changes in culture must make sense from within rather than being imposed by intruders.

8.4 HIV/AIDS.

HIV/AIDS may or may not be a gift from Africa to the world. Whatever its origin, it seems clear that the disease first appeared in Africa. It may have been present even before the late 1950s, when a few isolated cases appeared. The most commonly accepted conjecture is that the virus jumped across species from primates to humans, perhaps through capturing, killing, and eating chimpanzees. Whatever the case, it is clear that the widest spread of HIV/AIDS has been in tropical Africa, with the worst-affected areas being in eastern, central and southern Africa. The disease is also spreading widely in eastern Europe and Southeast Asia, even though it has been brought partly, but by no means completely, under control in western

AIDS and malaria control center in Liberia

Europe and North America.

In the case of HIV/AIDS, the gap between cure and prevention is widest in Africa. There is no cure, and the treatments available at vast cost in the developed world are simply off the economic scale for most of the tens of millions of African sufferers, despite drastic reductions in the cost of the most effective drugs. Palliative methods are being developed, including diet regimes, multi-vitamins, aspirin, and even the anti-malarial drug chloroquine, but none do more than postpone death for a few months or years. Opportunistic infections, such as tuberculosis and thrush, can be treated, although long-term persistence and recurrence are much more common in HIV patients.

As is clearly true everywhere, the real issue throughout tropical Africa is prevention, which is being used effectively in several countries. Senegal has kept the infection rate down, largely through strong top-down messages from religious and political leaders. Uganda too has done very well. In a May 2002 article in *The New Republic*, Arthur Allen quotes the work of Vinand Nantulya and Edward Green in documenting the remarkable reduction in HIV incidence and prevalence there. The reason, as in Senegal, lies in the vigorous attention to the issue by the president, the churches, the mosques, the NGOs, and the schools. The ABC method—Abstinence, Be faithful to one partner, and if A and B are not possible, as a last and not always safe resort, use Condoms—has greatly helped bring the rate down to single digits.

A principal motivation for President Bush's five-nation African tour in mid-2003was to publicize AIDS and to call attention to the success stories. Unfortunately, it appears that much of his publicity was precisely that—publicity. While he touts the U.S. initiative, his Congress is reducing his request for three billion dollars of assistance by a third. The AIDS initiative is also hampered by American insistence on giving support primarily to anti-birth control organizations.

Before prevention is even possible, the disease must be acknowledged and named. The great cultural gap between Western missionaries and ordinary Africans in their attitudes to sex is a big part of the problem. The public face of Western Christian missions is characterized by a cartoon on my study wall showing a missionary couple, he in a black suit and black hat, she in head-to-toe nineteenth century dress, walking along a jungle trail. In the water beside the trail are two beautiful, nubile maidens wearing nothing other than flowers in their hair. The missionary wife has her head bent down so as not to see the offending sight, while the husband looks sideways with a clearly disapproving frown.

European and American sexuality in the nineteenth century, when the missionary movement came into full strength, was a study in self-contradiction. The public picture consisted of women who endured sex in order to bring babies into the world and men who were strong, virile, and monogamous. The underlying reality, as historians, sociologists, and novelists have shown, was of a wide range of sexual activities, often far removed from the respectable public example set by Queen Victoria, although even in her case rumors spread about her relationships to the game keeper and gardener at her rural castle.

Most likely the majority of missionaries who came to Africa lived out the ideal in their own sexual lives. Missionaries set the pattern, despite that the pattern conformed neither to the realities at home in Europe or America nor to the reality on the ground in Africa.

Anthropologists and novelists in Africa have made it clear that sex and marriage follow patterns that are specific to ethnic and cultural groups across the continent. My experiences in Liberia, Botswana and Lesotho bear out the polymorphous character of sexual behavior. In Gbansu, where we lived for eight months, polygamy was the norm for wealthy men. When a wealthy man acquired a client worker, he might well give that worker one of his wives in order to bear children who would enhance the wealthy man's status and provide more workers on his farms. Yet if a man were to sleep with one of the big man's wives without permission, such action could be punished harshly. Polygamy in this case is simply one of the ways in which a patron keeps his clients happy and in line.

In a nearby village, a powerful chief with more than a hundred wives ordered an offender who had sex with one of his wives to be buried alive by his own family in full sight of the village. The offense was not immoral sex; instead, the offense was violating the system of power and possessions. The official missionary morality of faithful, lifelong marriage was only apparently, but in no way really, related to the case.

In other countries as well, the norms of sexual behavior were not the missionary norms. I was told in Tanzania that a visiting man would be provided with a woman to sleep with during his stay. Needless to say, I did not take advantage of the custom. In the golden age when Moshoeshoe ruled Lesotho, it is said that he would provide one of his wives for a visitor to enjoy during his stay.

My students at Cuttington College saw no point whatever in my personal affirmation of sex only within marriage. They not only knew the reality of sexual behavior in traditional Liberia, but they also knew that then-President Tubman was respected in a literal way as father of the nation. He had fathered children throughout the country by women other than his official wife, not just for reasons of sexual satisfaction, but in order to consolidate his authority and to gain respect. He exploited women as his prerogative, just as he exploited the whole country.

In Liberia, another factor entered into the relation between men and women. There, traditional life was built around the split between Poro and Sande secret societies. Women had their activities, men had theirs, and there was little real crossing of the line. Girls and boys did not play much together, nor were there many ways for adult men and adult women to socialize in a relaxed way. Women worked at cooking, keeping the house and yard clean, taking care of babies, planting crops, weeding and harvesting crops, and fishing. Men worked at building houses, cutting and burning the forest, setting traps and building fences around farms, hunting, and administering the village. A female Liberian priest, Abeoseh Flemister, wrote us in July 2003: "Where is the presence of the women at the Poro's celebrations? Nowhere. Where is the presence of the men at the Women's Sandi celebration? At the head table with the women given equal place of honor."

There never developed the kind of rapport and relation between the sexes that has often been present in Europe and America. A specific consequence is that casual forms of sex play, short of intercourse, that have become socially acceptable ways of releasing sexual energy without engaging in "sex" in Western societies, never really took hold in Liberia. Boys would walk hand-in-hand, girls would put their arms around each other, but I saw little fondling of this sort between the sexes during the time we were at Cuttington. Those who did begin to show affection in this way were the exception, although as more students saw Hollywood movies, it became more common. Underlying this superficial form of behavior, however, was the assumption that when men and women related deeply it was through intercourse.

We did our best at Cuttington to keep the male and female students from each other's beds, because we were, after all, a missionary institution. The parents expected us to maintain the public image of Christian morality, even though these very parents were known to violate the norms in their own lives. One leading clergyman, a key member of the Board of Trustees, was believed to have a mistress in every major town in Liberia—and yet this same man was among the strongest upholders publicly of the norms he violated in his personal life.

The pattern in Botswana was different, yet it led to the same split between public appearance and private behavior. I became good friends with some of our young research assistants, and one young woman in particular talked openly with me about relations between the sexes. She was beautiful and obviously promiscuous, but she was very clear about one thing—she had no desire to get married. Men to her were sex objects who were given to drink and violence. She hoped one day to have children, but she did not want to be burdened with a husband.

Aids poster in Liberia

I found attitudes toward sex resembling those of Western missionaries in the African-initiated churches. The church of Johane Masowe practiced endogamy in that people were required to marry within the church, even to marry the person chosen by the family elders. Yet polygamy was not only accepted but also actively encouraged. The patriarchs of the church had several wives, whom they managed with an iron hand. Within the Zionist church my impression is that endogamy also is expected and polygamy not discouraged.

To the best of my knowledge Lesotho is a hotbed of sexual promiscuity. Nothing I have learned contradicts the findings of an anthropologist friend that most people in the village where he did his field work were sleeping with people other than their spouses. Adultery is not approved, however. Far from it. There are ongoing reports of men coming home from the mines to find their wives in bed with another man, killing the other man (and perhaps the wife also) and not being convicted of any sort of crime. Yet, despite the strong emotional objection to adultery on the part of the victim, there is an equally strong emotional attachment to it on the part of the participants.

The surveys we conducted at Sechaba Consultants confirm that most young people have had several sexual partners during the course of their lives. Often they will have one regular partner along with other casual relationships. Such casual promiscuity leads to the spread of HIV/AIDS, but that is not the deep issue I want to raise here. I began by talking about the mismatch between the missionary view of sex and the reality on the ground. I feel that this has been one important factor in the inability of Africans to acknowledge the problem. Casual sex is known to take place, but it is not acceptable in terms of the public image that has been so thoroughly ingrained into the minds and hearts of Liberians, Tanzanians, the Batswana and the Basotho, to mention only those areas where I have worked. I suspect the situation is no different in other non-Muslim, sub-Saharan African regions.

There is a deep and strong reluctance among many Africans to admit either that there is a serious HIV/AIDS problem in their countries or that they personally may be victims. The sense of shame is extremely strong, leading to serious and firm denial. Perhaps the most vivid example of that denial is South African President Thabo Mbeki's now partly-withdrawn claim that HIV does not cause AIDS. Even in mid-2003 he resisted taking decisive steps to curb the spread of the infection. His stance is based not only in his hope that South Africans may find an alternative to the horror that awaits his country, but also in his unwillingness to admit the vast discrepancy between the public, missionary-inspired image and the private reality.

What is at stake is the admission that people in countries that are among the most actively Christian in the world behave in practice at complete variance with the missionary mandate. Sadly, one of the most powerful portions of what might be called the African Christian "creed" is that the Christian convert must appear to follow the nineteenth-century Victorian pattern of sexual behavior.

One related consequence of this creed is the horror expressed by so many African leaders about homosexuality. Adulterers do not state in so many words that they commit adultery. Homosexuals, on the other hand, have committed the grievous sin of stating their practices openly and publicly. The worldwide Anglican Church risks a serious split over the issue, which came to public notice after the church in England proposed in June 2003 to consecrate an openly gay bishop. Only after extreme pressure was placed on the diocese in question did the priest withdraw his candidacy. The more recent consecration of a gay bishop in New Hampshire in the United States has provoked howls of disapproval from African churches, the only significant exception being in South Africa, where Archbishop Ndungane has publicly stated his approval of the consecration (www.royclements.co.uk/links34.htm).

It seems that what matters in matters of sex is appearance. When appearance begins to be overwhelmed by reality, as in the case of HIV/AIDS, there arises a serious lag between having the problem, recognizing the problem, and dealing with the problem. My claim is that the missionary image of right behavior has resulted in the present unwillingness to name and thus to deal with the problem of HIV/AIDS.

Whether the West had anything to do with the virus in the first place is irrelevant. Of greater importance is the responsibility of the West in creating conditions under which denial is almost inevitable. What is needed now is for Africans to free themselves from the dual burdens of shame and guilt that lead to denial. Only then can we begin to move forward with effective ways to prevent the next generation of sexually active young people from killing themselves. There are other explanations that Africans bring forward to explain HIV/AIDS, including witchcraft, a Western plot to kill Africans, and even a supposed American Initiative to Discourage Sex. Nonetheless, I feel that deep within the hearts of the people I have worked with is a strong desire to appear "virtuous" in ways that deny the reality of their behavior.

At this point, the only truly virtuous acts any can perform are to slow the spread of the pandemic and to provide anti-retroviral drugs at affordable costs to people living with AIDS. President Museveni of Uganda took a strong stand for the ABC approach at the July 2004 conference in Bangkok, albeit with a stronger emphasis on Abstinence and Be faithful than on Condoms, to the disappointment of some of his audience. What was most disturbing about the conference was the ongoing stingy response of the American government to the crisis. Generic drugs that have been approved by the World Health Organization are still not supported by the US, which evidently prefers to maintain profits to American drug companies instead of responding to the desperate need for affordable drugs.

8.5 Introduction of strong alcoholic beverages.

Alcohol is one of the oldest of human discoveries; it probably predates agriculture. Elephants are said to enjoy getting drunk on marula fruits that fall from their favorite trees and ferment. Africans across the continent have their own special types of alcoholic drinks, from the pombe of eastern and southern Africa to Botswana's khadi (made from berries found in the Kalahari) to West Africa's palm wine. All have played an important role in brightening social life, encouraging cooperative work groups, and making libations to the ancestors.

What I take issue with are the strong liquors that were brought by Western traders, beginning with the slave trade. It is very difficult to drink oneself into oblivion on sorghum beer and palm wine, but the brandies and whiskies of the traders provided a short cut to alcoholic stupor. They quickly became popular and were part of what eased the way to the export of slaves to the New World. Brandy was one of the major trade items used to buy slaves in many west African ports. Strong drink has brought no good with them, but instead have enfeebled and unhinged Africans in all societies and at all social levels.

Cane juce mill in Liberia

A major example of the introduction of alcohol was what happened on the Firestone Rubber Plantation, though Firestone exploited Liberia in more ways than I can count. The company stole prime agricultural land, employed laborers at far below a living wage, housed workers under difficult conditions, bribed chiefs to force village people to leave their farms and make the long trek to the plantation, and manipulated the government to follow a political and economic path inimical to the best interests of the people. One more crime they committed was selling stills for the production of raw rum, called "cane juice" by the local people. Sugar cane has been grown for many years in the forests of Liberia. It then became an important commercial crop in the 1850s, with Liberian business men exporting refined sugar in Liberian-built ships (Crummell: 1969). It was only in the 1930s that people began to distill it on a large scale into a potent, knockout beverage. Subsequently, many rural business people took the short route to economic success by growing sugar cane to distill into cane juice.

Not only has hard liquor proved the physical and mental undoing of many rural Liberians, but it has also been used as a lubricant for exploitation. One of the prime pieces of farm land in Gbansu was "bought" by a high-level politician who made the local chief drunk and then persuaded him to sign over the land in return for a derisory sum of money and a few bottles of whiskey.

The problem is not confined to rural people who have no experience with the hard stuff and thus fall prey to alcoholism. I remember seeing a well-dressed young man sitting on the outdoor second-story veranda of the President Hotel in Gaborone,

Botswana, overlooking the central mall of that rapidly growing city. I was sitting with a friend and we watched while he systematically drank himself into a stupor. He was alone and seemed determined to make sure he passed out. I have already mentioned my three Batswana male research assistants who drank away their frustration and boredom instead of fulfilling our mutual agreement to do research. No wonder their female research associate wanted children but not a husband.

The former student of mine, Ghisler Mapunda of Tanzanian, won a full scholarship to study at the Patrice Lumumba Freedom University in Moscow. His friends, also former students of mine, reported that he fell victim to Russian vodka and eventually returned to Tanzania a hopeless alcoholic.

When I was in Uganda in 1987 for a brief International Labour Organization (ILO) evaluation of a rural development project in the recently-liberated Luwero Triangle, I stayed at the Speke Hotel in Kampala for the nights I was unable to be in the field. Every night the hotel dining room filled up with soldiers back from their successful campaign to free the country. They arrived with their child soldiers in tow and proceeded to drink away the evening, while the prostitutes waited on the street outside. My one visit with the Baganda elite at an exclusive local club was marked by the same excessive and ostentatious consumption of liquor.

Lesotho has also suffered from the affliction of alcohol. During colonial days, South Africa's racist liquor regulations meant that the Basotho had to get a license, not just to sell liquor but even to drink it. Importation of liquor was strictly controlled in the late nineteenth century (Epprecht: 81). Independence meant free access to alcohol, and as a result what were called "liquor restaurants" sprang up all over the country. I have occasionally tried to get food in such places, but the impression I got was that food was only a minor excuse to get a license. Once I observed a very drunk colonel in the army walk in, gun in hand, and demand food and more liquor. He was served without question before he returned to his car outside and drove off into the evening.

In Lesotho, weekends are a time for violence, which is spurred on by drink. Medical doctors have told me that their most common task on Saturdays, Sundays or Monday mornings is patching up victims of stabbings or beatings brought on by drunken quarrels. In a case I mentioned earlier in southern Lesotho, a man found his estranged friend in a bar where it was common for them both to drink, sat down next to him, took out his knife and stabbed the young man three times, leading to a quick death. The killer then turned himself in to the local police.

I could continue describing more horror stories, which I fear are replicated all over Africa. In at least two cases, however, potential alcoholics have found their way out of the hell of their own creation. In one case, a colleague of mine at the Transformation Resource Centre, who had been a refugee from apartheid, faced the choice between recovery and self-destruction. He joined Alcoholics Anonymous (A.A.), has been sober for almost ten years, and is doing first-class work as a rural developer in his original home in South Africa. In another case, a brilliant young biologist stopped at the brink of collapse after he had tried and failed in A.A. and took the surgical route of having an anti-alcoholic device implanted that makes him violently ill if he consumes any liquor.

The minority of people who succeed in overcoming their alcoholism must be set against the majority who continue to drink. Government officials, police officers, soldiers, the clergy, teachers, civil servants, and business people alike succumb, as do the poor and the newly unemployed, many who have just retrenched from South African gold mines. Not only do these people lose time at work, not only do they stretch the resources of medical facilities because of fights or car accidents, but they run the serious risk of forgetting to protect themselves when they engage in casual sex, thus running the risk of HIV infection. Basotho know the danger of alcohol, which interviewees in 1993 identified as the fourth most important cause of poverty, following hunger, unemployment and drought (Gay and Hall 1994: 96-97).

The variety of liquor that the wealthy consume is expensive and powerful. The poor, on the other hand, find that ordinary sorghum beer is too weak, and thus they seek solace in heavily doctored versions of it. A horrible example occured in 1990 in Nairobi, when over fifty slum dwellers died from drinking traditional beer that had been laced with methanol and other poisonous substances (www.namibian.com.na/2000/November/africa/00B5F8AFD3.html). In Maseru, I understand that the local traditional beer is enhanced with delights such as shoe polish and battery acid just to give it a powerful kick, but so far I have not heard of deaths from drinking the concoction.

The gift of strong drink by the West to Africa has been a curse that has led to the kind of personal devastation that also helped lubricate apartheid, when workers in the Cape vineyards were given tots of wine and brandy to keep them going (Brindley: 61). Alcohol has succeeded as a device to keep Africans down, keep them pliant, and keep them in a state of self-delusion. The gift has been given, and there is no way to take it back.

Support and guidance to help young Africans overcome this curse in their lives is needed. The Blue Cross from Norway established a strong, active center in Lesotho to help bring people back from the brink of alcohol and drugs. Such help is essential, but the real work must be done by the Basotho. Churches have feasts and parties, and many I have attended recently have not served alcohol. Student groups have urged their peers not to drink. Campaigns against drunk driving have been started. These examples are surely a step in the right direction, but more recognition of the problem and public pressure by churches and other non-government organizations is still needed.

8.6 Spread of alien diseases.

Diseases entered Africa that are the result of Western infection, adoption of the Western lifestyle, and working in Western-sponsored industries. In late 2000, a London court granted relief to thousands of South African employees of an industry that had mined asbestos, which had left its employees a life of increasing difficulty breathing, leading in many cases to painful deaths. The company tried to avoid paying compensation, was forced by the court to compensate employees in June 2003 (www.guardian.co.uk/business/story/0,3604,913769,00.html).

This is not the only example of sickness induced by labor practices. In the late 1990s a blue jeans factory in Maseru where women vomited and urinated blue as a result of continuous exposure to the dye that gives the jeans their fashionable color. Yet as recently as January 2003, labor union officials in Maseru reported that the dye is still polluting the river, which some now call the "blue river".

Though it is unlikely that the West introduced HIV/AIDS to Africa, it has spread, as in the case of other epidemics, due to the improvements in communication and transportation systems and to the rapid increase in population, which all have their roots outside Africa. Some have suggested that HIV/AIDS may have crossed the barrier between chimpanzees and humans several times before, but that it did not spread because of the isolation of the central African rain forest. Only when good roads, air travel, extensive colonial networks, and a more-or-less efficient Belgian bureaucracy came into existence could the virus spread beyond its presumed origins. A counter-argument is that if communications and transport are the issue, the virus should have spread at the time of the slave trade. This argument fails due to the remoteness and isolation of the places where simian HIV existed.

More recently new diseases, such as Ebola and Marburg fevers, have spread out of their isolated homes in the dense rain forests along the Zaire River and now threaten far-flung areas. In early 2003 Ebola killed more than 100 people in Congo Brazzaville (www.abc.net.au/news/newsitems/s819316.htm). In mid-2000 I was talking with a friend who teaches in Gulo in northern Uganda. We knew the dangers of disease from militias such as the Lord's Resistance Army, but at that time we did not think that Ebola would suddenly appear in Gulo, far from the Democratic Republic of Congo. The infection did arise, and it killed many people, apparently because Ugandan soldiers had spread it when they returned from the DRC to the Gulo area.

Increased mobility is also behind the recent rapid spread of cholera, which began its proliferation in Africa in the 1970s. There were sporadic outbreaks of cholera throughout recorded history in Africa, most recently in the late nineteenth century, but there had been little twentieth century evidence of the disease until Robert Stock traced a new variety called "El Tor," which evolved in the 1960s (Stock 1976). This new strain of cholera reached Guinea in mid-1970 by way of a Russian flight bringing home Guineans who had been infected in central Asia. We first heard about it in Liberia later that year, when it began to kill people in Monrovia's slums. Our medical doctor encouraged vaccination, though he said the vaccine did not have any lasting effect. The disease continues to pop up here and there across the continent, most recently in Kwazulu-Natal. Ultimately its spread must be attributed to the opening of Africa to trade and commerce and to population movement.

Cholera is an affliction of the poor. It spreads because of poor water, poor sanitary conditions, overcrowding, and ignorance. Far different are the diseases of affluence. Obesity, hypertension, diabetes, and tooth decay are not the result of direct infection, but arise as side-effects of the money economy. It is true, however, that prior to Africa's integration into the global economy, before food stocks and convenient transport were available to relieve the effects of drought and war, people often starved to death.

The introduction of imported foods has led to unexpected consequences. Right from the start in Liberia, I was struck by the number of grossly overweight women among the Monrovia elite who depended on imported food to maintain their superior status. One of the first truly shocking experiences was being served imported canned fruit cocktail at a supper in Monrovia, instead of the wonderful variety of local fruits. That the host could afford to serve boring Del Monte canned fruit was a mark of wealth. We missionaries were also victims of the desire for foreign commodities until we began to learn how to live more, though never completely, on what we could buy in the local market.

Sugar seems to be a key to the deteriorating health of those who can afford Western food. Yet it is not just the rich who fall victim to sugar. A Haitian dentist at Cuttington (one of the many Haitians in Liberia who fled the tyranny of Papa Doc Duvalier) had a mobile clinic he used to treat dental decay. He found that the proportion of decayed teeth was inversely related to the distance from the motor road, for the simple reason that Western imported candies could not be bought in the more remote villages, whereas they were universally available in Lebanese shops along the main road.

Two years ago, our family took a holiday trip in the sub-tropical parts of South Africa and Swaziland. We went first to the Indian Ocean coast and then drove north through Kwazulu-Natal, stopped in Swaziland for a few days, and then continued north to Kruger Park. All along the way we passed through long, uniform stretches of sugar cane plantations on land that had presumably once been used for grazing cattle or raising food crops. The history of these plantations goes back to the late nineteenth century when Indian workers were brought to South Africa to plant, tend, and harvest sugar cane. Commercial crops have displaced food crops throughout Africa, but sugar cane is different in that it does harm to local health and not just to the local economy.

Sugar cane in Swaziland

I cannot help thinking of the net negative effect of these vast sugar cane plantations. Not only does production of basic foods go down, not only are workers exploited, not only was the racial disharmony exacerbated by the introduction of a large Indian community, but the effect on health of cheap, easily available sugar is substantial. The incidence of diabetes is growing rapidly in Africa, due in part to readily available sugar, but due also to calorie-rich, protein-poor diets. The World Health Organization recently came out strongly against the overuse of sugar. According to a CNN report on 3 March 2003, "People should get no more than 10% of their calories from sugar, experts say in a major new report Monday on how to stem the global epidemic of obesity-linked diseases" (www.cnn.com/2003/HEALTH/ diet.fitness/03/03/fat.world.ap/). The sugar industry objected strongly to the recommendation.

Sugar is not the only problem. Eastern and southern Africa have become hooked on maize as a staple food. Maize only became an important crop in Central and East Africa in the eighteenth century. In Lesotho and South Africa it did not take hold until the nineteenth century, replacing older (but still not indigenous) crops such as sorghum and millet. Maize is not an appropriate crop for the drier areas of southern Africa, but it is easy to grow and easy to cook, provided it has been ground into meal.

The problem with maize meal became serious in the twentieth century with the introduction of a highly refined version devoid of most nutrients (cpsajoburg.org.za/hivaids/bckgr2.html). The nutrient materials are largely used for animal feed, leaving humans to eat the virtually vitamin-free, protein-free residue, called "Super Maize Meal" by advertisers. It is white, pure, bland, and very satisfying to those who do not want to put effort into preparation or cooking. One can still buy the rougher, less refined maize meal, but it is increasingly hard to find in shops. Paradoxically, the most expensive form of commercially available maize meal is called "Traditional Braai Pap" (an Afrikaans term), which is coarsely ground maize meal to which nutrients have been returned. This is eaten only by white folks; black Africans prefer the refined, nutrient-free variety.

It has been widely noted that poor, often poorly educated people prefer the most refined foods if they can afford them, while better educated, wealthier people go back to the rougher, more basic foods. For example, white bread is preferred by the poor, while brown bread, even though cheaper, is preferred by the wealthy. Similarly, the poor drink sugar-based carbonated drinks such as Coca-Cola, while the wealthy are more likely to drink fruit juice. The deciding factors seem to be ease of access, a quick sugar fix, the prestige of an international label, and the addictive melt-in-the-mouth taste.

The consequence for those who can afford the consumer goods that originate in the Western consumer society, which bring a faint reflection of Western affluence on the user, is an unhealthy life. The great popularity of fast-food restaurants confirms this tendency, as people crowd into MacDonald's for burgers or into Colonel Sanders' for Kentucky fried chicken. These foods are the ultimate in choosing what is fashionable, and they have the dubious advantage of being quick. It is clear that the combination of obesity, high blood pressure, and diabetes is the result of this preference. In July 2003, MacDonald's claimed that it would reduce the more dangerous elements in its products.

It is only now that the European and American desire to appear thin is catching hold in southern Africa. I regularly see advertisements—on T-shirts, on bumper stickers, and on car windows—for products that will help people lose weight. One of the most common reads: "Lose weight now—ask me how," which gives a telephone number for the purveyor of food supplements that are only necessary because their users have built a way of life that depends on unhealthy, quick-fix foods.

One of the consequences (perhaps unintended, perhaps intended and well-understood in advance) of global prosperity is global ill-health, which paradoxically accompanies what has been, up until the HIV/AIDS pandemic, an overall global increase in life expectancy. It is tragic when people become able to avoid the diseases of poverty only to fall victim to the diseases of wealth.

8.7 Expensive medical care unavailable to the poor.

On my study wall is another cartoon, this one by the brilliant South African cartoonist, Zapiro. It appeared in the South African paper, the *Mail and Guardian*, shortly after the ill-fated October 2000 conference of leading international financial institutions in Prague. The cartoon shows two black-suited, briefcase-carrying diplomats, one from the International Monetary Fund and the other from the World Bank. In the first panel, they are shown telling a Latin American family to cut down the forest in order to grow a cash crop. In the second they tell an Indian family to evacuate their village because, "You've decided to build a dam." In the third, they tell an emaciated African family who are lying on the ground under the burning sun, "You can have your clinic, provided you pay cost recovery." In the fourth panel, they are in Prague complaining about demonstrations against globalism, saying, "The trouble with these demonstrators is they just do not respect people."

The health systems brought to Africa are a good thing on balance. They have eliminated smallpox and almost eliminated polio. Unfortunately, Muslim clerics in northern Nigeria persuaded their state governors to stop the vaccination campaign, just as the World Health Organization felt it had come close to wiping out polio. Before they changed their unfortunate decision, hundreds of new cases in several African countries had been discovered. Hopefully vaccination will begin again in earnest. (allafrica.com/stories/printable/200407200695.html).

When I first came to Liberia, yaws and elephantiasis were still common, but now they are rare. Malaria can be controlled, though it is still a major killer and drug-resistant varieties are a threat. River blindness, which I remember as a major threat in Gbansu, is on its way to being wiped out. Life expectancy went up significantly, although it is now dropping sharply due to the HIV/AIDS pandemic. The birth rate has dropped dramatically in most African countries due to a public health campaign, improved education, and readily available birth control. Where war has not ravaged the population, malnutrition has been reduced and crop yields increased.

The problem is that many of these gains are not available to the poor, as shown in Zapiro's not-so-funny cartoon. Western medicine is very expensive, and someone has to pay the cost of doctors, nurses, equipment, drugs, lab and other supplies, teaching institutions, and transport. In Africa, good health remains a privilege, not a right, and those who can afford it will benefit from the rapid advances in medical understanding and technology.

The only people who can afford the luxuries of Western medicine are those who live near a clinic or hospital, people who have a reasonable income or at least available cash resources, people who are not caught up in war, people who have crossed the cultural barrier (created, as I said earlier, by the medical profession itself), people who have patron-client links with government or private donors, people who are not so sick that they cannot travel, and people who have not fallen into despair, drunkenness, or madness. These conditions severely restrict access to health.

A sad example of lack of access to health care is the cure for Guinea worm. The technology is available, but wars have prevented it being brought to the people who need it. In March 2001, the *New York Times* reported that Sudan has 80 percent of all the cases of Guinea worm worldwide, but that due to the ongoing war, treatment cannot be brought to the people most in need of it.

Slum housing on the edge of Cape Town

The IMF and World Bank exacerbate the problem. Following what the characters in the cartoon said to the dying African couple, poor people can have their clinic, but they must pay for it. Health is not a free good, not a right belonging to all people. As a result, the truly poor do not even seek medical care, except through their network of neighbors, relatives, traditional healers, and churches. That some recover is due only to the good will of these informal sources and to the spread of public health ideas, which have produced some beneficial results. Fortunately, voices within the establishment are being raised against the idea of cost recovery. Most notable among these is Joseph Stiglitz, whose recent book *Globalization and its Discontents* speaks strongly against socially destructive IMF policies (Stiglitz 2003).

In Lesotho, clinic use among the truly poor has declined in recent years. Beds are sitting empty in church hospitals, because the fees are so high. In turn, the hospitals face closure, because they do not earn enough from patients to pay salaries or buy drugs. The Methodist hospital in one remote part of Lesotho closed for that reason, leaving the people in Semonkong with only an inadequately staffed and provisioned government clinic.

The problem is most acute for those suffering from HIV/AIDS. Lesotho is just now beginning to experience the rapid increase in serious illness and death from the disease. Until recently only a small proportion of the more than 35 percent of the adult population infected with the virus has begun to experience the devastating effects of full-blown AIDS. In a survey we did at Sechaba Consultants in early 2003, we found that only 18 percent respondents knew anyone who had died of AIDS. According to the Glasgow Sunday Herald President Thabo Mbeki said in September 2003 " he doesn't know anyone with HIV, yet three of his officials died of aids ... like 600 South Africans do every day. So why is he still in denial?" www.sundayherald.com/36998.

Yet it is clear that many people are already sick, that they are unable to work, that they are totally dependent on relatives to care for them (with hospital beds already full with other AIDS cases), that they are in need of special attention, and that they are dying. AIDS can be managed through the use of anti-retrovirals, but these drugs are beyond the means of the vast majority of Basotho. Even low-level palliative care, using vitamins, carefully chosen foods, and immediate attention to opportunistic infections, is too expensive for most people.

The devastation seen in Lesotho is happening throughout tropical Africa as well. In some countries the trend is being reversed, while in others such as Botswana, anti-retrovirals are being made available, most notably through the Bill and Melissa Gates Foundation. The situation is even worse where it is exacerbated by war, as in Liberia and so many other African countries. It is not enough to hope for reduced prices for anti-retroviral drugs or nevirapine, which helps prevent mother-to-child transmission. Ultimately, the questions are political. Will foreign donors respond to the appeals of the Global Fund to fight malaria, tuberculosis, and HIV/AIDS? Will African countries respond to the dual imperatives of prevention and distribution of drugs? Whether African countries, donor countries, or international agencies have the political will to respond is the big question of the twenty-first century. Bill Gates is doing so. Former US president Bill Clinton has also recently joined the struggle against HIV/AIDS by starting a Foundation committed to reducing the price of anti-retrovirals (www.hivnet.ch:8000/africa/zambia/viewR?1337).

8.8 Hopeful signs.

The medical school at the University of Zimbabwe has developed close cooperation with **traditional healers**. A leading herbalist is teaching both in the medical school and in the social science faculty. In Lesotho, traditional healers have formed an association and promote professional behavior among their colleagues. Attempts are being made in South Africa to preserve sites in which valuable herbs are found, so that they are not over-cropped.

Holistic healing is no longer just a fad among aging hippies but is becoming a respectable alternative to mechanistic medicine. My South African friend regularly sees her "get-well doctor" for immediate needs, but she also consults her "stay-well doctor," who deals with her as a whole person rather than as just an organism with aches and pains. Additionally, public health is becoming a basic part of the medical profession. In a church hospital in the mountains of Lesotho, the public health physician plays a vital role in bringing a healthy life style to poor people, many of whom simply cannot afford to come to the hospital for healing.

Prevention of disease is a key to a healthy society. UNICEF, for example, is giving more of its resources to vaccination campaigns. Proper sanitation and clean water are emphasized by governments and aid agencies in order to keep people from having to seek treatment for avoidable diseases. Prevention of HIV/AIDS has taken center stage in many countries, where treatment is simply too expensive.

The campaigns to treat and prevent the spread of HIV/AIDS are now beginning to take shape. People in South Africa are moving beyond the doubt cast by President Thabo Mbeki and are attending to prevention and cure. The government has quadrupled its budgetary allocation to AIDS prevention and care. In particular, it is highly encouraging that drug prices have dropped, so that anti-retrovirals can be given to more people and so that nevirapine is available to sero-positive pregnant women at the time of delivery, thus reducing mother-to-child transmission.

Alcoholism is a social disease that can be brought under better control. Youth and church groups are trying to spread the message of sobriety to their members. Alcoholics Anonymous is active in southern Africa. The campaign to end drunken driving is also growing as a way to stop the carnage on southern African roads.

There is little that can be done to eliminate **alien diseases** in Africa. More possible is a healthier lifestyle among the wealthy. Obesity has been recognized as a major problem, and many southern Africans are now beginning to change their eating habits. Attention is also being paid to working conditions in factories and industries. The South African gold mines have tightened up safety procedures, asbestos is no longer being mined, and pressure is being brought to bear on textile factories to provide a healthy working environment. I know an ILO worker in Lesotho whose main commitment is to study and report on poor working conditions in these factories.

The Global Fund to fight AIDS, malaria, and tuberculosis has already awarded $1.5 billion to more than 150 programs in 92 countries (www.globalfundatm.org), but **free medical care** may still be a long way off for Africans. Africans are still suffering under the burden of IMF and World Bank requirements for cost recovery. Yet there are signs that even these institutions may change their ways, and move toward recognition of health as a right rather than a privilege. Until that movement is translated into reality, however, public health will continue to suffer.

CHAPTER NINE. WESTERN ECONOMIC CONTROL

Many people, including at times even me, have claimed that the real basis of economic development is the greed of the developer. I include myself, because the life I lived in Africa was both pleasant and profitable. I have no idea how I might have fared had I chosen to remain in the United States. Life there might also have been pleasant and profitable. Such conjectures are, of course, pointless after forty-two years in Africa that left me satisfied and able to retire in reasonable comfort.

I hope that my motivation was not totally built on greed. Global companies that span the world are clear on the point. The reason why Coca-Cola expands into Africa, to the point where Coke becomes "our national drink" as one Motswana told me, is to make money, not to promote the health and well-being of Africans. As I suggested in the previous chapter, Coca-Cola has likely had a negative effect on the health of Africans. Furthermore, Cecil Rhodes did not get excited about South Africa, where he moved ostensibly to recover his health, until the glitter of diamonds and gold caught his eye. And Firestone Rubber had to find a convenient and reliable source of rubber; exploiting illiterate Liberians was a good start.

It is not only global business that has seen Africa as a source of wealth. From the time of the slave trade to the present, European and American governments have encouraged the rape of Africa. Official support was provided, once it became clear profits could be made, not just to Lever Brothers and Anglo-American, but also to small Lebanese trading companies that made a good living selling Western goods to West Africans. And, if one proved successful at selling to the "natives," one could even be knighted by the queen.

In 1885, the Berlin Conference was used to tidy up the arrangements that governments had been making informally. German bureaucratic efficiency was not happy with the casual and informal theft of African resources that had marked the previous four hundred years. Let it be regularized and organized, the Germans decided—and so it was, with each country marking on a map the territories to which it would shortly thereafter lay claim.

The large historical pattern of exploitation is well known. In this chapter, I want to look at details familiar to me, including development projects, loans, donor funds, emphasis on urban areas, displacement of peoples, and export of raw materials. Each of these activities theoretically helps African development. Some have succeeded to a limited extent, but each has caused enough problems that the balance sheet is negative.

9.1 Externally-imposed development schemes.

The literature is full of broad-brush complaints about projects such as efforts to use the Niger River for irrigation, the attempt to grow peanuts for export in Tanganyika, dams on the Senegal River, and erosion-creating boreholes in the Kalahari Desert. Rather, I want to discuss why specific projects went wrong in countries where I have worked.

I was asked in 1975 by the Food and Agriculture Organization (FAO) to be the project sociologist on the Senqu River Agricultural Extension Project in Lesotho. I had done research on agriculture in Liberia, and after a year of study and teaching at Cambridge University, I felt called to try my hand at practical agricultural development. It was a personal experiment to see if I was able to assist in the concrete business of making lives better, instead of just talking about development.

FAO persuaded the Lesotho government to accept the funds for a project intended to identify constraints to rural development, to show how the constraints could be overcome, and to strengthen necessary government services. The areas where work was to be done included animal production, crop production, soil conservation, irrigation, credit for livestock and crops, and training of local staff. The activities were to include the following:
- Meet chiefs to identify progressive farmers whose fields could be included
- Organize farmer committees to manage extension services
- Provide extension leaflets and organize field days
- Set goals and indices for crop and livestock prodtion.
- Improve livestock through exchange, breeding and sale
- Set up block farming areas with detailed schedules for cropping activities
- Set up irrigation units in six riverine areas
- Organize training in farm mechanization

All these activities were carried out under the supervision of highly skilled expatriates, who were assisted by local staff trained in each of the areas. Careful land use profiles were prepared, showing the potentials and the constraints. Technical studies were carried out in specialized areas such as irrigation, pest control, weed control, cattle fattening, crop production, and extension methods.

Senqu Project harvester

Problems arose almost immediately. Crop farming innovations only succeeded when farmers were given material incentives, including money and farm inputs, for working on their own fields. The only livestock successes came when the project provided farmers with good animals and fencing for livestock areas. Otherwise, conservation works were not completed, grazing control was ineffectual, farmers trespassed on livestock control areas, yields were low, and records were not well kept. In the end, money was lost on twelve of the thirteen farmers' associations established. A half-hearted effort was made late in the life of the project to ask the farmers to repay the losses, but the ordinary people who had been forced to participate in the project were not able or willing to do so. The loans were written off, and the associations disbanded.

I was brought into the project well after it started. Much of the damage had already been done; the project was not achieving its goals, and farmers and livestock owners were losing interest unless they got material benefits. The experts had decided they must hire new experts to help sell the project to the people. I was one of the experts, and Tesfa Guma, an Ethiopian farm management economist, was the other.

I very quickly found that the real task was selling the people's viewpoints to the project rather than vice versa. I established a research base in a foothill village that was part of one of the consolidated farm blocks and far enough from project headquarters that I could be reasonably independent. I only survived in the job for a year and a half. I produced a report that was critical of the project and its top-down procedures and decisions. It was the project's obituary (Gay 1977). We parted company, each glad to say goodbye.

The project's fundamental problem was that the places where technical experts were working were already populated by people with their own history, knowledge, attitudes, practices, and priorities. It is ironic, but true, that probably the only way for the project to succeed would have been to remove all the people from the area and hire back laborers as needed. This approach was only possible in South Africa, where an integral component of the apartheid system was that the indigenous population could be displaced at will. In Lesotho, an independent country, such displacement was not possible, so there was an inevitable clash between international expertise and local culture.

Local people responded well to project advice only when there was a clear advantage, but otherwise they left the project to do its own thing. There was resistance from local people in areas where project plans conflicted with local priorities. This was particularly evident with the consolidation of farmers' fields into blocks managed by the project that allowed for only nominal input from farmers' associations. Farmers did not want their fields planted and managed by outsiders. If there was money to be earned by doing day labor, they did it, but not because they expected long-term benefits to production. Good farmers lost interest in the consolidated activities, since they knew they could do better on their own. Resistance also grew because livestock owners were restricted from using and managing grazing land in the ways they were accustomed to doing.

Village in rural Lesotho

It was the social clash between outside expertise and the Basotho way of life that doomed the project to failure. There were individual aspects of the project that were technically good, and there was much that future projects could have learned from its less-than-successful technical aspects. These lessons were unfortunately lost, primarily because of the overall sense that this project could not overcome local resistance. The project was viewed as a complete failure. It was not a complete failure, but the small successes could not be heard or seen in the light of the larger picture of the social disaster. There was no follow-up and no second phase in which some of the lessons learned might have been applied to achieve long-term success.

Many Basotho technical experts worked on the project and it is fair to ask why they did not foresee the problems and include traditional Basotho expertise. There were two reasons why they did not save the day. First, they were all in junior positions and were expected, as counterparts, to learn the foreign ways. Second, all their formal training had taken place in the same foreign countries that supplied the senior technicians, and they were selected for the project on the basis of their performance in those foreign universities and agricultural colleges. They had already been trained to do what proved counter-productive, and they were further trained on the field to do more of the same.

Such projects need not fail, especially with the involvement of such committed, serious, and skilled experts. In order to achieve success, however, a project must involve local people from the very beginning. Basotho farmers are not foolish, and they have legitimate values, priorities, knowledge, and practices that cannot be ignored. If the farm management economist and the sociologist had been involved from the start, if the technical experts had moved more slowly in trying to implement incremental changes in local knowledge, and if practices were based on a deep understanding of the positive aspects of local culture, the project could well have succeeded.

I have written extensively about this project, because I believe it illustrates all too well the failure of donor-driven development projects to take into account the needs, feelings, and practices of ordinary people. I tried to communicate that message to my colleagues on the project, but for their own reasons they were not able or perhaps willing to hear me. I was told by one colleague, when he saw a draft of my final report, "You can't write that sort of thing." His implication was that I would be eased out of the FAO professional staff—and he was right.

What sorts of people succeed in the United Nations development system? The other FAO sociologist working in Lesotho at that time was a reasonably intelligent party hack who wrote what the Lesotho government and United Nations bureaucracy wanted to read. He played golf across the border in Ladybrand, at that time off limits to those of us who shared in the struggle against apartheid. He wrote inoffensive and innocuous sociological reports and eventually became the FAO Resident Representative in Lesotho. His actions make me think of Gilbert and Sullivan's opera, *HMS Pinafore*, about the admiral who "polished up the handle on the big front door" and polished it up so carefully that he "became the ruler of the Queen's Navy."

The inner world of the United Nations Development Programme and its subordinate agencies is all too often sealed off against the real world, as I found in the Senqu project. I have already mentioned the project in Liberia that clear-cut the rain forest in order to plant rice and then coffee. It was an environmental disaster, because the officials did not listen to ordinary people who knew the fragility of their own soils. Similarly, other projects were imposed on Liberians, including one-person paddy rice schemes, which involved extremely dirty, lonely work without enough reward to justify violating the expected norm of having cooperative work groups help bring in the harvest and unite the village. Individualism in any intensely communal rural village rarely worked. Only a few people I knew were able to stick to the project, and often they felt cut off from their fellows.

The opposite is true in Lesotho, where individual enterprise is much more likely to succeed now that the old traditions of cooperative farming are almost dead. Yet in Lesotho the Scandinavians continue to fund the Lesotho Cooperative College, working at cross-purposes to the usual vertical patron-client relationships. And as long as the Swedes or the Danes provide money for the cooperatives, or as long as Canadian Catholics fund the Credit Union schemes, the members continue to do the work. As soon as the funding dries up, however, these cooperatives cease. Development efforts that try to circumvent the natural lines of respect, patronage, and authority will always fail.

I remember the disappointment expressed by USAID upon receipt of my report on small-scale informal sector businesses in Botswana. I pointed out the extreme difficulty these businesses had in trying to make a living and how the only successful ones were those that operated within a protective church environment.

USAID was committed to a secular separation-of-church-and-state ideology. They preferred to find ways for these small businesses to work together, such as through cooperative purchasing and marketing. Outside of Johane Masowe's church, however, small businesses were in fierce competition, with far too many trying to tap the same local markets, and these businesses were born and died with depressing regularity. The businesses we identified at the start of the six-month-long survey died by the time it ended, and we had to substitute new businesses in the same lines in order to complete our research. The image of the informal sector that USAID and the ILO desired was not the reality at that moment in Botswana. I told what I saw, but it was not a suitable basis for the kind of development that these foreigners wanted to introduce. I was reassured but saddened by a 2004 report confirming our findings about the informal sector in Botswana (allafrica.com/stories/200407210721.html).

I had a similar experience in Uganda. The ILO Luwero Triangle self-help project which I was asked to evaluate proposed what the experts thought were good ideas, but they were developed in Geneva and Kampala. As a result, the village people were doing the work for financial rewards. They were being given blankets, hoes, and money to do what they should have wanted to do for themselves, particularly local road rehabilitation. The object of the exercise, from the people's point of view, was the rewards, not the work. The community was compelled to create a committee that rubber-stamped the decisions made by the expatriate project leaders who were living in Kampala rather than in the village.

Blanket distribution in Uganda

The expatriate experts were offended when the evaluation team, which consisted of three Ugandans, one Swiss, and me, recommended that the experts should live at least part-time in the village and that they should respond to the ideas of the locally-organized, community-based committee. From a letter by a Ugandan sociologist (now, in 2003, Uganda's Minister of Local Government) who had been on the evaluation team, I learned that the experts tried to bribe the Ugandan members to change the report once I had left. It was very depressing, indeed, that the leaders of a good project failed to see the importance of deeply involving the local people in planning and decision-making. Expatriate selfishness served to divert resources, both financial and human, toward personal gain.

It is important here to underscore that a large proportion of foreign assistance money went into the pockets of the experts and into the coffers of foreign suppliers. Similarly, the Senqu River Project in Lesotho allocated the bulk of its money to foreign experts and expensive machinery. What little that was spent on Lesotho went to pay minimal local salaries and to buy heavy equipment for the Ministry of Agriculture, equipment much of which fell into ruin before the end of the project.

My wife and I must plead guilty to the charge of benefiting from foreign aid, including salaries and support from international agencies and from the Episcopal Church Mission Board. We did very well in our years working in Africa. We sent our children to good schools in Liberia and Lesotho as well as in the United States.

We received medical support when we were ill, including the time I was seriously ill in 1968. We accumulated solid and substantial savings for retirement, which came in 2001 after forty-two years in Africa. I believe and hope we tried to give value for value received, but I am sure that we too can be viewed as having gained more than we gave.

In the Transformation Resource Centre newsletter *Work for Justice* I wrote in September 1989 that according to the United Nations Development Programme, Lesotho received more than 4 billion rands in aid from 1978 to 1987 (then roughly equal to $2 billion U.S. dollars). At that time there were about three million hectares of land being farmed in the Orange Free State, and the land price in that part of South Africa was about 1,000 rands per hectare. That foreign assistance money given or loaned to Lesotho in only a decade was more than enough to buy Free State farmland in what the Basotho legitimately call "the conquered territories" is sobering. The actual benefit of that massive amount of aid to Lesotho has been much less.

The United States has gained far more from Liberia than it has given. The only Liberians to benefit were the elite, while the poor bore the brunt of the suffering. Charles Taylor's hypocritical noises about American exploitation unfortunately reflected reality (www.allaboutliberia.com/opinion354.htm). In 1982, the Reagan administration in the U.S. listed eight guidelines for giving aid to foreign countries. At the bottom of the list was international solidarity and general economic growth, well below political, military, and economic advantages for America. Certainly, access to Robertsfield International Airport, a massive Voice of America installation, and a link in the worldwide low-frequency tracking system were strong reasons for giving aid to Liberia. Value was given for much greater value received!

Americans often believe theirs is one of the most generous countries in the world. Far from it! At the end of 2001, the U.S.A. contributed 0.1 percent of its Gross Domestic Product to foreign aid, less than a tenth of Denmark's percentage of GDP. Yet a public opinion poll in 2001 showed a median score of a random sample of Americans believe that the U.S. spends 20 percent of its federal budget on foreign aid, whereas the reality is less than 1 percent (www.pipa.org/OnlineReports/BFW/finding1.html).

Foreign manufacturers have benefited greatly from African aid. I think of the hundred or more tractors brought to Lesotho in the 1970s as Austrian aid. They were not really needed, since South African tractors would have served the purpose better, but doing so allowed Austrian manufacturers to sell off surplus stock. I think of the flood of surplus, out-of-date, heavily polluting Japanese minibuses that have come into Lesotho. They were banned from the streets of Japan, but here they are, painted over and polluting the streets of Maseru and South Africa. I think of the D-9 Caterpillar tractors that sank out of sight in the swamps of Liberia, a form of overkill that could not survive the difficult conditions of the rain forest. I think of the rusting irrigation equipment I saw on the banks of the Niger River in Mali and on the banks of the Senqu River in Lesotho. Who benefits? Surely not the recipients of the "aid," and even more surely not those

Ruined irrigation structures on Niger

who have to repay the loans.

It is not only high-priced, low-quality goods that are imported into Africa in the name of foreign aid. An often unnoticed kind of aid is the importation of used clothes. Many Europeans and Americans think this must help the poor Africans who have no shirts to put on their backs. That may be true in many cases, but the macro-economic effect of importing used clothes has been far from positive. A striking article in the New York Times in 2002 showed what happened to a typical article of clothing, a T-shirt, which came from New York and ended up being sold in a market in a remote village in Uganda (Packer 2002). The micro-economics for the recipient and for all the hawkers along the way were good. Yet the net effect on domestic African industry is substantial and negative. Instead, Africans must develop textile industries of their own. They are doing so, as I have commented elsewhere in relation to the growth of the industry in Lesotho, but the goods do not find enough markets in Africa to justify the industry, in part because of the massive importation of used clothes. What starts and ends as an act of generosity becomes counter-productive.

I could go on to describe other foreign-based failures to think and act locally. I will not, because I think the point is clear. It is essential to be patient, to have a long-term perspective, to listen to local people, and to allow plans to emerge from the interaction between local people and foreign experts. I think back to the most successful development project ever undertaken in Lesotho, namely, the missionary work of Eugene Casalis and his French colleagues in the mid-nineteenth century. They took the long perspective and did not force the Basotho to follow instructions formulated in Paris. Instead, they learned what it means to be a Mosotho, submitted patiently and sensibly to the great king Moshoeshoe I, and helped him create a new nation. Much of what we see as the golden age of Lesotho and much of what we know as Basotho culture came out of this fruitful interaction between Moshoeshoe and the missionaries. It might even be said that Lesotho is one of the few African countries to benefit directly from foreign assistance at that time. Can we not learn from that great beginning instead of forcing the Basotho to dance to an expatriate tune that no longer benefits them?

9.2 Loans to create indebtedness.

In 1871, Liberian president Edward Roye took an ill-advised loan from Great Britain of £100,000 sterling, equivalent then to $500,000. The terms were such that Liberia would have to repay $663,000, while they only received $375,000, because the loan had been discounted. Worse was that the British agents deducted three years' interest up front, leaving Liberia with only $270,000, of which only a quarter was sent to Liberia. The remainder was held as credit. Moreover, the initial payment was in goods and worthless notes, so that according to Cassell (pp 274 ff), Liberia effectively got nothing and British bankers made a tidy profit.

Cassell continues the story up to the 1920s, as I summarize here. Edward Roye was a prominent business person in Liberia before he was elected president. He knew that a business could only succeed if it had capital up front, and so he extended that logic to the nation. It was a question of "willing buyer, willing seller." The bankers in Britain were only too pleased to give money to the President of Liberia, because they saw it as a good deal whereby they could get a semi-permanent source of interest payments and flog off relatively worthless goods as part of the first tranche of the loan. Roye was taken in by the smooth-talking British financiers. Roye was not smart enough to ensure his own personal financial survival, and the Liberian elite were quick to see how he could have enriched himself using the money he had brought, ostensibly to help the country develop. He was overthrown and tossed into prison, where he died.

Roye was replaced by veteran ex-president Joseph Jenkins Roberts, who did his best to try to restore political and financial stability to Liberia. But he could not shake off the international responsibility Roye had taken on, and committed the country to honor the debt.

Another loan of $500,000 was negotiated with the British in 1906 against a pledge of the entire customs receipts for the indefinite future. This debt also proved an impossible burden, leading the American State Department to renegotiate all previous debts through an additional loan of $1,700,000 in 1912. The condition of the loan was that the Americans would provide a receiver of customs, a financial advisor, and an auditor. The loan was refinanced in 1926; this time the Firestone Plantation Company provided the money and the newly established Finance Corporation of America was responsible for administration of the loan. The Liberian government could not incur any further debts without the permission of the Finance Corporation, and Liberia was responsible for all interest at 7 percent per annum. The proceeds of the new loan, which was valued at up to $5,000,000, were to be used to pay off all earlier loans.

What helped Liberia in this instance was that rubber proved to be a very valuable commodity on the world market, particularly when the Japanese closed off supplies from Southeast Asia. The rapid growth of income to Liberia from rubber during and after World War II made it possible in 1951 to retire the loan entirely, as American author Earle Anderson pointed out (pp. 93-94, 227). Yet retirement of the loan did not mean the end of dependency on foreign sources of income, including the export of rubber and iron and foreign monetary assistance.

Firestone plantation sign

Step by step Liberia worsened its indebtedness until the country lost not only its financial independence but also large portions of its territory to the almost autonomous Firestone Rubber Plantation, which displaced and then exploited the indigenous peoples. In the end, the loan was retired, but at the cost of Liberia becoming an economic dependency of the United States and its big businesses.

The story of Liberia's disastrous early experiments with international loans and the eventual rescue of Liberia through global business is a cautionary tale for African countries, so many of which have fallen into similar traps. The Liberia we first began to know in 1958 was not only an American appendage, it was almost an appendage of the Firestone Rubber Company. There was some diversification, particularly with the discovery and exploitation of iron ore and the construction of the Free Port in Monrovia, but the diversification was toward, rather than away from, capture by international big business.

In other African countries such as Botswana, rapid economic growth over the past twenty years has been largely the result of the diamond industry, and as a result, Anglo-American and De Beers have the economic muscle to determine Botswana's economic development. The livestock and tourism industries are important; they bring in foreign exchange and allow the wealthy to become even wealthier. But the real power is in diamonds, symbolized by the fortress-like mines at Orapa and Kanye in the desert and the impressive office block on Gaborone's central mall. Major loans have been given to Botswana by international corporations and financial institutions, loans that can be managed because the economy is alive and growing, due to its deep involvement with the big global financial players. The economy is generally believed to have been handled well, with diamond earnings being ploughed back into infrastructure and social services. A big problem, however, is Botswana's 40 percent HIV/AIDS prevalence among adults.

Lesotho has depended almost totally on the gold mining industry in South Africa and was able to avoid heavy commitments to international finance, because the miners brought income to the country. Yet now that retrenchment has brought the number of adult males working in the mines from 29 percent in 1988 to 12 percent in 2000, and even less in 2003, the country has acquired serious debt to foreign financial institutions.

South African gold mine

Loans were taken over the past several years for expensive prestige projects, such as paving the road to the interior mountain district of Mokhotlong and building a costly appeals court. Lesotho also took out extensive loans for building the dams that supply water to South Africa under the Lesotho Highlands Water Project. Repayment of these loans is beginning to hurt. The rapid expansion of the textile industry due to America opening its markets to African products has helped, but this expansion is not helping to build national infrastructure.

I have little experience with or understanding of the huge debts so many African countries have been persuaded to take. I only know that other countries where I have worked seem hopelessly in debt. Uganda, Ethiopia, and Tanzania pay a large proportion of their annual national incomes in debt service; in some cases, debt repayment is greater than the amount received in foreign assistance. It seems clear that these debts can never be repaid and equally clear that creditors must write off debts, whether they are nations, the World Bank, the IMF, the United Nations, or big global corporations. How much, where, and under what conditions, I am not sure. On the other hand, the banks do not complain when the interest continues to roll in and the principal is untouched. The Jubilee Movement, off to such a good start in 2000 under the leadership of South Africa's Archbishop Ndugane, is moving ahead, but slowly. The Jubilee Movement International (www.jubileeplus.org) tracks the progress of forty-two "Heavily Indebted Poor Countries" regarding the goal of receiving debt relief. As of mid-2002, seven African countries had jumped through the necessary hoops preparing them for assistance, and others were lining up. Debt relief is not an easy process, however, as in the case of Zambia, whose debt payments went up in 2001 in the course of implementing the requirements for debt relief (www.afrol.com/News/ zam004_debt_relief.htm).

The major Western countries started giving big loans to African and other Third-World nations as a result of the rapid increase in oil prices in the 1970s. These Western nations had surplus dollars, and they wanted to put them to work. They were willing sellers of dollars, and they quickly found willing buyers in poor nations. Some genuinely had the best interests of their people at heart, such as Julius Nyerere in Tanzania and Seretse Khama in Botswana. Others, including Mobutu in Zaire and a succession of crooks in Nigeria, were simply looking for the best deal for themselves and siphoned off substantial portions of the loans into offshore tax havens and Swiss banks.

In cases where the economy could support loan repayment, as happened in the 1950s in Liberia and at a later date in Botswana, the debtor nation survived, though it was deeply in thrall to Western powers. In cases where loans were unwisely taken and unwisely spent, including in Tanzania and Uganda, the result was impoverishment. In the most extreme cases, particularly where loans were eaten by the local elite, the result was economic and political disaster, as in Zaire (now the Democratic Republic of Congo).

Rarely hurt in this process are the willing providers of the loans. Even the earliest lenders to Liberia came out smiling. The Firestone Rubber Company has done extremely well there, and so have the Liberian elite. The people who suffered were families who lost their land and workers who were exploited over the years. In the case of Botswana, a larger portion of the elite benefited than in other African countries, partly because the diamond companies knew how to manage the resource in a way that the local people did not. In Botswana the losers have always been the Bushmen, who systematically get the worst possible deal from everyone.

But in almost every other African country the ultimate losers have been ordinary people, not just specialized groups like the Bushmen, who were outside the mainstream and were ignored. The elite may survive or even benefit, but the common folk get poor medical care, their children go to low-quality schools, civil servants receive salaries late if at all, the roads are neglected, food becomes expensive and scarce, and fuel prices rise sharply.

Apart from endemic corruption and wasteful expenditures on the military and on prestige projects, one reason ordinary people lose out is because the government must spend so much in debt repayment, sometimes in interest alone, that it cannot afford to provide basic social services. Another problem is that African countries cannot afford the investment in infrastructure and business development that allows money to be generated from within these societies. Yet it must not be forgotten that if the money sent abroad by politicians and entrepreneurs were repatriated, there would be enough to begin rebuilding African economies. Debt forgiveness is necessary, but so are honesty and prudent financial management at the national level.

9.3 Export of raw materials.

As a result of ongoing indebtedness, countries go broke, continue to pay back more money than they earn, and in desperation sell raw materials in the open world market without being able to locally transform them into finished goods. One of the main reasons why industrialized countries sought to give loans was to expand their supplies of basic commodities such as rubber, tin, copper, iron, aluminum, coffee, cocoa, tea, and cotton. The producers of these primary commodities took the loans without realizing that the increase in export supplies would lower prices, thus reducing the value of the loans by making them more difficult to repay from proceeds. Countries with oil and diamonds were more fortunate, since the world continues to pay high prices for these goods.

The port in Monrovia

I saw the vicious cycle of increased output and lower prices not only in Liberia, where the price of rubber, iron, cocoa, and coffee dropped in direct proportion to the increase in supply, but also in Tanzania and Uganda. In both countries coffee was a major export crop, and in both countries farmers got steadily lower prices for the increased harvest. In 1999 cocoa farmers burned 20,000 tonnes of their surplus stock in order to keep prices up (www.indianexpress.com/fe/daily/19991202/fco02017.html). It seems a mad scheme to burn crops in order to sell crops, but it is an obvious and logical consequence of being encouraged to over-produce. Overproduction was in part a response to World Bank pressure to produce cash crops rather than food crops for home consumption. The underlying theory was that growing cash crops would have a higher return per input than food. In practice, shifting to cash crops produced real failure and, in the end, hunger.

The price does not drop only because of overproduction. It has become clear in recent years that a major problem is subsidies by rich nations of their own wealthy farmers. The most recent case is cotton production in the savanna zones of West Africa. Mali and Burkina Faso have depended heavily on cotton for foreign exchange, but with the massive subsidies the U.S. government gives its own cotton producers, West Africans cannot compete. Blaise Compaore, the president of Burkina Faso, and Amadou Toumani Touré, the president of Mali, wrote a compelling article for the 11 July 2003 issue of The *New York Times*. In it they beseeched the American government to give a fair deal to African cotton producers. Otherwise, they said, poverty will get continually worse in their countries, which could lead to disaster, not only for Burkina Faso and Mali, but for a world that depends on keeping global peace.

During my time in Liberia, there was frequent discussion of building tire and steel factories in West Africa, but nothing came of it. Liberia wanted to be able to process its own rubber and iron, and not just sell what was, in the case of iron, a limited and finite resource. West African countries could not come to an agreement about which country should host the factory, and individual countries could not raise the capital necessary to go it alone. In the end, rather than succeed together, they preferred to fail separately.

The problem is not simply one of cooperation and capital. Other factors enter the equation: competence and management. I remember eating some Ghanaian chocolate candy when we visited that country in 1966, but it was a poor imitation of Swiss or Belgian chocolate. To succeed in the chocolate business, they would have had to import skilled professionals and would have had to maintain tight quality control. They did not, and their chocolate was only marginally worth eating.

Gold in South Africa, as well as in Ghana, Mali, and Tanzania, is another resource that is rarely beneficiated in the supplier country. South Africa has been producing gold since the late nineteenth century, but the vast bulk of it is exported in the form of gold bricks. A small quantity is pressed into gold coins or sold to collectors, but other processing is done in countries such as Italy, where the expertise exists to make fine jewelry. The depressing truth is that both Ghana and Mali once made fine gold jewelry, ornaments, and works of art during its pre-colonial days, but these are arts that have largely been lost today.

South Africa should have had the foresight long ago to process its gold locally, but did not begin to do so until recently. Its industrial expansion has been in other areas, financed by profits from selling gold. Fortunately, South Africa is now turning its attention to manufacturing and services, businesses that are far more profitable than primary production. There is hope that South Africa will be the engine for economic growth in southern Africa, because it can provide export goods as well as create jobs in manufacturing, engineering, sales, and services. South Africa's prospects, however, are sadly dimmed by the economic crisis that afflicts both Zimbabwe and Zambia and by the continual state of war farther north.

Other countries in Africa have been much less fortunate. Even the big oil producers such as Nigeria, Angola, and Gabon have little to show for the sale of crude oil. Nigeria has even gone backwards because of black-market sales of the petrol it produces and because of the sabotage of its pipelines and other basic means of distribution. Hundreds of people have been killed by petrol fires when oil lines have been cut by people wanting to make a few naira stealing and selling fuel. In June 2003 mover than 100 people were killed in southeastern Nigeria when a spark ignited pipelines which had been cut in order to steal the precious fuel (/news.bbc.co.uk/2/hi/africa/3009756.stm).

It is ironic that Nigeria regularly runs out of petroleum products, which forces prices up and causes huge traffic jams around petrol stations. At the same time, Nigeria continues to export the raw material that it could refine in much larger quantities locally. In July 2003, for example, Nigeria's economy was crippled over the price of fuel, raised for what are probably legitimate macro-economic reasons, but heavily damaging to the livelihoods of ordinary poor people who depend on cheap transport and cheap cooking fuel.

In each of these cases, the losers have been the people who owned the land in the first place. I have already pointed out how rural Liberians lost not only their prime farmland, but also lost their independence as they were forced into rubber production. Liberia's iron mines are now played out, and the result is forests that were ruined in the process of extracting the iron.

Furthermore, American interest in an African country grows when oil is found in it. If it were not for the threat of terrorism and for oil, now exported by Nigeria, Gabon, and Angola, and soon to come online from Sudan, Equatorial Guinea, and Sao Tome e Principe, I wonder if President Bush would have even made his mid-2003 African tour.

All across West Africa, once extensive virgin rain forests have been cut down for the profit of foreign capital and local elites. When I flew over Côte d'Ivoire in 1997 I was struck by the almost total absence of forest. Instead, palm oil, cocoa, and coffee plantations dotted the landscape. Who benefits? Certainly not the local people who get only meager profits from the sale of these crops and who are compelled to agree to the destruction of surplus cocoa.

Much of Liberia's forest, which was still more or less intact at the end of the Liberian civil war in 1996, is now being bulldozed in order to get the few high quality trees that dot the landscape. In the process, one of the last remaining reservoirs of equatorial plant and animal life is being blotted out of existence, not to mention the trees that are the lungs of the West African weather system. The real beneficiaries of this rape of the forest were Charles Taylor and his cronies, as well as the European suppliers of the weapons that fueled Taylor's ambitions.

The ultimate of evil exploitation is the extraction of diamonds and oil. I have not worked in an oil-producing country, but I have seen the greed that glazed the eyes and hardened the hearts of Nigerian friends. They know full well that Nigeria has been cursed by the oil that ought to have been a blessing. Gerard Manley Hopkins' poem *God's Grandeur*, written about the polluted life he saw in England, anticipates how the Niger delta has been "seared with trade; bleared, smeared with toil;/And wears man's smudge and shares man's smell: the soil/Is bare now, nor can foot feel, being shod."

The people of the oil-rich regions of Nigeria have made every kind of protest imaginable, but to no avail. Their leaders, notably Ken Saro-Wiwa, have been murdered. Their rivers are polluted. The fish they catch are inedible. And yet the Nigerian elite and the major oil companies continue to profit, making only meaningless gestures toward recompense of the people and the environment.

I know that oil is the source of the money that Colonel Gadhafi used to fund Charles Taylor in Liberia and to sow seeds of distrust among other African countries. Oil will soon be the force that will bring Equatorial Guinea out of being a backwater in the competition for the most unjust and corrupt country in Africa and into being a major player in that most wicked struggle. Oil is what kept the government of Angola going while war raged between two equally horrible competitors: the president of Angola, José Eduardo Dos Santos and the rebel, Jonas Savimbi. Dos Santos lives on oil, which benefits him, his cronies, and their war machine. Savimbi is dead, but his legacy lives on. Recently, explorations offshore show that Sao Tome and Principal is the next nation to be enriched (or impoverished?) by oil.

What kept Jonas Savimbi alive until his 2002 murder was diamonds. The diamond trade is fueled by the desire of wealthy socialites to appear richer and more glamorous than their rivals and by the desire of ordinary people to have shiny rocks that "are forever." The diamond trade is a horror, except for the reasonably well-run industries in South Africa, Botswana, and Namibia. If it were not for the genuine benefits that diamonds bring to these three countries, I would argue for the trade to be banned or at least shamed, just as the fur trade was shamed.

A geologist friend in Liberia, who was at the time Minister of Mines, told me about a pair of diamond miners in the remote Gola forest. They worked as a team, with one of them deep in a hole they had dug, passing up buckets of mud and gravel for the other to sieve for diamonds. One day the man on the surface found that the bucket contained a large and potentially very valuable diamond. His response was to cut the rope by which his partner was able to come back up to the surface, leaving him there to die. The surface partner then left the scene, took the next taxi to Monrovia, and sold the diamond to an unscrupulous trader, who probably gave him far less than it was worth. He bought a big car, drove it around town until he wrecked it, rented the movie theater and invited all his friends to celebrate, gave a big party, and the next morning was once again just another penniless diamond miner—and a murderer.

That story to me encapsulates the horror of the illicit informal diamond business. It is only a small step from there to situations such as when Charles Taylor funded the Revolutionary United Front in Sierra Leone, which turned children into drugged, brain-washed soldiers and encouraged them to cut off the hands and feet of those who blocked their greedy quest for riches. Taylor destroyed not only Sierra Leone but his own country in the process.

Once again, who is hurt? The ordinary people, the farmers who have no hands to cultivate their soil, the child soldiers who may be detoxified and then discover what they have done, the men whose greed has stripped them of the last vestiges of humanity, the countries whose hopes for development have been hijacked. Even after the end of the war in Sierra Leone, child soldiers have been recruited into diamond-mining in the interior of the country, and reports continue to surface of young children dying as they are lowered into water-filled and rain-swollen pits to scoop up diamond-bearing gravel.

The raw materials of Africa are still there to be exploited. Another kimberlite pipe has recently been found in the Liberian forest. Côte d'Ivoire is hoping to bring an offshore oil and gas field into production. Equatorial Guinea is suddenly becoming of interest to big oil companies. Chad has received the first down payment on a big loan to build an oil pipeline to the coast. The Democratic Republic of Congo sits on huge untapped reservoirs of minerals, including diamonds. Because of its oil and diamonds, Angola is potentially one of the richest countries in the world. The story goes on, across the continent.

But what in fact is happening? The raw materials are indeed being exploited, but so are the people of the land. Exploitation occurs because African countries cannot cooperate, because skilled technicians are leaving Africa in droves for industrialized countries, because short-term gain so often leads to long-term loss, and because there is massive corruption in high places. Coffee, cocoa, iron, timber, diamonds, gold, and the whole catalogue of African wealth are being exported at low prices to Europe and America, where they are processed for sale at high prices, even being sold back to the elite whose selfish folly has been partly responsible for making local processing impossible.

Commodity prices are manipulated in European and American stock exchanges in order to maximize foreign profits and minimize returns to African farmers. Evidence indicates that child laborers are the main workers on family farms in Côte d'Ivoire and that their wages are minimal, if they are paid at all (www.usaid.gov/press/releases/2002/fs020726.html). Some have called this slavery. I would challenge that label at the micro-level, since these children are helping their parents survive, but I would agree at the macro-level, saying that African producers are now enslaved to a Western economic system they cannot control.

There is still more to the failure of African nations to be productive than the factors I have listed. My friend and colleague Alan Price in Maseru pointed out that poverty is deeply embedded in the process of under-development, both as an effect and a cause. Low income or even no income at all is both a source of the problem and a result. Poverty comes in part from low productivity, which in turn stems from poor health and poor education. This, combined with poor management skills, leads to low investment per capita, meaning low wages and low on-the-job training. To the extent that a large, inexpensive labor force is available, manufacturers will continue treating African countries as sources of cheap, expendable labor and will do their high-tech processing at home in Europe or America.

Still worse are the horrors being committed in the lust for gain. Not only are profits being exported to Europe and America, not only are loans being skimmed by leaders and put in Swiss banks, not only are creditor banks squeezing African governments dry in order to claim their exorbitant interest payments and reclaim their loans, but the worst of it is that the very governments who are sitting on this wealth are abusing it, abusing the earth, abusing the people, and destroying each other.

In the unseemly lust for wealth in Côte d'Ivoire, the southern forest belt rulers denied the rights of the northern savanna dwellers for years, claiming that they were "foreigners," without recognition of the long-term inter-ethnic movements of the West African region. The result was a destructive but wholly unnecessary civil war that has set back progress not only in Côte d'Ivoire but in that country's northern neighbors.

As oil wealth rolls in, the amateur brutality of the Ngoema family in Equatorial Guinea will become fully professional. In Nigeria, children are accidentally burned alive in fires started as the poor of the Niger delta try to tap the oil and petrol pipelines for a bit of the wealth that is being exported from their region. In Chad, the first installment of a World Bank loan intended to pay for an oil pipeline was used to buy armaments to put down rebel forces that want to take over the cash cow that oil will soon become. In Angola, the civil war has ended, but all sides are still busy exploiting resources to benefit themselves rather than the country as a whole.

Many have been deeply involved in the Democratic Republic of Congo, fighting over control of the vast riches of that country. When I joined a group of men cutting up an elephant in the remote rain forest of Liberia, I found that it was not long before we were visited by every fly from every corner of the forest. They smelled the rotting meat. How similar to the situation in Congo, except that the human flies there feel it necessary to make hypocritical speeches about the protection of sovereignty and human rights. A good example in eastern Congo is the shameless exploitation of hungry day laborers who work to mine the mineral coltan (used in cell phones, laptops, and other electronic devices). The *New York Times* printed a powerful article in August 2001 on the horrors of digging for this substance, which apparently is necessary for those like me who depend on computers (Harden 2001). I hope that the new government of national unity in Congo, agreed upon in South Africa in early 2003, will hold, but I have to admit I am skeptical.

9.4 Displacement of peoples.

I refer again to the Zapiro cartoon on my wall, showing the World Bank and IMF experts informing a poor Indian family that they must evacuate their village, because "you've decided to build a dam." In Lesotho, several thousand people were forced to move because of the Lesotho Highlands Water Project. I think the Lesotho project is justified because of the overall benefit to the region of providing water to the industrial center of South Africa. Lesotho will benefit, not only from sharing in the economic growth of the southern African region, but also from the royalties accruing from the sale of water. I realize many people object to the project as destructive to the environment, as wasteful of water, and as exploitative of poor people, but I support it. The best arguments against it are given by Patrick Bond in the book *Unsustainable South Africa* (Bond 2002).

I cannot deny that many of the people required to move have been harmed. The treaty giving legal force to the dam project requires that their condition should not be worse at the end than before construction began. Those working on the project have not done a bad job. The first phase of resettlement and compensation was not fully up to expectation, but amendments were made to the program so that some of the worst excesses were ameliorated. The second phase has been handled better, and monitoring, from outside and within, is being put in place to ensure compliance over the next decades. Even in the second phase, all has not been perfect, especially for the people who were moved to Maseru and subsequently received ill treatment by the politicians who were their new neighbors. A third problem is the potential destruction of the main river, which takes what remains of the water from the dam and channels it eventually into the Orange River in South Africa.

Village water tap in Lesotho

All these issues are being taken into account and it appears that much is being done to minimize damage. In the end, I support the project because it can lead to long-term economic growth for South Africa and spillover economic growth for other countries in the region.

Far more serious are the displacements I witnessed in Liberia, Tanzania, Botswana, and South Africa, where almost no compensation was provided and where people are worse off than before. It is very hard to turn the clock back. People who have been moved into new areas, away from their original homes, can only with great difficulty be given back their land.

I have already mentioned the forced removal of Liberian farmers from their land as a result of creating the Firestone rubber plantation. That removal led in part to a decline in exports because of the decline in markets for hitherto profitable commodities such as palm oil, pepper, coffee, and cam wood. Additionally, Liberia was backed into an economic corner, not only through ill-conceived loans by unscrupulous foreign financial institutions, but also because of Liberian incompetence. Liberia escaped from the financial trap, but ultimately at great cost to the little people who lost their land.

Further displacement took place because of the civil war. The Liberian interior was extensively depopulated, because people were killed or died due to lack of medical care, and because people fled to the coast in fear. The same displacement happened to Charles Taylor's former playground, Sierra Leone. In both countries, traditional rural agriculture is difficult, starvation is rife, death and maiming abound, and the only hope for many is to escape from what once were and still could be good rural homes.

The problem in Tanzania was created in Tanzania without help from foreign advisors. Julius Nyerere, the first president of independent Tanzania, saw the necessity of providing water, education, roads, and medical care to rural people. The problem was that in many parts of the country families lived on isolated homesteads rather than in concentrated villages. It would therefore have been difficult to locate

Destroyed homestead in Tanzania

schools and clinics near every home, and equally difficult to construct the roads and water systems needed by remote households. The traditional system, however, had the advantage that people lived next to their fields, which meant they found it easy to cultivate the fields without having to walk great distances.

The decision was made to relocate people to newly created villages. Houses were destroyed and families were forced to abandon their plots and move. A system of top-down village democracy was forced on them, complete with "ten-cells." Each ten households watched one another to ensure compliance and also elected representatives to a village council. The theory had some good features, and a solid network of schools, clinics, roads, and water systems was put in place around the nation.

Yet the net effect in many areas was disastrous. Agricultural production dropped, because people lived too far from their fields. As a result, people complied with relocation with extreme reluctance and foot-dragging. The problems in some of these villages included the situation I mentioned where the chief exploited his people and even tried to buy off my research team. In several villages, the communal farms that were required by the system were poorly managed and erratically cared for. For example, I saw a significant contrast between two rice farms in an area near lake Nyasa at the border with Malawi and Mozambique. The communal rice farm was a disaster, full of weeds, and unlikely to have more than a tiny harvest. The adjacent rice farm, run privately by an entrepreneur who resisted the communal process, was beautiful.

The only successful villages were ones where the local leadership was keen and where people had not lived in isolated homesteads prior to independence. The system depended too greatly on human energy, honesty, and sharing for it to work, particularly in places where ordinary villagers were coerced into cooperating.

Regarding the displacement of hunting and gathering people in Botswana, I did not have the chance to visit the Kalahari Desert where Bushmen formerly lived a nomadic existence, but I saw the consequences in nearby villages to those families displaced from their traditional land. The squalor and hopelessness of some of the Bushmen families was pathetic in the extreme. Unfortunately, there is probably little that could have been done or can yet be done to save their lifestyle. Across the world, pre-agricultural peoples have been the victims of so-called progress, and Botswana is no exception.

In South Africa, displacement of peoples was part of the apartheid scheme to create true separation of the races. Prior to 1948 when the National Party took control of the country, blacks still lived on bits of their traditional land among the whites who had wrested political and economic control from them. The so-called "black spots" were accepted by the ruling whites, partly because they had no choice and partly because it was convenient to have a black working class within easy reach.

The apartheid theorists were not happy with this casual and incomplete separation. They wanted blacks out of white areas and in their own "homelands." The result was one of the most systematic and massive efforts to relocate people anywhere in the world; the Liberian and Tanzanian exercises pale in comparison. New countries were invented, though no other nation recognized places such as Ciskei, Transkei, Bophuthatswana, and Venda. About 3.5 million people were taken from their ancestral lands and force-marched into new, barren areas. Their houses were bulldozed into piles of rubble.

This process stretched from the most remote rural settlements in isolated parts of the semi-desert north and west right into the heart of the cities. I was shocked at my first sight of District Six, which had once been a vibrant multi-racial community in the center of Cape Town. In the first post-apartheid years it was not initially rebuilt. It was left a wasteland that symbolized the inhumanity of the National Party regime. Only recently have rights to original land been restored, and owners are now planning to rebuild on sites they remember from forty years earlier. I spoke with former residents in Cape Town in January 2003 who are planning to move back. But it is difficult, not only because of the expense but also because so much time has elapsed since they were forcibly moved out. The social fabric that made District Six such an exciting place, and which is memorialized in a wonderful museum in the heart of the district, has been torn asunder, and it will be extremely difficult to put back what has been lost.

The newly democratic South Africa has passed laws for restoration of land to displaced people. Few communities have actually succeeded in reconstituting themselves, but the effort is being made. Fortunately, the original forced removal was never completed. As a result, many areas remain complex mixtures of white towns and black farms, particularly in densely populated Kwazulu-Natal. Furthermore, the so-called "locations" such as Soweto, where black employees could live while they traveled to their places of work in the white areas, were never dismantled. Today local residents have largely taken over the political administration of redefined municipalities, which include both the white and the black settlements.

It has proved difficult for integration to take place between these areas, though some blacks and people of mixed race have moved to the white towns. The town of Clocolan in the eastern Free State is an interesting case. The former Anglican bishop of Lesotho has moved to Clocolan, where he bought a house close to the center of the town. My wife and I attended a party at his house and rejoiced in the new community he has found. The local Anglican church choir sang and danced in full African dress, and the house was overflowing with friends and neighbors. The sad fact remains, however, that Judy and I and a British friend were the only whites in attendance, despite that all of Bishop Duma's nearest neighbors are white.

Integration is tough, and it will take a long time before whites and blacks in South Africa, indeed anywhere, fully accept each other. The scars of the past dislocation of blacks are still very real. For some blacks, like my bishop the former Bishop of Lesotho and other Basotho friends, to move into Free State towns is a beginning—but only a beginning.

Yet there is hope. The formerly Afrikaner town of Kroonstad in the Free State now has a black mayor, who entertained us for lunch in January 2003. Black farmers are now moving back to the land and, with help from my friend and colleague Baba Jordaan, a former freedom fighter turned agricultural developer, are selling their produce to the supermarkets that once catered only to white farmers. The new beginning is happening in Kroonstad.

While I was there, I visited a former all-white girls' high school on the outskirts of Kroonstad. Its history is a parable of the apartheid era, the difficult years of transition, and the beginning of a better future. A group of Catholic nuns ran the school until the early 1980s. Then the school closed and was taken over by the South African army as a training camp for its soldiers. In the early 1990s the army closed the camp, leaving it empty to squatters. Some stabled their animals on the ground floor; others moved from rural farms and used the classrooms for accommodations, and still others used the place as a center for urban resistance. Now the Kroonstad council has given the school and grounds back to the church, which is rebuilding the center as an industrial and trade school. The first task of the students is to learn on the job by renovating the buildings after the years of abuse by the army and by squatters. The end product will hopefully be skilled workers who can take an active role in creating a vibrant, non-racial economy.

9.5 Misplaced emphasis on urban development.

School being renovated in South Africa

Urbanization is a worldwide phenomenon, and there seems to be no way to stop it. Probably, it should not be stopped, since it is what the majority of mobile people seem to want. In the twenty-five years we lived in Lesotho, we have seen Maseru grow from a small town, where horses could still be hitched at shops along the main street Kingsway, to a sprawling community covering about seventy-five square kilometers and including nearly 300,000 people. People know, or want to think they know, that jobs are easily found in Maseru. They are partly correct, since what few jobs there are in Lesotho are in the urban areas, not just in Maseru, but also in other centers along the western border.

Botswana's capital, Gaborone, also has grown incredibly over the years I have known it. It was already bursting at the seams in 1982 when I first went there. On my most recent visit, I hardly knew the place because of all the expansion.

I have seen the same thing in South Africa. A remarkable and frightening example is the rural slum created by the apartheid regime in Botshabelo, fifty kilometers east of Bloemfontein, which was intended as the home of forcibly resettled Basotho in what was then the Orange Free State. There must be a quarter of a million people there, in what did not even appear on the map of South Africa during the old days.

Botshabelo is a city of about the same size as Maseru, but it is a city without real hope for economic development. The fact that Botshabelo has no real economic future goes to the heart of the problem. To the best of my understanding, most of the cities and towns I have known in Africa are not sources of economic growth. They are sinks into which resources are poured without visible benefit. The major urban centers of South Africa—Bloemfontein, Cape Town, Durban, East London, Johannesburg, Port Elizabeth, and Pretoria—are exceptions, since they are the engine for economic growth in the southern African region. But the other big cities I have visited in Africa, from Lagos to Nairobi to Harare, do not add value to the wealth produced in the remainder of the mostly rural countries.

Monrovia is probably the worst case. Even at Liberia's time of greatest economic health during the 1950s and 1960s, Monrovia had essentially no productive industry. A few factories grew up, producing commodities such as paint, glass, cement, and frozen fish, but nothing substantial. The most profitable business (the only enterprise not damaged by any army in the civil war) was the brewery. Liberia's wealth was all in its rural areas and was based on rubber, iron, coffee, cocoa, and timber. The roughly 200,000 people in Monrovia before the war were parasitic on the rural interior for food and for saleable commodities. Now there are more than a million people in Monrovia, many without any place to lay their heads at night. During the worst of the intense civil war of mid-2003 there were estimated to be roughly 200,000 refugees moving from place to place in search of food and shelter. Needless to say, any infrastructure that might have held promise for economic growth has been trashed.

Gaborone, Dar-es-Salaam, Kampala, Addis Ababa, and Windhoek, to name a few of the capital cities where I have lived and worked, are no different. They are safe, reasonably secure, and have much better social services than the rural areas so many people are leaving in order to enjoy better lives. They have some small industrial output, but not enough to justify the capital expenditure on them as cities. In them I see a reversal of economic logic in that the greatest resources are spent on the least productive areas. This reversal is driven by the fact that policy makers live in and enjoy the resources of the cities. They build good roads, provide electricity and water, construct teaching hospitals, subsidize housing, and minimize urban taxation in order that they may live well. They justify their actions by pointing to the role they play in administering the development process, despite their obvious inability to do more than skim off the profits from the system of donor assistance and non-economic loans. As aid diminishes and loans become intolerable burdens, the cities deteriorate and become increasingly unliveable.

The problem is most acute in war-torn countries such as Liberia. In 1990, a Liberian friend, an economist, and I put together a proposal for reconstruction of Liberia after the war. As I look back, I realize our great naivete in thinking that rationality and patriotism would prevail once people understood the folly of killing each other. Our proposal centered on rural reconstruction with a minimum of emphasis on rebuilding Monrovia's severely damaged infrastructure. We believed that if Liberia was ever to recover from the war, recovery had to be based on kick-starting the rural economy, so that food supplies would be restored and natural resources redeveloped.

None of this has happened. Monrovia has swollen to a population of one million, and the rhetoric of development that a few months ago focused on bringing back electricity, clean water, housing, schools, clinics, and other infrastructure has now shifted to strategies for post-war survival. Investment for productive development was not then part of the plan, and at this point it is not taking place. Charles Taylor may be safe and comfortable in exile in Nigeria, but the city he left is dying. The only bastions of any economic strength remain in the rubber and timber industries, which are economically, socially, and environmentally destructive.

In Lesotho, our recent study of poverty shows that the towns and cities will continue to attract rural people. Agriculture there is steadily losing ground as the population grows and the soils continue to be exhausted. In the case of Lesotho, however, there is more justification for building up Maseru than for building up Monrovia. It is important to remember that investment for economic growth must build on strength. For the time being, Maseru will have to remain a large agricultural village with house sites large enough for to feed families on garden produce for those who fail to find jobs even in the growing number of textile factories.

In short, urbanization cannot be stopped. But it must be treated with caution. Where cities are economic parasites on rural areas, the emphasis for development must be shifted away from the city. Where cities are necessary for growth in countries where agriculture is failing, the emphasis for development must be shifted toward providing facilities for urban productivity.

9.6 Hopeful signs.

It is encouraging that some far-sighted nations are changing their approach to **development projects**. Ireland Aid in Lesotho has been very creative and thoughtful in its planning. The Irish consuls and technical advisors have looked closely at the results of social and economic surveys and have laid their plans accordingly. Starting with an exciting effort in the 1970s to upgrade the stock of the traditional Basotho mountain horses to their recent effort of funding a locally run school furniture industry, the Irish have responded to need. Similarly, the Swiss agency Helvetas was a pioneer in sponsoring the Machobane agricultural system and an innovative rural water supply project.

The campaign to reduce, if not entirely eliminate, **unrepayable debts** has gained force through the strong intervention of churches. I have been very proud of our southern African Anglican Archbishop Njongonkulu Ndugane for spearheading the Jubilee campaign. The Biblical concept of a year of Jubilee when debts are forgiven—in this case at the turn of the millennium—has been applied to the back-breaking load of debt on African countries. Already, Uganda, Ghana, and Mozambique have been given partial relief, and more relief is scheduled to still other countries.

Local processing of **raw materials** is a slow and difficult process, but it is beginning to happen on a small scale. South Africa has led the process by exporting diverse products such as Mercedes-Benz cars, fine wines, and indigenous delights such as my favorite rooibosch tea. After a bitter legal fight with the European Union, South African products have been allowed almost duty-free entry into the European market. It has been more difficult for other African countries to break into the field. Botswana has for many years been exporting canned beef to the rest of the world, but there are not many such examples. The American African Growth and Opportunities Act (AGOA) opens the American market to products such as Lesotho's textiles, and Lesotho is now the major exporter of textiles to the USA from Africa (Gibbon 2003). Pressure is being exerted on European and American governments to reduce domestic subsidies and foreign tariffs in other areas so that Africa can engage in profitable trade.

Forced resettlement of peoples throughout Africa continues, whether due to industrial development or to war. Yet some efforts are being made to bring the process under control. The Lesotho Highlands Water Project has improved its record of the resettlement of displaced households after its first inadequate response in the early 1990s. South Africa has tried to overcome the legacy of apartheid's human engineering by building houses for the poor and restoring land to its rightful owners, but the legal requirements have meant an intolerable delay for many deserving people. It is to be hoped that resistance to the proposed Epupa dam on the Cunene River, which forms part of the border between Namibia and Angola, will succeed, as international outrage grows against the willful destruction of the territory of the Himba people (www.tve.org/earthreport/archive/10Aug2000.html).

Some African **urban areas** are almost beyond hope. But there are countries attempting to better the lives of their slum dwellers as well as attempting to diversify industries away from the cities. South Africa again is a leader in the field, with serious efforts being made to provide housing to squatters in peri-urban Cape Town, Johannesburg, Durban, and even in many of the smaller urban areas such as Grahamstown and Kroonstad. The problem is that as soon as one family gets a good house, the next family arrives from its rural home and builds a shack, often on the very land vacated by the family that succeeded in moving. In Lesotho, Maseru sets a good example of humane urbanization, in that new families can relatively easily (although only quasi-legally) acquire plots of about a thousand square meters on which they can build a small house and grow a vegetable garden. As a result, there are almost no slums or squatter areas in Maseru. Urbanization in Africa is here to stay, but there are signs that it can be put to good economic and human uses.

CHAPTER TEN. IMPOSING WESTERN POLITICAL FORMS

Politics have existed everywhere and at all times wherever there are two or more people living together. The number of possible cabals and factions increases dramatically as soon as a population grows beyond a few families, but even in the smallest societies, politics exist and powerfully influence the course of events.

My experience of African communities and nations, even without the introduction of new forms of political organization, is that they behave in complex and often unpredictable ways. In Sinyea behind Cuttington College, choosing a new chief to replace the charismatic old man, Sebe Dorweh, depended on balancing lineages, friends, brains, strength, and glib talk. Moreover, the stories of the past history of that village reveal that a careful alternation between peace-loving reconcilers and tough-minded warriors marked the political transfer of authority well before the coming of the Liberian nation.

This chapter is about the changes that have been brought by Westernization, a process in which European and American forms transformed the political process, while reinforcing some of its underlying features. In many cases, the changes were harmful, bringing still further disharmony and disunity to societies that had worked out elaborate means either to keep fighting to a minimum or to ensure quick victory over an enemy.

It is likely, but unprovable, that African polities were in the process of developing toward increasing complexity and sophistication when the European powers interrupted and in most cases destroyed indigenous political evolution. The kingdom of the Kongo in the late fifteenth century was in many ways as sophisticated as the Portuguese kingdom that used slave trading to destroy it. What made the difference? The Portuguese had guns and ships, the Kongolese, neither.

10.1 Disrespect for customary leaders.

The stereotypical new visitor to a hitherto remote African community is supposed to have said, slowly, loudly, and in childish intonation, "Take me to your leader." This request (or order, as was all too often the case) was then translated by someone who often had a minimal command of both languages and an equally minimal understanding of the two competing cultures.

Graham Greene, the most sensitive of all observers of the Liberian scene, makes it clear just how wide of the mark outsiders were in dealing with rural Liberian life, whether the outsiders were coastal Americo-Liberians or Europeans. He too was bemused by what he saw, but he neither sentimentalized tribal society nor looked down on it. It was simply another of the host of very peculiar ways in which human beings disported themselves (Greene 1936).

Of course, I came on the scene much later; Graham Greene walked through the forests of Liberia, innocent of known trails and guidebooks, in the early 1930s. When I arrived in Liberia many years later, I could see the negative side of the interaction between Western politics and rural traditions. The greatest disrespect for customary leaders was offered by self-important government officials. The man to whom Dr. Stewart and I gave books at the remote village on Liberia's border with Côte d'Ivoire was a petty despot to the people in the village, as we later found out.

The first government officials in remote northern Liberia, where the American Episcopal Church eventually established a pioneering mission, were brutal in their treatment of traditional chiefs. Stephen Hlophe points out how in 1912 government agents hanged eight traditional chiefs who had complained about Liberian extortion and exploitation (Hlophe 1979). Oral history, as recorded by Liberian Episcopal minister Benedict Vani, has preserved the story that these officials invited the chiefs to a meal, apparently with the connivance of another chief who wanted unchallenged power.   Once the dinner guests were surrounded in the government compound, the government representative had his soldiers slaughter the dissidents and gave power to the turncoat, who was later murdered for his deed (Vani 2002).

The Liberian government generally used the chiefs for its own purposes, including the one just mentioned who betrayed his fellow chiefs. I have already mentioned how the government ensured the supply of laborers on the Firestone plantation by working through the chiefs.   To make sure the laborers were forthcoming, the chiefs were given a bounty for meeting or exceeding their quotas of laborers and were warned that their status would be in danger if they did not deliver.

A government-invented hierarchy of clan chiefs and paramount chiefs was superimposed on the traditional system not long after the Liberians pacified the interior. These super-chiefs were given higher salaries and status, but they were expected to keep the people under them in line and to produce hut taxes on a regular basis. The hut tax was reintroduced under Charles Taylor, to the dismay of human rights workers (members.aol.com/csiedit/HeadTax.html). The hut tax was the most regressive of all tax systems, in that the poor had to pay the same as the rich, who knew how to escape the levy in a variety of way. In the old days, talking drums—as tall as a man and with a deep and penetrating tone—had been used to send messages between villages. They were banned in the 1930s so that warnings could no longer be sent out that the tax collector was coming. In some villages, houses were made with temporary thatch walls that could be disassembled once the tax man was in the neighborhood so that the tax could be avoided. The walls and roofs would be hidden in the nearby forest, and only put back together after the tax man had left. As far as the tax collector was concerned, there was no house!

What may be surprising to some is that many African societies did not have "chiefs" before they were imposed by outsiders. A pioneering book, *Tribes without Rulers*, made that point clear in 1958 by its title, focusing on six ethnic groups that did not have chiefs but which gave influence to different categories of people, depending on context (Middleton and Tait 1958).

Customary rulers have a very useful role to play in rural areas in Africa, and should not be exploited. The "Take me to your leader" cliché is only a cliché because it refers to a deep truth. Every African village in which I have worked had a gatekeeper who was usually called a chief. It is a matter of routine courtesy to visit the chief before attempting to do any work or visit anyone in a village, unless the visitor is already well known. In theory, village chiefs in Lesotho have the right to arrest (or in the old days kill) the stranger who violates the norm. Even today the unannounced visitor who arrives at night or under some suspicious circumstances is viewed

A traditional chief at a meeting in Lesotho

with great suspicion as a potential thief or disturber of the peace. In Lesotho, there are now community watch groups that patrol the village at night to prevent livestock theft and burglary. These watch groups have been known to take the law into their own hands and kill strangers.

I am impressed with how closely some town chiefs know their people. In mid-2000, my colleague David Hall and I went to a Lesotho village with research assistants to re-interview people who had been surveyed in 1993. We went, as expected, to the chief and read the list of names to him. The chief, a calm and thoughtful man, well-dressed and living in a comfortable home, not only knew every name but also knew where each person was at that moment. This one was at home three houses away, the next one had gone into Maseru for the day, the third had died two years ago, the fourth was also home but on the far side of the village, the fifth had moved to a nearby village, the sixth was in South Africa—he knew them all. He then gave us permission to visit those who were available at the time. It was indeed an impressive performance.

Not every chief is as knowledgeable or even as coherent. My research assistants and I have encountered drunken men, old men long past their prime, women standing in for their husbands who were unwilling to give us an official welcome, suspicious religious fanatics who took us for Satanists, and hard-core members of a political party who did not want any opposition nonsense. No matter in what state we found them, the chief, the headman, the wife, or a young substitute was a necessary gatekeeper without whose help we could not work. Normally this gatekeeper would ask us our business, we would explain about surveys and national development, and we would be given access. Only in a very few cases (the religious fanatic, the political true believer, the drunken sot) were we forced to go elsewhere to find another village where we could work

The chief performs a variety of functions within the village. One of the most important is listening to disputes and trying to rule wisely. They do not always succeed, but I have the feeling that the success rate is high. In the 2003 survey of African political opinion mentioned above, we found that most conflicts are resolved either with the help of traditional chiefs or with the intervention of the police. Only a few people go to the central government for conflict resolution. Less than 10 percent had ever contacted a national government official, while more than 60 percent had been to a local chief for some official purpose.

A case in which I was an interested party involved one of my research assistants in Gbansu. He had been caught sleeping with a local woman against our agreement that the researchers would avoid local involvement. His problem was that he was indiscreet and did not cover his tracks. The chief convened all the parties, listened to everyone, and at the end gave a considered judgment in which our researcher had to give compensation.

What was impressive to me about the occasion was not the wisdom or lack of it in the judgment; I was not sufficiently aware of the complexities of the case to judge. What was impressive was the existence of a mechanism by which violence and revenge could be avoided. At its best, in Liberia or Lesotho, the chieftaincy keeps the peace and allows people to finish a case with at least the feeling that they have not been seriously cheated. At best, the chief is wise, and even if the judgment is not wise, the community finds a way to heal itself, realizing that the alternative to listening to and respecting an unwise chief is social confusion. Unfortunately, confusion often does arise, leading in the worst cases to violence and even community fission.

Social chaos was precisely what happened in many Liberian villages as a result of the civil war. Chiefs were deposed or even killed by young, drunken and drugged revolutionaries. Many stories emerged about conscious and explicit disrespect for constituted authority. Boys, often in their early teens, swaggered into villages and announced that they were taking over. They demanded food and commandeered all the village wealth. A close friend was once in a rural village when the child soldiers arrived. They had AK-47 rifles and thus could not be refused. In the course of a week they ate every living domestic animal in the village and looted the rice storage sheds before moving on to the next village.

When I visited Liberia in 2001 I saw almost no animals in the villages and was informed that the number of sheep, goats, and chickens in rural Liberia had dropped to almost zero as a result of the civil war. Similarly, rice farms had not been planted, and those that were planted were looted even before harvest. The result in many villages was an orgy of feasting by the boy soldiers and destruction of the future for the residents of the rural villages.

Lesotho has been attempting to build a system of village development committees that will take on many of the activities of the chieftainship. They have not been successful. Because of political infighting, greed, lack of support, and most significantly, the silent undercutting by the customary chief or headman, few are functioning as planned. The survey mentioned above showed only a quarter of the people had ever contacted village development councilors as opposed to almost two-thirds who had spoken with the chief.

One of the reasons the new system has not worked is that the illegitimate usurper, Prime Minister Leabua Jonathan, created the village committees in the 1970s as a way to ensure his control of rural politics. This created bitterness that has never completely gone away. Subsequent efforts to reconstitute the committees, including the naive means of changing their names from committees to councils, have failed. Elections at the village level were ordered, but few have been actually held.

Deeper than political bitterness is the feeling that the central government has not given proper respect to local self-control. Chiefs have been leading villages for almost two hundred years, and the system has more or less worked. People believe that the alternative systems do not respect what villages have been able to do for themselves. Even where there are drunken or incompetent chiefs, they represent the villages and not the central government.

Some educated urban Basotho would like to see the end of the chieftaincy, but 44 percent of respondents in the political opinion survey would like to see a return to traditional rule by chiefs. I have sometimes spoken against the chieftaincy system, but no longer. I would not like to see Lesotho put the king in power as happened in Swaziland, but I respect the system at the village level.

One reason I now support the chieftaincy is that educated urban Basotho do not have a viable system to replace it. Urban people must first learn how to make the system work in their own backyards before imposing it on rural areas. Corruption and failure to perform basic services have been rife. The lesson of the failed village development councils is mirrored by the very serious inability of the Maseru City Council to administer the city. Reforms may be possible, but they should be gradual and should take advantage of the very real benefits of the customary system.

South Africa is currently facing the same problem, but on a larger scale. The traditional leaders are being eased out of their posts by enlarged metropolitan councils whose jurisdiction is extending in ever-widening circles into the countryside. At the same time, I am not sympathetic with the excesses of the Zulu monarchy and chieftaincy system. The chiefs have fallen into all the traps that Shaka set for them as he created the Zulu nation out of war and death. Mangosutho Buthelezi is a depressing example of a tribal chief seeking national power, and the Zulu monarchy has few of the redeeming features I see in Lesotho. Swaziland is in even worse shape, with a silly, polygynous, young king attempting to rule the country single-handedly and in the process alienating ordinary people with his greed and lust.

Yet I do not believe that the rush to sweep away the authority of the customary chiefs is going to benefit any of the countries that currently retain a system of rural chiefs. A top-down urban ruling class will not be able to do all the small things that the chiefs have done in the past without a period of careful preparation for the transition. Where the past has been swept away in a rush of mindless modernization, the result has been disaster. When we were in Liberia in the 1960s, we watched with dismay as Sekou Touré ruined Guinea. Much of what went wrong in Ethiopia under Mengistu Haile Mariam in the 1970 and 1980s was due to throwing out what was good in the old feudal system and replacing it with a brutal, centralized, poor imitation of Marxist-Leninist structures. Among other reasons, the creation of centralized villages in Tanzania went wrong, because the government political party imposed its leaders on the new, very fragile villages.

10.2 Politics without policies.

In the great days of anti-imperial, anti-colonial rhetoric, politics were real and vital. I can still remember the thrill I felt when reading and hearing Kwame Nkrumah strike out against the oppression Africa had known over the centuries. Jomo Kenyatta spoke with fire about the British stranglehold on his people in Kenya. The politics of the time had one simple policy, directed to the British, the French, the Belgians, the Portuguese, and the white South Africans: get out and let Africans have Africa once again.

Colonial governments had clear, simple policies as they administered their colonies: gain as much profit as possible and make sure that the colonies do not cause trouble. This policy did not change materially as independence approached or even after independence was a reality. Neo-colonialism was, and in a few countries still remains, a reality in which independent African countries remained loyal to the former rulers, provided raw materials for foreign industries, and were patient and faithful consumers of goods, both intellectual and material.

This situation left little room for the newly independent countries to develop policies of their own, policies that could guide them into new paths. Leaders who struck out on their own to create a new and authentic African society were few in number. Kwame Nkrumah did indeed try to build a new way of life in Ghana, though all too soon he identified that new way of life with his own hunger for power as ruler over a United States of Africa. Jomo Kenyatta of Kenya, on the other hand, relaxed into the easier alternative of enjoying the overt fruits of independence while retaining all the benefits of covert links with the former colonial powers.

How did the post-colonial situation translate into the reality of day-to-day politics? In Liberia the post-colonial situation mainly meant the removal of the old oligarchy. The last generation of old-style rulers in Liberia had real policies to go

Inauguration of Tubman in Liberia in 1960

with their politics. President Tubman, for example, sought the integration of the hinterland with the coastal people and also sought to develop the use of Liberia's natural resources. President Tolbert wanted to transform the rural areas so that Liberia could simultaneously achieve self-sufficiency and reduce the gross inequities between the elite and the rural poor. It is an oversimplification to reject all that Tolbert tried to do simply because he overreached and was brought down by a group of illiterate soldiers. In a moving tribute to her father, my former student Christine Tolbert-Norman grieved: "You could not complete your promise to build for your people a Wholesome Functioning Society, which you had envisaged."

It is a matter of real regret that both presidents failed to achieve their objectives, in part because of the extreme difficulty of bringing the so-long-despised indigenous people into the main stream of national life and in part because both fell into the trap set by over-centralization and greed. The policies of development and egalitarianism yielded to the politics of power and profit. Both men had good ideas and a genuine vision of where Liberia could go. Tubman had the undisputed power to change Liberia, but in the end preferred to cherish and nourish power rather than to cherish and nourish his nation. Tolbert did not have the free hand that Tubman had. He outlined a grand vision for moving Liberia "from mats to mattresses," but the combination of his own selfishness and the web of conflicting aspirants to power around him made it impossible for him to reach his goal. His recourse to repression in the last year of his life was an act of desperation and led directly to his downfall.

It is not surprising that their successors, Samuel Doe and Charles Taylor, have played similar, although far more vicious and self-centered, games. Tubman and Tolbert were serious when they talked about national regeneration and a fair deal for the poor and downtrodden masses. Doe and Taylor used the same words, but the reality for both was the desire to amass quick profits for themselves and their cronies. None of Charles Taylor's grandiose claims about freeing his country from poverty and oppression was realized, except that he replaced one ruthless, greedy tyrant, Samuel Doe, with another—himself. Before Taylor left there were no visible national policies for reconstruction despite the rhetoric at which he was so skilled.

The political leaders in Lesotho have not been as vicious or as successfully greedy as those in Liberia, but they too are more motivated by power than by principle. I have tried hard to find out exactly what the major political parties in Lesotho stand for, and I have succeeded only slightly. Before independence, the predecessors to the Basutoland Congress Party did seek a secular, egalitarian, modern society and set themselves over against the chiefly parties. The choice for or against tradition was at that time based on political principles. There has been a residue of that sentiment since independence, but it has shifted more and more into family-based alliances.

In the most recent survey of political opinion, however, I did find a statistically significant tendency for members of the ruling Lesotho Congress for Democracy to stand for strong government control of the economy, while adherents to opposition parties favor a more hands-off "liberal" economic policy. I found this significant, since it shows the beginning of politics based on principles and policies, which has been rare in Lesotho. It should also be acknowledged that three-quarters of the Basotho we interviewed in the political opinion survey genuinely believe that Lesotho is a democracy, even though flawed.

There have been exceptions elsewhere to the general rule of politics without policies, power without principle, and privilege without public interest. The great men of recent African history stand out. Julius Nyerere was still president of Tanzania during my stay there, and he operated on the basis of deeply-felt policies, principles of integrity, and with great concern for the public interest. The only problem is that some of the most important of his policies were misguided, such as the policy of forcing people into consolidated villages, in theory attractive but in practice a disaster. He was a serious believer in African socialism, but his followers could not or would not live by his principles. He promoted collective agriculture, but it did not work. He created parastatals, but they were both corrupt and inefficient.

Nyerere is remembered with affection and respect, not for his economic and socialistic policies but for his deep humanity. He did not enrich himself but gave himself fully for what he believed to be the betterment of his people. His retirement from power, emulated by only a few other leaders, including Alpha Oumar Konare of Mali, Jerry Rawlings of Ghana, Leopold Senghor of Senegal, Kenneth Kaunda of Zambia, and Nelson Mandela of South Africa, was the act of a statesman.

Nelson Mandela in particular was a leader with genuine principles—principles, moreover, that benefited the people of South Africa. His policies of redistribution of wealth, reconciliation among races and classes, compensation for past crimes and errors, and his evident willingness to listen to the voice of the people, make him one of the great men of history. Sadly, his successors do not seem to have the same humanity and broad vision. In particular, the ruling African National Congress appears less concerned about the well-being of the people than about maintaining power and acquiring personal wealth. Mandela's policies were often excellent but often were not put into practice by the politicians whose job it was to implement general guidelines.

Politics are about power. Policies are about people—all the people. Politics may prevent good policies, not only from being enunciated but also from being implemented. If the quest for power, long-term power and unchallenged power, continues to dominate, Africa will continue to decline.

10.3 Political parties as ethnic and social clubs.

Political parties are an invention of Western democracy. We who have grown up in Europe or America believe that competing parties are necessary in order to keep any one person or faction from gaining absolute power, and thus being corrupted absolutely. Many respect Churchill's belief that democracy, whereas a terrible form of government, is better than the alternatives.

Idealists and do-gooders in the West encouraged Africans to create parties in the colonial era. Even without foreign encouragement, educated Africans sought to emulate what they saw in Western democracies. Liberia pioneered the forming of political parties shortly after the Americo-Liberians landed in 1822. Sierra Leone, Ghana, and Nigeria formed their own parties around the turn of the century as they looked forward to independence and self-rule.

It is instructive to trace the course of these parties. There was competition between parties in Liberia until the ascendancy of the Tru[e] nineteenth century. Sporadic challenges to True Whig regularly, but by President Tubman's time there was only to point, Tubman apparently persuaded one of his friends to run old man could show his magnanimity by voting for the op[position]. Tolbert tolerated opposition parties, mostly on the left, but in a move that contributed in part to his overthrow.

Elections were held in 1985 under Samuel Doe and in 1997 under Charles Taylor. A broad collection of opposition parties ran candidates, but they were overwhelmingly defeated by a combination of brute force and chicanery. People have generally conceded that there was no vote-rigging in the Liberian election of 1997, but they also point to serious intimidation. It was said at the time that people were saying about Taylor: "He killed my ma. He killed my pa. I will vote for him." The reason was the fear that if Taylor lost he would go back to the bush and restart the war.

It is important nonetheless that opposition parties continue to exist in Liberia, because they may eventually provide a basis for something like Western, multiple-party democracy, as is already happening in Côte d'Ivoire, Ghana, Kenya, Malawi, Nigeria, Senegal, Tanzania, Zambia, and Zimbabwe. The big problem now is preparing for elections in 2005 due to Taylor's removal from power, while avoiding a replay of politics by intimidation. The last thing most people want is for one of the rebel groups to force itself into power in the same way as Taylor did, where a formally and meticulously free election is won by force majeure.

Liberian election tee-shirt

Lesotho has had a multiple party system since before independence in 1966. The elections of 1965 and 1970 were closely fought, even though the losing party hijacked the results in 1970. There are still several parties in Lesotho, although the leading party, the Lesotho Congress for Democracy, commands the loyalty of more than 60 percent of the population. The same phenomenon exists in South Africa, where multi-partyism prevails, but where one party, the ANC, will probably continue to have easy victories for several elections to come.

What is disturbing is that political parties in Africa are often built on religious, tribal, and family lines. A partly-resolved conflict in Côte d'Ivoire pits northerners, mostly Muslim and related to groups in Mali and Burkina Faso, against southerners, mostly Christian and related to Liberians and Ghanaians. Nigeria's parties are divided along geographic lines with the Yoruba in the southwest, the Igbo in the southeast, and the Hausa in the north forming the nuclei of political groupings. Kenya is strongly divided along tribal lines, and in Ethiopia, the lowland Muslims are pitted against the highland Christians. In South Africa, the main divisions are along racial lines.

Lesotho is a curious case. The Basutoland Congress Party, which eventually gave birth to its rival, the Lesotho Congress for Democracy, is a commoner party that to a large extent has roots in the Lesotho Evangelical Church. The Basotho National

...rong Catholic and monarchist origins. These affiliations are not absolute, ... tend to persist. What makes them persist is their clan-like character. People ...orn into Catholic or Protestant families and into BNP or BCP (or now LCD) ...milies. These loyalties are strengthened by the unresolved bitterness arising from the events of 1970 when the BNP, under the late Leabua Jonathan, stole the election from the BCP. Many people were imprisoned, hurt, burned out of their houses, and exiled as a result of the resulting civil strife. Since Lesotho has never had a Truth and Reconciliation Commission like that in South Africa, the bitterness is only slowly being healed, and some families are still fighting the inter-party, inter-church, inter-clan war.

In short, the transplantation of political parties into Africa has been seriously problematic. It may have been an inevitable transplant, given the overwhelming desire of most ordinary people for a voice in politics, but much of recent African political history shows the tendency of African society to reject the transplant. On the other hand, one-party states have been notoriously corrupt and arrogant. The idea of the no-party state, as introduced by Yoweri Museveni in Uganda, may prove more successful, but even there many people have doubts about its long-term sustainability as Museveni grows older and more comfortable in his permanent presidency. In the end, who knows? Churchill's conviction that democracy, bad as it is, is the best system may well be right, even in Africa.

10.4 Swollen government bureaucracies.

There are many reasons why working for government quickly became the ideal for schooled, and even unschooled, Africans. One important reason was that power was found in offices headed by Europeans. In Europe, the mere fact of holding a post in the civil service was no guarantee of power. There, the traditional aristocracy did not deign to be civil servants, and business people knew that power grew out of money. There, military men knew the importance of the gun and the sword. There, politicians could get far more, far more quickly, from political manipulation than if they took up white collar administrative jobs. And there, the lawyer and the judge knew how to twist the law to their own ends.

In Africa, however, the bureaucrat combined almost all these roles. He (and bureaucrats were almost inevitably male) controlled the traditional native aristocracy, approved or disapproved business ventures, usually at substantial profits to themselves, had the army and the police under his control even if he was not a member of the army or police, arrogated the role of politician to himself by insisting on making basic political decisions, and exercised the legal roles of legislator, lawyer, judge, and executioner. The all-pervasive patronage system evolved in relation to bureaucracy as Africans began to take over the reins of power. No wonder upwardly mobile, educated Africans saw government bureaucracy as the way to the top.

A second reason Africans enter bureaucracies, as stressed in an earlier chapter, is that colonial curricula emphasized white-collar skills at the expense of all other learning. One had to master reading, writing, and rhetoric in the colonial language in order to succeed in school. Little training was offered for people to become future business people or politicians, and those interested in such vocations were often strongly discouraged or even tossed out of school once their political interests became apparent. Africans were schooled to be subaltern functionaries in the government bureaucracy as clerks, teachers, or administrative assistants.

A third reason why those who completed school went into administration is that there were very few productive industries that offered security and a good salary to young Africans. Businesses were generally run by foreigners, who at best hired Africans as junior clerks, typists, messengers, and receptionists, and in most cases as unskilled labor. There was little chance for advancement and less chance for competing with the foreign managers and capitalists. European- or American-based industries were mostly run as "old-boy" clubs, and the only place at the top of the hierarchy for Africans was as public-relations officers. Public-relations people made sure that companies had a good local image and also made sure that the local employees stayed in line.

A fourth reason Africans chose bureaucracy is that government jobs are secure. No one is likely to fire bureaucrats, provided they keep their heads down, do not rock the boat, make no independent decisions, and follow the party line. Salaries go up regularly, at a rate often better than inflation, and perquisites such as housing and transport are guaranteed at the senior level to which all civil servants aspire. Obtaining a white-collar job may initially depend on passing exams, though even that requirement fades in the face of strong family or clan connections. Thereafter, permanence depends on political loyalty and not upsetting the patronage system. Clients and patrons need each other, and a smooth, well-oiled bureaucracy is one result of the system.

Liberia president's mansion 1960

In colonial days, the future for most people lay in government, church, or business, either as administrators, lawyers, doctors, teachers, accountants or even as secretaries or clerks. Africans who made money outside the corridors of government bureaucracy or who could not find legitimate employment in the private sector, often did so as successful informal sector entrepreneurs or as criminals. Clever albeit unscrupulous people looked for a living in the sale of diamonds, gold, or drugs as well as in protection rackets, armed robbery, or smuggling. The situation is not much different now, since government remains the principal employer.

My students in Liberia aspired to jobs within the government, if they could find them. A small survey was taken in Liberia by a friend, who found the same result. In Lesotho, few university graduates look for employment outside the government. The poor and less educated find jobs in the textile firms or in South African mines, but the educated, in almost all cases, go into teaching, which is paid for by the government, or directly into government service.

The result is a huge imbalance in the use of human resources. Government by its very nature is not a producer of goods. It takes resources out of the economic system rather than creating new products. Thus, when the best and the brightest opt for security and power by joining government, the whole society is weakened. Less harm is done when the harmless and the ineffectual become civil servants, but even in these cases the nation is not well served. I am not suggesting total dismantling of civil service, but rather a redressing of the balance.

Yet there are many ways in which the civil service can give over work to the private sector. In Lesotho, government parastatal organizations covering water, electricity, and communications are now being privatized. A July 2003 article in the *New York Times* shows how in Ghana the cell phone business grew exponentially once it was privatized. Such privatization may be overkill, however, and serve to open the door to a wider gap between rich and poor. Sadly, privatization may be necessary because of mismanagement by civil servants. In an ideal world, basic services would be provided by government in collaboration with the private sector to benefit all the people

I have already mentioned the serious incompetence, inefficiency, and corruption displayed by government agricultural production and marketing organizations. The only way some crops could efficiently be planted, tended, harvested, and sold in Tanzania at the height of the *ujamaa* philosophy of government was when smart individuals bypassed the Ministry of Agriculture. I spoke in 1987 to coffee farmers in Uganda who felt that the only way they could benefit from their production was to avoid official marketing procedures, since by the time they got their much-delayed payments, inflation had turned their profit into loss.

Some of those who are now employed as civil servants or parastatal workers will be hurt if the fat is trimmed out of the system. In the late 1990s I visited an office in Maseru where there were six workers, all young women. One of them was sleeping, the second was reading a magazine, the third was plaiting the hair of the fourth, the fifth was eating a mid-morning snack, and the sixth looked up from her desk to ask what I wanted. I am sure they are not needed by the government bureau where they were working. But I am also sure that each of these ladies is supporting a family and depends on her salary to avoid poverty. It is somehow cruel to weed such people out of the system. Humane methods are needed by which such people can be retrained, retired, or reassigned, but, I hope, not retrenched.

Retirement and retrenchment of civil servants will not be popular, since so many people depend not only on having such jobs themselves but also on patronage from friends and relatives in the civil service. In our 2003 study of political opinion in Lesotho, more than 80 percent of respondents agreed that civil servants should be allowed to keep their jobs.

Clearly, South Africa cannot continue to provide jobs for its huge mass of civil servants, if the economy is ever to grow to the point that it creates new jobs for the 30 or 40 percent who are unemployed or underemployed. South African television broadcast a protest by municipal workers in Johannesburg toward the end of the year 2000. They were protesting the thinning of their ranks by privatization and wanted to ensure lifetime employment with regular salary increases. The labor unions certainly have the right, and even the duty, to protect their members, but we cannot assume that their choices will benefit the larger society.

South Africa made a brave effort in the mid-90s to reduce public sector employment by offering generous retrenchment packages to those who volunteered to retire early. Unfortunately, the net result was to lose the most efficient and competent of civil servants, since they knew they could get jobs outside government. What remained was a small cadre of committed and serious civil servants, but also a large mass of the people who should ideally have been persuaded to take early retirement. Instead, they will continue to work until they are finally retired by virtue of age. The end result, as occurs elsewhere in Africa, is that unproductive government workers in unproductive cities will eat up the resources needed to help the economy come alive.

10.5 Inconsistent and corrupt borders.

The artificial national boundaries created by colonial powers and kept in place by power-hungry African rulers continue to hinder cross-border African trade and development. The border guards range from petty tyrants, who impose rigid controls, to corrupt officials, who demand bribes (particularly for those who bring contraband across the border), to incompetent officials, who could not care less who crosses where or why.

There is abuse of the system above and beyond the protectionism and selfishness of the nation-states. These borders offer petty officials an ideal opportunity not only to squeeze money out of travelers but also to puff up their self-images by using power in an arbitrary and high-handed way. I have the impression that the power motive is at least as important as the money motive. In 1966 my family and I were crossing the border from Liberia into Côte d'Ivoire and arrived at the Côte d'Ivoire border at 12:01 p.m. The official in charge was closing his office for the noon siesta and informed us he would return at 3:00 p.m. We waited in the hot African sun until he came back promptly at 3:00 p.m., looked at our passports for all of ten seconds, stamped them, opened the gate, and let us through. We could see the smile of satisfaction on his face. No money was passed, though at the Liberian side a few hours earlier we had been forced to provide the Liberian border guard with a dollar for "cold water."

The border between Lesotho and South Africa is a special case, because Lesotho and San Marino are the only countries in the world entirely surrounded by one other country. I have done studies of Lesotho's relations with South Africa, and it is clear from data that the border is a big nuisance to everyone, except possibly to border guards and customs officials whose salaries are dependent on it. Despite the inconvenience, in the 2003 political opinion poll attitudes were divided regarding the value of border controls, probably because many Basotho still fear South African raids and military exercises, as happened often during the 1980s and 1990s.

Most citizens of Lesotho have relatives across the border, and nearly all the Basotho we have interviewed had been across the border within a year or so, mostly for shopping, visiting relatives, medical care, school, and work. Yet every day, rain or shine, cold or hot, hundreds, and on some occasions thousands, of Basotho line up at the main border gates to get their passports stamped so they can cross. Most are back by evening, having wasted a good part of the day standing twice at the border gate. Sometimes the wait can be as much as two hours on each side.

Those who are impatient or have their own private reasons cross at well-known informal border crossings that include shallow sections of the Caledon River, holes in the fence in the southwestern border, and steep donkey trails in the east. Those who use the informal crossings in the west are often children who attend South African school (not quite legally), patients who want to use South African clinics, farmers who have arrangements to graze their cattle on the lush Free State pastures, or women who cut firewood to supplement the meager supplies on the Lesotho side of the border. The South African stock-theft police also cross the border at these informal crossing points in order to capture cattle rustlers.

What happens at the eastern side of the country, where a steep and rugged escarpment separates Lesotho from South Africa, is a different story. Mountain farmers grow marijuana as a major crop there, often using maize as a cover to hide the real crop from the police. They export the crop at a good profit by sending donkey trains down the escarpment to the Eastern Cape, to KwaZulu-Natal, or to Qwaqwa. In 1996 at a high mountain border post I was offered a large bag of marijuana at a very low price by a man who wanted to save himself the trouble of taking it down to Natal. I refused the offer! Truckloads of goods, including stolen cattle, drugs, small arms, and other illicit goods are brought in or out of Lesotho at a disused border post on the southeast, and customs officials are not willing or able to control the trade.

Whether on the east or on the west, anyone who really wants to get to South Africa invisibly can do so with little difficulty. The border officials go through the motions at the official border posts in order to keep their jobs and justify their salaries. Those who cross on foot are clocked into the Home Affairs computer by South African officials, but the same officials ignore many of the people with border passes who cross in cars, allowing them to pass freely. Therefore, the statistics mean almost nothing. On the Lesotho side, the guards wave people through, often without looking at passports.

The border pass is a prize that requires either standing in a queue twice a year to get a stamp in a passport or paying a minimal bribe not to be bothered. Each time I collected my six-month pass, the South African rules have been different. The result is that almost anyone willing to stand in the queue for thirty minutes is passed through.

A careful study was conducted by Sechaba Consultants in 2001 and 2002 on the future of the Lesotho-South African border (Sechaba Consultants and Associates 2002). The consensus was not that the border should be eliminated, but that controls should be greatly relaxed to allow free movement wherever possible. Business people on both sides of the border will be delighted to have greater access to markets offered by Basotho shoppers. Additionally, it is important to remember that despite the majority in favor of keeping the countries separate, there are 30 percent who think that the two countries should unite.

Other African borders are also a thicket of bureaucracy, corruption, and neglect. My Namibian friends tell me that they can cross back and forth between Namibia and Angola without hindrance, unless the government is on the lookout for smugglers or rebels. The Mozambican and Zimbabwean borders with South Africa are patrolled more carefully, but hundreds cross daily, including those who were sent back home the previous day (Tevera and Zinyame 2002). In 1981 my second son Stephen arrived at the Tanzanian border, having traveled overland through Malawi to see me, and was initially told he could not cross. When he sat down and told the officials he would prefer to die there than go back to Lilongwe, they yielded and let him pass. I once followed the route of cocoa smugglers between Tanzania and Malawi, and no one blocked me.

10.6 Rulers for life.

A common election joke in many African countries is, "One man, one vote...once." The situation is changing, however, as democratic institutions and values spread. Yet much of the decline and civil disturbance in Africa are due to the desire of leaders to entrench themselves for life.

Liberians watched wily old William Vacanarat Shadrack Tubman go downhill from being a reasonably progressive, but nonetheless dictatorial, president in 1958 to being a suspicious, vindictive old man before he died in 1971. Doubtlessly, he was a breath of fresh air in 1944 when he took power, and his efforts to promote the emancipation of the interior and to open up the economy to a larger world were generally good. But toward the end he had surrounded himself with luxury and suspicion, to the extent that we at Cuttington feared to speak freely about the country. We knew that we, just like our Peace Corps colleague Tom Lane, could get our marching orders for being too frank in our classrooms. Had Tubman left office after ten years or so, the whole history of the country could have been different and, I think, better.

I speak of ten years because of my empirical "Gay's Law of Diminishing Returns." I believe no one should rule or administer any organization for more than ten years. Throughout history there is evidence that leaders have done their best work in the first ten years and afterwards declined into corruption, incompetence, and suspicion. Some go bad even earlier, such as Ghana's Kwame Nkrumah, who was thrown out of office in 1966, a year or so before he reached the ten-

Statue of Tubman

year mark. The American constitution was changed in a very sensible direction after Franklin D. Roosevelt's historic fourth term. Now no president can be in office more than two four-year terms.

Lesotho's Leabua Jonathan was in power for twenty years, and the last ten were all downhill. Zimbabwe's Robert Mugabe has long passed the twenty-year mark and is still showing every sign of being willing to destroy his country in order to remain in power. When I was in Zimbabwe during the election of June 2000 it was clear to me that if his party were to retain control of the Parliament it would be the ruin of the country. When I last visited Nairobi in the late 1980s, Kenya was still a well-run viable country. Yet much of Kenya's structural wealth was lost due to former president Daniel Arap Moi's mad desire to hold onto office despite the decay he helped create in his 24 years in office. We can only hope that Mwai Kibake's new government, which took power in January 2003, will do better, although the diatribe by the British High Commissioner to Kenya in July 2004 suggests otherwise.

Fortunately, some African leaders have had the good sense to quit. Julius Nyerere showed his true mettle when he resigned after realizing the failure of his economic policies. Leopold Senghor retired as president of Senegal and remained an elder statesman and intellectual in France until his death in 2002 at the age of 95. Nelson Mandela knew that he could not continue after his first term as president because of his advanced age, and Botswana's Ketumile Masire gave up his post to a younger man.

Toure, Tubman, Nkrumah 1960

As opposition parties gain more respect and the ability to command votes, some leaders have been forced out of office by military means. The most notable examples are Mobutu Sese Seko in the former Zaire and Milton Obote in Uganda. Others have been voted out, including Abdou

Diouf of Senegal and Kenneth Kaunda of Zambia. Jerry Rawlings' party has been voted out of office in Ghana, and in South Africa, even the entrenched African National Congress is being given serious competition. It appears that the day of life-long presidents is drawing to a close—none too soon, in my view. Yet there remain men like Bakili Maluzi in Malawi who seem determined to hang on to power indefinitely (www.dalitsotrust.org/oct02.PDF), even though he was finally forced out of office.

10.7 Rulers and their yes-men.

Sycophancy is an elaborate word, but it carries the flavor necessary for the situations I want to describe. The Oxford English Dictionary defines it as: "servile or abject flattery" and "obsequiousness." Sycophancy certainly describes what was taking place in Liberia toward the end of Tubman's rule in that no one dared speak out openly against him. Tubman had "Public Relations Officers" whose assignment was to smell out dissent, causing people to say they could "only tell the truth in their iceboxes." In public, one had to agree with Tubman. In Lesotho, when Leabua Jonathan neared the end of his rule, he spoke more and more wildly, and his supporters were less and less willing to contradict him. In Zimbabwe, only the Movement for Democratic Change (MDC) dares to speak out against Mugabe, and even then the result is often harassment, jail, or death. Criticism is the last thing that a ruler wants to hear who has continued in office beyond his "sell-by" date. The leading opposition newspaper in Zimbabwe *The Daily News* has been repeatedly closed through a number of effective legal devices (www.sundayherald.com/36873).

Yes-men are an inevitable part of any fully functioning patron-client network. Patrons who have attained sufficient power do not want to hear that they are wrong. It is true that at the top it is lonely; it is also true that the person who has reached that point must make independent decisions. At first the powerful listen to those who helped them reach the top, but they eventually begin to fear that those very people will be the ones to pull them down, so they surround themselves with safe, unambitious followers who assure them that they are doing everything correctly. The power brokers who helped them get to where they are, are then rejected. In some cases, the early supporters are killed, as happened in Zambia when President Chiluba's former principal advisor was shot by unknown gunmen the night before he was to give testimony about possible government corruption.

What is the effect on African development? In the countries I know, sycophancy has slowed down or even reversed progress, justice, economic growth, and community participation. Liberia stagnated during the last days of Tubman, just as Lesotho did while Jonathan was trying desperately to hold onto power. We see signs of the same syndrome developing in South Africa and Namibia as Thabo Mbeki and Sam Nujoma tighten their grips on power. If it continues, this patron-client sycophancy will be a disaster, since these two countries hold out much of the promise for the southern African region.

I find the situation most depressing in Zimbabwe, where Robert Mugabe has drawn the wagons close around him. His advisers include men such as Jonathan Moyo, a formerly respected political scientist who now says whatever his boss wants him to say, to the extent of pronouncing gross public lies. Mugabe's foreign minister Stan Mudenge was once head of the Institute of Southern African Studies at the National University of Lesotho, where he was a strictly self-serving, greedy academic. Mudenge left behind him an Institute that was demoralized and ineffectual. At this point in history, the only forces able to speak out about the destruction of Zimbabwe are the courts and the opposition MDC. In response, Mugabe announced that the decisions of the courts are not to be honored if they go against the will of the war veterans and Mugabe's ZANU-PF party. He has also placed every possible obstacle in the way of the MDC in order to keep them from expressing what appears to be the will of the people.

It is important, however, not to blame only Africa's leaders for such blatant sycophancy. Many of the international donor agencies are equally guilty of allowing yes-men to flourish. I was told when I worked for the FAO and then USAID that one must follow the party line if one wants to advance. I believed instead, probably naively, that I had been hired to work for the people of Lesotho and not only for an international body. When the agency and the people disagreed, I felt honor bound to respect the view of the people with whom we were working. That position did not make me popular, since I was no longer polishing up the handle of the big front door, which is essential to getting ahead.

I honor and respect people who speak their minds, regardless of the personal and political fallout. One USAID educator in Liberia, who preferred to spend his time finding ways to help village people build and manage their own schools, lost his job, because he did not meet his target number of finished schools during the lifetime of the project. The researcher who showed that an officially approved erosion control system was causing as much erosion as it cured was prevented from getting further work within the aid system. Sadly, such people are rare in international circles.

More common are people such as the man who wrote new agricultural projects in Lesotho identical to old ones that had failed, because that was his assignment. When I pointed out that his ideas had been tried and failed, he only said he had no time to think about the past. Another example is the man who wished very much that the Basotho would leave the rural areas so that he could implement standard range management schemes. These people, just as their national counterparts who say what the boss wants to hear, will be promoted until they too are the ones who dictate nonsense to the new boys in the club.

There are certainly many yes-men and sycophants in Europe and America. They just as certainly do their countries no good, though they may bring great benefit to themselves. What is sad is that the Western nations can afford the loss to national productivity, while, as my friend Melvin Mason in Liberia said about the corruption in his country, Africa cannot afford it. It is also true, of course, that the media in Western nations are able to blow the whistle and call attention to corruption, whereas in too many African countries the media are muzzled.

10.8 Hopeful signs.

Respect for **customary leaders** continues at the village and community level across most of sub-Saharan Africa. Local politics would be confused and badly disrupted if the chiefs were not in their offices, willing to listen to complaints and manage local activities, such as cleaning trails. In the more successful ujamaa villages I visited in Tanzania, the natural traditional leaders were important in keeping that society on an even keel.

Political policies are coming to the fore in countries where opposition parties are beginning to play an important role. Policy differences exist in South

Africa, Namibia, and Zimbabwe between the major parties. Whether parties differ on substantive points, as opposed to differing only about patronage and power, is less clear in tropical Africa. I feel hopeful as I read speeches by politicians and technocrats in Liberia, several of whom are now developing a rational plan for moving Liberia forward during the post-civil-war period.

It is hard to find **political parties** in Africa that transcend traditional patron-client lines. The opposition to Jerry Rawlings' chosen successor may be one of few successful examples. Voters in Ghana united to put into power a genuinely non-military government. And the Movement for Democratic Change in Zimbabwe brings together labor unions, unemployed urban people, and white farmers under the umbrella of opposition to the slow national suicide engendered by Mugabe. Yet many worry what will happen if the opposition actually gains power and wonder if it too will split into ethnic and social factions. Ultimately, it may be economics that breaks up Africa's **swollen bureaucracies**. They exist to give jobs to clients within the ruling patrimony, among other reasons. But in recent years civil servants have increasingly gone without salary, because there was no money to pay them in government coffers. Bureaucracies may shrink naturally because of attrition, as stranded government employees leave their jobs for something, anything, to keep them alive.

Future political leaders in Lesotho

National boundaries are being increasingly thinned, as cross-national relations are improved. There is a serious move at the highest level to remove many of the regulations that now restrict movement across Lesotho's border with South Africa. The Southern African Development Community (SADC) is seeking ways to rationalize relations between its member countries. Additionally, it is hoped that eventually the almost continual war between Liberia, Sierra Leone, Guinea, and Côte d'Ivoire will end and a new era will issue in a more effective confederal relation between these nations. Perhaps the new African Union, which replaced the Organization of African Unity, will be in a position to be creative in its approach to the problem.

The era when leaders became **rulers for life** is coming to a close. Senegal, Côte d'Ivoire, Ghana, Malawi, and Zambia all had successful elections to replace long-serving presidents. Togo's President Gnassingbe Eyadema, in power for thirty-seven years as a result of his election in 2003, and others, such as Mugabe, are relics left over from the past. At the same time, there is strong pressure in Africa to get rid of leaders whose ambitions are to be president for life. Mandela's example of stepping down when he could easily have won another election sets a very important precedent.

Sycophancy, in part a result of long-term rulers, is hard to root out. Yet there is arising a new generation of educated people, many in mainline churches which previously had often been silent in the face of oppression. The young and active have never experienced the full strength of the old patron-client networks, and who have been schooled in Western-type democracy. These sophisticated young people are not going to be as satisfied as their elders were when they received patronage in return

Church leaders marching for the ANC

for loyalty. These days, "no-men" are becoming more common and more powerful than **"yes-men."** The negative consequence of this resistance to sycophancy is the multiplication of political parties and sub-parties. Presumably, that result is healthier than the old-style "president knows best" politics.

CHAPTER ELEVEN. CENTRALIZED COMMAND ECONOMIES

African countries have almost without exception suffered from mismanaged economies. The fear of losing control, which has prevented governments from decentralizing their political systems, has also led them to maintain tight grips on their economies. Every country I have worked in, including South Africa, has sought to dominate economic activity, all the way from the biggest corporations down to the smallest informal sector operator.

I have already mentioned some of the big issues. Government remains the biggest single employer in most countries. Huge debts have been incurred, often through the connivance of both lenders and borrowers. Unemployment is widespread and under-employment is even greater, reaching about 50 percent in most countries. Resettlement schemes in some countries have slowed or even reversed development due to a heavy-handed, compulsory approach. Government parastatals have been created to do the work that private enterprise can do better. Serious corruption has sent money out of the country and into foreign banks. The infrastructure impacting transport and marketing in remote areas has been allowed to deteriorate; instead, the bulk of resources for building infrastructure has been concentrated on major cities.

In this chapter I consider the consequences of the development and decline of Soviet-style five-year plans as well as top-down collectivization, state control of labor unions, centralized food-for-work instead of community-run self-help projects, inappropriate price structures, massive and inappropriate prestige projects, and bureaucratic controls on the informal economy. Decentralization in each of these areas, to the extent it is allowed by the patron-client networks that dominate Africa, will lead African nations further toward democracy and economic growth. I conclude with a discussion of the media, since without freedom of the press it will be hard to expose further economic false steps.

11.1 Five-year plans.

One of my first assignments when working with USAID in Lesotho when I was assigned to the Ministry of Agriculture was to help write the agriculture section of the next five-year plan. I soon found that it was composed of economists' pipe dreams. Figures were taken from previous plans and projections made for the future without any sense of the vagaries of weather, of shifts in politics, or of the lives and deaths of animals and people. Linear projections were made from scanty data, and the results were enshrined in a thick book. I was convinced of the futility of the exercise, at least in the area of agriculture.

I think back to the time I taught modern European history at Cuttington College when the Soviet Union was a major focus of the course. Five-year plans were Stalin's invention; he used them as he pushed the Soviet Union into a mad rush toward development. Goals were set by bureaucrats and then fulfilled on paper by terrified apparatchiks throughout the country. The plan was the scripture, and Stalin was the god who dictated it. This was especially true in the case of farming, since at that time Lysenko was dictating the new orthodoxy in plant genetics.

China fell into the same trap. Chairman Mao Tse Tung was determined to bring about a steady march toward a bright communist future, complete with backyard smelters and collective farms. The plan had to be met, if only on paper. Otherwise, heads would roll. As it was, not only did heads roll, but millions died of starvation due to the forced march toward collectivization.

In general, careful planning makes sense. The number of children eligible for school can be calculated, subject to careful demographic projections. Thus, the number and level of training of teachers can also be predicted with reasonable accuracy. Health is another straightforward planning exercise—or at least it was before the HIV/AIDS pandemic. Plans can be drawn up for transport and communication. Roads deteriorate at reasonably well known rates, and therefore plans for the maintenance and construction of roads can be projected. Energy and fuel needs can be calculated. A serious problem arises, however, as soon as more volatile sectors, such as agriculture and employment, are factored into the plan.

Children and teacher in rural Liberia

Lesotho, like so many other African countries, felt it had to have five-year plans, partly because international donors required them. Certain ministries were able to set out their needs, particularly those needs mentioned in the previous paragraph. Yet overall, the grand plans made little sense and may well have hindered real development. Speaking as a statistician, it makes no sense to me to add sets of numbers with wildly different margins of error. If I can predict the increase in the budget for schools to within 5 percent accuracy but can only guess at farm production to within plus or minus 50 percent (which is the case, if one looks at historical trends), then the overall prediction of a national budget, which requires summing all the component parts, each with its own level of inaccuracy, is notoriously imprecise. Thus, in order to give the appearance of precision, arbitrary and artificial goals were established in the five-year plans for the guesswork sectors, and nonsense growth rates were imposed. This removed the projections in the guesswork sectors from reality and pushed them into the realm of fantasy.

Large projects were then created by Lesotho's planners to implement their own as well as their donors' fantasies, particularly in the agriculture and employment sectors. An unfortunate result of working with unreal numbers is that the same mentality spills over into sectors where planning makes more sense. For example, though the need for new roads can be realistically projected, planners feel pressured into coming up with an economic rationale. They feel they must first explain that a certain amount of increase in trade will take place, which will result in more businesses being established, which in turn justifies the new roads, because so many more vehicles will use them. The economic meat grinder takes the imagined data and produces mince meat, which appears edible but in reality has no substance.

All this building of imaginary structures would not cause great harm if there was proper dialogue between planners and people in the productive sector, as happens in most Western economies. But economies such as Lesotho's are greatly dependent on and subordinate to centralized government, which is the country's biggest single employer. This centralized government operates as the central traffic controller for the flow of donor funds into the country, which my wife Judy calls the "donor mode of production." These donor funds are then applied according to the national plans, which are built out of office-made smoke and mirrors. The result is serious misapplication of funds toward activities that in themselves make little sense. In particular, funds are administered at the center so that local administration, however much it may be praised, is starved of the funds it needs to implement locally designed activities, unless it tailors those activities to fit the central model.

I have seen this happen in Lesotho over the years. I have had less experience with other countries, but it is my impression that development efforts in Ethiopia, Uganda, and Tanzania, where I was peripherally helping provide data for national plans, are no different. Those working in the Tanzanian Mbeya Regional Integrated Development Plan (RIDEP in the project's jargon) in the early 1980s wanted figures so they could plan ahead for the next five years. The administrators of the plan had little real interest in what was going on in the villages. They wanted numbers they could plug into a growth chart showing the effect five years down the line of imposing certain interventions on people. I was working as a sociologist in the field, and the qualitative (and at times quantitative) impressions I brought back from the villages did not lend themselves to precisely projected growth rates. From what I have read over the years of the news in Tanzania since I left in 1981, I am sure that my qualitative comments on the Mbeya region more accurately portray what has happened than the economists' growth charts.

It could be argued that I am advocating a purely ad hoc laissez-faire policy with no attempt to look ahead. Perhaps I do overstate my case. What I recommend is smaller, more specific, and more local planning. Most long-term plans have a strong urban bias that needs to be corrected. Real precision may be possible in education, although even in that case it matters greatly whether plans are being made for the mountain areas of Lesotho or the plains of Tanzania, where boys are often pushed into herding, or instead for urban areas where the pressure to attend school is greater than in livestock country. Much more attention must be paid to local conditions in the agriculture sector, unlike plans that assume a certain number of tractors and a specific amount of fertilizer are needed without incorporating how they are to be used or the possible dangers of relying on them.

I am saying that national, top-down planning, based in the unreal world of the capital city, is dangerous and ineffective. It has induced countries to take loans that cannot be repaid. It has imposed strategies on farmers that were irrelevant. It has required curricula in rural schools to ignore the needs of rural communities. It has induced government bureaucrats to fulfill paper targets, often by distorting on-the-ground realities rather than by thinking through issues of local change and local problem-solving.

11.2 Top-down collectivization.

Top-down collectivization is often closely related to centralized five-year plans. The Stalinist approach to national development was to invent a plan and then mobilize the population to carry out the plan, by force if necessary. Fortunately, most of the countries where I have worked were unable even to conceive of mobilizing populations to carry out their plans, because they did not have the structures to enforce such action.

Yet in three cases just such a scheme was attempted and, inevitably, it failed. The temptation remains alive in other countries to try the Stalinist approach, but circumstances militate against it being put into practice.

The first such effort I observed happened in Guinea when Sekou Touré in the 1950s and 1960s imposed a national plan and tried to force every one of his subjects to cooperate. I use the word "subject" deliberately. Although the French cultural inheritance in Guinea allowed the authoritarian government erroneously to describe every person as a "citizen," control was firmly in the hands of the Democratic Party of Guinea (PDG), which allowed no dissent against national decisions.

I visited Guinea for a short time in late 1959, not long after independence, and I saw the beginnings of the collective experiment. Brutal government agents were put into place across the country and were told they must organize their subjects to do what the government in Conakry told them to do. I met one of these leaders in Kankan and was quite shaken by what I saw. He was a large, determined man, surrounded by fully-armed soldiers who claimed that my colleague, Dr. John Stewart, and I were smugglers. We had some difficulty getting out of his police office and on our way back to Liberia; visitors who might see what was actually going on were considered dangerous.

Refugees from Guinea fled to Liberia in the 1960s on a regular basis, and the stories they told us were frightening. They claimed that dissidents who wanted to carry on their independent lives as entrepreneurs were arrested and thrown into overcrowded jails with little ventilation, where many died. Most of the Guineans I met in Liberia were the free-wheeling Mandingo traders so common across West Africa, and thus their stories were likely to be one-sided. But what they said confirmed what we read in newspapers and magazines: that Guinea was destroying its economy and killing its people by forcing a Marxist-Leninist-Stalinist-Maoist regime on the country. Sekou Touré had high hopes that both Russia and China would help him in his efforts, but ultimately they both disappointed him and pulled out. His death in 1984 was greeted with great relief by a ruined nation.

Tanzania was the second country where I observed how top-down collectivization was tried. I have already spoken about the troubles that Nyerere's economic philosophy brought to that country, but a footnote to that story concerns the Mbeya integrated development project I worked on. A former student of mine, one of those who so inspired me when I first arrived in Liberia when they had just come back from the Pan-African Congress in Ghana, was in 1981 the Mbeya District Commissioner. He was the person-on-the-spot to implement any development plans that the project might generate.

I had a lengthy conversation with him, during which it became clear that there was no way in which bottom-up, people-centered ideas could be implemented. He was under orders from the central government to organize agriculture, commerce, education, health, communications, and, indeed, every aspect of life according to the national model. This included requiring villages to produce their crops communally. As I have already pointed out, the communal farms I saw were in most cases dismal failures. People wanted to develop themselves, and they were not allowed to do so.

The only redeeming feature of the Tanzanian experiment was that Nyerere was not the monster that Sekou Touré was. Whereas in the collectivization model that was followed it was likely that Stalin's real intention was to destroy the peasantry rather than to increase farm production, Nyerere instead had the genuine interests of the rural population at heart. People were not arrested, tortured, or killed, as they had been in Guinea or in the model countries of Russia and China. Humanity eventually prevailed. Nyerere ultimately realized that his ideas could not work, and so he resigned.

The third country was Ethiopia, where collectivization under Mengistu Haile Mariam also failed. Mengistu was no Nyerere. He was much closer to Sekou Touré in the brutality of his methods and in his systematic drive to collectivize, thus destroying Ethiopia. The majority of the people I met in Ethiopia had no use for him or his methods, but they had no choice but to appear obedient. Sekou Touré was more thorough and more willing to kill or imprison dissidents in his drive for obedience than Mengistu, the result being that there was more open opposition among the general public in Ethiopia than in Guinea.

I had several conversations with leading academics at the University of Addis Ababa in 1982. They had nothing but scorn for Mengistu's goals and methods. They went through the motions of agreement to the extent that senior professors at the University attended weekly classes in Marxist-Leninist thought in order to keep their jobs. Yet they laughed openly at what they learned. At the time I could see that collectivization would not work and that people would "obey" by continuing the sort of passive inactivity I saw at a forced resettlement camp.

When Mengistu gained control of Ethiopia, Haile Selassie's overthrow had been long overdue. Before his death, Selassie was old and nearly senile, and his regime continued because no one had the temerity to topple it. What is truly sad about the overthrow was that it was done so badly. If Mengistu had been a Nyerere, he would have at least caught people's imagination and devotion, as was the case in Tanzania's failed experiment at African socialism. Better still would have been a moderate leader trying to bring democratic change to a potentially rich country. It did not happen, and, unfortunately, it is still not happening.

Top-down collectivization is not among the mistakes of other countries where I have worked. The leaders of Liberia (before Charles Taylor) and Lesotho were neither ruthless nor single-minded enough to have done it, nor would they have wanted to do so. Even the most wicked of Uganda's rulers, Idi Amin, did not have a grand plan for organizing the nation. He just ruined it without having a template for its destruction. Botswana, South Africa, and Namibia are content to continue in an exploitative capitalist fashion that at least allows development, however corrupt, to take place.

Yet in countries where there is IMF involvement, there is a paradox inherent in the dictates of that organization. The IMF opposes the rigid plans made by socialist centralized governments, but their own requirements of fiscal austerity and cost recovery force countries to adopt something very like a command economy.

11.3 State control of labor unions.

Labor unions have an important role to play in keeping an economy honest and on track. Governments who prefer it otherwise do their best to control workers and prevent them from striking to seek better working conditions. Lesotho, for example, has several trade unions, some of them independent of government and some not. The government has never actually forced the independent unions to close but at times has come very close.

A good example is in the area of education. There are two unions—the Lesotho Association of Teachers (LAT), which has a very cozy relation with the Ministry of Education, and the Lesotho Teachers Trade Union (LTTU), which often opposes government. LAT is mainly composed of principals, headmasters, and senior teachers, and is compliant with government wishes, preferring to work within the system rather than speaking boldly about teachers' complaints. As a result, LAT receives top-down support, has regular government-sponsored seminars, has a direct line to policy makers in the Ministry of Education, and receives regular country-to-country support for its seminars. LTTU, on the other hand, has been outspoken and has led several strikes. In the most notorious of these strikes, which occurred during the military government, LTTU teachers and supporters were badly beaten and some were dismissed. It is impressive that ordinary teachers still respect LTTU (rather than LAT), because it is their voice.

Another example from the period of military rule in Lesotho involved two umbrella trade unions, one affiliated with the anti-communist International Federation of Free Trade Unions. The first umbrella trade union, The Lesotho Federation of Free Trade Unions, had a close relation with the military and could be counted on not to rock the boat. The alternative union, The Lesotho Federation of Democratic Unions, was more radical and supported a major strike against the Lesotho Highlands Development Authority, which was supervising the construction of the huge dams that would supply water to South Africa. Strikers were beaten and even killed. The Lesotho Federation of Free Trade Unions, supported by government, had an adviser, who in my view was very likely posted to Lesotho by the American government to make sure that radical policies did not prevail.

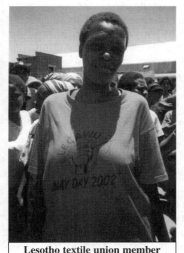

Lesotho textile union member

Fortunately, government-sponsored unions have never gained popularity among workers, and as a result, workers have a voice with which to speak. Having a voice has been particularly important for workers on the dam construction projects as well as workers in the textile factories that are increasingly important sources of employment. A strike by the Lesotho Clothing and Allied Workers Union in 2001 helped bring about increased wages and improved conditions in the textile industry. Lesotho has been, at least to some extent, a success story in the matter of labor relations.

Another success story, which in its midst involved bitter conflict, was the struggle in the 1980s of the National Union of Mineworkers (NUM) for recognition in South Africa. I was working at the Transformation Resource Center at the time and was deeply involved in supporting Basotho migrant workers who were part of NUM. Lesotho's military government was strongly opposed to the NUM activists, and so we at Transformation had a hard time providing the necessary logistical and moral support for the union. The military government in Lesotho knew which side its bread was buttered on and was willing to obey orders from the Nationalist government in Pretoria. Yet in the end, NUM was victorious, and it ultimately played an important role in undoing apartheid. Unfortunately, many of our Basotho friends lost their jobs in the process. At the same time, the politically powerful president of NUM was a Mosotho, James Motlatsi, a man who has long argued for closer political links between Lesotho and South Africa.

International politics played a small but negative role in my work with NUM when I fell into a trap set by the American and Swedish governments. In the process,

I came close to losing all credibility, because we at Transformation naively thought they simply wanted to help, when in retrospect it appears that the Reagan government wanted to influence the course of events. I made the mistake of arranging for some of the NUM leaders to meet with Swedish and American diplomats at a party at the Swedish ambassador's residence, where liquor flowed so freely that I fear confidences were betrayed. I had to fight my way back to having the trust of my South African colleagues, a trust I may never have fully recovered.

The point of my story is that governments know the power of labor and want to influence its leadership. The same story is being played out today in South Africa, where the Congress of South African Trade Unions (COSATU) is an integral part of the ANC-Communist Party-COSATU alliance that rules the country. At this point in history, labor has an inside track to government, but the government is seeking to control labor through the tripartite alliance. It appears that so far workers are holding their own against the increasingly right-wing policies of the ANC, but the alliance could crack at some point. If it does, the result may be beneficial, since the result would be a realignment of forces in which the ANC would no longer hold an overwhelming majority in Parliament. Real competition is always a good thing.

At present, organized labor has a love-hate relation with the South African government. But that is a sign of health. Just as in Lesotho, independent labor unions have maintained their integrity in South Africa. Yet the role of the unions in defending the rights of workers would be enhanced if they did not have to buy into the rather conservative economic policies of the ANC government. Having a share of power has its costs.

In other countries labor has been less fortunate. In Liberia, the rubber workers have tried to organize but have had little success because of government opposition. There is little they have been able to do to get a better deal from any of the successive governments from Tubman to Taylor. The Public Relations Officer at Firestone was always a Liberian whose job it was to make sure that the tappers were kept in line, by persuasion or by force. The result was that the workers had no chance to have their grievances heard or attended to. The government may have been able to retire its international debt by ensuring that rubber workers were kept down, and in the same way the elite may have been able to enjoy good incomes. It is clear, however that real national development, that is, development among the ordinary working people of Liberia, was blocked.

Rubber workers went on strike at Firestone in 1999 for better working conditions and wages substantially higher than the very low $2.53 per day they were receiving at the time (www.state.gov/g/drl/rls/hrrpt/1999/254.htm; also mailman.efn.org/pipermail/pie/2003-August/000087.html). At that time, the Taylor government was still more or less in control of the country.

Whether because of Taylor or despite Taylor, the workers were able to win some concessions after seven weeks of strike action. Taylor played all sides in his constantly shifting strategies for keeping power and making money. Throughout the civil war life has been very difficult, and jobs were more scarce than they were before Doe and Taylor upset the status quo. The experience of exercising labor power remains with the rubber workers, however, and when peace comes once again, surely the unions will take advantage of past achievements.

11.4 Centralized food distribution.

Governments and donor agencies across Africa have used top-down schemes to distribute surplus food to those who were in need because of drought, war, floods, famine, or politics. Often the food is sorely needed, people are genuinely starving, and the normal mechanisms for getting food into their mouths have broken down. I do not have a serious complaint with the system when there is a real emergency, many of which have arisen in recent years in Africa. I admire the World Food Program and its work and hope it can continue to support the truly hungry. I particularly admired the school feeding program, which over the years has made school meals available to hungry children. Unfortunately, this program is being phased out in favor of school gardens that in the past have been only marginally successful.

What concerns me is the patronizing assumption that only central administrators can bring food where it is needed. I had that experience when I worked with the Catholic Relief Service (CRS) in Lesotho in the mid-1980s. They, together with their government counterparts, insisted on doing the whole job from their central base in Maseru. They did not trust local institutions, whether village government or private enterprise, to move food, despite what was obvious, that the villagers knew the extent of the need far better than any outsiders. I urged that the surplus food, brought in by CRS from international donors, either be monetized or given to the communities themselves to distribute.

The CRS officials raised every possible objection and refused to allow me to publish my recommendation that food distribution be localized, either in the form of food or money. They said it was against their head office regulations, would cause enormous corruption, would bypass government procedures, and in short was against the whole ethos of food aid around the world. At the core of their position was the conviction that they were the chief patrons and all others were their clients. To have allowed others to distribute the food, according to local need and understanding, would have been to give too much power to those at the margins. The underlying issues are control, and who holds it, and power, and who wields it.

In the end, I had to submit to the wishes of the Catholic Relief Services. Yet in my own copies of their commissioned report about the distribution, I retained the final chapter containing my recommendations, which I subsequently distributed to interested parties. I continued to push the same approach in other reports I issued through Sechaba Consultants, because I believe strongly in decentralization. Central authorities cannot understand what is really going on in local communities, even when local people under them manage the distribution process. Decentralization and dependency can only coexist when local patron-client networks are created, resulting in conflict between center and periphery. Such conflict is necessary for an effective balance of power between central powers and local, ordinary people.

Dependency on central authorities is strongly reinforced whenever local people are bypassed and treated as passive recipients and instruments of social policy. Furthermore, there is evidence that much of

Food for work in Lesotho

the food that is intended to feed the poor is in fact "eaten" by national authorities. The argument that village-level corruption would violate the integrity of international and government assistance assumes that central government authorities are honest, something known to be far from true. Moreover, the main people to advocate decentralization of food aid to the villages are women, who have notoriously little political clout in Africa. Men at the central government level say they should manage food distribution, by implication saying they don't trust rural women to do the job.

It is true that village authorities can be corrupt. Yet corruption at the local level is much less likely to go unnoticed, since one can do little that is wrong in a village without at least some people being aware of it. Feedback that corrects the system is much more likely to work at the village level than at national level, where it can easily go unnoticed. On the other hand, villages are becoming more heterogeneous, so that the misallocation and even the sale of food can escape detection. Even if that were to happen, however, the quantities involved are small, and the food would remain in the same community. Food assistance, including food for work, is best by many problems, not just corruption. There is always a tendency to overestimate the amount of food needed, especially since Lesotho is a country with strong links to the South African economy (www.fews.org/fb970728/fewsid3.html).

Food aid in Liberia still suffers from centralized top-down assumptions that the poor simply exist to be fed and are unable to learn how to feed themselves or manage their own affairs. Massive quantities of inexpensive, low-quality rice were imported into Liberia during the Tubman and Tolbert eras and sold to people at subsidized prices. In this way, rural rice farming was discouraged, and people in the urban areas or along the roads were content to buy and eat the so-called *puu-saaba* rice, a word that I believe refers in the Kpelle language to its cost at thirty cents per pound in the local market. It was a distinctly poor grade of rice, and rural people who knew good rice would not eat it. It was cheap, however, and easily available to the poor. The big international rice producers knew that sale of this rice to donor agencies for distribution in places like Liberia would help them dump their surplus and distinctly inferior rice. Such dumping also means lower prices for rural farmers, which further depresses local production.

African leaders sometimes do the right thing, sometimes even for the right reason, but do it in the wrong way. I think of occasions, such as the national meltdown in Nigeria in July 2003, when governments have doubled or tripled prices for petroleum products overnight and then were forced to face the wrath of the people. In Nigeria there were strikes and riots over petrol prices in most major cities and at least ten people were killed in the economic capital Lagos (www.guardian.co.uk/oil/story/0,11319,993419,00.html).

In Liberia's case, the product was rice. In 1979, President Tolbert, following the recommendation of the Ministry of Agriculture, decided to raise the price of rice from $22 to $30 per hundred pounds in order to promote local rice production. It was a good idea, though it was clear even beforehand that many senior government officials and private individuals would benefit, because they had large rice plantations in the interior. The rise in price, however, turned out to be too much, too soon.

Nascent opposition political parties rallied to the defense of poor people who had to pay more for their staple food. They sought to avert the price rise and at the same time hoped to gain a greater voice in Liberian politics. Yet the long-term ascendancy of the ruling True Whig Party meant that its leaders were not willing to listen to views raised outside the inner circles of power. The price rise was confirmed, and a public rally by the opposition was brutally suppressed. According to the *Historical Dictionary of Liberia*, seventy people were killed and hundreds injured (Dunn 2000: 325).

The ultimate result of this far-too-firm clampdown on the protests and the subsequent proscription of opposition political parties was the 1980 coup by Samuel Doe and his associates. The link between doing the right thing in the wrong way and the eventual destruction of Liberia is quite clear. Self-reliance in rice would have benefited by a rise in the artificially low market price. Yet, as has happened in so many countries where popular feeling has been ignored in making what are potentially rational economic choices, those most likely to suffer from economic rationality were not consulted. It is another example of the fallacy that a rising tide lifts all boats. In this case in Liberia, all the boats sank. In the end, even more rice had to be imported to feed a much larger number of destitute people.

Hunger, as Amartya Sen has often pointed out, is a political problem. The book for which he won the Nobel Memorial Prize in Economics asserted that famines do not occur because of a shortage of food (Sen 1982). Instead famines occur in wars. They occur in non-democratic countries where the press is muzzled and where people's voices are not heard. They occur especially where those at the top are not accountable to the people but can do what they wish with national resources. Hunger, according to the World Health Organization, is the biggest health risk in the world, higher even than HIV/AIDS (www.globalhealth.org/news/article/2435). Hunger continues unabated in countries such as Malawi and Ethiopia, and is always ready to kill and maim people all over Africa. Yet politics continues to keep hunger from being overcome.

Test cases have arisen in 2002 and 2003 in southern Africa. Admittedly, serious droughts afflicted Zambia, Malawi, and Zimbabwe, but the political structures were such that the government felt it did not need to respond to advance warning signs of starvation. Zambia was in the throes of political infighting, admittedly within a democratic structure, but it was a structure in which jockeying for power within the ruling party took priority over attending to people's needs. Malawi accumulated major food reserves during two good years, but government officials were tempted and sold off the food reserves for personal profit, bringing on serious hunger during the 2003 drought. In Zimbabwe, the Mugabe government's lust for power has destroyed an agricultural economy that should have been able to supply the needs of its hungry neighbors. In all three cases, Sen's hypothesis was proved true. And in each case, food relief was required. The desperate need for food for Sudanese refugees in mid-2004 is another clearly political crisis.

I do not have personal experience with food relief procedures in the other countries where I have worked, since I have not been there during times of famine or war. I have followed the news, however, and it is clear that food aid has always been centrally organized and that rarely have people administered their own affairs or become more self-reliant. Governments say they want to help people avoid starvation by becoming self-reliant, but when self-reliance involves giving the people a measure of autonomy, governments prefer to sacrifice self-reliance, because it is too dangerous politically. The result is the decline of rural production, increased migration to the urban areas, and confirmation of the belief that government exists to give people what they want.

The attitude that government will help and that people only need to ask exists in many African countries, including Lesotho. Yet donor agencies are finally changing their tunes and are trying to find ways to escape dependency. They want government and foreign development programs to create what is called in today's jargon "an enabling environment." When this phrase is translated into reality, it means that the central authorities are tired of spending money on aid when it does not yield productive results. But people are not ready to buy the idea. All the interviews we have done at Sechaba Consultants show that dependency is a firmly established habit. To many, democracy means a government that satisfies people's needs and wants. Our 2003 survey of political attitudes in Lesotho has borne that out fully. The top four tasks that people assign to their representatives in parliament have to do with economic development; less than 20 percent of respondents stress political issues. In short, many years of top-down donor assistance, including food aid and all the other ways in which the economy is subsidized from above, has created a mentality that is very hard to change and which has contributed seriously to Africa's decline.

11.5 Inappropriate price structures.

Pricing is a mechanism that can promote or hinder economic development. Governments want to use rural farmers, who are "subjects," to benefit urban dwellers, who are "citizens," by paying low prices for foodstuffs. I mentioned the disaster that the rice riots triggered in Liberia when prices were raised. There have been insensitive and arbitrary increases in the price of petroleum products, not only in Nigeria but in many African countries. Fortunately, South Africa (and by extension Lesotho and the other SADC countries that are totally dependent on South Africa for petroleum product imports) has introduced gradual changes, and even reductions, in price, and thus has avoided the riots experienced elsewhere.

For a long time, the market price of maize in Lesotho was driven by duties on maize imported from South Africa. The result was that the Basotho were paying more for raw and processed maize than were South Africans. The situation gave the Basotho incentives to produce more maize locally, but the unfortunate result was an over-emphasis on what is not a sensible crop for many areas of Lesotho. People grew maize on marginal soils not only because they liked it, but also because they did not want to pay into government coffers the duty on imported maize. In order to grow maize on these marginal soils, people have had to spend too much on seeds, fertilizer, hiring tractors or oxen, and labor, causing them to lose money. In the late 1990s, the levy on imported maize was dropped. Now maize can be brought freely into Lesotho from South Africa. Poor people are thus spending less on their staple food, and they can plan more rationally how to use their fields and their other resources (Gay and Hall 2000: 39).

Another example of inappropriate pricing was the harm I saw done to tea, cocoa, and coffee production in Tanzania. People had little incentive to produce these crops, because they knew they would get low prices from the government buyers and that they would get the payments so late that inflation had already eaten the profits. Farmers preferred to sell their crops for poor prices to local smugglers, because at least they received timely payment.

I encountered a similar situation in the resettlement camp I visited in southern Ethiopia in 1982. At the end of our visit, several of these dispirited, formerly urban people approached the Ethiopian research assistants on our team and offered to sell at a reduced price the teff and wheat they had produced on what, in theory, was a collective farm. Both parties were pleased to make a deal. The farmers were pleased because they would get some timely money for what they had produced, rather than having to wait an indeterminate length of time for what might never come. The researchers were pleased because they could buy the grain at substantially lower prices than they would have had to pay at government markets in Addis Ababa.

Inappropriate exchange rates are another set of price structures that create problems. The official rate for the Zimbabwe dollar has been so out of touch with reality that business cannot take place. As a result there is almost no currency in the country, and exchange takes place primarily informally and on the black market (allafrica.com/stories/200309110664.html). When I was in Zimbabwe in 2000 one American dollar would buy about 55 Zimbabwe dollars. The official rate as of July 2004 is about 824 Zimbabwe dollars for one American dollar, and the inflation rate had reached 455 percent in November 2003 (www.zwnews.com/issuefull.cfm?Article ID=7746).

Exchange rates are not only a problem with currency, however. One of the main reasons Nigeria is perennially short of petroleum products is its subsidized price at home. Lower prices have meant that enterprising Nigerians—and what Nigerians are not enterprising?—buy petrol and cooking fuel cheaply and sell these products across the border at a substantial profit. Petroleum products are, in this case, another form of currency, and the domestic price comparison amounts to an artificial exchange rate.

11.6 Expensive prestige projects.

Having an airline is one way for a country to gain international visibility. Unfortunately, many African airlines have gone broke. Lesotho Airways was at first a small, moderately efficient airline that only ran flights into the interior as well as a couple of flights a week to Johannesburg. It had no competition and so it survived without losing money. It was an essential service, because many remote rural villages could only be reached by airplane.

But the airline began to have pretensions, partly due to the isolation brought about by Lesotho's stand against apartheid during the 1980s. Planes had formerly used a small airstrip near the bus stop in the center of Maseru from which two-engine planes could fly to their destinations. Then the government decided it needed an airport long and modern enough to accommodate jets and bought a used Boeing 707 as the flagship of its fleet of planes. The new airport was located about thirty kilometers south of Maseru and took a substantial amount of what had been good, arable land. The villagers whose land was taken were supposed to be compensated, but my interviews in neighboring villages uncovered dissatisfied people who had lost their land without payment.

Lesotho spent a large sum on the airport and even more on the 707, which hardly ever left the airport and in the end was sold for a substantial loss. Lesotho Airways continued to limp along, but was losing money regularly. A South African company bought into it, thinking to make a profit, but that venture too collapsed. At present, South African Airways flies into and out of Lesotho twice daily, using the same two-engine planes that could have continued to use the air strip in Maseru. Otherwise, the airport sits empty. Its duty-free shops sell nothing, its bank agency is hardly ever open, and its elaborate air traffic control buildings and equipment are rarely used. Lesotho not only does not get any prestige points out of the airport, but people who are forced to use it instead of the more convenient in-town airport (which has been turned over to the army) are annoyed at having to travel so far.

Lesotho has been the victim of other prestige projects. The Appeals Court in Maseru is a huge, elegant building that is used just a few times a year; it cost a very large sum. A highway from the lowlands to the mountain headquarters of Mokhotlong was paved at high cost to the government. The loan from Kuwait that paid for it must be paid back, but the money will not come from revenues from any increased economic activity in the mountains. Not only does the road cost Lesotho money, but it caused serious environmental degradation during the construction period.

The United Nations Development Program has constructed a four-story building in Maseru to house all the U.N. agencies. There is value in having a headquarters building where all the agencies can work together, but the building itself is grandiose out of all proportion to the work conducted in it. Roughly half the floor space is wasted on hallways, on reception rooms that lead to more reception rooms, and on large offices that could have been half the size and still hold meetings. The building is a monument to the ego of the resident representative who proposed it and supervised its construction.

Liberia also had its share of white-elephant prestige projects. During the wealthy days of the Tubman government in the early 1960s the country built huge prestige projects. The government insisted that Liberia should appear to be a country all Liberians could be proud of, even though they could not personally afford to use them.

Luxury hotel in Liberia

Probably most harmful to the nation was the John F. Kennedy Memorial Hospital in Monrovia. As one of the most modern, well-equipped hospitals in all of West Africa, it was intended to be the apex of the Liberian national health system. The Americans built it in the 1970s as a monument to their own generosity, and the Liberians accepted it as a monument to their pride, but the annual cost of staffing and maintaining it was more than the entire health budget of the country. Sadly, neither party thought enough about the health of the poor Liberians who they hoped would be referred there after they had exhausted the facilities at regional clinics and hospitals. Few rural people could afford to be transferred there, and the hospital was not able to provide the services and specialized treatment had rural people been able to come.

The money would have been far better spent upgrading hospitals and clinics throughout the country, along the lines of Phebe Hospital. In the interior, the Lutheran Church built a simple, clean, functional one-story hospital at Phebe, which served the needs of a quarter of a million people in the interior until the civil war forced it to close in March 2003, and subsequent looting stripped it of all that is needed as it now struggles to reopen. At the time the Kennedy Hospital was built, Monrovia's population was also 250,000, and it would have been well-served by a hospital similar to Phebe's. Such a hospital would have also provided emergency and referral facilities, though not as elaborate as what was built.

Kennedy Hospital began to deteriorate right from the start. The air-conditioning packed up years ago, and it cannot be staffed, because there are too few doctors and too small a health budget to pay them. Before the civil war it had become a monument to folly, and a place where even simple, decent medical care was not be provided, to a large extent because of the complexity of the structure. The Taiwanese promised to renovate the hospital, and when we visited it in November 2001 reconstruction had already begun. But that does not solve the remaining problems of paying staff and maintaining the physical structure even without a civil war. Moreover, news reports following the invasion of Monrovia in June 2003 show that basic medical care is being provided in the more basic structures maintained by the international NGO, Doctors without Borders (www.doctorswithoutborders.org/).

What is the effect of such prestige projects on the countries which insist on having them? They drain the national budget of funds needed for simple, functional buildings or activities that can serve the needs of ordinary people. Thus, the needs of ordinary people are not met, and the government struggles to pay debts and to maintain buildings that might better be allowed to collapse, as I fear will ultimately be the case with Kennedy Hospital.

11.7 Bureaucratic controls on the informal economy.

Informal businesses form the most vibrant and fast-growing sector of African economies. In our report on poverty in Lesotho in 2000, we showed that the informal sector is central and links together all other sectors in society (Gay and Hall 2000: 150ff). These businesses are absolutely essential to keeping a large proportion of the population alive and include a wide range of activities from the most respectable to the frankly criminal.

Businesses such as knitting, sewing, watch repair, photography, tent and chair rentals, catering, and brick making fall into the legitimate category. At the other end of the legal spectrum are carjacking, prostitution, drug sales, protection rackets, and pyramid schemes.

In the middle falls the mother of all informal businesses, brewing traditional beer, which is the principal support for many mothers across Africa.

Brick making in Uganda

The beer can be a mild, nutritious, even healthy fermented version of maize or sorghum porridge. At the opposite extreme, it can be a wicked concoction, often with traditional brew as the base but laced with everything from battery acid to shoe polish to methanol, guaranteed to send consumers out of their misery and in some cases on a one-way passage out of the world.

The main feature of the informal sector is that it is precisely that—informal. The entrepreneurs work anywhere and everywhere, looking for a niche in which they can make a profit. The businesses are highly competitive, and people move into and out of activities with remarkable speed, as I found when trying to compose a comprehensive list of informal businesses in Botswana.

Governments in general do not like informal activities, because they cannot control them or force participants to pay taxes. What governments want is order and regularity. They want to know who is doing what and where it is taking place. They want to issue licenses that can be noted on lists kept in office filing cabinets. That Mrs. So-And-So has decided to hawk the dresses she has just made on the streets of the capital city can neither be captured on government records nor her goods taxed to fatten government coffers. She stands in the street with her wares on a table and pushes herself as far as she can into the path of pedestrians so they can see her and, she hopes, buy from her.

Mrs. So-And-So is not much of a nuisance, and she may be helpful to customers who want to avoid the shops. She avoids a middleman, gets her goods to the customer directly, and saves everyone money. Some of the other small businesses may pose a problem for the public, however. A woman cooks and sells fat cakes on the main street, leaving rubbish behind her, and spattering the street with oil. A young man hawks watches not far from the store where he stole them. He denies his crime as the foreign shop owner accuses him in front of the store, bringing about a near riot in which ordinary people defend him against people they see as exploiting outsiders.

The result often is overkill by the government. Bureaucrats prefer to regulate everything, and in particular they want small businesses off the streets. This came to the fore in mid-2000 in Lesotho when the Maseru City Council tried to relocate businesses to official market places that, unfortunately, the public will never visit. The entrepreneurs knew this, and so they staged strategic withdrawals from the main streets only to come back the next day.

A particularly striking case occurs on the bridge over the Caledon River between the Lesotho and South African border posts. Hawkers line the bridge selling fresh bread, Basotho hats, fruit in season, horsewhips (horses still remain a dominant mode of transport in Lesotho), walking sticks, passport cases, stolen sunglasses, and what could possibly be diamonds but might also be cut glass. Some hawkers provide a legitimate service to people waiting to have their passports stamped, while others are clearly lawbreakers. What the two governments regularly try to do is to drive the hawkers off the bridge. They go, but they come back as soon as the coast is clear.

The problem is simple. How can the disorderly be ordered, the unstructured be regulated, the casual be made formal? I do not have a clear answer, but I know that informal businesses are the main hope of a large proportion of the population in most African countries. I also know they provide important services to many people. If some of those who sell food and drink on the street are providing cover for the sale of drugs, that is hard to avoid. If the women who sell me bananas so I do not have to go to the supermarket leave rubbish on the ground, that too is hard to avoid.

What I am arguing for is flexibility and sensitivity to the needs of a flourishing informal economy. When I did my survey in Botswana, it seemed that the government wanted to find ways for the informal sector to grow (Alexander et al 1983). Some of the regulations it tried to impose were too rigid, however. The government wanted informal craftsmen to have certificates proving their skills. It wanted stall holders to work from places far from the main streets where their customers normally walk. There must be a willingness to compromise. Without that willingness, the entrepreneurial impulses that lead an economy out of stagnation are likely to be crushed, and Africa will continue to decline.

Research into the proper use of informal businesses needs to continue, not in order to control and crush them, but to make best use of them. The National Research Foundation in South Africa has set this issue as one of its most important areas of study for 2003. The focus of this study is "the problem of persistently high rates of unemployment in South Africa, which indicate that the formal economy is unable to absorb the available labor. It investigates how people construct livelihoods in ways other than joining the formal economy in a range of contexts, both urban and rural." (www.nrf.ac.za). Such research is needed in order to free up the innovative ideas of ordinary people who can never find work in paid wage labor, but who have skills and initiative.

11.8 State-controlled media.

Toward the end of 2000, a woman who had resigned from Malawi television complained on the BBC about her inability to broadcast what she knew the public wanted to see and hear. She was forced day after day to screen reports about one minister opening a school to another minister giving a speech to the president traveling to a foreign country. She could not do investigative journalism, and she could not report the activities of opposition political parties. In short, she was forced to broadcast, day by boring day, programs that no one (except the ministers being portrayed and perhaps their wives and children) wanted to see.

The boring quality of official government television would not be a problem if there was competition from the private sector. It appears from the woman's comments that there are no private television stations in Malawi. As a result, the public is exposed to only one perspective on national affairs, and national debate on critical issues is stifled. Still, the situation in Malawi today is not as bad as it was under former president Kamuzu Banda, who put outspoken opposition figures in jail.

Lesotho is fortunate in that it has a free press, which speaks its mind on almost every public and private issue. But the word "media" is a plural noun. I am always unhappy when I hear statements such as "The media is..." because the media are manifold and reach different sectors of society in different ways. Whereas there are many independent newspapers in Lesotho and many radio stations are beginning to be heard, there is only one television station, which broadcasts what the government wants people to hear and see.

Liberia also had a free press when I visited it in 2001, with many newspapers jostling each other for the public eye. Charles Taylor allowed it, because he was not afraid of the small minority of Liberians who read these papers. He knew that there were so few that they posed no threat to him. Yet as the noose began to close from opposing forces in the ongoing civil war, he closed newspapers and restricted journalists from entering the country because of the bad publicity being leaked abroad. It was one thing for these newspapers to speak to a few Monrovia intellectuals but something very different for them to tell the rest of the world whatever negativity was happening in Liberia.

A much more serious threat to Taylor's power was radio, particularly FM radio, which reaches into the interior of the country and broadcasts in indigenous languages. Star Radio was established during the mid-90s under the sponsorship of a Swiss foundation and with support from USAID. It had a highly professional staff which broadcast honest, independent news and beamed it to every corner of the country in about fourteen different languages. Taylor could not stand hearing the truth told to the public, and so he ordered the radio station closed (www.fol.org/freedom_of_speech.html). International protests did not move him. Instead, he made false and defamatory comments about the content of the broadcasts and had his police chief, Paul Mulbah (a former student of mine in charge of maintaining civil order while all around him the society collapsed), remove the high-tech equipment, lock the door, and ban the broadcasters from further work.

Similar pressure was placed on the Roman Catholic Church, whose archbishop Michael Francis has been over the years a fearless proponent of justice and truth. He received the Robert Kennedy award for human rights work in 1999 and continues to be personally unscathed by the criticism to which the church is subjected. Sadly in early 2004 he was felled by a serious stroke and at this writing is still in hospital. The Catholic Justice and Peace Commission has been threatened and raided several times, and the former head of the commission has been sent into exile. The Catholic radio station, Radio Veritas, was closed on several occasions. It opened again because of international pressure from the Catholic Church and the world media, but under strict supervision. In the meantime, harmless, politically naive radio stations such as ELWA (Eternal Love Winning Africa), which is sponsored by right-wing fundamentalist churches, were allowed to operate freely. Taylor's own station, KISS radio, beamed broadcasts in FM and AM to every corner of the country, spreading his propaganda. The decline of Africa is epitomized by this subversion of the truth.

South Africa's government sees its country's newspapers as more "dangerous" than Taylor's government saw the Liberian papers, because South African papers have many more readers. In 2000, the ANC government attempted to limit the freedom of the press in South Africa through its Human Rights Commission, which based its argument on purported racism in mainstream, largely white-owned, white-written newspapers (cjonline.com/stories/ 111798/new_southafrica.shtml). In the end an investigation took place, but the only outcome was to urge the newspapers to be more careful of implicit racism. There still may be racism, both subtle and overt, in these papers, but clearly the intent of the Commission was to control what the public was reading.

That effort to curtail freedom of the press along with other recent actions has caused many to worry that the ANC-led government is losing touch with its founding principles. Political corruption is growing, and officials with little competence and a poor track record are being appointed to senior positions. It is difficult, without outside pressure, to remove politicians who control large segments of the nation, despite their reactionary politics, their obvious incompetence, or their known corruption. That is not to say that there should not be a vertical, patron-client network, which is the character of many African societies. Every political system in the world must pay back its supporters, especially those who bring constituencies with them.

Yet a vital role of the independent press is to keep up that outside pressure on government by exposing corruption, including in papers such as the Johannesburg-based *Mail and Guardian*, which is regularly accused of racism because it points the finger at incompetent and corrupt black politicians. It is true that more black politicians are named by this paper than white, and it could be argued that this is due to racism, but I have decided to base my viewpoint on statistics. Blacks form 83 percent of the population of South Africa, and a similar proportion are now in high government and private positions. It seems obvious that more of them would be corrupt or incompetent, simply because of their greater numbers. The *Mail and Guardian* has also regularly pointed to white politicians and business people of doubtful ability and morality. I think that the Human Rights Commission has conveniently overlooked this fact in order to protect the ANC-led government.

The situation is much better in South Africa and Lesotho than it is in Liberia; other countries where I have worked also have a reasonably free press, including Namibia and Botswana. In visits to these countries over the past few years, I have been impressed with the outspoken character of their criticism of government. Such open criticism is essential if African countries are to find ways to stem the decline. Zimbabwe, where independent media are being systematically brought into line by economic pressure and strong-arm tactics, is an obvious exception to my hope. One of the few hopes for that poor country, which is in a terminal state of decline, is that the remaining independent media are able to continue to speak out without fear of harassment, imprisonment, or death—circumstances that sadly have happened in some countries.

The theme of this chapter has been the importance of a balance between central and local control. My main thrust has been economic, but my emphasis here is on the media as part of the whole picture. Economic malpractice can only be corrected if free speech prevails. As Sen points out, hunger can only be relieved if it comes to the attention of the public, and that requires a free press. Otherwise, all the destructive economic trends I have mentioned, including five-year plans, collectivization, state-controlled labor unions, centralized food aid, wrong price structures, expensive prestige projects, and bureaucratic domination of the informal sector, will never be overcome. That which takes place in the dark will never be seen. As the book of Genesis says, "Let there be light."

11.9 Hopeful signs.

Lesotho seems to be running out of steam for publishing **five-year plans**, and I hope I am right in feeling optimistic about this change. When I left the country, the new emphasis was on a continually upgraded rolling plan. Instead of churning out a big book describing what should happen over the next five years, the government committed itself only to modest and regularly updated projections, sector by sector. Donors are also beginning to bypass cumbersome government planning procedures as they make direct approaches to community-based organizations.

Collectivization is dying of its own weight. The only country that at the moment is bucking the trend is Zimbabwe, whose war veterans are taking over white-owned farms. In some cases these nationalized farms are operated by individuals, but in others it appears that the state wants to manage the work on behalf of ordinary farmers who do not have the skill or training to do it themselves. The ruinous consequences of these actions are what will bring them to a halt, and perhaps other countries tempted in this direction will learn from Zimbabwe's disasters.

Labor unions are vital to the health of an economy, provided they are not under the control of the state. The growing separation between COSATU and the ANC-led government in South Africa is a very healthy development. Competition between labor unions is also a benefit, notably in Lesotho and South Africa. With competition, the unions are forced to help their members and are not able to simply remain content with a guaranteed income from workers' dues and guaranteed support from government.

The increasing frequency of famine and war in Africa has led to decentralized **food distribution**. The reason for the change is not good, but the end result may be beneficial. In particular, the World Food Program has been forced to bypass corrupt and inefficient governments in order to get supplies to victims of disasters, both natural and man-made. Humanitarian efforts by churches and private agencies, such as took place during the floods that struck Mozambique in recent years, are proving effective. Moreover, the Market Society in South Africa organizes and distributes food using community-based committees.

Lesotho has benefited from changing the **price structure** for its staple crop, maize. Now there is less pressure on farmers to produce the crop on unsuitable soils. Additionally, Zimbabwe is being forced to change its agricultural prices the hard way, by the ongoing collapse of the Zimbabwe dollar against world currencies. This collapse is another example of the right thing happening for the wrong reason. Farmers will not produce for the market if the market does not give them a reasonable reward.

Expensive prestige projects are no longer the goal of many African governments. National airlines have been collapsing everywhere. Air Afrique was one of the latest forced into liquidation, though it is hoped that its new foreign management will help revive it. The day of huge stadiums, grandiose new airports, and monumental presidential mansions has passed. I have heard of no such projects being approved over the last year or so.

The **informal economy** still suffers across Africa from official disapproval and neglect. The good news is that it flourishes almost everywhere. What is needed is more recognition of its role in providing jobs and promoting trade. One promising approach is that of the Market Society in South Africa, which is establishing regional rotating markets in peri-urban areas (http://www.wisc.edu/ltc/r498.html). The idea is that the market can bring traders, customers, and service providers together weekly in convenient locations so that big businesses and middle-men are bypassed.

Finally, the record of the **free press** across Africa is mixed. South Africa and Zimbabwe are well served by their independent newspapers, though their governments want to restrict them. In the case of Zimbabwe, several apparently state-sponsored attacks on newspapers have caused great damage. Though BBC reporters are banned from working in Zimbabwe, the BBC continues to broadcast fundamentally truthful reports, thus reclaiming losses suffered by other suppression of the free press. And where there are radios there will be listeners, meaning that the truth will be broadcast to people who might otherwise not know what is happening.

CHAPTER TWELVE. INCREASED MILITARIZATION

Breakdown of moral order, neglect of indigenous technologies, domination by elites, alien educational systems, demographic shifts, religious conflict, new medical systems, outside economic control, Western political forms, and centralized command economies have led many sub-Saharan African countries into serious decline. There is one last step toward total collapse, a step that is an inevitable consequence of the other steps. That last step is for people to cross the brink into civil and international war.

Sub-Saharan Africa today is almost totally a battleground, with only a few southern areas spared from the scourge of mutual destruction. From Mauritania, where light-skinned Moors are oppressing dark-skinned Africans whose only resort is to fight back, to Senegal, where Casamance rebels continue a long struggle for their autonomy, to Guinea Bissau, only recently rid of a predatory and trigger-happy general, to the Guinea-Sierra Leone-Liberia-Côte d'Ivoire complex of chaos and hatred—the far west of Africa is steeped in war and blood.

Muslim-Christian strife continues in Nigeria. Southern Sudan has fought for years to free itself from the Arab north and now in 2004 genocide is taking place in the far-west region of Darfur. The Lord's Resistance Army causes panic and mayhem in northern Uganda. Internal conflict breaks out regularly in both the Central African Republic and Congo Brazzaville. The Democratic Republic of Congo is a basket case, with vultures from all the neighboring states seeking to pick over the corpse, despite the tenuous peace agreement and the internal creation of a government of national unity. Rwanda and Burundi are wracked with internal ethnic hatred, while the leaders of both are looting the former Zaire.

Skulls from war in Uganda

Southern Africa is somewhat better off, although not Zimbabwe, which is spiraling downward toward serious internal conflict. Sadly, hunger threatens the fragile democratic stability in both Zambia and Malawi. Fortunately, the remainder of the SADC region is at the moment reasonably free of overt conflict, although the roots of potential conflict remain in all the member countries.

This chapter looks at the course of conflicts in post-colonial Africa, but only to the extent that I have followed them. The picture across all of Africa, however, is not much different from what I have seen in Liberia, Uganda, Ethiopia, Zimbabwe, South Africa, and Lesotho. War in these countries has followed an almost predictable course, with enlarged armies, alignment with foreign powers, tightened internal security, and military coups. These conflicts are triggered by the breakdown of national and international order and the emergence of new styles of war, which leads to the use and abuse of child soldiers and further descent into drugs, alcohol, and brutality.

12.1 Enlarged post-colonial armies and budgets.

The most dubious gift that Great Britain gave to Lesotho at the time of its independence in 1966 was an army. After all, every "civilized" country is supposed to have an army—though it is not clear why. Certainly it is evident to almost every observer of Lesotho that it has no need for an army; it is entirely surrounded by South Africa, a country that under normal circumstances is highly unlikely to invade.

There were two circumstances in the apartheid days when South Africa invaded Lesotho, both times in order to kill freedom fighters who had escaped there as refugees. In the first case, on 9 December 1982, the Lesotho army was warned in advance that the raid would come. Leabua Jonathan realized that his tiny, ill-trained army was helpless against the South Africans, and so he told his forces to lie low. They sought cover, realizing they could do nothing against such an attack. At midnight, black-faced South African commandos entered Lesotho and proceeded to slaughter forty-two people, most of them ANC activists, but a number of them visitors or ordinary Basotho.

The second intervention by the South Africans came as a direct result of the Lesotho army's own folly. The incident began in September 1998, a week before the South Africans became involved. Instead of keeping to their purpose as a defense against invasion, a faction of Lesotho's soldiers mutinied against government-appointed senior officers. In all likelihood, they were preparing to mount a coup.

The mutinous soldiers had already engaged in a practice fight between two regiments in 1994. By the end of that bright January day, only minimal damage had been done, but for about eight hours, until a heavy rainstorm quieted the fighting, the town rocked with heavy artillery fire. I remember that morning vividly. We were in church when the window-shivering gunfire began. We wondered if we would be able to go home, or if we might become, at least temporarily, internally displaced persons. The two factions in the army, one loyal to the old regime and the other loyal to the recently elected BCP government, went back to their barracks by nightfall, but the quarrel continued to fester.

Fighting started again in 1998 after three months of simmering rage between opposition parties. Soldiers who were increasingly dissatisfied with the results of the May 1998 election had the weapons and the manpower to do whatever they wanted, and the Lesotho government could do nothing to stop them, except to call for help from their big brother next door. On the morning of 22 September 1998 South African helicopters and armored vehicles invaded Lesotho, followed by a contingent from Botswana. This led to three days of chaos, bloodshed, burning, and looting. The looting was, according to informed reports, planned well in advance. While the SADC forces fought a three-day battle to put down resistance from the rebellious soldiers, the capital and two other cities were ransacked by supporters of the opposition political parties and also by looters who simply used this as an occasion to fill their houses with stolen goods. We watched the smoke rise from shops and government offices just a five-minute walk from our house. People from the U.S. Embassy finally persuaded us to leave the country for a few days until things quieted down. If there had been no Lesotho army, none of it would have happened.

An army is often like a genii that cannot easily be put back in its bottle. The British created it, Lesotho's annual budget subventions sustain it, and the public suffers because needed funds are taken from social services in order to pay for it. The Lesotho army's track record is negative, but the army is here to stay. It has the weapons to enforce its own survival and growth, and it provides work for otherwise unemployable youth. There is some talk about using the army for public works or other nation-building exercises, but so far nothing concrete has happened.

Liberia too in the past has had a useless and counter-productive army. The Liberian Frontier Force engaged in a few foreign skirmishes during the early days, but did not win any of them. Yet Tubman and Tolbert, the modernizing presidents of the second half of the twentieth century, continued to feed the army with weapons and money. Ultimately, the monster turned on its maker when Master Sergeant Samuel Doe killed President Tolbert, taking the country for himself and his fellow soldiers and tribesmen.

Disabled Liberian fighters

Death breeds more death in what becomes a vicious circle; it is said that those who live by the sword will die by the sword. These words came close to being literally true when Doe killed Tolbert with a large knife, probably a cutlass or a bayonet. Doe was later killed, presumably with something akin to a sword, as bits and pieces were cut off his body by his erstwhile military associate, Prince Johnson.

Charles Taylor came into power by putting together a second Liberian army, funded and trained by meddlers in warfare such as Libya's Colonel Gadhafi and Burkina Faso's Blaise Compaore. Taylor's National Patriotic Front fought its way to power through seven bloody years of civil war and then pretended to be a civilized government elected by the people of Liberia. Unfortunately, the people who voted for him were too afraid of Taylor in that 1997 election to allow him to lose.

Two of several losers in the war that brought Taylor to power continued to fight even after he was elected president. In 2000, a group of dissidents—Liberians United for Reconciliation and Democracy (LURD)—supported with money, arms, and logistics from Guinea, established itself in northeast Liberia with these stated objectives:

- "...to repatriate all Liberian refugees and resettle all internally displaced persons in Liberia;
- to professionalize the military and security forces;
- to rehabilitate all former combatants; and
- to work tirelessly with the other countries (Guinea and Sierra Leone) of the Mano River Union to ensure lasting peace and stability in the sub-region"(www.copla.org/aboutlurd.htm).

Yet it is clear from following LURD for three years that they were doing no such thing. They caused more people to be displaced, they copied Taylor's tactics by filling their ranks with boy soldiers, they produced more wounded and disabled fighters, and they promoted regional instability. Taylor did the same, and so their underlying objective, getting rid of Taylor, made some sense. It is their methods that did not.

The last party involved in the fighting, The Movement for Democracy and Elections in Liberia (MODEL) was no better. They were supported by Côte d'Ivoire in much the same way as LURD was supported by Guinea. They captured much of southwest Liberia, and LURD captured much of northern Liberia. Between the two, they still control about a quarter of the total area of the country, despite the Accra agreement of September 2003 to create a government of national unity. LURD drew largely from the old Mandingo forces that called themselves ULIMO-K, and MODEL drew largely from the old Krahn group, ULIMO-J. Both were in Accra in July 2003, negotiating for their part of the cake in the new government, and both supported the final agreement. For either to win substantial power would be a disaster. Taylor's rule would be replicated, and militarism would win again. Yet it appears clear that neither has really given up its ambitions for total power.

A recent distressing example of how armies fatten themselves at the expense of the people is South Africa's much-reviled plan to spend more than 43 billion rands on sophisticated military equipment. Foreign arms dealers are supposed to be providing jobs in South Africa through investments, while South Africa buys their military toys to defend itself against presumed enemies. Why South Africa should need most of these arms, I have no idea, and so far no one has identified who these supposed enemies are. Even the ANC's military police objected to the plan, saying it provided unnecessary security and served only to enrich politicians and business people inside and outside South Africa (www.telegraph.co.uk/news/main.jhtml?xml'/news/2001/02/10/wsaf10.xml).

Certain enhancements of South Africa's military are probably necessary. It needs the capability to control the sea route around the Cape and to provide an instant reaction force in case its smaller neighbors need help. The intervention during the Lesotho mutiny was a sensible response to a difficult situation, though it was badly executed. A more clear-cut case of positive intervention was the rescue effort mounted in Mozambique after the devastating rains and floods of early 2000. South Africa is the only regional power and as such needs a limited capacity to help its SADC colleagues when called upon.

Yet the huge increase in military expenditure seems totally out of line to me as well as to many South African commentators. Some have suggested that there may be corruption involved. The supplying countries have in theory agreed to invest substantially in the South African economy with the aim of providing jobs and industries. Yet the potential penalties for not completing the deal are sufficiently low that it would be in the interest of the investing nations to default on the agreement, pay the penalty, and get out.

Armies do not have to be official—organized and led by United Nations-recognized governments. Anyone can construct an army by looking to adventurist backers and by selling whatever commodity may be internationally attractive. Currently, diamonds and, since the diamond embargo, timber are the fashionable currency for buying weapons and fighting wars. Charles Taylor bankrolled his wars, after its initial capitalization by Gadhafi and Campaore, by exploiting the diamond and timber resources of Liberia and Sierra Leone. Jonas Savimbi of UNITA in Angola was able to continue his twenty-year civil war until his death in 2002 through the sale of diamonds. Laurent Kabila in the Democratic Republic of Congo stayed in power as long as he did because his backers were sure they would be well-rewarded by sales of diamonds as well as other minerals if he were eventually to consolidate his position.

Who benefits from the continually escalating costs of maintaining and expanding African armies? Surely not the ordinary people of any of these oil-rich, diamond-rich, mineral-rich, donor-rich countries. When money that should be spent on social services goes to the military, ordinary people are cheated out of decent schools, well-equipped clinics, a competent and well-paid civil service, clean water supplies, and good roads. It is the soldiers and their leaders who are parasites on the rest of society that benefit, although common soldiers get considerably less than their officers, who in turn get less than the big men at the top.

Other beneficiaries are those who make and ship weapons in return for raw materials that go to convenient, discreet markets. Cheap diamonds, which can be resold at vast profit, give considerable incentive for unscrupulous dealers to provide guns and ammunition to African leaders. In mid-2000, Ukrainian-born Leonid Minin was found and captured by Italian police in Rome in an apartment full of diamonds, drugs, and delivery orders for weapons (web.amnesty.org/pages/ttt4-article_2-eng). He was described as a long-term associate of Charles Taylor and was said to have made millions by supplying Taylor and others with surplus eastern European weapons with which to fight their wars.

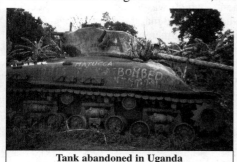
Tank abandoned in Uganda

Exploitation of pre-colonial states in Africa was, of course, not much different. European and American traders got palm oil, pepper, and rubber, but above all slaves, in return for supplying local leaders with trade goods, weapons, and liquor. Now the currency is in oil, diamonds, and precious metals, with which Africans are exploited by each other and by the armaments manufacturers. I am sure there was rejoicing at the July 2003 coup in Sao Tome e Principe, in which an army of about four hundred soldiers took over from a democratically elected, though doubtlessly corrupt, government. What motivated the coup, and what motivates arms dealers to back them? Reports about the country say that , "Oil companies including ExxonMobil and Shell hope to produce up to one million barrels per day in 10 years time if exploration drilling confirms their expectations of massive reserves in deep water. Nigeria will get 40 percent of revenues from all oil extracted, while Sao Tome will get 60 percent" (allafrica.com/stories/200307160283.html). Oil, indeed, may be more of a curse to Africa than a blessing.

12.2 Alignment with foreign power blocs.

Behind those who buy and resell illicit diamonds and who make and sell weapons that bring carnage to Africa are the big powers that claim to have nothing to do with this inhuman trade in blood and death. Officially, their hands are clean, but their economies thrive because Africa suffers. The first and most direct means the big powers used to control Africa was through the division of the continent into spheres of British, German, French, Belgian, Portuguese, and Spanish control. That historical phase ended when African states began to win independence, culminating in 1994 with South Africa's first democratic elections.

The time after independence and before the collapse of the Soviet Union was one of indirect control in a cold-war world divided into huge geopolitical blocs. The communist nations had their clients, with states such as Guinea, Ghana, and (later) Ethiopia depending on Soviet support. There was no single Western bloc in Africa, but the French, British, and Americans ensured their hegemony over most of their former colonies. They supplied them with aid, and in particular made sure that their armies were able to withstand outside pressure.

The Western nations closed their eyes to the iniquitous behavior of leaders such as Mobutu Sese Seku in Zaire, P. W. Botha in South Africa, and Samuel Doe in Liberia, because they were considered bulwarks against communism. The United States spoke about "constructive engagement," which was a euphemism for keeping client states in line, maintaining a steady supply of raw materials, and preventing the spread of communism. They gave what they called humanitarian aid to these nations, but much of the aid went into shoring up tyrannical governments against internal opposition. The military in such countries were the big winners. That they often were not motivated by ideology is suggested by the behavior of Ethiopia and Somalia, which shifted allegiance between West and East according to which gave the best deal.

The Russians did much the same thing. I remember having supper in the hotel in Addis Ababa in late 1982 when a large contingent of Russian generals arrived. They were a remarkable collection of well-fed, well-decorated, hard-drinking patrons, who were clearly at the hotel that night to ensure that their clients behaved themselves. I was supposed to be awed by the sheer number of medals on their jackets, as I am sure were the subservient Ethiopians who had supper with them. The young man who was my research assistant on the project was both amused and saddened by the spectacle.

I also understood the power and influence of the Soviet bloc when I talked politics in the 1980s with my ANC friends in Lesotho. The Soviet Union could do no wrong, in their view. Many of them had studied in Eastern Europe and had been treated most royally—and, significantly, in a non-racist way—by their hosts. Our close friend, Phyllis Naidoo, a long-term communist and member of the ANC, praised East Germany as a socialist paradise. She had been there for medical treatment and knew the East Germans as loyal friends and supporters. I am sure that is true, and I am sure that I would have felt the same loyalty. But behind the generous and even loving treatment she received was the communist quest for power in southern Africa. Not all Africans got the red-carpet treatment, and many complained of racism and discrimination at the hands of their communist hosts.

We entertained Chris Hani in our house in 1983 at considerable personal risk. Not only was he the leader of the military wing of the ANC, but he was also a key member of the South African Communist Party. He was loyal and committed and saw the communists as saviors of the region, while we Americans dithered and talked out of both sides of our mouths. The United States talked publicly about "constructive engagement" under the Reagan administration, while it supported the UNITA army in Angola and refused to support the campaign to boycott South African products. I cannot challenge Chris Hani's choice of loyalty. I am sure I would have done the same in his position, and I found myself being ashamed of being an American who by implication would support his government's policies.

What was remarkable about the ANC was not their military struggle, supported as it was by the Eastern bloc. They won the struggle in a much healthier way. Together, they used people power in South Africa, the remarkable leadership of Nelson Mandela and Desmond Tutu, and the moral support of outsiders like the communist nations and, I am pleased to say, like us. I thank God they won in a peaceful fashion rather than through the barrel of the Soviet gun.

The third phase in the relation between African countries and the great powers is more subtle. Except for oil and terrorism, Africa is no longer of any real geopolitical interest to Western nations. It is true that weapons are still flowing into Africa, probably in greater numbers than before, but the sources of these weapons are disguised. No longer do Western powers need to bribe Nigeria, Liberia, Angola, or Kenya with shipments of weapons.

In particular, rarely seen now is the famous USAID black and white hands logo. The United States is in the political-military business mainly in Israel and Egypt. It does not need to do so elsewhere, because the black market in weapons is working perfectly. Russia, Britain, France, Italy and, at the top of the list, the United States remain the world's biggest suppliers of weapons (www.fas.org/asmp/library/articles/tamar_commondreams_02.html). But it is not at all clear where these weapons are going and who is buying them. There are public deals, as when South Africa negotiates for large shipments of sophisticated weaponry and delivery systems, but the flow of small arms continues and may well be more profitable than the big stuff. Where do these small arms come from? Israel and Ukraine are obvious examples. But how do these nations manage to keep up economies that can supply such exports? Who else supports them, and thus indirectly supports the arms trade, other than the big powers?

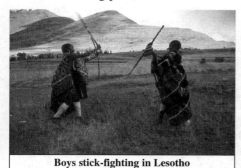

Boys stick-fighting in Lesotho

Whether I am talking about the partition of Africa after the 1885 Berlin conference, or I am talking about the formation of great-power client blocs after independence, or I am talking about the more subtle shipment of arms into Africa in return for minerals, it is all the same phenomenon. Europe and America are making profits, and African peoples are being killed in the ensuing wars that continue and continue and continue.

12.3 Tightened security and suppression of dissent.

Military governments, as well as the supposedly democratic governments that have surrendered much of their real power to the army, quickly lose their popularity with ordinary people. Many who once were citizens are moved into subject status by these governments. Social services are curtailed, and the armed forces begin to arrogate power to themselves. Even the police, who in most countries have traditionally played a neutral and honest role, have begun to take on the features of the army in the quest for armed control of a restless populace.

As discontent grows, governments must choose between reining in the so-called disciplined forces and reining in the people. All too often they have chosen the latter. In Liberia, both the army and the police were used to keep the people in line and to keep Charles Taylor in power. Extra-judicial killings have become increasingly common, and dissenters are told in no uncertain terms to keep out of government matters. The national chief of police in Liberia suppressed independent radio stations and on several occasions, including during an attack on University of Liberia students, sent his men on overt and covert missions to put down the opposition.

The present situation in Zimbabwe is depressing. The veterans of Zimbabwe's independence war, which is known to the freedom fighters as the *chimurenga*, supported the ruling ZANU-PF party in destroying all opposition. They have a legitimate claim on land, in the face of excessive ownership by white farmers, but their claim becomes a hollow sham when it is set against the land-grab by senior ZANU-PF politicians over the past years. When land reform was supposed to be taking place, the war veterans were unleashed to do as they wished to white farmers, to members of the urban-based Movement for Democratic Change, and to their old enemies, the Ndebele of western Zimbabwe (www.telegraph.co.uk/news/main.jhtml?xml=/news/2002/08/18/wzim18.xml). They were told by President Mugabe that they need not respect the judgments of the courts if those courts try to apply the rule of law. The soldiers, ex-soldiers, and camp followers—some of whom were too young to have fought in the 1970 battles—were given carte blanche to do as they wish. The only rule they currently must obey is, "Keep Robert Mugabe in power."

Political disappearances remain all too common in African countries. They were a staple part of Sani Abacha's rule in Nigeria. Many bodies were uncovered in Côte d'Ivoire after the disputed elections of 2001, bodies the government forces tried to hide. The Truth and Reconciliation Commission in South Africa continues to explore unexplained deaths and disappearances from the apartheid era. Idi Amin of Uganda did not commit atrocities secretly, he simply had his men go out and slaughter those whom he did not like. In Nigeria, the governor of Anambra State was kidnapped in July 2003 but fortunately was released a few days later (www.suntimes.co.za/2003/07/20/news/africa/africa06.asp). I think of Nigeria as the "Wild west", because political action is so often blunt, direct and governed by who has superior firepower.

Lesotho has had its share of apparently extra-judicial murders, none of which have yet been solved. Colonel Sekhobe Letsie spent years in jail for his part in killing two senior government officials, Sixishe and Mokhele, during the military government, but it is widely believed there were more people involved in the killings. Two Catholic bishops died within a couple of days of each other, and it is rumored that the reason is that they knew too much about the murders of these two men. Even before that time, Leabua Jonathan had his secret service henchmen imprison opposition figures, a number of whom died in detention or shortly after being released.

12.4 Military coups.

What were these unpopular governments afraid of? The answer throughout much of the last forty years has been simple—military coups. I wrote a small article in the Transformation Resource Center newsletter *Work for Justice* in March 1989 entitled *"Whose coups are news?"* The article listed a number of recent coups and made the point that of all the countries in Africa only Botswana had never had a coup, not even an attempted coup. I also asked in that article who would be next. Naively, I suggested, "No one—we hope!"

Unfortunately, there have been coups and counter-coups aplenty since that time. In 2000, Guinea Bissau had two attempted coups, followed by a further coup in September 2003. The Central African Republic continues to have attempted coups, attempted by the same crowd that has never given up trying to take power. The July 2003 coup in Sao Tome e Principe did succeed. Whatever the case, I fear I was naive in thinking that coups were a thing of the past.

None of the coups in Africa have benefited the countries where they took place. There has been massive corruption, gross incompetence, military adventurism, ethnic hatred, and religious prejudice in all corners of the continent, and these have been made worse by the coups that were supposed to cure the problems.

The two coups that I have personally kept close watch on are test cases, although they are too few to prove anything. The 1986 overthrow of Leabua Jonathan in Lesotho left the country worse off, because it went from an oppressive civilian regime to an oppressive military regime. Some might say that the replacement of General Lekhanya by General Ramaema in Lesotho in 1991 was also a coup. I prefer to think of it as the military coming to its senses and realizing that the experiment in military government was a failure. The return to civilian rule in 1993 was a great blessing and redounds to the credit of Ramaema, who really did not want to rule.

The 1980 coup in Liberia was an unmitigated disaster. Some say that it was inevitable, as Tolbert proved incapable of managing both the desire for greater democracy and the desire for promoting agricultural production. Inevitable or not, it brought unrelieved pain and suffering to ordinary people. First Samuel Doe metaphorically bled the country dry and then Charles Taylor added real bloodshed to the metaphorical.

Displaced Liberians

Coups are a shortcut to the democratic way of resolving conflicts and building up a country. I have mentioned the Churchill hypothesis that though democracy may be bad, other forms of government are worse. Surely at the bottom of the heap is government by the military, which has brought misery almost everywhere in Africa it has been imposed. Some have started well, such as Lekhanya's coup in Lesotho, but in the end these governments have shown their true nature by becoming more repressive and corrupt than their predecessors. A solid 84 percent majority of respondents in the 2003 survey of attitudes to democracy in Lesotho objected strongly to any military coup.

How military governments can be prevented from coming to power in the future is a difficult question. The Organization of African Unity and the regional power blocs have said they would refuse to recognize coups in the future. But it must not be forgotten that many of Africa's heads of state themselves came to power through coups and thus are likely to sympathize, or at least find a way to disguise their approval of a coup, as for example in the September 2003 coup in Guinea Bissau (www.africaonline.com/site/Articles/1,3,54068.jsp).

12.5 Internal and external conflicts.

Coups have obviously not been the only form of warfare in post-colonial

Africa. Internal strife is all too common. When we lived in Liberia, such strife was suppressed, to a large extent because of the superficially benevolent paternalism of President Tubman. We were encouraged to believe at the time that ethnic differences were disappearing, even the difference between Americo-Liberians, descendents of the recaptured slaves called Congoes, and the indigenous people. The village nearest Cuttington College had Liberians from many ethnic groups as well as Sierra Leoneans and Nigerians. At one point I counted more than ten different languages being spoken in that one village.

We also hoped that religious conflicts would disappear. President Tubman did his best to reconcile or at least paper-over such conflicts. On one occasion when a fundamentalist Christian group tried to burn secret society paraphernalia, Tubman intervened to stop them, saying that since Liberia is a Christian country, traditional religion and Islam should be allowed to practice without hindrance.

We did not know what might lie under the seemingly peaceful surface. I wanted to believe at the time that Liberia was on its way toward being a truly multicultural nation where people could find jobs, spouses, and residences without harassment due to religion or tribe. I believed that our friends Moulai and Ruth Reeves were forerunners of this multiculturalism, since the grandparents of their children spoke four quite different languages. At Cuttington we encouraged people to work, play, and live together, and we were pleased to see cross-tribal, cross-religious, and cross-racial romances taking place there.

Samuel Doe ruined all that. Yet perhaps it should be stated differently: he let loose the divisive forces that possibly still existed under seemingly superficial harmony. The conflict between the coastal aristocracy and the rural peoples was always under the surface, but Doe encouraged it to rise again. Ethnic conflicts between Krahn and Mano-Gio may have been simmering before, but Doe raised them to a serious level. Mandingo have always been perceived as different from everyone else, but now being Mandingo puts a person at risk of abuse, robbery and even physical violence. The long years of civil war made a bad situation worse, and now there are regular outbreaks of fighting involving peoples of different languages and religions.

When I was in Ethiopia, most of its people were united against the brutal regime of Mengistu Haile Mariam, and as a result ethnic and religious differences were less important. Since Mengistu was overthrown, many suppressed conflicts have come to the surface, most notably the fight for independence by the Oromo people in the southeast and the brother-against-brother quarrel between the Amhara and Tigre peoples. Once Eritrea achieved its independence it was inevitable that Ethiopia would pick a fight, hoping to gain back its lost provinces and with them access to the sea. In theory, the border dispute has been settled, but the Ethiopian government still harbors resentment over the World Court decision to grant the tiny town of Badame to Eritrea.

Uganda and Tanzania are not exempt from these inter-ethnic quarrels. During my fieldwork, I intuited that the Maasai would eventually have to fight for their rights to grazing land, when I saw how limited were their prospects in southwestern Tanzania. In 2001, full-scale ethnic conflict broke out between pastoralists and farmers in Tanzania's central plains. Sadly, I was not surprised. In Uganda, the north-south divide was made harsher during the bloody rule of Idi Amin. Now that the Rwandan faction has achieved power under Museveni, there are continual challenges from Nilo-Hamitic peoples in the north and west. The Lord's

Resistance Army is an example of a group that continues a bloody and barbaric fight, and the Ugandan army is unable to stop it.

The long-standing enmity between the Ndebele and Shona peoples in Zimbabwe threatens to erupt again. The crushing of the Ndebele opposition by Mugabe's North Korean-trained Fifth Brigade has never been forgotten or forgiven. Now the evidence is coming out, and with the economic and political situation of that country in terminal decline, it is possible that Matabele-land will fight for autonomy.

Botswana, as always, remains an exception in southern Africa. I sensed only a small mutual resentment between the mainstream Batswana and the northeast Kalanga people. The Bushmen always lose out in Botswana, but that is not a conflict likely to tear the country apart.

Namibia is a different story. The dominant Ovambo and related peoples in the north will rule as long as Sam Nujoma remains in power. But there are restless people in the south and in the Caprivi Strip to the east, who staged a mini-rebellion early in 2000. Caprivi has always been an historical accident, unjustified geographically and ethnically. Union with Zambia would make more sense than remaining in Namibia, but it must not be forgotten that economically it would be disastrous to join forces with a Zambian economy that is running on empty.

Internal conflicts are a serious matter, but more serious still are the external conflicts raging in two key areas of the continent: the Great Lakes region of east and central Africa, and the Guinea forest of west Africa. It is clear to any outside observer that the DRC has never been a united country, even under the Belgians and certainly never under Mobutu. The unity government of 2003, with its four vice-presidents representing four political and military movements, is a candidate for further fighting.

The conflict I can speak more intelligently about is the ever-shifting and broadening war in West Africa. Charles Taylor had a much larger goal than simply replacing Samuel Doe as chief bandit. Right from the start of his war in1989, he was grooming Foday Sankoh to be his lieutenant in Sierra Leone. Sankoh almost prevailed, but fortunately international forces led by the British won at least temporary peace, leading to Sankoh's arrest and eventual death in a Freetown jail. Taylor turned his attention to Guinea, supporting rebels against the repressive government of General Conté, but with help from the Guinea government, LURD stopped Taylor's expansionist plans. His allies in Côte d'Ivoire came close to toppling that government, first in 2001 with the help of General Guei and then with a shadowy rebel group in early 2003, but with French help the government of President Gbagbo survived. However, Côte d'Ivoire remains divided, with rebels having pulled out of the agreement to form a government of national unity.

Taylor tried to use his glib tongue, his apparently unlimited supply of weapons, and his ruthless will to gain hegemony over the entire far west section of West Africa. He is still a threat, despite the indictment by the international court in Sierra Leone and his enforced exile in Nigeria. It has been reported that he maintains regular contact by telephone with his lieutenants in Monrovia (www.globalpolicy.org/intljustice/wanted/2003/0917control.htm). He remains a gifted and forceful leader of men and will stop at nothing to get power. He uses the Hitler approach, that the bigger the lie the more likely it is to be accepted by gullible people. He is a menace and must be extradited to Sierra Leone to stand trial as soon as possible, even though the crude American device of offering a two million dollar reward is hardly the way to get the desired result. The problem is that other leaders in the region are weak and indecisive. The presidents of Sierra Leone, Guinea, and

Côte d'Ivoire did not know what to do with the geopolitical adventurer in their midst. It is not at all surprising that Taylor had such a close personal relationship with Colonel Gadhafi in Libya. They are two of a kind. I watch with interest and hope as Nigeria resists the effort to bring him to trial. I fear he will escape from this charge also, just as he escaped from a Boston jail twenty years earlier.

One other motivation for war brought to my attention by anthropologist Thayer Scudder is conflict over the fruits of development projects. He points out in a book now in draft form that the conflict between blacks and Arabs in Mauritania stems from the relative success of dams built on the Senegal River in making irrigated agriculture possible. Similarly, as the worldwide hunger for hardwoods grows, Taylor's war in Liberia has been partly about who controls the timber in the last intact rain forest in West Africa.

12.6 New/old styles of war.

Classic warfare, with set battles, regular armies, and Geneva conventions, is a thing of the past in Africa. What has replaced it is a combination of the future and the distant past. The techniques of war observed in pre-colonial days are returning, though more so in the forest zones than in the open savannas. When the last Kpelle wars ended in 1919, the world assumed that lightning raids in the bush, complete with the destruction of villages and the murder of civilians, were over. Not so. Wars are increasingly fought by irregular soldiers, who are hyped up on drugs and alcohol and "protected" by traditional medicines guaranteeing their invincibility, rather than by members of regular, officially trained armies.

The old style in Lesotho

In addition to the privatization of national resources I have already addressed, security forces and the military are also being privatized, as was pointed out to me by a friend. "Proper" armies, trained by the British, French, or Americans, have been singularly unsuccessful in Africa, with the possible exception of Nyerere's invasion of Uganda in 1979 that led to the overthrow of Idi Amin. Big men have surrounded themselves with bodyguards, armed gangs, security forces, and small armies, sometimes taken from disaffected members of the national army, but more often recruited from unemployed and disaffected youth.

Charles Taylor's campaign for the conquest of Liberia depended on such a militia and involved every type of warfare I know about, including the frontal assault on Monrovia in June 1990. It is striking that this assault was one of Taylor's only failures, and because of it he learned that Liberia would not be won in the classic way. Rather, he eventually prevailed by sending groups of marginally trained soldiers to take over villages and towns, using brutal tactics that violate all the laws of so-called "civilized" war.

Who were these soldiers? The initial invasion of Liberia on Christmas Eve 1989 was by a well-trained, small militia of Liberians and Burkinabe. They

Displaced child

entered Liberia with conventional weapons and established a "liberated" base area along the Côte d'Ivoire border. Taylor's soldiers were joined by enthusiastic civilians, many who were disaffected, unemployed drifters. They quickly built up Taylor's ranks as he moved down the main roads toward Monrovia. He hoped for a quick victory, but was blocked by American and other foreign powers just before final conquest. Taylor's hopes were dashed, the Liberian Frontier Force consolidated its position, and an uneasy stalemate resulted that lasted six years, with Monrovia and environs on one side of a truce line and the rest of the country on the other.

After Taylor's defeat in Monrovia, he lost much of the national support he gained during the first few months of attacks against Samuel Doe. Soon, other militias sprang up, hoping to get either their share of the spoils or the grand prize of Liberia itself. The fighting degenerated quickly into drugs, alcohol, and mindless brutality. One of Taylor's strategies was to find young boys in the bush, kidnap them, and turn them into killing machines. I was told that his most inhuman approach was to take a boy, ten, twelve, or fourteen years old, teach him to shoot, and then show him a second boy in the camp. The first boy was instructed to kill the second, and if he refused to do it, then the first boy would be the target for still a third boy. In this way Taylor's child soldiers had their humanity beaten out of them; to replace it they were given drugs and liquor. The same pattern has been repeated in many wars across Africa (www.iss.co.za/ Pubs/Monographs/No82/Ch2.pdf). I describe the process in my novel *Long Day's Anger* (Gay 2004).

Rape, brutality, mutilation, and armed robbery were common practices and remain an unfortunate legacy of war, not only in West Africa but in other African countries as well. Where poverty has led to violence for survival, that violence is not perpetrated only during military combat. Though peace treaties were signed in Liberia and in Sierra Leone, the militias continue to harass and brutalize ordinary people. Similarly, the Liberian insurgents in LURD and MODEL are also boy soldiers, drunk and drugged out of their right minds.

A boy soldier's pay was a gun with ammunition, which he was to use to subdue and lay waste village after village. A friend of mine was in such a village when boy soldiers arrived to loot it. When nothing was left, the militia went on to the next village. My friend told me that his wife witnessed her father's decapitation, because a soldier from an opposing militia had been seen entering that house.

There was little difference between the various ragtag armies that despoiled Liberia during those terrible years from 1989 to 1997. Almost a quarter of a million people were killed, and more than a million fled from their homes. The wealthy escaped to foreign countries, and many of the poor fled to neighboring Sierra Leone, Guinea, and Côte d'Ivoire. The rest withdrew to the temporarily secure enclave of Monrovia.

Taylor won a Pyrrhic and very temporary victory in Liberia, lasting from 1997 to 2003. He ruled over a devastated country, but that did not seem to bother him, since he came out of the war an extremely wealthy man. He exported diamonds, rubber, and timber to pay for his military supplies, to secure his own nest egg, and to finance the next campaigns. He was the patron of a network of armed clients who depended on him for their support. Without Taylor, the ordinary people would have turned on the militias that Taylor protected. Such patron-client networks are a major component of Africa's post-colonial history, and war is no exception.

Taylor's surrogate, Foday Sankoh, learned all Taylor's techniques and added some of his own. He too built up a network of clients, and his subordinates still remain loyal to him, even after his death in prison in Freetown. Sankoh's war in Sierra Leone made Taylor's war look gentle. The amputation of hands and feet became his trademark. What fueled his war was diamonds, exported first to Liberia, enriching Taylor still further as middleman, and from there to the rest of the world.

Diamonds from Sierra Leone and Liberia appeared everywhere on the world diamond market, including, we believe, in Lesotho. My wife Judy was approached toward the end of our stay in Lesotho by a man from Guinea, who asked her if she would like to buy a diamond. Of course, it is possible that the diamond came from Lesotho's mountains, where there are well-known and thoroughly mapped kimberlite pipes. But the combination of the man being from Guinea and his offering to sell an illicit diamond is quite striking.

Child soldiers have been used in many of the African civil wars. They are not recruited into the so-called "disciplined forces" that are the regular armies and police forces, but they are the mainstay of irregular militias. *New York Times* reporter Somini Sengupta, on 23 June 2003, made a poignant comment regarding the war in eastern Congo: "The warlords have killed even childhood here." Use of child soldiers is against the U.N. Convention on the Rights of the Child, but that convention is scarcely honored in many African countries.

Sorious Samura's video, *Cry Freetown*, has a particularly moving sequence in which the producer, himself a Sierra Leonean, interviewed a boy, at that time about 15 years old, who was responsible for committing atrocities during the war. He was numb, withdrawn, deeply troubled, and at one point said that he wished he were dead. Numerous accounts of child soldiers can be found at www.wuomi.ca/SierraLeoneLinks.htm.

I have personally met boys in Monrovia who are disabled and beg in order to survive. They were recruited during the civil war and doubtlessly committed horrendous crimes during their brief moments of glory. They are described by Stephen Ellis in his fine book, *The Mask of Anarchy* (Ellis 1999). I only saw a few of these ex-combatants and can imagine what the rest of them must be like. Integrating such people back into society will be immensely difficult.

The war tactics used in Liberia and Sierra Leone are not much different from those being used today in the Democratic Republic of Congo, Burundi, Rwanda, Uganda, and southern Sudan. Many were dismayed and sickened by the guerrilla-style brutality of the genocide in Rwanda and Burundi. Zimbabwe also experienced inter-ethnic hatred as the Shona fought both the whites and the Ndebele. In Mozambique, boy soldiers from the South African-supported RENAMO militia in the north were trained to kill even their parents, though the Maputo region in the south was largely spared. The liberation of Namibia fortunately did not depend heavily on cruel and brutal guerrilla tactics, such as those still practiced in Angola. The war for liberation in South Africa was a major exception. It was really hardly a war, with only a few bombings and acts of sabotage in isolated incidents. The ANC freedom fighters were far less brutal than their white opponents, who killed and tortured on a regular basis, as the Truth and Reconciliation hearings have shown.

I do not believe in war, although I have to admit I make an exception for the fight against real tyranny, such as that which took place under Hitler, in African countries where colonialism was particularly vicious, and in South Africa under apartheid. In those cases, genuine patriots organized their forces to put down evil. There are few wars in Africa today that fall into that category, except possibly for the successful efforts of the southern Sudanese to free themselves from Arab overlords.

Otherwise, Africa's wars prove how right my basic instinct is. The continent has damaged itself severely and continues to destroy its own future through greedy, senseless wars. I pray that South Africa can be a model for the rest of the continent for how to obtain a non-racial, democratic government through peaceful means.

Armies have also played a significant role in the spread of HIV/AIDS. A *New York Times* report in November 2002 said, "For better or worse, no institution is more central to the stability of many African nations than the military, and few institutions in Africa are more threatened by AIDS." The armies carry the infection with them and often use rape as a military tactic; the most recent reports of rape come out of eastern Congo. The report by Physicians for Human Rights on the post-war situation in Sierra Leone gives horrifying statistics on the role of rape in that civil war. Even without rape, soldiers are notorious for sleeping with any woman they can find.

What is truly horrifying is that the chaos arising from war "suits many parties just fine," to quote Adam Hochschild in the 20 April 2003 issue of the *New York Times*. His comment confirms the thesis that Chabal and Daloz so presciently pointed out in their book, *Africa Works* (Chabal and Daloz 1999). Confusion and disorder make it easier for warlords and "big men" to control their clients and to make sure that they are the sources of any social services. If a warlord is clever and lucky, as Charles Taylor was, he can become a very rich man through managing local marketable resources. Gold, diamonds, oil, and coltan have been the basis of many fortunes. The poor people on whose land these resources are found and who do the labor to extract them do not benefit and remain as poor as ever.

12.7 Hopeful signs.

There are fewer hopeful signs regarding increased militarization than in the other topics I have explored. In some African countries, however, there are voices being raised against **expanded military budgets**. The South African opposition, both on the left and on the right, has objected to the huge military spending spree dictated by the ANC-led government. Voices also have been raised in Lesotho about seriously reducing the size of the army, especially after its adventures in the 1990s. And as countries that are of similar size, comparisons are being drawn between Lesotho and Costa Rica, where the army was eliminated.

Foreign power alignment has decreased markedly since the death of the Soviet Union, not so much because of enlightened African policies, but rather because the major powers have lost interest. Also helpful is the pressure being brought to bear on European suppliers of weapons to African warlords. The United Nations sanctions against Liberia were welcome as the world tried to find a way to deal with Charles Taylor and his threat to West African security.

Suppression of dissent is still strong in many African countries. Rulers who have passed their sell-by date, including Gnassingbe Eyadema in Togo, Robert Mugabe in Zimbabwe, and Yoweri Museveni in Uganda, sense that their backs are against the wall and thus are doing their best to silence the growing opposition in their countries. It is encouraging, however, that opposition parties have been allowed to speak out, to campaign, and even to win elections in countries such as Senegal, Ghana, Zambia, and Malawi.

There have been fewer successful **military coups** in recent years. The most recent to achieve temporary power was that in Guinea Bissau in September 2003, but in that case the army quickly turned over power to a civilian government. The possibility of coups is still present and is not far beneath the surface of politics in a number of countries. The fighting on the border between Guinea and Liberia could give rise to a coup in either country.

There have been a few cases of successful mediation of **internal and external conflicts**. Mozambique is a good example, where RENAMO and the ruling FRELIMO party have achieved an uneasy peace. RENAMO threatens regularly to pull out of the government, but so far it has not made a firm and final decision to do so. Unfortunately, in most cases, war goes on until either one side is victorious or both sides are too exhausted to continue the bloodshed. Mediation in the Democratic Republic of the Congo has produced periodic withdrawals of rebel groups from the government of national unity. One can only hope that unity will survive and opposition forces will choose the political process rather than war as a way to gain their end. The war in southern Sudan also stops and starts; its peace talks take place regularly and just as regularly are aborted, even though in November 2003 it appears that a real peace treaty may be around the corner. Ethiopia and Eritrea have given up their pointless border war, more out of exhaustion than out of principle. It is only in insignificant quarrels such as that between Namibia and Botswana over a small island in the Zambezi flood plain that international mediation been effective.

International conventions against **irregular styles of war** are flouted almost everywhere. International humanitarian workers have been fired on in many places, most recently in Bunia in eastern Democratic Republic of Congo. The work of the World Food Program has been stopped frequently in countries such as Liberia and Burundi when it becomes too dangerous for aid workers. I must admit defeat in trying to identify cases where humanitarian styles of war, if they are really possible, have been agreed upon and enforced by warring parties. Tribunals in Belgium and in Arusha, Tanzania have begun to bring perpetrators of genocide to justice, but the killing often still continues.

CHAPTER THIRTEEN. WHERE NEXT, AFRICA?

I asked one of the readers of my first draft his suggestion for this final chapter. In effect he said, "Don't write it. Leave it to Africans to write it in their own way, in actions more than in deeds." He may well be right, but I have chosen to disregard his advice—but only in part. I cannot and will not write a detailed blueprint for the way I think the future of Africa should go. Instead, I suggest, as succinctly as possible, broad areas for Africans to decide for themselves "where next" and "how."

In the sections listing signs of hope in the various chapters, I have already given hints of the directions that Africa and Africans can go. My suggestions here underscore the most important and productive of these signs of hope and perhaps show a way for Africans to remake Africa.

13.1 Internal democratization.

Liberia calls its soldiers home "without gun"

Democracy means different things to different people. Our study of democracy in southern Africa elicited more answers relating to economic well-being than to political freedom, for example. Foreign governments sometimes impose a parliament or a politburo on African countries to satisfy their own visions of what democracy should be. African rulers often say they know what their people want and believe, but nonetheless impose a firm totalitarian grip on their subjects. Pronouncements by politicians to the effect that all Nigerians or all Somali or all Zimbabweans want what the politicians are selling are, by any standards of democracy, lies covering up anti-democratic power plays.

If democracy means rule by the people, then what people are saying should be listened to, from the top to the bottom of society, whether or not their views fit with some preconceived idea. But it is vital to listen to everyone. The people's voice has to be heard, and there have to be independent mechanisms for listening honestly and effectively, whether through surveys, local assemblies, or elected representatives.

If the government in an African country does not meet these two criteria, namely listening to the people and making sure that the listening process reaches outside the power elite, then the country allows only a false imitation of democracy.

13.2 Education and health are rights, not privileges.

Donors, international financial institutions, and government officials need to understand that education and health are human rights. If they cannot hear the message, then more protests against the arrogance of international organizations should take place. Africans can lead the way, as did the presidents of Mali and Burkina Faso before the Cancun meeting of the World Trade Organization in September 2003 when they protested against unfair Western subsidies to farmers in their own countries (www.mindfully.org/WTO/2003/Farm-Subsidies-Strangling11jul03.htm).

Money is available to help the poorest of the poor, but budgets and financial recovery conditions are skewed away from their needs. It appears that wealthy international agencies and government officials are only willing to provide social services for the poor once other "needs," such as debt repayment and prestige projects, are funded.

Who can speak for the poor? Ideally they speak for themselves, but in reality their voices are not heard. Advocates for the poor must have the courage and personal integrity to point out just how badly the poor are hurting. Useful as current research may be, more is needed. Results must be publicized, for only then can the plight of those without schooling and without health services be heard. Forums where people can speak for themselves are useful. Community-based organizations can speak for their members. If honest advocates do not come forward, then demagogues will arouse and lead the poor in their places. When that happens, only the demagogues benefit; the poor remain poor.

13.3 Serious anti-HIV/AIDS campaign.

The biggest single health issue in Africa, in fact the biggest single issue overall, is the HIV/AIDS crisis. AIDS leads to death, HIV leads to AIDS, undisciplined sexuality leads to HIV, and blinkered life-skills training for children leads to undisciplined sexuality.

Each step in the sequence needs to be addressed. Those with full-blown AIDS need guidance regarding how to live the remainder of their lives in as full and healthy a way possible. Those who are HIV-positive need help, through drugs and lifestyle changes, to postpone the onset of AIDS and to prevent transmission of the disease to others. Those whose sex lives are already set in patterns of promiscuity need to learn at least how to depend on condoms. Those who are still being formed need serious, frank, and open guidance on how to live responsible lives.

It is everyone's task to educate and help others, from fellow villagers who must not stigmatize those with HIV/AIDS, to church people who must not take a holier-than-thou attitude toward victims and toward those who transmit the disease, to parents who need help in talking to their children, to governments that must face the issue head-on and develop realistic programs for prevention and maintenance, to families who must care for the sick, to business people who must manage an economy bereft of some of its most productive citizens, to foreign donors who know that the future of Africa is at stake, to pharmaceutical companies who must no longer just take profits from selling drugs, to researchers who need full funding for developing vaccines and treatments, and to all those who are trying to communicate public health messages. There is no one who should be exempt from the task of controlling the pandemic. Models for effective HIV/AIDS control can be found in Uganda and Senegal. May other governments follow them.

The alternative is too horrible to contemplate. Is it possible that in a few years African countries will not be able to handle the sheer volume of dead bodies that will lie in the streets unburied? Is it possible that the number of orphans will so far exceed the ability of relatives, churches, or government to support them that there will be hundreds of thousands of child-headed "families" living in squalor and disarray? Is it possible that social devastation will remove all the controls that maintain the moral order? Africans and friends of Africa can surely find ways to avert or at least minimize that awful prospect.

13.4 Promote personal initiative in agriculture and business.

People need to be able to order their own lives. Personal initiative is essential and must not be stifled either by the Coca-Cola-ization of the world or by top-down development structures. Ultimately, economic well-being only comes when people build up and amplify their own resources. Farm produce only comes from farmers. Businesses are only built by business people. I am speaking now to Africans who can make their world better by doing their own part to increase production. It is true that they need substantial assistance from European and American governments to open markets to African produce and to reduce subsidies to their own farmers and businesses. But without African initiative, better First-World policies will not serve the purpose.

World economic history is made by individuals who have ideas, initiative, resources, and courage. African governments need formal businesses, but they also need the informal sector, for it is the nursery for new ideas. Individual entrepreneurs need protection in order to get started; thus I am arguing against instant globalization, though ultimately entrepreneurs will also need help if they are to compete on the international market. If the long-term goal is to promote economic health, then we must work to help ordinary people make a decent living in their own ways. National and international domination is not enough.

13.5 Promote regional integration.

Africans must realize that their future depends on working together at an international level. Sadly, national pride and xenophobia have been fostered by African rulers who know that they more easily retain power if their subjects are united against some supposed common enemy, which is often an African neighbor. The reality is that these enemies are almost always artificial creations.

Regional integration does not just mean minimizing the barriers between nations. It means finding ways for different ethnic and religious groups to work and live together. It means understanding that they must stand together in the struggle for economic well-being and political freedom. If the nations of Africa do not stand together, they will fall separately, and the only winners will be foreign exploiters.

13.6 Starve wars and isolate warlords.

First, I urge foreign powers to find ways to stop the supply of weapons and related war equipment to people such as Kagame in Rwanda or El-Bashir in Sudan. It is not enough for Western nations to wring their hands and deplore the trade in blood diamonds or the wicked export of petroleum used to fund repression. If foreign powers want to restrict the arms trade, they can do it. Otherwise, they only continue to make hypocritical pronouncements about African warlords, while ensuring that the material conditions for their wars remain untouched.

Ordinary Africans, for their part, should work as hard as they can to reduce military expenditures. Regional leaders, such as South Africa, may need armies, but most African countries need only internal policing. Citizens must make their voices heard by requesting lower budget expenditures on armies, unless they are willing always to remain subjects. This means lobbying political leaders, writing letters to newspapers, casting votes only for those who see the necessity of limiting the military, and ensuring that present members of the army are not replaced when the time comes for them to retire.

13.7 Repatriate illicit foreign savings.

The immediate picture that comes to mind when thinking of illicit foreign savings is of leaders such as Abacha or Mobutu, who in former days stashed huge fortunes in foreign banks and tax havens. These banks surely know where their profits are coming from. But it is not only the Abachas and the Mobutus, fortunately now absent from the political scene, who have defrauded African people. It is also the banks, donor agencies, and international financial institutions that persuaded African rulers to take ill-advised loans. Countries that are returning more money to their creditors than they receive through exports, loans, or grants must reverse the flow. The year of Jubilee is at hand, and odious debts must be canceled.

In addition to the iniquities of government policies that have impoverished Africa, it is often simple incompetence that has wasted resources needed for the betterment of the local economy. Those who have fallen victim to their own weakness deserve a second chance. After all, a second chance was an important part of the Biblical message of the year of Jubilee. People, families, or even nations must not have to suffer forever, even if the fault is their own. Forgiveness is what makes life livable and is what brings the world community to a proper sense of humility and unity.

13.8 Restructure foreign assistance.

Let me recapitulate and in so doing point out the international implications of my suggestions. The world community must encourage democratic practices. Health and education can only be provided for all if the schools and clinics are seen as the responsibility of all human beings for all human beings. Clearly, the HIV/AIDS pandemic is not just a local matter. Local initiative in agriculture and business is required if dependence is ever to end. Regional integration is necessary so that African peoples no longer are trapped into thinking that for every winner there must be a loser. The whole family of nations, African as well as non-African, must agree that the wars being fought in Africa today are an international responsibility. The return of looted goods and money can only happen if the international community deals with the issue in a responsible and honest way. Thus, it is also necessary that foreign assistance should continue, albeit on a sensible basis.

Let me not repeat the details of the negative character of much foreign aid. There have been good programs, including water supplies, roads, schools, and clinics. There have also been real disasters, including almost all the agricultural development projects in Lesotho. Africans and donors can learn something from this history, from the good as well as the bad, as they design aid projects. A cliché that happens to be true is that the person who does not learn from history is condemned to repeat it. Only so can countries avoid becoming aid-addicted.

First, it must be asked, does the assistance program meet ordinary Africans halfway? Have Africans done what they can do in a given sector or community to solve a problem or meet a need? Are they genuinely ready for help and ready to take the next steps? If yes, then a small, inexpensive, and specifically tailored project can meet a precise need.

Second, are the problems and needs clearly identified by the nation, region, village, or household as their own? If so, they will already be looking for ways to solve the problems and satisfy needs. If not, there is no point in trying to create problems and needs for people.

Third, can the problems be solved and the needs met through a reasonable use of local resources? If a continual injection of outside resources is required, then the problems and needs should be written off as hopeless, with the exception of a major disaster. But even then, care must be exercised lest assistance go into a bottomless pit.

13.9 Moral and spiritual renewal.

Individuals do not only make money. They make lives. When Africa finally becomes what it has the potential to be, African lives can be rich and full. This is not merely an economic question; it is also a moral and spiritual matter. In the previous section I argued for individual initiative as one way among others to achieve economic and social betterment. But initiative and drive are not enough.

It does not solve Africa's disease for some of its people to be clever or to create technologies and enterprises that generate and distribute wealth. Simply being clever is not the same as being wise and certainly is not the same as being loving. I remember a profound comment made by the great Jewish philosopher and theologian Martin Buber. He was giving a lecture at Cornell University when my very bright undergraduate friend Harold Bloom began to argue with the positions Buber had taken. Buber responded, "You are very clever, young man, but you are not sincere." Honesty and sincerity, rather than taking advantage of others for personal gain, are necessary for renewal.

13.10 A personal postscript.

I speak now from a frankly Christian perspective, and I hope I am sincere. Two friends who read this section in draft claim that what I am now about to say is discontinuous with and undercuts what I have written up to this point. They say I now reveal openly what had hitherto been a partly hidden Christian missionary agenda. They assert that Christianity, just like every other Western ideology, has harmed Africa and that what I am now saying proves their point. I respectfully disagree, and I believe I would be a hypocrite for not revealing my position openly instead of relying on transparent hints throughout the body of the book.

Let me be honest as I close. I believe that the gospel of Jesus Christ can bring renewal to Africa. I understand that all too often those of us who preach the gospel have denied its basics in our lives and words. Often in our preaching we have been clever and yet have failed to be sincere. Failure is part of what it is to be human, and failure is certainly a disease that affects Christians who are called to bring fullness of life to the world.

We who are Christians can begin by confessing our own sinfulness, which is a theological way of saying that we did things—some of them right and some of them wrong—for selfish reasons. We rarely gave full respect to the evidence of God's presence in Africa, and we often ran roughshod over beliefs and life styles which were well rooted in Africa before we came. Some of us, even up to the present, have used our Christian faith as a way to promote Western economic and political objectives. In particular, we have confused the life-affirming religion of the Hebrew Bible and the Christian New Testament with the gospel of wealth and progress. We have forgotten that much that is good in Africa has been due not only to Africans themselves but also to secular and even militantly anti-Christian outsiders. Hopefully after confessing our shortcomings, we can ask God to help us show wisdom and love through our lives.

In the end, it is God, and not us, who works to redeem mankind, and I am sure that God can and will redeem Africa. African Christians—and I would like to be included in that group if my African friends will allow it—can open their hearts to their Lord, acknowledging that they too are part of all that has gone wrong in Africa. I have listed so many problems in this book that I may be accused of just propagating doom and gloom. But listing these problems is in large measure, as I said above, a confession of my own sins of commission and omission, as well as the sins of others. I ask other African Christians to join me in that confession, for in that way we can go forward toward solutions to the serious problems I have outlined in this book.

Christianity is growing more rapidly in Africa than anywhere else in the world (Jenkins 2002). What a blessing it would be if the Christianity which is growing so rapidly would be faithful to its founder. If so, Africa, broken and distorted as it may be now, can help heal all humanity. But first Africa must heal itself, with all the help that wise and sincere—and, I hope, clever—friends can provide. I have noted at the end of each chapter hopeful signs, and I believe that many of these hopeful signs are what Christians should embrace as they seek a better and more godly future for Africa.

I conclude this book, therefore, by asking my readers, both Christian and non-Christian, to support and adopt a strong and liberating Christianity that will help this wonderful continent re-shape itself and shape its future. God the Creator has made and rules the world. Jesus Christ the Redeemer is alive and brings new life. The Holy Spirit is always ready to breathe power into those who open their hearts and minds. The Triune God is alive and well in Africa. I pray that God's people will also choose to be alive and well for the sake of Africa and of themselves.

I speak directly to myself, to ordinary Africans, and to friends of Africa everywhere. Let us open our hearts and minds and let God in, so that God can use us, ordinary and simple as we are, to change ourselves, our community, our nation, our continent, and, in the end, our world. God bless us all in the effort.

REFERENCES CITED

Acheson, Dean, 1969. *Present at the Creation: My Years at the State Department.* New York: WW Norton, Inc.

African Futures Project, 2002. *Profiling Africa at the Dawn of the 21st Century.* New York: United Nations

Alexander, Elsie, John Gay, Nomtuse Mbere and Moshe Setimela 1983. *Informal Sector Businesses in Four Botswana Communities.* Gaborone: Ministry of Local Government and Lands.

Allen, Arthur, 2002. "Sex Change; Uganda v. condoms", *New Republic*

Ambrose, D., Pomela, E. M and Talukdar, S., 2000. *Biological Diversity in Lesotho: A Country Study.* Maseru: National Environment Secretariat

Anderson, Jon Lee, 1998. "The Devil they Know, *The New Yorker*. July 27 1998. www.republicofliberia.com/thedevil.htm

Anderson, R. Earle, 1952, *Liberia: America's African Friend.* Chapel Hill: University of North Carolina Press

Arbousset, Thomas, ed by David Ambrose and Albert Brutsch, 1991. *Missionary Excursion.* Morija: Archives

Bales, Kevin, 2002. "The Social Psychology of Modern Slavery", *Scientific American.* April 2002

Barnett, Tony, and Alan Whiteside, 2002. AIDS in the *Twenty-First Century: Disease and Globalization.* Palgrave MacMillan: New York.

Bellman, Beryl Larry, 1975. *Village of Curers and Assassins.* The Hague: Mouton.

Beti, Mongo, 1960. *King Lazarus.* London: Frederick Muller

Bledsoe, Carolyn, 1980. *Women and Marriage in Kpelle Society.* Stanford: University Press.

Blyden, Edward W., 1967. *Christianity, Islam and the Negro Race.* Edinburgh: University Press

Bond, Patrick, 2002, Unsustainable South Africa: Environment, Development and Social Protest. Pietermaritzburg: University of Natal Press.

Bratton, Michael, and Nicolas van de Walle, 1997. *Democratic Experiments in Africa: Regime Transitions in Comparative Perspective.* Cambridge: University Press

Brindley, Marianne, 1976. *Western Coloured Township: Problems of an Urban Slum.* Johannesburg: Ravan Press.

Brown, Leslie, 1965. *Africa: A Natural History.* New York: Random House

Cassell, C. Abayomi, 1970. *Liberia: History of the First African Republic.* New York: Fountainhead Publishers

Central Bank of Lesotho, 2001. *Quarterly Review.* Maseru: Lesotho Govt.

Chabal, Patrick, and Jean-Pascal Daloz, 1999. *Africa Works: Disorder as Political Instrument.* Bloomington: Indiana University Press

Chakela, Q. K., ed., 1999. *State of the Environment in Lesotho 1997.* Maseru: National Environmental Secretariat.

Clower, Robert W. et al., 1966. *Growth without Development: An Economic Survey of Liberia*. Evanston: Northwestern University Press

Comaroff, Jean and John, 1991 and 1997. *Of Revelation and Revolution Volume One: Christianity, Colonialism and Consciousness in South Africa and Volume Two: The Dialectics of Modernity on a South African Frontier*. Chicago: University of Chicago Press

Crummell, Alexander, 1969. *The Future of Africa*. New York: Negro University Press.

Davidson, Basil, 1992. *The Black Man's Burden: Africa and the Curse of the Nation-State*. New York: Random House

de Craemer, Willy, 1977. *The Jamaa and the church: A Bantu Catholic Movement in Zaire*. Oxford, at the Clarendon Press.

Dillon-Malone, Clive M., 2000. *The Korsten Basketmakers : a study of the Masowe Apostles, an indigenous African religious movement*. Denver, Colo. Academic Books.

Diop, Birago, "Breath", translated by John Reed and Clive Wake, in Soyinka, Wole, ed., 1975. *Poems of Black Africa*, African Writer Series. London: Heinemann

Diop, Birago, "The Vultures", translated by Ulli Beier, in Hughes, Langston, ed., 1963. *Poems from Black Africa*. Bloomington: Indiana University

Dunn, D. Elwood, et al., 2001. *Historical Dictionary of Liberia*, 2nd edition. Lanham Maryland: The Scarecrow Press

Ellis, Stephen, 1999. *The Mask of Anarchy*. New York: New York University Press.

Epprecht, Marc, 2000. *'This matter of women is getting very bad': Gender, Development and Politics in Colonial Lesotho*. Pietermaritzburg: University of Natal Press.

Gay, John, 2004. *Long Day's Anger*. Northridge California: The New World African Press.

Gay, John, 2003. *An Application of Amartya Sen's Development as Freedom to Data Collected in the Afrobarometer Survey*. Michigan State University: Afrobarometer Publications

Gay, John, 2002a. *Red Dust on the Green Leaves*. Northridge California: The New World African Press.

Gay, John, 2002b. *The Brightening Shadow*. Northridge California: The New World African Press.

Gay, John, 1999. *Attitudes Toward Migration of Skilled Professionals*. Maseru, Sechaba Consultants

Gay, John, 1983, "The Uses of Social Psychology in Agricultural Development", in F. Blacker, ed. *Social Psychology and Developing Countries*. New York: John Wiley

Gay, John, 1977. *Rural Sociology Technical Report*. Rome: Food and Agriculture Organization of the United Nations

Gay, John, et al., 1991. *Poverty in Lesotho: A Mapping Exercise*. Maseru, Sechaba Consultants.

Gay, John, and David Hall, 2000. *Poverty and Livelihoods in Lesotho, 2000: More than a Mapping Exercise*, Maseru, Sechaba Consultants: 84-86

Gay, John, and David Hall, 1994. *Poverty in Lesotho 1994: A Mapping Exercise*, Maseru, Sechaba Consultants: 112-114

Gay, John and Robert Mattes, 2003. *The State of Democracy in Lesotho: A Report on the 2003 Afrobarometer Survey.* Michigan State University: Afrobarometer Publications.

Gay, John, and Michael Cole, 1967. *The New Mathematics and an Old Culture: A Study of Learning among the Kpelle of Liberia.* New York: Holt, Rinehart and Winston.

Gay, John, and Thuso Green, 2001. *Citizens Perceptions of Democracy, Governance, and Political Crisis in Lesotho.* Michigan State University: Afrobarometer Publications No. 13.

Gay, Judith, 1980. *Basotho Women's Options: A Study of Marital Careers in Rural Lesotho.* Cambridge University doctoral dissertation.

Gibbon, Edward, 1995. *History of the Decline and Fall of the Roman Empire.* New York: Modern Library.

Gibbon, Peter, 2003. "AGOA, Lesotho's 'Clothing Miracle' & the Politics of Sweatshops" *Review of African Political Economy* No. 96

Gifford, Paul, 1993. *Christianity and Politics in Doe's Liberia.* Cambridge: University Press

Gill, Stephen J., 1993. *A Short History of Lesotho.* Morija: Museum and Archives

Greene, Graham, 1936. *Journey without Maps in West Africa's Black Republic.* London: Heinemann

Harden, Blaine, 2001. "The Dirt in the New Machine", *New York Times.* 12 August 2001

Harley, George Way, 1941. *Native African Medicine*. London: Frank Cass.

Harwood, Bill and Katy Anis, 2001. *A Resource Guide for Education in Crisis Situations*. Developed in Preparation for the 2001 Human Capacity Development Workshop in Bethesda, MD, August 20-23, 2001, CARE USA

Hlophe, Stephen S., 1979. *Class, Ethnicity and Politics in Liberia*. Washington: University Press of America: 118

Institute for Contextual Theology, 1986. *The Kairos Document: Challenge to the Church*. Revised Second Edition, Grand Rapids: Eerdmans.

Institute for Contextual Theology, 1989. *The Road to Damascus: Kairos and Conversion*. Johannesburg: Skotaville Publishers.
Jenkins, Philip, 2002. *The Next Christendom: The Coming of Global Christianity*. Oxford: University Press.

Kapuscinski, Ryszard, 2001. *The Shadow of the Sun*. New York: Alfred A. Knopf

Kulah, Arthur F., 1999. *Liberia Will Rise Again: Reflections on the Liberian Civil Crisis*. Nashville: Abingdon Press

Low, Allan, 1986. *Agricultural Development in Southern Africa: Farm-Household Economics and the Food Crisis*. London: James Currey.

Lugard, Lord Frederick, "The Dual Mandate in Tropic Africa", in Collins, Robert O., ed., 1970. *Problems in the History of Colonial Africa 1860-1960*. Englewood Cliffs: Prentice-Hall

Lye, William F. and Colin Murray, 1980. *Transformations on the Highveld: The Tswana and Southern Sotho*. Cape Town: David Philip

Majeke, Nosipho, 1952. *The Role of the Missionaries in Conquest.* Unity Movement History Series. Cumberwood: APDUSA

Mamdani, Mahmoud, 1996. *Citizen and Subject: Contemporary Africa and the Legacy of Late Colonialism.* Princeton: University Press

Mather, Charles, and Freddie Mathebula, 2000. "Mozambican farmworkers in the Mpumalanga lowveld" in Crush, J. ed. *Borderline Farming: Foreign Migrants in South African Commercial Agriculture.* Cape Town: Southern African Migration Project.

Mathot, Gerard, 2000. *The 1999 Poverty Assessment: Educational Component Report.* Maseru: Sechaba Consultants

McCann, James C., 1999. *Green Land, Brown Land, Black Land: An Environmental History of Africa*, 1890-1990, Portsmouth, NH, Heinemann

McDonald, David, et al., 1998. *Challenging Xenophobia: Myths and Realities about Cross-Border Migration in Southern Africa.* Cape Town: Southern African Migration Project

Mda, Zakes, 2000. *The Heart of Redness.* Oxford: University Press.

Middleton, John and D. Tait, 1958. *Tribes without Rulers.* London: Routledge and Kegan Paul

Mokhehle, Ntsu, ed., 1976. *Moshoeshoe I Profile Se-Moshoeshoe.* Maseru: Mmoho Publications

Mokuku, Tsepo, 1999. *Education for Environmental Literacy: Towards Participatory action Research in the Secondary School Science Curriculum in Lesotho.* Rhodes University doctoral dissertation

Murray, Colin, 1981. *Families Divided: The Impact of Migrant Labour in Lesotho.* Johannesburg: Ravan Press

Ngugi, James, 1965. *The River Between.* London, Heinemann Educational Books Ltd.

Nkrumah, Kwame, 1970. *Consciencism; Philosophy and Ideology for Decolonization.* New York: Monthly Review Press

Otti, Pauline N., and S. Benson Barh, 2001. *A Study on Socio-Cultural Barriers to HIV/AIDS Prevention Initiatives in Monrovia Liberia.* Monrovia: United Nations Development Programme.

Psacker, George, 2002. "How Susie Bayer's T-Shirt Ended UP on Yusuf Mama's Back", *New York Times*. 31 March 2002

Palmer, Robin, and Neil Parsons, 1977. *The Roots of Rural Poverty in Central and Southern Africa.* London: Heinemann

Physicians for Human Rights, 2002. *War-Related Sexual Violence in Sierra Leone A Population-Based Assessment.* Boston: Physicians for Human Rights with the support of UNAMSIL

Presler, Titus, 1999. *Transfigured Night: Mission and Culture in Zimbabwe's Vigil Movement.* Pretoria: University of South Africa Press.

Reno, William 2003. *The Collapse of Sierra Leone and the Emergence of Multiple 'States Within States'.* ccasls.umontreal.ca/contents/sierra_leone.htm

Rush, Norman, 2003. "Apocalypse When?" *The New York Review of Books*, 16 January 2003

Samite,1997. *Song of the Refugee*. Ithaca NY: Glenn H.Ivers Productions

Sechaba Consultants and Associates, 2002. *The Border Within: The Future of the Lesotho-South African International Border*. Cape Town: Southern African Migration Project, Migration Policy Series No. 26

Sen, Amartya, 1999. *Development as Freedom*. Oxford: University Press

Sen, Amartya, 1982. *Poverty and Famines: An Essay on Entitlement and Deprivation*. Oxford: Clarendon Press.

Sengupta, Somini, 2003. "The Child Soldiers of Ivory Coast Are Hired Guns", *New York Times*, 27 March 2003

Shattuck, Roger, and Simon Watson Taylor, ed, 1965. *Selected Works of Alfred Jarry*. New York: Random House.

Smith, Robert A., 1964. *The Emancipation of the Hinterland*, Liberian Writers Series 1. Monrovia: The Star Magazine and Advertising Services

Soyinka, Wole, 1963. *The Lion and the Jewel*. London: Oxford University Press

Stiglitz, Joseph, 2003. *Globalization and its Discontents*. New York: W. W. Norton

Stinton, Diane B., 2004. *Jesus of Africa: Voices of Contemporary African Christology*. Maryknoll NY: Orbis Books.

Stock, Robert F., 1976. *Cholera in Africa: Diffusion of the Disease 1970-1975, with particular emphasis on West Africa,* African Environment Special Report 3. London: International African Institute

Sundiata, I. K., 1980. *Black Scandal: America and the Liberian Labor Crisis*, 1929-1936. Philadelphia: Institute for the Study of Human Issues

Tarr, S. Byron, D. Elwood Dunn and C. William Allen, 2002. *Liberia Reform Agenda: A Framework for Comprehensive Reform of Governance in Liberia, A New Vision.* unpublished report

Tenner, Edward, 1996. *Why Things Bite Back: Technology and the Revenge of Unintended Consequences.* New York: Alfred A. Knopf

Tevera, Daniel, and Lovemore Zinyama, 2002. *Zimbabweans Who Move: Perspectives on International Migration in Zimbabwe.* Cape Town: Southern African Migration Project

Thomasson, Gordon C., 1987. "Primitive" Kpelle Steel Making: A High Technology Knowledge System For Liberia's Future? 149 , *Liberian Studies Journal*, Volume XII Number 2.

Transformation Resource Center, 2002. "The People's Verdict", *Work for Justice*, issue 62. Maseru.

Turnbull, Colin, 1973. *The Mountain People.* London: Jonathan Cape

US Dept. of State, 2001. *Trafficking in Persons Report*

Vani, Benedict, 2002. *Echoes from Bandiland.* Unpublished manuscript.

Vidal, Gore, 1981. *Julian.* Franklin Center, PA: Franklin Library.

Whiteside, Alan, ed., 1998. *Implications of AIDS for Demography and Policy in Southern Africa.* Pietermaritzburg: University of Natal Press